Ch0n

Book One of the Arw'an Chronicles

Gavan Connell

The author's initial cover design concept as sent to Miguel López Bernal!

Front cover artwork by Miguel Angel López Bernal, Mexico City, 2015

Thanks to Tim Bartlett of Merida, Yucatan amongst other places for his work editing the book.

Book Layout © 2014 BookDesignTemplates.com

Ch0n/Gavan Connell. – 2nd Edition

ISBN: 9780994574343

To Matt

Don't die with your music still in you. (Wayne Dyer)

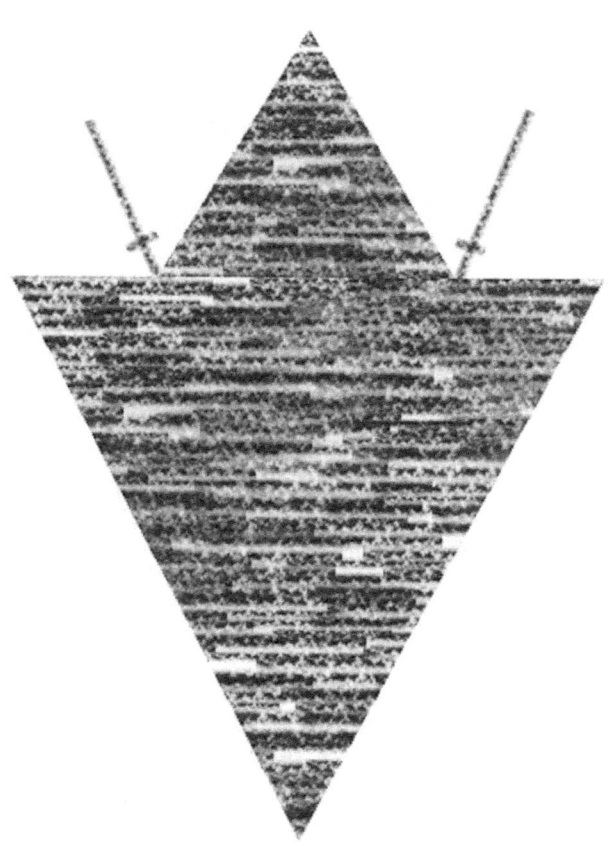

Prologue

One never knows where the chronicles of what one perceives as one's life's work will end up or how they might be interpreted by future generations. In my case, I was ordered to document every activity of every day in the event I were to perish before any rescue mission could be mounted. I was under strict instructions to list, categorize and 'photograph' every new item or event involving weather, minerals, flora, fauna and especially sapient life on the planet where I had become an unwilling inhabitant. Fortunately, those around me, most notably, Karín and Jez were able to contribute extensively to the mountain of information contained in these chronicles. As the years passed I see that I developed from being a pure space commando cloned for one purpose into a more rounded individual. This was possible due to my being in the company of an intelligent alien race on a planet that surely is the jewel of the entire universe. These chronicles as I re-read them have become less mission-oriented and more rounded as my people's situation became safer and more predictable. Now, I entrust my original tablet with all its files to the former priest Temen for his safekeeping in the hope that he or his novitiates would one day be able to place them in the hands of someone who would use them for the better good of all. It is my hope that my descendants will keep similar diaries for the same reasons. If you are reading this, it must be that Temen or someone who followed his path has finally committed them to a readable format and released them. In that case, try not to judge me too hastily but try to think what you might have done in my place....

Ch0n.

Chapters:

Chapter 1: The Awakening

The first thing the clone was aware of was the headache. He felt it long before the opaque helmet with its invasive points and tubes was removed by his attending droid. It threatened to explode his brain so acute was the sensation of pain in his frontal lobes. After a time it diminished, due no doubt to the cocktail of chemicals he could feel warming his innards. He knew what would come next. It was the dozenth time he had been awakened from a long period of hibernation since he had been cloned. As a boy and a youth he had grown and developed physically in the nursery, being fussed over by droids and humans like worker bees in a hive but once he had turned eighteen, he had slept the long sleep in one of the hibernation tubes, his subconscious brain being filled with all the information he would ever need to fulfil his particular role. There had been dozens of kids like him. Each had been cloned for a particular task. He was a soldier. Others were operators of equipment, navigators, scientists and doctors. The nursery was full of groups of children and teenagers who all looked alike. There were no women. None.

He waited for the droid to remove the helmet. He felt the tubes being pulled from his nose and mouth. He felt the probes being removed from his ears and the pressure from the other sensors at the back and top of his head as they were released. At that point he closed his eyes tightly against the light he knew would dazzle him, even through closed lids. Then he was free of it.

The intense glare was almost instantly replaced by a dull glow as the droid placed a filter over his eyes. He was able to open them at last. They were bright green with vertical black pupils, a legacy of the sea-turtle DNA knitted into his human strands. He was in fact a conglomerate of several species. He was a miniscule part sea turtle, selected for its ability to shut down its systems for long periods of time and endure extreme cold without tissue damage. He also shared the DNA of a few plants and mammals that allowed him to live for longer than a normal human, to withstand various viruses and bacterial infections and to regenerate tissue, even skin and digits. Most importantly he shared a strand of feline DNA that gave him extraordinary eyesight, reflexes and strength for his size, which was not inconsiderable. To the naked eye he was all human until he opened those green eyes. He was totally bald and had no facial hair. This was a product of chemically neutralizing every hair follicle on his body during sleep. Without that, he would have filled the tube with hair long before he was woken and that was an issue of hygiene. His bodily waste could be evacuated through tubes and catheters but his hair had to be killed off. His nails had already been cut away by the droid. He had seen them once before in the trash container. They were almost a metre long and curled around like large diameter springs. His hands and feet were housed in special gloves and boots to force the nails to grow in such a fashion so they would not create a problem with cables, tubes and sensors.

He took in the familiar surroundings. He was lying in a metal tube, the top of which was now standing open. A droid was fussing about his person, making sure his vital signs were within the acceptable range for him to stand up. It had as yet not disconnected the suction caps from his back, arms and legs. They were still stimulating his muscles and had been doing so since the same droid had prepared him for his potentially years-long hibernation during which time the craft of which he was a crew member would hurtle through space at faster-than-light (FTL) speeds in search of planets which fulfilled certain criteria that might render them suitable for higher life forms. He knew from previous experience that the ship was right now in orbit around such a planet and that in a few days he would be leading the advance ground party to establish a beach head. What would follow would be all manner of human and robotic scientific data gathering and sample collecting. The landing craft would then return to the mother ship and the data would be analysed and transmitted back to earth to be minutely examined for future use.

The droid disconnected his cables and rolled back. A mechanical voice told him he was clear to stand. He did so and almost fell over again when the blood rushed out of his head and down to his feet. That in itself was accompanied by painful pins and needles that rendered him motionless for several seconds. He walked unsteadily to a room where he was weighed. Then he walked slightly less unsteadily to his locker room and showered. Showers were limited to thirty seconds of actual water flow. The clone chose an initial five seconds of water flow before turning the faucet off. He washed himself thoroughly with a damp, soapy cloth and then stood under the warm water for twenty-five glorious seconds at which time the water abruptly stopped. He dried himself in front of a turbo fan-assisted heater and strolled naked to his locker. His nomenclature was stencilled on it. CH0N. It stood for: Clone: Marque H: Serial Ten: Batch N. He was one of two in each batch who could generally make a name out of it. In his batch, there had been Chin (CH1N) and himself. Ch0n. Chin was long dead. He had not woken up after a lengthy hibernation and his ashes were now part of the great cosmic cloud.

He dressed in his on-board uniform. It was little more than a skin-tight, two-piece high-tech suit designed to massage his muscles as he moved so as to get him into condition more rapidly. He knew that in exactly five days he would have to be physically able to take the landing craft to the planet's surface and defend it if necessary. That meant toning up every muscle in his body. The massage electrodes could only do so much. He went to the dining area. There were several other crew members already seated, including one other soldier. One from Batch M. Serial seven. As such he was known as Seven M. He formed part of the advance party like Ch0n. They greeted each other like the friends they were. 7M was a year older than Ch0n and they had grown up together when they were released from their tubes. They had practised their combat skills together since their teenage years and had fought one frantic battle side by side a couple of planets ago. Ch0n looked around. He was usually the third to be woken.

"He didn't make it this time," said 7M. I saw them taking him to the crematorium when I was on the way to the locker room.

'He' was 5M. The three of them were usually the first to set foot on a new planet. They were selected for their capacity to fight and nothing else. The other half of the team were soldiers as well but usually served to defend the landing craft only if the other three were overrun. So far this had never happened.

Ch0n shrugged. Life was cheap to the clones. They were conceived, they grew up and they fought till they died. No emotions allowed. They formed fighting units and any friendships they had were born on the training square.

"I suppose 3M will get a promotion then," he answered.

"I guess. If he wakes up."

Their rations were spartan. The kitchen droids spent the years of FTL travel growing protein and vegetable matter in their small 'garden'. The fruits of their labour were compressed into bars and flavoured with some chemical or other for use as hard rations during the time the crew was awake. That was after they had produced enough to sustain the near-dead clones in their tubes and why it was so important that the sea-turtle DNA be incorporated into the clones. They needed almost no sustenance for their almost frozen bodies. They were barely alive but enough so to allow sustenance to be transported by their cold blood to their extremities. Even so, many died during their sleep.

"I wonder what's for breakfast," wondered 7M aloud to ChOn. The kitchen androids told me they are almost out of spores for the vegetable matter and their protein plant can barely keep up with demand. They say the ship has been programmed to return to earth after this stop. That way, if we all die on the trip, it won't matter. Even so, I'd like to see earth."

ChOn nodded. He had been 'born' during this voyage and was now more than thirty earth years old. He had seen and set foot on three other planets but had never seen earth. Perhaps he would. Perhaps not. It mattered little to him. He didn't miss what he didn't know. All his knowledge of Earth he had gained subliminally via his minitron. It had painted a picture of a planet always at war. According to it, the ship he was on had been launched after the great religious war of the 23rd century when Christians and Muslims had finally tried to wipe out each other and the rest of the human race in the name of peace and love. The Chinese had tried not to get involved but the Muslims had decreed that all Infidels, as they called them, were to be exterminated if they didn't convert. That was the last piece of information programmed into the minitron. All of the history of the world leading up to that time had been loaded into it. It was the font of all information and merely by asking it, it could display results on the small holographic screen.

"Whatever," he answered. "If it's still there."

Chapter 2: The Quickening

Their ship, a joint Chinese, Indian and Brazilian project, was part of the space colonizing and mining program launched by the three world superpowers. Its mission was to search for planets that would support human life if the mineral wealth of the planet was worth exploiting. Simple. It was apparently a timed mission if the kitchen droids were to be believed. They obviously talked to the navigator droids when the humans were all in suspended animation. Maybe they had parties together and distilled alcohol from their plant material.

They ate their protein meal and drank their ration of precious water. The water itself was obtained by trapping the condensation formed inside the ship's water plant. Moisture in the air produced by the exhaust outlets of the sleep tubes was pumped to a special chamber which had no insulation from the outside vacuum. The very air froze on the ship's condensation plates and then fell onto a mesh where it built up to useable levels. Special droids collected the precious ice crystals and transferred them to holding tanks. The water for the showers was similarly obtained but was distilled also using the waste from the humans and even the vapour from the crematorium. It was then re-processed after use in the showers and the cycle continued. It was an ecosystem in its own right. Nothing wasted. Nothing lost.

More and more humans trickled into the food area. 7M and Ch0n left to go to the locker room again and change for training. This next five days would be spent in combat training and physical conditioning. They would be briefed in good time but they already knew their roles. They always knew their roles, thanks to the ever present probes in their ears which were never silent during their FTL sleep. They were in a never-ending state of information transfer and could use weapons they had never handled, thanks to the visual element of their 'training'. They were, in a sense, no less programmed than their droids.

They went to the training room. It was reserved for the soldiers. Each of the specialities had its own training area. Theirs was by far the biggest because it involved running, weights and sparring. It could house three pairs at any one time and the schedule was posted by muster. Forward scouts first. There were six of them. Three pairs. Two section, Second and Three section, third. Eighteen soldier-clones. The teenagers in training were allocated time fourth. There were also six of them. Or there had been last time they woke up.

Five forward scouts started the first session. They were joined by 3M who had been a Two section trooper. Someone from Three section would go to Two section and the best of the teenagers would get his chance in Three section and leave the nursery for the hibernation tubes. That's how it had always been.

"The rear echelon has arrived to join us," joked 1M. "What you got, Pogo?" 2M would be 3M's partner as it was he who had been partnered with 5M. They started immediately on their team drills and finished up with a light run around the room. They were tired already after just half an hour. They were programmed back in the training room in one and a half hours. For the rest of the day they went at it for half an hour at a time with one and a half hours off. It was their standard routine. Tomorrow it would be one hour with three hours off. Just enough time for all four groups to have their turn.

Ch0n slept like a child. His tube had been converted to operational mode, which meant it had been converted into a cot. Nothing else was different. When he slept he was required to insert the ear probes. At first they emitted a hypnotic sound pattern to induce sleep and then the subliminal training would start again. The minitron just ploughed through its memory bank in a pre-ordained sequence involving weapons, hand to hand combat katas, survival skills, language pattern recognition using all the known languages of earth and space, military history, causes of conflict, religions of the world and tactics and strategy. It was a never ending loop that lasted three months at a time. ChOn had heard it dozens and dozens of times in his sleep.

Day Two upped the tempo of training. They did more aerobic work and little real physical stuff. The training area was at slightly less than one atmosphere of pressure and the oxygen level was slightly below 19 percent with the carbon dioxide and helium levels elevated. Their expenditure of energy was designed to allow them to operate better when they were using their backpacks, which had an oxygen content of twenty two percent. By the end of the second day, the stiffness had disappeared from their joints and they were ready for Day Three, which would be two hours of exercise for the forward scouts and remain at one hour for the others, and then three hours off as for Day Two.

During Day Three, the weapons were drawn from the armoury during the first rest period. They were kept in a vacuum sealed container and never needed oiling or cleaning whilst they were so stored. As soon as they were exposed to the training area, however, they became the subject of multiple strip and assembly exercises and cleaning naturally followed. There was no firing range. The solid projectiles represented too much of a risk to the hull of the ship and the metalstorm kinetic projectile guns and pulse guns had no recoil and could be sprayed like water, so aiming and firing wasn't a priority. The main weapon training involved close quarter fighting with simulated steel weapons including synthetic katanas, hammers, pikes and short swords or daggers. They had the katas subliminally imprinted in their brains and when they sparred, they were dancing a highly choreographed routine, one for the main partner and the mirror image for the secondary one. That is why they were in pairs. They could spar for several minutes at a time at full speed, knowing that they would not be able to touch their partner because he was just as adept at his kata and attack and defence were inbuilt for both parties. To an untrained onlooker, these sessions would appear to be actual combat, so well were they choreographed and enacted. After several sessions of sparring a day complemented by running and weights routines, the soldiers were showing signs of recuperation from their long sleep. Of course, none of this would have been possible had it not been for the electric stimulus to their muscles for several hours a day during their hibernation.

On Day Four, the metal weapons were produced. The katanas were made of a special carbon fibre-titanium alloy, which made them light and almost indestructible edge to edge. They held their edges like no other material in the history of weaponry and they could cut through wood and heavy leather as if they were paper. Their weakness lay in their propensity to break if they received a solid blow on the flat of the blade. The daggers and short swords were more traditional stainless-blue lightweight steel. They also carried nylon tonfas for non-lethal situations. Training with metal weapons was no less frantically approached than with their synthetic substitutes and merely showed the soldiers that they and their partners were battle-ready. Hardly anybody was ever cut whilst sparring and those that were, simply bandaged their wounds and continued. Usually within eight hours, the scars had sealed and the rest of the healing process was usually completed within a day or two, thanks to their reptilian DNA.

It was usually at the end of Day Four that they were invited to the bridge to see the planet they would be exploring. The main ship by this time had been in orbit for three weeks conducting scientific experiments and testing the atmosphere, gravitational pull, solar radiation as well as mapping the terrain and looking for any sign of life, either plant or animal. The planet above which they were orbiting was remarkable in its similarity to earth. It was smaller by about one quarter in mass and its physical dimensions were accordingly reduced. It rotated every eighteen earth hours and it was calculated that it orbited around an orange star once every three hundred of its own days. There were two small polar ice caps and two major oceans, separated by several large land masses, some joined and some islands. At least one active volcano had been discovered and there were signs of sapient life in the form of small tent villages and at least one major permanent camp, town or city. The geological survey showed clouds, water, ice, permafrost and potential mining sites for iron, aluminium, copper, nickel, cadmium, silver and gold as well as the precious rare-earth metals that were so sought after on Earth. This planet was the jewel of their mission and the ship had been transmitting pictures back to earth for the entire period it had been in orbit. The geology clones were in a state of shock and amazement at such a treasure. To a man they wanted to set foot on the planet below and collect the precious samples they would need for analysis and projected percentage yields of the various metals. They believed they would need at least a month on the surface, including various landing zones in order to achieve the ship's mission. The logistic team was no less enthusiastic, talking animatedly about the possibility of obtaining fresh soil, plant and protein matter for the droid 'garden' and the ability to void the ship's water tanks and refill them with the real thing for the first time in six years. The soldiers were laconic in their assessment. They could see the camps and knew that a camp might mean a fight. For them it was either a fight against a few or a fight against many but a fight was a fight and they had eighteen soldiers, five teenagers and eight pre-teen clones who could all handle a weapon. All they needed was the ability to

Gavan Connell

choose the landing site so they would have enough time to establish a beach head before the white-dust-coat brigade arrived.

5M was the senior soldier-clone. He didn't consult the others, he just looked at the landscape laid out before him on the huge screen and pointed a laser at a point on it.

"That's where we should land," he said. "It's right inside the richest mineral zone so far identified and it's a long way to the first camp. We can land, shuttle Two and Three sections down with defensive weapons and sensors and have a perimeter established inside the first day. Judging from the camp setup, the inhabitants are sapient humanoids and probably will be frightened of us. I am guessing from the lack of structure of the camp that they are nomadic shepherds with no fighting force and so will probably not attack us at any stage. We should try and establish contact with them as early as practical after we are settled."

He looked around. Nobody disagreed with him. Not that anybody would. The soldier-clones all stood six-four and weighed 220 pounds and weren't known for their patience. Besides, if they were unable to protect the mission, there was no point landing at all.

He continued.

"I will need this room in an hour for briefing purposes. Anybody who needs to be here may stay but I will need silence while I give orders to the soldiers. ChOn, get Two and Three sections ready. Cartologists, I want a relief hologram of this area here within twenty minutes. I'll remain here and study the terrain." He nodded his thanks to the Chief Officer of the bridge and sat down. ChOn and the other four Forward Scouts left the room along with several other humans and a couple of service droids. ChOn went directly to the training room where Three Section was training and told them of the briefing. He then went to the tube room and informed Two Section and the teenagers what was happening and that Two Section would be needed for a briefing. At once the place became a hive of activity as Two Section unpacked their battle order and laid it out on their cots. ChOn went to his own cot and did the same. The other four scouts were already half done.

Gavan Connell

Chapter Three: The Planning

Ch0n opened his war locker. In it was his battle dress. It consisted of a two piece black cut resistant suit with Velcro seams and fastenings. It could be worn sleeved or sleeveless, high or low collar, long or short trousered and had provision for a webbing weapons belt. Ch0n invariably chose the full coverage as a first option. Long sleeved high necked long trousered, turned over calf-length boots. Even the boots were Velcro fastened at the front, ankle and top so as to give a glove-like fit. There were two narrow tubes on the outside of each boot into which Ch0n fitted a pair of gleaming sais.

He took out his body armour. It was lightweight, cut-proof and spike resistant and was made specifically for him. It was the latest in sprayform technology when the ship had left. He had stripped naked to the waist and had been covered in a plastic film. Then a robot had sprayed his torso with an expanding foam compound. Fittings were placed on the sides of the outside surface and then a second coat was applied. All in all it was just under an inch thick and weighed less than a pound. It would take anything up to and including a projectile from a rail gun. The raw armour was then cut along the edges using a laser and the bottom flap tailored to fit inside the waistband of his trousers. It was similar to the images he had seen of ancient Roman armour except that it was synthetic.

On his head he would wear a lightweight sprayform helm with a tiny false-fusion power source, a miniature digital telescopic vision camera, a holographic video camera, sinewave radio, white and black light and heat vision and starlight amplified vision devices attached to nanotechnology storage devices. A full face gold UV screen visor could be retracted to form a short visor to cover his eyes and allow him to see naturally or switch to a heads-up display of any or all of his vision devices or what any or all the other five cameras in the team were transmitting.

ChOn laid his weapon belt on the cot. It held a metalstorm kinetic pistol that fired .177 inch ball bearings at 3000 feet per second either singly or in barrages. It was good for anything up to fifty feet but was too affected by wind resistance and gravity after that. A second smaller pistol fired blue pulses at infinitely variable pulse rates to stun, disable or kill or even to blow holes in masonry walls. It had a range out to 200 feet but was best at close quarters. Fragmentation grenades and smoke generators the size of a thumbnail were contained in two magnetic magazines and then there were the spring-loaded tonfa and a taser. A false-fusion pack maintained the weapons fully charged at all times and the only concession to individual needs, a water canteen, made up the complete kit.

The clock told ChOn there were twenty minutes left until the briefing started. He reached into his locker and took out a long silk bag made from a parachute. He undid the knot at the top and withdrew his katana, two short swords and two sine wave generators that looked like two-tined forks. The katana was housed in a scabbard made of some sort of rigid, synthetic leather. The two short swords were naked. He slid them lovingly into the fittings on his armour and withdrew the katana from her scabbard. At the humming sound of it, all the other soldiers looked towards him. The sword was pale green in colour and had been given to ChOn by a metallurgist during exploration of the previous planet. It was of a metal unknown to anybody and spectrum analysis of its properties had yielded little information other than it was of something not listed on the periodic table. The metallurgist had named it 'Chontium' for the man who had found it. ChOn had found a large lump of the green stuff whilst patrolling his perimeter and the metallurgist had received it gratefully and then excitedly. It was so hard that it was only by accident that he had discovered a piece of it could be shaped by a hammer if it were being subjected to sine-wave frequencies so low they were inaudible to any living thing. He had crafted a katana for ChOn and by experimentation he had honed the blade with high-frequency sound and a diamond wheel. He had then cut a steel sheet with it and named it 'Shiew' for the sound it made as it cut the metal.

ChOn carved a long arc in front of himself with the katana. He fingered it lovingly and returned it to the scabbard. The others returned to their tasks.

At the appointed time, seventeen fully kitted and armed soldiers entered the briefing room as one. 5M was waiting. A hologram hovered above the table in front of him. He started immediately.

In twenty minutes the briefing was over. It was essentially the same as every other briefing they had had with just a few concessions to the terrain and the possibility of hostile action. ChOn didn't need to be told he would be in the bubble at the base of the landing craft. He was always there and knew what he had to do. 3M was given some extra detail on his role as it was his first time in the Forward Scouts. They stood in a single line and waited for 5M to inspect their kit. He didn't really need to do it because he already knew that they were ready and that all their equipment was ready for instant use. Nevertheless, he walked the line tugging and testing different items before dismissing the team until the following morning just before first light.

ChOn and the others went to the landing craft. It was a pilotless shuttle, capable of deploying six persons and their equipment plus an additional 100 pounds of cargo. It was roughly the size of an elevator car with three hydraulic legs and a bubble underneath for the loadmaster to manually navigate the last few metres. That was ChOn's main task until the vehicle actually landed. After that he reverted to combat soldier. Each of the sections and civilian teams had a loadmaster as a secondary task. There wasn't much to it, the velocity of the craft was controlled from the main ship but things like rocks and holes were only visible from close up. The loadmaster would manoeuvre the craft either left, right, forward or backwards by enough to avoid hitting something that might topple the craft. There had been two landing craft but one had gone unserviceable some years ago between planets and had since been used to cannibalize parts for the second one, the one they were to use the following day.

ChOn climbed into the bubble. It was big enough to hold him in a seated position and to allow him to operate the controls. His weapon belt would accompany him but his armour and backpack would travel in the main body of the craft. He opened the valve on his oxygen bottle and shut it when he heard the hissing of escaping gas in his mask, turned on the master switch and tested the manoeuvre-controls, the heat shield controls, his seat and harness, the hatch door and latch, and was satisfied with what he found. He switched off the master switch, climbed down from his bubble and climbed the five steps of the ladder to the main door. Inside, 3M was checking the door and the restraining belts inside the main chamber. The five pax would be standing in harnesses so that at the point of contact with the ground they could lift their feet to avoid the shock. Their kit was stored in webbing pockets at their sides and there was a space for the loadmaster's kit and for the extra one hundred pounds of cargo. They usually took movement sensors and a longer-range metalstorm rail gun that fired .22 inch bearings out to 150 yards. They also took water receptacles and sun shelters. These had already been stored by 6N. An Oxygen bottle showing 'full' on the gauge was attached to the main door and a tube led from it and branched off to five masks where the pax would be strapped. ChOn tested the restraining latch for the ladder, which would be hidden inside the main door during flight. He climbed down the ladder to the floor, raised the ladder and stowed it. Then he released it and lowered it again. This was his second task after guiding the feet of the landing craft: releasing the ladder so the other five could dismount safety. He was done.

Outside, droids and mechanic-clones were checking the mass-driver and other technical bits of the craft. They didn't acknowledge his presence as he left 3M to the rest of his pre-flight checks.

Gavan Connell

Chapter Four: The Landing

At the appointed hour, the six members of the Forward Scouts arrived at the flight deck. They stowed their personal equipment, strapped themselves in and waited while the ground crew closed hatches, stowed the ladder, raised heat shields and occupied themselves with other pre-flight checks. ChOn was in tannoy contact with 5M and in radio contact with the bridge of the main ship, where the landing craft pilot was located. They conducted their comms checks, put on their oxygen masks, pulled their webbing one last time and listened for the count. Inside, 5M was counting down from ten with his fingers for the others. ChOn could hear on his headset. On 'zero', the craft lifted soundlessly away and floated outside the flight bay into space. The flight would take ten minutes until touchdown. They would lower the heat shields and ChOn would leave the bubble and release the ladder. When the craft was empty, ChOn would stow the ladder, enter the bubble, raise the heat shields, leave the bubble and close everything down and the craft would be remotely piloted back to the ship. The next two flights would contain Two and Three sections and then after that the civilians would arrive in whatever order they had determined. ChOn wasn't the least bit interested in that part of it. By the time they arrived, he would have long ago secured his perimeter and would be asleep until his turn to keep watch.

The craft started to vibrate and shake and ChOn knew they had entered the planet's atmosphere. He hunkered down in his straps and tried not to have his head shaken off his body. The temperature inside the bubble rose to an uncomfortable level and stabilized. Then he felt himself being pushed harder and harder into his seat and he knew they had decelerated to landing speed. At this point he was able to move his head into a position where he could see the ground. They were flying laterally at several hundred feet per minute and were still well above the surface. They passed within distant sight of a camp but as the craft was silent and it was still just after dawn, he wasn't concerned at having been seen. He recognized the landing site from the hologram and the craft slowed to a few feet per second and commenced its pre-determined descent speed. ChOn turned on the master switch and took hold of the lateral movement stick. He called 5M to tell him they were within a minute of landing but there was no answer. He tried again but to no avail. He called the main ship and told the pilot he was ready to take control. The pilot indicated it was too soon and that he would continue to land the craft until it was within thirty feet of the ground. ChOn shouted that they were already within thirty feet and he had visual and wanted the override. By the time the remote pilot received the message and realized there must be something wrong with his altimeter, it was too late. ChOn got the override and tried to avoid a narrow fissure but the craft was already less than two metres from the ground. Two of the three legs went into the fissure and snapped off a third of the way up. The third splayed outwards and the craft landed heavily at an angle. ChOn knew it would never fly again unless the soldiers could somehow get it standing vertical. He thought that with six of them they might be able to raise it and then it could return to the main ship and get new legs from the other craft. He called 5M again. There was still no answer. He started to feel uneasy. The internal comms channel had no reason not to work. It was a simple tannoy connected by two strands. Perhaps the cable had broken during flight.

ChOn managed to lower the heat shields and exit the bubble. He dropped lightly the few feet to the ground and stretched. The ladder release latch worked fine and he lowered it to the ground. It was a little crooked but otherwise OK. He climbed up and looked in the small porthole. He could see two of his comrades still strapped in their harnesses, not moving. A sudden fear gripped him. It was a sensation he was unaccustomed to. He opened the hatch and surveyed the space inside the craft. None of the soldiers was moving. He checked each of them in turn for a pulse. They were all dead. He took the headset from 5M and radioed the ship with the news. The landing craft was wrecked and he was the sole survivor. He would not be able to right the landing craft and so he was effectively marooned in space.

The radio was silent for some time. The chief officer spoke next.

"Soldier, I want you to spend the next half an hour surveying the physical damage to the landing craft. I want you to look around you and see if there is any way you could winch it into a standing position. If we can do that, we can get it back here and fix it. Then we can continue the mission. The mission is the important thing here. We have found something that nobody has ever found before and we have to maximize the moment. Now get to work and find a way to get that thing standing up. We have two cargo drones that we can send to you but they are strictly one way. They hold two hundred pounds of cargo and are about your size and shape. Do you understand me soldier?"

"I understand you just fine but I can tell you I don't need the half hour. Two broken legs and one bent one tell the story. Without the bubble and with no legs it might work but the bubble is part of the craft. Without it, it would just burn up in the atmosphere on the way up. I'm sorry but you'll just have to map the co-ordinates of this place and come back for me and whatever I find here. In the meantime, I'll think about what you can send me to make my life a bit safer and more comfortable."

The Chief Officer was emotionless on the other end of the radio.

"OK soldier, we'll send what we can send. Now we have no landing craft we'll plot a course for earth. We should be there in three or four years and then you can expect relief and a probable mining boom in another three or four. Give it seven or eight all up for luck. Now go ahead and make that list."

Ch0n sat down under the landing craft. The first thing he had to do was get the bodies out and salvage the equipment. He had six people's weaponry and other equipment including their false-fusion generators and armour. He would need shelter and food but he knew he could get food and water here. He thought back to his training days and survival. Then he tried to consider what he might encounter here. If he had to fight, he would need lots of weapons and ammunition. He already had most of that. If he expended all the munitions he had at his disposal he would only be prolonging a fight he could never win anyway. He would need metal. Steel. Copper wire. Sprayform canisters. Lots of them. Cordage. Soap! Hand tools. Portable lighting. A tarpaulin. A metal cooking implement. No, two. Waterproof clothing. A hat. Bandages. Sewing equipment. Storage containers. Waterproof, as big as they can fit in the drones. Boots. Uniforms. Body bags. A hat with feathers.

He realized he was laughing. Then he realized he was in shock. Then he realized he had work to do.

Chapter Five: Getting Organized

He radioed his list, leaving off the hat with feathers but including explosives and a few remote firing devices. He knew the miners had lots of fusion explosives. A few boxes of those could change a lot of odds.

He set to removing the bodies of his comrades in arms. He stripped them naked and laid out their equipment. He had five spare everything. Except that nobody else's minitron would work for him. They were programmed at the factory to be operated only after verifying the iris of the user. Ch0n decided to try and reprogram them all just in case. He took his comrades one by one and removed their helms. Then he took their minitrons and one by one, started them, holding each soldier's eye open in front of the sensor to enable the device to boot. Three of the five worked and he was able to reprogram them to his own iris. He had no idea whether or not he would ever need to use one or more of them but at least he had a contingency to fall back on if he lost or broke his own.

Six of everything. He would have to stash the stuff he couldn't carry on his person, including the rail gun and all the spare ammunition and explosives. He recalled seeing a cave on the hologram. 5M had also mentioned it as a reason for landing where he did. Shelter and storage he had said under logistics in his orders. The off-duty troops will shelter in the cave, store their heavy weapons and the scientific equipment there. He scanned the surrounding area looking for a landmark and saw the low, broken rock face he was looking for only a hundred metres away. He started to roll the equipment in the uniforms and placed them on the armour. The helms he wrapped, conscious of their sensitive equipment. He started the first trip to the cave carrying part of his comrades' kit. He was surprised

25

at the ease with which he could lift it all and realized that the lesser gravity here would make him stronger and probably faster than he had been before.

The entrance of the cave was barely high enough for him to enter without bending. He went in with his white light showing the way. It smelt musty but there were no tracks of any kind in the dusty floor. It went back for about twenty feet before it opened up into a larger cavern. His light showed some hand prints painted on the walls as well as some spirals and human-looking stick paintings of humanoids with bubbles for heads. It was confirmation that he was on a planet inhabited by sapients. He hoped they were friendly because he figured seven years was a long time to live undiscovered in a cave that had once been the home of at least one artist. He put the first load of stuff down and returned for more. He had transferred all the kit plus the first load of cargo, including the rail gun, when he heard the radio in the ship burst into life. It was the Chief Officer and the pilot of the drone.

"We've been watching you at work from up here while we put your list together. You've still got a lot to do so the pilot is going to try and land the cone at the entrance to the cave. He'll approach from where the landing craft is so he can see the cave entrance and not have to worry about the rock wall."

"Well," replied ChOn, "I hope he makes a better fist of it than he did with the landing craft and if he is going to crash one of them, try not to make it the one with the explosives."

"The first bird is away," announced the pilot, cheerfully ignoring ChOn's comment. "According to the manifest it has tools, utensils, a tarp, cordage, wire and steel pieces but not many. They're too heavy. Clothing and soap. They're all in stacked storage containers with lids but there isn't much space in that thing. The explosives are in the next one."

"We threw in a few extra things to make sure we didn't waste any space or weight. I hope you get to use everything. We'll stay here until dark tomorrow night and then we'll have to go. You have all the skills to do this thing easily. You're a soldier and a good one. You have all the knowledge we can give you with the minitron and if the locals are friendly you will do it easily. If you have to fight, you certainly should have the advantage. We have changed orbit slightly and can tell you the locals are not too advanced technologically. They're still in the iron-age and your neighbours are definitely nomadic or semi-nomadic herders. If you play your cards right you can set yourself up as God Himself!" He laughed at his own joke.

Ch0n didn't feel much like laughing. He had about three hours of light left and he was hungry and thirsty and for the first time in his life, alone.

He didn't hear the capsule until it whined close over him. It floated near to the cave entrance and then a small explosive device popped a plug and a parachute deployed from inside it. It just dropped the last few feet on the parachute and lay still. Ch0n was stationed at the landing craft and told the pilot he had seen it arrive and it was safe and in one piece.

"The second one is on its way as well. You'd better stay where you are in case you get blown up. That'd really ruin your day."

Ch0n tried to picture the drone pilot. He remembered seeing him in the briefing room and thinking how young he looked. Maybe twenty. He'd been born on the ship too and yet Ch0n had never met or spoken to him in all those years. Admittedly half the time they'd been asleep but that didn't excuse things.

They were all too caught up in their own little roles to worry about anybody outside their muster. He was still musing about the lack of social interaction between groups when the second cone hummed by, popped the 'chute and landed safely close to the mouth of the cave.

"It's here," he reported. "I'm going to leave the landing craft now and set up the cave and look for water. I can't recall seeing any on the hologram but I wasn't looking for it either. Can you see any?"

"There's a stream about two hundred yards past the cave entrance. It looks like it's coming out of a cleft in the rock. It's just a trickle but it's a hell of a lot more than we have here. Check in first thing in the morning. We're going to do some strip imaging and geological analysis. We have to get as much information back as possible."

Ch0n looked at the landing craft. He decided he could make a reasonable shelter out of it. It had unlimited power, the heat shields worked, it was strong enough to resist small arms fire and it wouldn't take much to roll it on its side if he dug the fissure out a bit. He walked away with that thought in mind and went instead to the cones. They were heat-resistant cylinders with a point at one end and a flat base, like a giant bullet. Each one was about six and a half feet long and two feet in diameter. He opened the door in the base of the closest one and found it full of plastic, labelled cylindrical storage containers. Three in all, each one filled with treasure. Rather than delay proceedings by unpacking everything, he took the containers inside the cave and then rolled the cones inside. He unclipped the nose-cones, located the container that held the cooking containers and fire starters and decided to walk to the creek. He determined from the outset to never go anywhere without his weapon belt or his helm. That way he could see everything and defend himself if needs be or hunt. Which is what he was planning on doing now.

He walked steadily towards the location of the creek, all the while looking for tracks or movement. Or anything. He reached the place where the stream fell from a cleft in the rocks and tasted the water. It was fresh and cool and even a little sweet compared to what he was used to. He drank his entire canteen and refilled it. Then he started looking for food. His survival training, most of it subliminal, told him that around water was the place to look for small game. But he didn't even know if there was any small game on the planet. He almost laughed at the inadequacy of that one small piece of advice. Just the same, he had no real alternative so he decided to wait for an hour. He sat still. It was a skill all soldiers had developed since soldiers first appeared in history. Absolutely still. He had the pulse gun set to low intensity. Suddenly his eye caught movement and he resisted the temptation to turn his head. Instead he focussed on the stream and the place he had decided a creature would find it easy to drink from. His self-discipline was rewarded when a small mammal entered his vision and went to the water's edge. The pistol hummed and the animal just dropped in its tracks, stunned and unconscious. ChOn ran to pick it up and hefted it. It was rabbit-like in appearance and weighed at least a pound and a half. He broke its neck, skinned it deftly with a sharp cut to the rear knees and a quick pull. A slit down the belly, a couple of seconds work and he had a rabbit ready to cook. He washed his hands in the creek and wandered back to the cave. He wished he'd asked for a stove but there was nothing for it now but to make the most of what he had. He lit a fire inside the mouth of the cave and skewered the rabbit on a stick. He was very hungry and the smell of the meat reminded him of the last time he had eaten cooked meat, several years ago now on the last planet they had discovered. That time it had been a vegetarian lizard, the only higher life form they had found on the entire planet. It had been quite palatable compared with the protein and vegetable bars they lived on aboard the ship.

He devoured the cooked rabbit and found it delicious. Things were already looking up. He guessed he had an hour of light left so he started to unpack his new provisions. If he were going to sleep easy tonight he would need movement and vibration sensors deployed near the cave entrance.

He opened the webbing sack that held the devices. There were six of them. Six of everything! They were hollow aluminium spikes that could be driven into the ground a foot, topped with a small housing with a three molecule thick seismic skin attached to a fixed frequency sine wave transmitter. Atop the device was a real-time, image-intensified, heat-detecting camera and a tiny false-fusion power cell. The whole device stood six feet high when assembled. The spike could 'feel' surface vibrations caused by animal, human or vehicle movement to a range of fifty feet. Those vibrations would register on the seismic skin, which was capable of analysing the intensity and direction of the source and aiming the camera in the appropriate direction. It would automatically transmit the video, intensity and direction to a receiver panel, with its audible alarm or to any or all of the helms. If two or more detectors transmitted at the same time, the location of the cause of the vibrations could be triangulated to within one foot. A trigger mechanism attached to the receivers could detonate any explosive devices in the zone. The entire network was designed to be mutually supporting and in depth so that a narrow front could have saturation coverage out to 150 feet. A wide frontage would be deployed differently but could have reasonable coverage at 150 feet, good coverage at 100 feet and saturation coverage at fifty feet. It was not designed to be a stand-alone form of defence, only an early-warning system with human coverage. ChOn planned to use it just to wake him and so deployed it only out to 100 feet. He set the rail gun to cover the entrance of the cave, made sure there was an escape route if he needed one, stashed a spare weapon belt where he could pick it up on the run and retired for the night.

He slept with his ear probes inserted, more out of habit than anything but also because they were attached to his helm as well as to the minitron using the multi-connect function of Bluetooth XV. The hypnotic sleep inducement sounds filled his brain and calmed his mind. In less than two minutes he was asleep. The minitron changed its transmission to one ChOn had pre-programmed. It reeled through audio and video of survival techniques, katana katas and language patterns. It also gave him a half-hour revision lesson on the rail gun every two hours. He slept soundly, his eyelids fluttering the entire time. He wasn't dreaming, he was absorbing the subliminal training. The sensors silently monitored the area in front of his cave. They picked up the signals of several rabbits and lizards but did not assess them as a threat.

ChOn slept undisturbed for seven hours when the dawn woke him. He ate a protein bar for breakfast and drank his entire canteen of water. He checked the memory on the receiver and was pleased to see that he had plenty of small, nocturnal game to hunt. He stripped his uniform to short sleeves and short legs. He opened the six storage containers and took stock. The first item he found in bin number one was a writing tablet, designed to maintain a log. It was a hardened, white glass touch screen the same as the scouts all carried. It didn't seem to be anything else but, between what was in reality two laminated layers, there was a one-molecule thick computer board complete with 512 terabytes of storage space, a built in power source, a holographic camera and sound recording and playback system and the main feature, a voice to text capacity with a range of twenty feet. ChOn turned it on. The image of the Chief Officer appeared on the screen. He had left instructions that ChOn was to log every single thing he saw and did until a ship arrived. A homing device on the tablet would enable the device to be recovered in the event ChOn were dead. So ChOn started what was to become routine for him. He instructed the tablet to adopt the voice to text mode and he made a list of his provisions.

Sent from ship:

<u>Tube 1, Bin #1:</u>

Tablet 1

Hammer 1

Rotary cutting tool 1

Power saw 1

Cordage ¼ inch 3000 ft

Chain alloy 25 feet

Axe lightweight 2

Slingshot ammo 500

Remote firing device 6

Pliers 1

Gas blowtorch 1

Protein bars 12

Cold chisel 1

Substance analyser

<u>Bin #2</u>:

Forage cap 6

Uniform 10

Aluminium blankets 6

Wet weather gear 2

Tent two man 1

Fishing eqpt 10 set

Gavan Connell

First aid kit (6 man) 1

Solar stove 1

Scope 60 x 60 1

Sprayform cans 14

Helium canisters 4

Balloons 50

Bin #3:

Soap 16 pkts

Razor 1

Sewing kit 2

Cable ties pkt 5

Fusion explosives pcs 6000

Water bladders 6

Spring trap 4

Seal-all cans 10

Laser cutting pen 1

Synthetic blankets 3

Synthetic tarpaulin

Sprayform cans 20

Spanner set 1

Crossbow 1 Bolts 160

Slingshot 1

Tube 2 Bin #4:

Water bladders 6

Spring trap 1

Fire lighter 24

Entrenching tool

Crossbow 1 Bolts 160

Slingshot 1

Slingshot ammo 5000

Remote firing device

Sprayform cans 17

Bin #5

Anti-armour firing tube 1

Energy rounds 40

Explosive rounds 40

Sprayform cans 15

Ammo .177, 50,000

Ammo .22, 100,000

Bin #6

Fresnel lens 2

Signal mirrors 18

Silk parachute packing

Climbing rope 100ft

Gavan Connell

<u>To be salvaged from the landing craft:</u>

Radio

Water pump and hoses.

Hull and legs

Seats

Mirrors

Tannoy, Wire

Heat shields

Glass

Electro magnets

Webbing harnesses

Oxygen equipment

Mass driver and false fusion power cell

Ladder

Parachutes 3

<u>Cargo Cones:</u>

Bodies, mass drivers, parachutes

<u>Salvaged from the squad:</u>

Minitrons 6, 4 usable

Tablets 6

Metalstorm Kinetic Pistols 6

Ammo .177, 6,000

Metalstorm Rail gun 1

Ammo .22 60,000

Sine wave pulse guns 6

Frag grenades 36

Smoke various 36

Sensor kit 1

Katanas 6

Short swords 6

Knives/daggers 6

Tonfas 6

Sai 12

Weapon Belt 6

Torch 6

Armour 6

Boots pr 6

Helm 6

Watches 6

Water canteens 6

Green laser pens 6

Uniforms 6

Cable ties (packs of 200) 6

Horse bows 2

Arrows 48

Entrenching tools 6

Incendiary pens 6

karabiners and assorted spring clips 24

That was it. He had to survive for up to seven years with that. He had taken the false-fusion packs from the two unusable minitrons and had dismantled them for useful bits and pieces.

The next problem was where to secure his cache. If the cave were ever entered, whoever had done so would just waltz in and have an instant treasure bonanza. The storage bins weren't enough to bury everything in but he had to decide what to bury and what to hide. He decided the weapons were the most important thing to hide so he started out by stashing five kinetic pistols, five pulse guns and the box of detonators in the first bin. He used the entrenching tool to dig a decent hole and buried it outside the cave entrance but under the overhang. That way he could walk on the spot and compact it and nobody would be the wiser. He rigged a fragmentation grenade inside the bin and also inside a small container at the top so it would detonate if not disarmed first. That way the pistols would be damaged. Certainly the detonators would be destroyed.

The second bin to be buried was the one with the explosives. It also contained the spare ammunition for the kinetic pistols and rail gun. As with the first bin, spare clothing was used as packing. And as for the first bin it was protected by a fragmentation booby trap.

Ch0n allocated as much of the sensitive equipment to the bins as possible. He stashed them around the middle of the cave where he or anybody else would be walking and sitting. The long equipment he rolled in a set of wet weather gear and stashed high up the wall in a crevice. Only the personal equipment he would use often, the spring trap, the cooking pots, the remote sensors and the rail gun were left out. He was ready to begin his ordeal.

The day was drawing to an end. Ch0n suddenly realized he was hungry. He went back to the stream and shot another rabbit and while it was cooking, decided to try the ship on the radio. As he approached, he could hear the radio crackling. He talked into the mike and the Chief Officer answered. He was not amused.

"Listen, Soldier, I told you to check in this morning. We've been trying to reach you all day. That isn't good enough. We have priorities up here"

Ch0n involuntarily went to attention and was on the point of apologising when the irony of the situation struck him.

"Well," he replied, "I have priorities down here too and they didn't include wasting valuable time chatting. You can be sure I am well established, the day's activities have been logged and I will do my best to survive the time it takes for the next ship to arrive. Feel free to leave any time you like. You have a long trip back and you can't start until everybody is bedded down and tucked in so I suggest you get started. This is Clone, CH0N signing off. Out!" He let the mike fall from his hand and walked back to his rabbit. Two hours later, he was in a deep REM sleep guarded by the sensor unit.

Gavan Connell

Chapter Six:The First Foray

On the morning of the third day he found a rabbit in the spring trap. He cooked and ate it and reset the trap. He had decided the night before that it was time to take a look at his surroundings. He still had to salvage the landing craft but he had decided to slip it by a day and get to know his future home. He walked first to the top of the hill and looked around. He decided to walk in a Westerly direction because he would need the sun to navigate home by. If he walked along the line of his shadow for slightly more than half the time he had allocated himself, he would be able to walk back along his shadow in the evening until he saw this hilly outcrop. Having made his decision, he returned to the cave and prepared himself for a lone patrol. He put on his long sleeves and long pants option, his armour and helm and on the weapon belt he put his kinetic pistol, a pulse gun, two water canteens, his entrenching tool and a length of cordage. He slung the green Katana, Shiew and the crossbow across his back. If he were surprised by a band of sapients he would have the means to defend himself at medium and short ranges, either silently or noisily. If he encountered any large game he could shoot it with a variety of weapons and carry it back. It was mid-morning when he set out past the little creek, filling up his canteens as he went.

The 'home hill' was some half a mile long on the western side of the cave. He kept to the creases in the land and followed his shadow past various green wadis and flat areas devoid of any forestation. In the middle distance he could see a large saucer-shaped depression where the vegetation was quite substantial and green. He reached the edge of it in about two hours. The trees were fairly straight for several metres to the first branch, which meant there was enough light for a scrubby understorey of bushes and tufty grass. It also meant he could use them for making a wooden cabin or stockade or even a tree house, safe from non-climbing carnivores if any existed on the planet. There were orange fruits on the bushes below the trees and no sign that they had been eaten or harvested in recent days. The grass was undisturbed and the tips of the branches intact. That told him they were either poisonous, they were not ripe or there were no large fruit eaters in the vicinity. He removed his pack and took out the plant analyser and the tablet. He took several images of the fruits using his canteen as a size comparison and then squashed the pulp of one of the fruits onto the analyser. It was soft to the touch and quite aromatic. The smell was pleasant enough to make his saliva glands activate. In less than ten seconds the light array came up all green and one orange. That meant it was safe to eat, could be eaten without preparation but that it may cause diarrhoea if eaten in large quantities. ChOn decided to try one and found it delicious. He couldn't really compare it with anything because he had never eaten a piece of fresh fruit in his life. He only knew he had been missing out. He took another image of the cut section of the fruit with its multiple seeds and ate two more before moving on. He arrived on the other side of the forest in an hour of walking, checking over his shoulder at the sun because his shadow had been lost to him in the trees. He found more edible fruit and sampled several likely looking bushes and roots, finding everything edible but as the analyser advised him on a few occasions, not palatable. He registered all his findings on the tablet, as much for his own use as for that of future explorers and decided to continue across the next open plain to another rocky outcrop.

When he gained the slopes he climbed to the top and surveyed the plains further to the West. He was surprised by the sudden flurry of wings as a small flock of birds flew into his vision and wheeled to the ground near a crop of trees. He adjusted his visor and zoomed in on the area. His heart beat rapidly because there was the unmistakeable sign of branches that had been cut by a sharp tool. He lay down on his belly and waited several minutes but decided that had there been anybody in the copse, the birds would have been frightened away. He suddenly wanted desperately to see the humanoids that had cut those branches. He planned another excursion for two days hence, knowing that in the interim he would have to hide the landing craft and dismantle as much of it as possible. He did not want anybody knowing he was around until he was ready for it. He scanned the horizon with the zoom activated and saw in the distance the movement of a herd of herbivores. They were barely specks on his monitor but there was no mistaking them moving slowly and stirring up the dust. He would have an endless supply of meat and vegetable matter it seemed and water seemed to be relatively plentiful, although he had no idea of the seasons. He lowered himself down from the hill and trotted towards the copse where the birds had shown him the cut branches. He slowed down as he approached, even drawing his pulse gun but when he gained the first trees, the birds took off again in a rush and he knew he was alone.

In the middle of the copse was a spring gushing out of the ground and running away down a shallow wadi. Beside the spring was a flat rock that had been used by humanoids to eat. Bones were scattered nearby and ChOn followed his nose to where he found his first proof of higher animal life on the planet. An ape-like creature had been butchered and left beside the remains of a fire pit. The maggots were all through it, which told ChOn that it had been there several days at least. It reminded him of an image of a chimpanzee. He didn't believe this was the hunter but rather the game. The dead animal had orange coloured short fur and no tail. He took an image of it and examined the corpse as best he could without losing his stomach. From what he could tell, the animal had been killed by several chopping blows about the head and shoulders. That meant the hunters had probably had to surround the animal and kill it as it tried to run the gauntlet, probably with swords and clubs. So they had no medium range weapons such as bows or spears. Or if they did, they didn't have them with them when they perhaps surprised the animal watering. All his thoughts were registered on the tablet, somewhat like a doctor might register his findings during an autopsy. He was curious to know more about the humanoids who had hunted and killed this creature and then eaten so little of it. He was as yet, however, in no state of preparation to do a long range expedition in case his own camp were discovered. His next expedition might take him overnight at best but to trek for days on end he needed much more preparation.

He checked the position of the sun and decided to return to his base. His shadow was all important after he reached the interim hills because the otherwise flat landscape he had traversed offered little aid to navigation. His shadow was the key so he had to allow plenty of time before the sun disappeared altogether. He turned to start back and found himself looking into the eyes of a large canine-like animal which he assumed had come for water or to dispose of the remains of the ape. It was crouched in a menacing fashion, its lips drawn back in a silent snarl. Without warning it sprang at him, knocking him to the ground. It attacked him fiercely, its fangs catching the armour breast plate and its front paws astride his body. ChOn was able to wrestle himself to one side and draw his short sword before the creature recovered. It paced around him for a few precious seconds while ChOn unsheathed Shiew. The next time it sprang, only the front half of the body and a spray of blood reached ChOn. The other half dropped half a yard short, severed cleanly by a downwards sweep of the green katana. The beast continued to growl and scrabble at ChOn's feet before its brain realized it was dead. The light in its eyes faded to grey and went out. Ch0n wiped the blade on the beast's fur and stood *en garde* for long seconds before sheathing his blades and examining the creature. He decided it was a type of wolf but with pale orange fur and green eyes or at least they had been green in life. It was otherwise a typical carnivorous quadruped with long canine fangs and crushing teeth at the back. It was a lactating female, which indicated that within a short distance she would have a lair and pups, maybe a mate who would come looking for her. Perhaps he was being watched from close by. He turned his ocular to infra-red and heat seeking mode and scanned his immediate surrounds. He saw no canine but what he did see frightened him a lot more. Approaching from a distance of some fifty yards was what appeared to be a dragon. It didn't have wings but it was less like a crocodile and much more like he imagined a dragon would be. The creature was sniffing the ground and the air, its long forked tongue testing the breeze, which was at Ch0n's back. It could smell him and the wolf. It rose on to its hind legs and crept stealthily forwards. Ch0n lifted his visor for a better look and the creature disappeared before his eyes. That is, it almost disappeared. Where it had been was now a shimmer and nothing else. Ch0n looked again through the ocular and there it was. A perfectly camouflaged chameleon the size of a small dinosaur. It was not built for speed it seemed because its approach was steady and silent. Ch0n assumed it would spring at the last moment and kill its prey with its large jaws. He backed away from the wolf's carcass, making sure it was in a line with the creature's approach. He couldn't tell through the ocular if he was being seen or not because of the lack of detail but he planned that if the creature wanted meat, it was going to have to walk over some to get to Ch0n himself. He drew his pulse gun and set it to maximum. It would no doubt kill the chameleon but he didn't really care. All at once he realised that the planet was not going to be an easy place to survive with man-eating carnivores and invisible reptiles tracking him. He stepped behind a stout tree and watched as the chameleon reached the wolf. It went to all fours and picked up half the body with its tongue. With a deft flick, it disappeared into the reptile's maw and was soon followed by the other half. The chameleon stood up on its hind legs again and its tongue started flicking the air. It looked in ChOn's direction. It looked straight at his tree and started forwards again at a walk. It was in no hurry. ChOn waited until it was fifteen feet away before he fired. A sub-sonic, cone-shaped shockwave pulsed through the air and struck the beast full in the chest and it fell immediately to its knees and then tumbled onto its side. It was completely immobile. ChOn kept the gun trained on the creature's centre of mass as he approached it. He kicked the chameleon's mouth but there was no reaction. He lifted the ocular and watched in amazement as the creature started to take shape. Its body had lost its shimmer and was transforming into a pale orange colour similar to the wolf's. Its eyes were the same opaque grey that wolf's had become in death.

ChOn looked at the sun. It was getting too low in the sky for his liking. He wanted the safety of his cave but doubted there was enough time to reach it by nightfall. The near hills, however, did have some caves where he might spend the night closed in against predators. He lowered his monocular again and scanned the surroundings for a second time. He saw nothing. He returned to his daypack and set of at a soldiers' run for the hills. He had about half an hour to get himself established for the night.

He reached the first cave in less than twenty minutes. He was surprised at the lack of effort it had taken to run the three or four miles. He recalled the doctor telling him that a product of a small planet might be enhanced strength because of the low gravity and put it down to that. The cave entrance was too big for what he had in mind so he continued a little further to one which was more suitable. He was able to enter by stooping but the roof was high enough to stand. He turned on his flashlight and looked around. As far as he could tell, he was alone. It took him all the remaining time available to gather wood and rocks. The wood he stacked up close to the entrance and the rocks he used to block all but the top few inches. He hoped it would be enough to draw any smoke out of the cave. With some slight adjustment, it proved satisfactory and so he settled in to a long night with no food and as he discovered, no water either. His spare canteen was missing. He thought back to the scene of his two battles and remembered dropping his backpack before he took on the chameleon. He would have to return for it the following day.

Whether or not any predators attempted to enter the cave, Ch0n didn't know. As usual his minitron sent him to sleep, this time with images of canine predators, dinosaurs and various reptiles programmed into his night's training schedule.

He awoke refreshed but hungry as the first rays of light filtered in past his rock wall. Instinct told him that first light was probably not a good time to go to the spring because it was likely any nearby animals would do the same and he wanted to eat breakfast, not *be* breakfast. He left the cave and carefully patrolled to a point where he could see the spring. He zoomed in on it in time to see that a small group of large moose or giant elk-like creatures was watering there. They seemed unconcerned about any impending danger and lingered, pulling at the grass. Ch0n decided he was safe to retrieve his canteen and examine the chameleon further before returning to his hide. He set off at a jog, only slowing down when he was close to the spring and the elk. They were wary of his approach but didn't bolt when he arrived. They were obviously not hunted by the humanoids if that was the case. It reaffirmed to Ch0n that the locals had no long or medium range weapons or they could have easily speared or shot one of these enormous elk. That in turn would make them wary of humans. He imagined one of the wolves would not have been able to get so close. He was tempted to shoot one of them for food but reasoned that he could never carry it to his hide. He would have to be content with smaller prey for the time being. Instead, he tried to get as close to them as possible and found he could walk among them without their getting concerned. They looked at him with curious eyes but would just walk away a few yards if he got too close. It was almost as though they were domesticated but there was no evidence of it other than the fact they had no fear of him. He took images of them for the tablet and then wandered to the chameleon. It had been worried during the night by some carnivore. Its cheeks had been eaten away and there was a gaping hole in its rear end. The rest of it appeared untouched and when ChOn felt the creature's hide, he understood why. It was like thick armour and would probably be able to withstand an arrow. Certainly a spear would not penetrate it. He unsheathed Shiew and with a few passes, cut a section of the hide away. It was as stiff as wood and would make a good shield or breastplate for any able to harvest it.

The elk started to get a little skittish behind him so ChOn lowered the visor and scanned his immediate surrounds. The elk were standing, looking at a low scrubby bush some short distance away so ChOn concentrated his search in that direction. His heat detector saw a small point of red under the bush. It was too small to be a chameleon. He finished his study of the dead reptile, took several images of it and went to retrieve his canteen, which was where he had dropped his daypack. All the while he kept an eye on the red splash of heat under the bush. The elk had settled down somewhat but every now and then, their heads would rise as one to look at the bush. ChOn took out his pulse gun and walked warily towards the bush. The red splash got gradually bigger until it took form. It was a wolf. Suddenly it darted at him and the elk scattered behind him. He steadied and fired and the wolf fell almost at his feet. It was dead. ChOn had last fired the pulse gun at the chameleon, which was many times his own size and he had not changed the setting. The red fur was singed and smoking on the wolf's chest where the pulse had struck it. It smelt acrid and bitter on the breeze and the elk remained nervous and flighty in the middle distance. ChOn looked ruefully at the dead beast and realized he had killed practically every creature he had encountered in his short stay so far. He took photos for the tablet and was about to turn for his equipment when he saw movement under the bush. He set the gun to stun and waited. A red and grey furry ball had emerged from cover and was sniffing the air for its parent. ChOn stalked it quietly and the cub froze, blending instantly with its surroundings but finally ChOn changed course and pounced. The cub bit down hard on his gauntlet but did no damage. ChOn held it firmly to his chest, went for his daypack and unceremoniously shoved the creature into the main compartment. It weighed about six pounds and he had no idea how old it might be. As he followed the sun back to the base, he considered naming it. He had no real idea of how one should name a pet animal. He was CHON. A series of letters and numbers. He didn't think it fitting for a pet. He wanted to call it something more. Something suitable. He recalled a story he had read the first night he had been marooned. 'Robinson Crusoe'. He decided to call the pup, 'Friday'.

ChOn passed through the fruit groves checking all the while for chameleons and other hunters that might be stalking him. Behind him in the pack, the cub had stopped wriggling and trying to escape and was presumably asleep. By mid-afternoon, he had arrived, checked his perimeter and his traps and he settled down to make a cage for the cub. He used the aluminium cargo shelves, which were made of an open mesh, light but sturdy and far too strong for a cub to bend or twist. He installed Friday inside it and threw a piece of rabbit through the mesh. The cub approached it with caution, sniffed and licked it and finally started to eat. It struggled with the fur and bones but was obviously part-weaned. ChOn was pleased with himself and his find. He sat eating his own fare, talking constantly to the creature as though it could understand him. He told it how he had arrived and what he had done. He pointed out the recesses of the cave and the cache of weapons and stores. He even explained how the movement sensor worked. At last he was finished talking. The cub had eaten what it could of the rabbit and was exploring the cage, trying to escape. It whined and whimpered and almost drove ChOn to distraction but he resisted the temptation to let it out until he had fashioned a suitable lead and collar out of Velcro and a light chain. He finally released the cub, holding it while he put on the collar and then he took it outside to do its toilet before returning and tying it to the cage where it could not reach him but where it could sidle up near him when it was ready. ChOn was cooing to it and trying to touch it but it was wary of him. Finally, ChOn went to check his perimeter again, made sure all his traps were set, filled his water containers and settled for the night with the cub whining in its cage, the minitron plugged in to his ears and listened to a program on a loop on how to train animals. During the night, the movement detector monitored the movement of various small creatures but nothing large enough to set off the alarm. The cub eventually went to sleep and ChOn passed an uneventful night. The minitron whirred away telling ChOn about animal training and the the capacity of the tablet and all its miscellaneous functions as he had programmed it to do.

He woke the next morning to the sound of Friday whining to get out of the cage. ChOn let him out, attached the lead and dragged and coaxed him outside to relieve himself. The cub was pleased to be out of the cage and did his business immediately ChOn stopped tugging at his lead. ChOn knew from the minitron's night education program that the cub would want to pass water as soon as it woke up and left its bedding. He also knew he would have to trap more game if he were going to feed two hungry mouths. He tied the cub to its cage and checked his perimeter. He did it without thinking. It was part of his training and came as naturally to him as eating or sleeping.

"All patrols must establish and maintain a perimeter with separate day and night routine checks. Where a mechanical device forms part of that perimeter, each component of said device shall be checked in turn and repaired or replaced as deemed necessary."

It had been drilled into him by the minitron and years of practice as part of the squad. But now he was the entire squad and he had to do all the checks. It was an hour by the time he returned and he found the cub had dragged the cage to his food store and spread meat and fur over what seemed like the entire cave. He realized then that he should have fed and watered the creature before he did his rounds. He cursed himself for a fool and for not tethering the cage more securely. The pup had gorged itself. It was asleep inside the cage. ChOn smiled at it. It would be a separate challenge from those he had already encountered.

Gavan Connell

Chapter Seven: Consolidation

He had planned to move and store the heavy sections of the landing craft. He had also decided that he would make a schedule and stick rigidly to his plan. When the cub awoke, he took it outside, gave it a drink, waited until it had done its business and then led and dragged it to the craft, where he tethered it to a small bush. The cub wanted to play but after bouncing at the end of the tether a few times realized he could only go so far and so he settled down to watch ChOn at his work. Within minutes he was bored and tried the length of the tether again, only to discover that it was still the same. After complaining for some time, he realized nothing was going to change so he crept under the bush into the shade and went to sleep. Meanwhile, ChOn was using his small quantity of tools to dismantle the landing craft and haul the pieces into the cave. After a few trips he heard the radio crackle into life. It was the main ship of course but it startled him. The Chief Officer's voice sounded clear and close.

"ChOn this is Commander Guerra, do you read me?" It took him a minute or more to reach the handset.

"I read you loud and clear. I thought you had left me."

There was a long delay while the signal left and returned. Maybe half a minute.

"We left your orbit two days ago but we are still in normal flight mode. It will take another three or four hours for the droids to get the last of us settled in for the trip to Earth. Do you have anything to report?"

ChOn thought about his tablet and the images he had taken.

"Give me a few minutes and I will send you some images," he replied. He jogged to the cave and took the tablet to the radio. He plugged in the data transfer cable and pressed 'transmit.' A burst signal sounded and stopped. At the other end there was silence for several minutes and then Guerra.

"That's interesting but are there any minerals? Gold? Rare-earth elements?

"How the hell would I know that?" answered Ch0n angrily. "I've been here three days. I've made a shelter. I've found a way to eat and drink and sleep. I've been stalked by a chameleon-dragon and a wolf, both of which poor bastards I had to kill. I can say I haven't tripped over any gold or jewels or found any rivers of mercury. But I'm still alive and I aim to be when the next ship comes to plunder the place of everything it has. Meanwhile, I'll log everything and leave instructions right here as to where the tablet can be found. That is all."

He was about to rip the cable out of the radio in his anger and frustration but decided it wasn't such a good idea. He would need that radio years from now when the next vessel arrived in range. It was his lifeline. He would have to ensure it was safe from any danger. He turned it off and started to unbolt it and the cradle from the wall. He took them to the cave, placed them inside tube #6 and added it to his inventory. He took a section of cooked rabbit and a bowl of water to the cub on his return. It allowed him to feed it with not much more than a token growl before setting to eat. By the end of the day, the capsule was mostly dismantled into manageable sections. It would take another day inside the cave to break it down into its components. There was an enormous quantity of useful material including panels, fibre optic cables and synthetic strapping, shelving and heat shields. His first brainwave involved making a cot from the webbing seats. He suspended it two metres above the ground on four legs, one of which was made from the ladder. He figured that if a wolf came into the cave he could at least fight it off from a safe distance. A look at the sun revealed he had time to check the perimeter before nightfall. His traps were full again. The pup was whining for food as usual but ChOn decided he would have to earn his supper. He took the kinetic pistol from its holster on his belt and turned it on. The red light on the rear of the loading tube shone a dull red. He cut the cub's ration into small cubes and led him to a spot in front of the tube which ChOn used as a seat. The cub pulled against the lead. ChOn called softly to him.

"Friday!" He levelled the pistol and pressed the trigger mechanism. It made a loud 'click' to advise him the safety was engaged. The dog was startled by the sound and looked at ChOn, who had obviously been responsible for it. When the cub's eyes met his, ChOn made another 'click' and threw a cube of rabbit at the cub's feet. The creature pounced on the morsel and wolfed it down.

"Friday!" *CLICK!* ChOn threw another piece of rabbit when Friday's eyes met his. Five minutes later, the cub was sitting on command. ChOn was feeling very pleased with himself and the minitron. He took Friday outside, to the place he wanted him to toilet, waited until he was done and returned to complete his evening's work with the pup tethered to the cage. By the time ChOn had broken down the landing craft's console and stored all the LEDs, switches, buttons, diodes, cables and sensors, the pup had crawled into his cage and was asleep. ChOn followed his example and, tired from his day's hard labour, slept like the dead with the minitron refreshing his memory on survival techniques and weapon handling, its default setting.

It took ChOn more than a week to dismantle and store all the parts of the landing craft. The radio and homing beacon he took to the site where he thought another craft might eventually land, climbed the tallest tree he could find and installed it with Velcro. He turned it on, laughing out loud at the futility of doing so when he knew the probability of another craft landing inside five years was a million to one or worse but he left it on anyway. He went back to the cave and surveyed his final work. The part of his camp set aside for daily use was at the right-hand side of the main entrance so as to not be overcome by a rushing force but so ChOn could fire right handed from his cot. The Rail gun was mounted on a tripod under an overhang where it could be deployed along the rock face on either side of the cave. His cot was standing alone where he could defend it from all sides but nothing could jump from a ledge on to it. The cache of stores he would not need for some time was buried under what was now a flattened hard earth floor with only markers on the walls to line up the individual tubes. His dried meat was hanging out of reach of Friday, who now had the run of the cave. The motion sensor monitoring equipment was stored where ChOn could see it from his seat and his cot. His weapons were hung under the cot within easy reach. Shiew, the Chontium katana, was sheathed and stored on the cot so he slept with the blade against his body. Friday's cage was just inside the entrance to the cave where he could eventually provide early warning and defend the entrance against intruders alongside ChOn. He had depth, concentration of firepower, all round protection, good lines of fire and overhead cover. That was the best he could do by himself. The other principles of defence relied on being part of a multi-person team. He would have to do without them.

Friday had provided a pleasant diversion up till now but ChOn realized he would have to postpone his next exploratory trip until the cub would follow him and not need too much attention. He figured that would be at least a few weeks away so he decided to fortify his camp further. He was a little concerned that there was no outer wall to protect the entrance. He wanted at least some obstacle that would make an attacking force have to approach from a flank and not just rush straight in from the frontal approach. That applied to animals as well as humanoids. He was happy he could defend the cave for a short while but he needed to be able to inflict casualties on an attacking force or risk a siege situation with no means of escape or seizing the initiative. The rock face provided a natural channelling obstacle on two sides. The top of the hill was relatively stable but would need work so the entrance couldn't be blocked by a rock fall. He designed his outer wall with a defile at one end and a sally port at the other, hidden from the front. It led to a cleft in the rock where he could climb unseen to the top of the hill and make a run for it or fire long range weapons from the heights. It took him three weeks to build, not the two he had allowed, even though his strength amazed him in the low gravity. He built a two and a half metre high rock wall using stones he pushed from the top of the hill down the rock face. He used tree branches and trunks to make a ledge on the inside along which he could run and fire over the top of the wall. His sally port was stepped for rapid climbing and so Friday could negotiate it as well. At the top of the cleft, ChOn buried some rations from the ship, a couple of blocks of explosives and detonators and a grenade. The movement sensors were moved slightly to cover better the more exposed side of the outer wall and the rail gun was sited to fire into the only opening big enough to take a man. That man would then have to run along the rock wall for several metres before turning at right angles into the cave. ChOn was delighted with his design. The only problem was that it could be seen for hundreds of yards. He set to, transplanting shrubs along the wall and even in the cracks and crevices on the vertical face. That led in turn to the need for more water so he had to use one of his tubes as water storage. All the while Friday was growing and learning. By the time the fort was complete, he was following ChOn everywhere and had an impressive array of tricks at his disposal.

ChOn set a day for his next exploratory trip, one that would take him away from the fort for a few days at least. He would leave as soon as he was happy his plants were likely to survive. He had had the chance to survey his entire surroundings at length whilst getting the rocks at the top of the hill for his wall and had decided to head in the same direction as his first foray but to continue for two days unless he encountered humanoids before that time in which case he would follow them and observe them from a distance for at least two further days. He would then return to the fort and review his entire situation. His expedition would be a fact-finding mission looking for sapients, animals and edible plants. He wanted to map out his territory in every direction starting with the 'West'. He spent the next three days arranging his equipment for a long trek. He decided to try and live off the land rather than take several days' rations. He would take a couple of food bars from the ship, enough water for a day for him and Friday and the rest would be weaponry and the tablet, on which he would set up the cartographic mode he had learned about. It would then be able to create a map using his original start point and displacement in every direction using the planet's magnetic field to calculate distance and direction and its gravity field to calculate altitude. He could store waypoints easily plus points of interest including food and water sources, mineral deposits, caches, caves and safe areas and of course areas of danger such as quicksand, enemy habitations (including chameleon lairs) and safe passages though swamps and the like. All that information could be stored on the machine's drive and later transmitted via radio to a ship or via Bluetooth XV to his helm where the local map would automatically be displayed on the heads-up display on demand.

Chapter Eight: Long Range Reconnoissance

Three days later just before first light Ch0n woke and checked his perimeter. The night before, he had hidden everything of value in the spare tubes in case some creature wanted to strew things about or some inquisitive humanoid wanted to search his cave. The rail gun was the most difficult item to hide because of its size but it was also the most important weapon Ch0n had at his disposal and he could ill afford to lose it. The sensors were small enough to leave out but the monitoring equipment he had to secure along with the rail gun before he left. He dressed in his full patrol order with the long sleeves and long trousers. His daypack contained the tablet, cordage, food bars and water. Otherwise it was empty and available to store anything new and interesting he might come across. He had a crossbow and quiver slung across his back and Shiew sheathed between his daypack and his person with the handle protruding over his right shoulder at a jaunty angle next to his head. His weapon belt was full. The pulse gun and kinetic pistol were at the front, the grenades in their pouches and the tonfa and sais down his thighs and in his boots. The helm came last. He tested its various lenses and the heads up display. The microphone and receiver he removed after he had called for a radio check and realized nobody was going to answer. He was ready to explore and he was ready to fight if things turned sour.

They set off as soon as Ch0n was satisfied with the security of his stores. Obviously there was some degree of risk to everything not buried in the tubes but he had to accept that fact. He could withstand the loss of his cot and the dog cage. The sensors were unlikely to be found but if he lost them, he had to wear it. The cub was now able to warn him of the approach of anything or anyone. It had taken to leaving the cave at night and hunting locally anyway. The sheets of metal would be attractive to any iron-age culture and would be carried off but the reality was, they were just too big to hide. They were tucked away behind a few rocks but would never withstand even a cursory search of the cave. The tubes on the other hand would take some finding even if someone were looking for them because any evidence of their existence was long ago tamped down by human and canine feet.

By late afternoon they had traversed the terrain Ch0n was familiar with. They looked at the oasis for some time before approaching it cautiously. Friday went to the bush where Ch0n had found him and sniffed around somewhat excitedly before resuming his place at Ch0n's heel. They fed on rabbit and watered before continuing their westward journey. All the while the tablet was relentlessly processing information on direction and altitude and Ch0n was manually entering in the information he wanted known, such as the location of a stand of what looked like bamboo but was almost a hundred feet high and so dense in parts he could barely make way through it. He cut off a long section with Shiew to reveal a hollow tube with super strong walls. The trunk was as thick as his forearm and straight as a laser from base to tip with little variation in diameter. He could see from one end clean through to the other but when he put one end on a fallen tree, and sat on it, it barely bent under his weight. Ch0n had no idea what he might need the trunks for but he did know they were not to be ignored. Towards late afternoon, he started to survey the terrain looking for a suitable bivouac site. He was hungry and tired. Friday had galloped away several times and caught and devoured what looked like tiny rodents plus he could drink any old ground water so he was well fed and watered. Ch0n wanted a cave if he could find one and headed for a low rise in the distance where he thought he might find one or at least an overhang he could secure. On the way he discovered a spring and a colony of rabbits living off the sweet grass that surrounded it. He entered it in the tablet before shooting several of the unfortunate creatures and filling up his water bladder. An hour later they reached the outcrop and ChOn found what he was looking for, a huge fallen rock with a crawl space underneath and only one entrance. He entered it on the tablet, cooked his rabbits and fed one to Friday before moving rocks from below the boulder to the entrance of the crawl space. He put grass and small branches into the space, told Friday to go to the toilet and then they both crawled under. ChOn reached out and dragged rocks so as to block the entrance. Nothing bigger than a rabbit could get in without a fight. He positioned Shiew at his side, took the pulse gun out of its holster, inserted his earphones and went to sleep. Friday curled up by his side and every now and then twitched an ear as he heard the sounds of the minitron passing ChOn information about survival and weapon handling.

ChOn was woken up when Friday decided it was time to leave their den. The sun was dawning and chinks of light struggled through the rock barrier. ChOn cleared the entrance and the two travellers started their day with cold rabbit, some fruit ChOn had picked from his fruit grove the previous afternoon, a drink of water and a look around. ChOn climbed to the top of the outcrop to survey the surroundings and in the morning light saw a vast green plain stretched out before him. It was dotted with the orange elk he had seen a few 'weeks' earlier. A small herd of larger, buffalo-like animals was also grazing and in the distance the morning sun reflected off water. ChOn decided not to explore the plain because it had no features of obvious interest apart from the water. He was more interested in humanoids and the location of shelters, game, unusual trees and plants for consumption and deep down, he wanted to find gold. Gold was of no use to him at all but he knew it would be highly sought after by any exploratory vessels and so if he knew about it, he had some level of control over his possible rescue.

If he found it and reported it, a landing craft would have to land. Otherwise they could just upload information and leave. But not for gold and not for silver and not for rare-earth elements. Or diamonds.

At the end of the second day he had still not seen any humanoid village. He knew there had been one somewhere near his current location because they had seen it from the main ship when in orbit. Despite his lack of success, Ch0n decided to stick with his plan and return to his fort. He would be able to explore again. After all, he had nothing else to do but explore and map his territory and maybe expand it in time. He turned 'north' and trekked for an hour before turning 'east'. He was returning via a slightly different route so as to make the map a little more complete. Box patrolling, it was called. They had done it several times on different planets when the entire squad was deployed. Being a creature of habit and training, Ch0n just set out doing it. He also started to look for a place to bivouac and there didn't seem to be much on offer but he eventually found another boulder with enough space underneath it to secure them both. They passed the night exactly as they had passed the previous one.

They traversed the country all the third day without incident. Ch0n marked down his points of interest including a fast-flowing stream with pure white quartz cuttings and broken rocks in its bed and another grove of the same fruit trees he had encountered on his first trip. There was also a huge tract of the bamboo-like trees towering over the plain. Ch0n noted that both stands of bamboo had been close to permanent water and decided it must need its roots wet to grow so prolifically. They set up camp in a shallow cave. Friday slept at the opening most of the night as well as roaming the immediate area in search of small game. At first light they set off for their final leg of the patrol. Ch0n was looking forward to returning to the fort. He had realized on the second day that, rudimentary as they were, the fort had sufficient creature comforts for it to be classified as 'home'. He quickened his pace, only stopping to enter the location of a small lake full of flowering lilies. He thought he caught a flash of movement in the water and resolved to return with his fishing equipment and try his luck. He was getting decidedly sick of rabbit and coarse, edible leaves and roots punctuated by fruit.

In the late afternoon, they had their fort in sight when Friday started to growl and show his hackles. ChOn looked where Friday was pointing but could see nothing. He lowered the visor and selected heat vision, and saw the chameleon moving across their front. The wind was in their faces and so it had no idea they were so close. ChOn put his hand on the wolf's muzzle to quiet him. Ahead the chameleon raised its head and its long tongue flickered in the breeze. It turned away from ChOn and Friday and started moving purposefully towards the fort. ChOn assumed that it had caught their four-day-old scent and was moving to investigate but then he saw a small herd of elk put their heads up as one and look straight at the dragon. They could obviously not see it but it must have made a noise to startle them. It stopped when they turned to look. It stood stock still and ChOn lifted his visor to look. He could see nothing apart from what looked like a slight blur against the background. He lowered the visor again and there it was. It was not moving, apart from its tongue, which continued to taste the air. Then it put one foot forward and stood again. It repeated this creeping forward while the elk grazed somewhat uneasily, raising and lowering their heads in turn. Suddenly there was a rush of movement in ChOn's visor and the beast darted the last dozen feet into the elk, grabbing a calf in its jaws and clawing at the mother which was trying to fight off whatever it was that had her calf. The chameleon turned towards Ch0n and started forward, the weanling elk still in its jaws. Ch0n was certain he must be seen at any moment and set the pulse gun to its maximum power in case he had to kill the chameleon. Luck, however, must have been shining upon him because it suddenly turned at an angle and strode away with its prey still kicking and squealing. The elk, meanwhile had scattered in all directions and little puffs of dust and moving bush gave away their positions as they stampeded. All except one that he could see. The mother of the dragon's prey was standing still where she had been clawed. Blood was running down both her front legs from the withers. Her head was down and she looked beaten and in shock. Friday caught the scent of blood and darted forward, only to be checked by a stern word from Ch0n. Together they approached the wounded animal. Like the herd he had encountered before, she showed no fear of Ch0n but she was nervous of Friday. Ch0n sent him to wait downwind and he himself went to the creature. She allowed him to touch her with nothing more than a flinch as a reaction. She certainly was in shock and when Ch0n put a rope around her neck, she allowed him to lead her towards the fort. They had not gone more than twenty yards when a second animal fell in behind them from out of the scrub. It was a large bull calf with a rack of antlers, perhaps the brother of the slain animal. Ch0n arrived at the fort and led the cow through the outer perimeter into the enclosure within. The calf followed and Ch0n closed the wooden gate. Friday was sniffing around the cow which appeared to be interested in nothing more than lying down, maybe to die, thought ChOn. But he wanted the doe to live. His original plan was to lead her to the fort and kill her for meat but its plight touched him. He quickly went to his store of medicine, which he had hidden in a shallow hole in a tube and painted a salve on the wounds. They were deep but relatively clean-edged. ChOn took out a needle and thread and sewed them shut. It took him more than half an hour before he finished. The doe was lying on her side with her head on the ground and ChOn was not sure she would last the night. He went out and cut some bushes for the calf to eat and prepared the fort for habitation, taking everything from its hiding place and setting his home up again. Friday went to the cow and started to lick the blood from her wounds and ChOn feared the wolf would kill her during the night if she didn't die first. By the time he had checked his perimeter, set his traps, replenished the water supply and was ready for his cot, the doe was less of a mess. Friday had licked her wounds clean. The calf was backed into a corner with its head down defensively. Friday was eager to get more blood and ChOn had to tie him up for the first time in weeks. ChOn then climbed up to his cot, lay next to Shiew and put the earphones in his ears. The minitron started its hypnotic tone and sent ChOn to sleep. It then changed to a loop describing the husbandry of bovines as ChOn had programmed it to do.

Gavan Connell

He woke at first light as was his custom. Friday was already standing at the end of his tether watching the doe. She was on her feet in the corner with the young buck. The brush he had collected the previous evening had been eaten and the water half drunk. He climbed from his cot and let Friday loose. The wolf ran outside immediately and jumped the gate. Ch0n surveyed the two elk. After his earlier doubts, he now knew in his own mind that the doe would live but would need rest and plenty of food. Ch0n noted the doe's udder was swollen like the night before. He wondered if he might be able to milk her in her weakened state and after consulting the minitron, had a container of the warm fluid, which he tasted, drank and then shared with the wolf.

Ch0n ran his eye over the doe. Her eyes were quite bright. The wounds were not septic. Ch0n knew that the wolf's saliva had helped in that regard, even though he had licked off most of the antiseptic salve. She had no antlers. She stood some six feet tall at the shoulder and was perhaps nine feet long. Her legs were strong and long. She had a shortish mane of dark hair some three inches long, running from her ears to her shoulders and down towards her chest. She was chewing, which told Ch0n she was a ruminant. Best of all, she was docile and the rest of the herd he had seen were of the same nature. Therefore, they could be domesticated. And domesticated meant being used as beasts of burden as well as providing a source of meat, hide and milk. Ch0n had 'seen' images of oxen in their yokes and llamas and yaks carrying heavy loads on their backs. He had also 'seen' images of humans riding cattle and deer. He had no idea how they controlled these animals underneath them but he knew the minitron would be able to enlighten him. He was impatient to know but force of habit and self-discipline took him outside the fort to his perimeter. He made himself do a thorough check. His spring trap yielded the daily rabbit and his snares another two. He saw a large lizard basking in the early rays of the sun and shot it with the pulse gun. He was able to manage everything back to the fort, where he set to skinning the rabbits and tying the lizard to the wall. It was more than two feet in length and weighed about ten pounds he guessed. It had two even rows of teeth, lacking canines, which indicted it was probably vegetarian. The skin was an even greenish orange hue and ChOn wanted to know if it had the chameleon qualities of its enormous cousin. He had to wait half the morning before the creature showed signs of life. Its first action was to blink and look around. Its second was to bolt straight up the wall, only to be stopped in its tracks by the tether around its midriff and shoulders. It stopped still, straining against the chain and then flattened itself against the rock and tried to make itself invisible. Its skin did not change colour. It just ceased to move. It closed its eyes and ChOn had the impression it was just pretending not to be there. When he approached it, it scrabbled against the rocky wall and finally jumped to the ground and ran the length of the tether in all directions. ChOn left it to calm down while he took images of the deer and then the lizard. He collected more brush for the deer, saw they had water and painted the doe's wounds again. When he was done, he allowed himself to insert the plugs and turn on the minitron. He asked it how humans could ride and control quadrupeds. Almost instantly he had a menu of options to choose from. He programmed the machine and lay back on his cot.

Friday returned from his hunting and went to his cage. He had almost outgrown it by now but he liked the security of it. He looked up at Ch0n. It was unusual for him to be still in the cot at this time of day. Normally they were outside exploring or hunting. He was bored.

Ch0n was not. He was receiving 'images' direct to the image-processing lobe of his brain through the minitron's earplugs. He 'watched' the domestication of the horse, the camel, the cow, the elk and the water buffalo. Each was different but the same. The humans that used them employed a variety of methods to control them, depending on their role. He saw the Lapps riding their caribou and decided that was the closest thing to the elk he had here on this planet. He did take note of the plains Indians and their use of the travois to haul their belongings from camp to camp. He decided that was the best way for him too. He wondered how he might make a saddle for the elk. It would have to be the buck he was to ride. The doe was big but the buck would be bigger and stronger when it was full grown. It was already as big as the doe and Ch0n could guess it was still young because it had been allowed to stay in the herd. He guessed it to be about two years old, based on the comparisons e had made with elk antlers. It was still immature or the dominant stag would have driven it from the herd but Ch0n was thinking that it would not be long before the buck were a mature male and he would have to train it before then. He resolved to start the process immediately. With a quick bound he landed lightly at the foot of the ladder. He went to the two deer and talked to them in sweet tones, all the while getting closer and closer. The doe was the quieter of the two and Ch0n wondered if it were because of her wounds or just because she was more mature. The young buck let Ch0n feed it some sweet leaves and to touch its muzzle. Ch0n went beside the buck and ran his hand down its back and rump. The creature remained still but Ch0n could feel the muscles tense and ready for flight at the slightest moment. He went back to the buck's head and stroked the huge ears. Then he turned his attention to the doe. She was still in a bad way. The scars would heal in time but for the moment she would have to be kept quiet and contained. As he studied her, Ch0n was mentally designing the harness he would put at her broad chest and back over her shoulders. The two poles that would make up the travois would be joined above her back and trail behind her by some fifteen feet. That meant he would have to find poles about twenty feet long for the sides and then more for the load carrying platform. She could be led by a head halter attached to the saddle he would have to make for the buck. His mind went to the image of the complicated western saddle he had 'seen' earlier. He could never make something like that with the tools and resources at hand. He could, however make something less weighty and still comfortable. He would use a hide as a blanket over the buck's back and make a girth strap and stirrup leathers out of webbing, of which he had a great amount. Finally he would try and make a shell to fit his backside using the sprayform. He thought he could spray it over the beast's back with a synthetic sheet to protect the beast's fur. That way he would have something that fit the beast and if he were to spray layers on top of that and then sit on the foam before it set, he could make quite a fair substitute for a saddle. He could control the creature using a head halter. But first, he had to get a hide to use as a blanket, one that wasn't too big or hard to cure. It would probably have to come from another elk but ChOn didn't want to start hunting them. The fact one could get to within touching distance was a bonus. If he started killing them, they would soon learn to fear him and he would never be able to take advantage of their placid nature again. His eye was attracted by Friday leaving his cage and padding towards the entrance. It put the idea into ChOn's head that a wolf pelt might be just the right size. He had only seen the single adult wolf that had been Friday's mother and he had no idea where to look but he knew there was at least one den within half a day's forced march. He would start by looking there.

That night he dined on his first non-rabbit meat. The lizard was good eating. ChOn discovered in its stomach some snails and mushy vegetable matter. He hadn't seen any snails but now he knew they existed and could provide a change of diet. In addition, the skin was soft and pliable. He pegged it out and scraped it.

"Just in case I need it," he told himself. He saved the neat, white teeth even though they seemed too small to be of any use.

Gavan Connell

Chapter Nine: On the Move

Seven weeks passed. Friday grew into a big, playful animal. The doe recovered from her wounds but was weak and needed to graze outside to get enough forage to recover her strength. The buck was quite tame and would allow ChOn to walk around him and touch him on any part of his body without flinching. ChOn had taken to brushing him with damp grass to keep him clean and get rid of loose fur. The lizard hide was now worked into a soft roll almost two feet by one foot. ChOn had not found the wolf he needed to make a rug but he had instead made it from forty, sewn-together rabbit hides, dried on a stick triangle and scraped with the edge of a short sword. The buck was quite used to having the rug on its back and a strap around its belly. The halter had been more difficult to design and make and even harder to put on the beast. It didn't like having ChOn's arms around its head and so it took half a day to get it in place and velcroed together. ChOn discovered the deer liked the sweet fruit from the copse by the oasis and he gave it to them as a treat and a reward for letting him handle them and prepare them for their new roles. He used two of his same-day patrols to recover the bamboo poles for the travois. He had made it and fitted it to the doe and had led her around with no weight on it at first, increasing the load until she was content to pull several hundred pounds. One other thing ChOn had learned from his sessions with the minitron was how to hobble the deer so they wouldn't roam too far. He didn't have the cordage to tether them and he didn't want them all tangled up anyway. He had fitted the hobbles several times to get the beasts used to wearing them but had not let them outside alone. He decided it was time to try it. Apart from anything else, he was sick of having to forage further and further for their fodder and was even sicker of the stench of their droppings and urine. Friday often ate their droppings but ChOn still had to clean up several times a day.

On the sixtieth day of his enforced stay on the planet, ChOn led the two deer outside. He took them to the stream where there was plenty of sweet grass and open ground so he could watch them from the entrance to the fort. They were content to stay where the pick was good and so ChOn went inside to plan his next trip. If he could ride the buck, he would do so. He was confident the creature would not find his weight too much but had delayed the making of the saddle as long as he could in case the buck was still growing. It was over six feet at the shoulder. ChOn could not see over it without standing on tip toe. It was also ten feet from nose to rump. ChOn had tried to guess its weight several times but couldn't. The minitron told him a full-grown moose could weigh up to 1800 pounds so he figured it would have to be something similar. ChOn in battle order weighed two hundred and fifty pounds and the buck could easily manage that.

He decided to go more 'North' of his last patrol. He was certain he had not missed the humanoids' camp by much the last time. He also knew that he had to range further, but mounted that would be easier. There was no map to use of the area so he would be making one as he went and not trying to plan too far in advance. The important thing now was that he could stay away longer because he could carry more provisions and weapons.

It took three days for ChOn to properly design and make the saddle. It turned out to be a complicated process and the buck didn't like the noise of the foam coming out of the container. Or the smell it seemed. Finally, though, the first layer was completed and from there it was a matter of adding layers sufficient to make a comfortable seat. The stirrup leathers and girth straps were incorporated into the design. Velcro was used to fasten the girth in place after passing through a carabineer to get it tight enough. To mould it to his backside, ChOn used a large rock to sit the saddle upon and then he sprayed the foam thickly on the top surface. A thin sheet of synthetic sheeting kept his backside from getting covered in foam as he lowered himself to the saddle and held himself in position for some minutes without putting his full weight on it. Twenty minutes later, the seat was as firm as any leather saddle would have been and probably much more comfortable, ChOn decided. The next step was to fit it to the buck and let him get used to it before any attempt to mount up. Just the same, ChOn decided that he would start his patrol in three days' time. He figured if he couldn't ride the buck in three days, he would lead him and learn on the way. He went to the stream where the deer were grazing. They looked up at him and started walking awkwardly towards him. He took fruit out of his pockets and fed them what they were looking for.

ChOn didn't know whether to fit the saddle inside the fort or outside. He didn't know if the buck would thrash about and damage something or indeed if he would bolt into the distance and never come back. In the end he decided that outside with the hobbles would be best. He led the two back to the entrance and went in for the saddle. He showed the buck the blanket and threw it over its back. Then he put the saddle in place and tightened the two girth straps. The buck just stood still. It looked around at the strange thing sitting on its back and shook itself like a dog. Then it ambled to a nearby bush where its mother was already pulling at the leaves and started to graze. ChOn was dumbstruck. He decided to chance his luck mounting the beast. He had no idea what would follow or even if he would know what to do himself if he were able to mount. He attached the reins to the halter and hoisted himself into the saddle. His feet found the stirrups. The buck jumped in the air once and stood still. ChOn dug his heels into the beasts belly and it started to run awkwardly in the hobbles. Five yards later, ChOn found himself on his backside. The buck stood still and waited for him. He mounted it again and dug his heels into the belly again and fell off again. He loosened off the stirrup leathers so he could ride straight legged and this time he was able to stay aboard albeit with some effort on his part. He had assumed it would be easy but now he knew he would have to practise over the coming days. The buck was unfazed and allowed him to mount and dismount at will. After an hour, he could ride in a straight line without falling off and could make the buck walk and change direction. He even made it stop once but usually he had to let it stop when it felt like it. He rode for the best part of another hour. When he removed the saddle he was feeling pretty pleased with himself.

The following morning, Ch0n woke with his thighs screaming in pain. He knew why. He was sufficiently in tune with his body to realize he should have stretched his inner thighs before riding in the position he had. He also knew the best way to loosen up was to get back in the saddle and stretch them again. And again. His perimeter check was conducted slowly and painfully.

By the end of the day, he had had three separate one-hour sessions. He could stay on the buck at a run, make it change direction and make it go and stop. He fell off three times during the day. He knew he would be sore again the following morning and decided to postpone his next foray for a few more days until he could ride for a few hours at a time and not feel sore the next morning. It took another four days before he was confident. By then he was going stir crazy. He had planned and planned but couldn't leave until he was ready. His initial plan to lead the buck and practise riding had not come to fruition but now in retrospect he wished he had tried it anyway. The reality as he saw it was that he would have to spend a lot of time walking and he might by now have been far away. He decided to leave two days hence, time enough to pack up his fort and bury his cache again until he returned. His plan was to be absent for some weeks if things allowed. He decided to pack everything away on this occasion and so buried the movement sensors. He decided not to take much water with him because he had discovered so many small streams and springs on his previous trip that he was confident he would do so again. He estimated that one bladder for him and the dog plus one each for the deer would suffice for two days. If he went one day without seeing water he could simply return to the previous source and then set off in a different direction. He loaded the travois carefully, allowing himself the luxury of the solar stove, an air mattress and a synthetic tarpaulin. For the sake of balance, the water was located centrally. It had to be towards the front so it was the highest thing off the ground for clearance. There were other things tucked into nooks and crannies on the travois. Mostly they were weapons or ammunition that he could hide out on the plain somewhere for future use if and when he needed them. His 'military' training made him plan strategically as well as for the short term.

Ch0n considered his night routine. He wouldn't be able to sleep under rocks this patrol because the safety of his deer would be paramount. He would have to camp in caves or at the minimum, with his back to an obstacle to be able to defend his group to the front and flanks. The wolf would have to be his early warning. The rail gun was last to be packed so it could be unloaded first. This time he decided to carry some extra grenades, smoke and an anti-armour tube with one of each type of rocket. As a last minute addition, he threw in a sprayform canister.

At first light on the day of his departure, he checked his perimeter as usual. There were only two rabbits in his traps. He was starting to thin out the warren and the break would allow them to breed. He took the traps and stowed them on the travois. The buck stood for him while he saddled it up and the doe waited patiently for him as he fastened the complicated harness across her chest and shoulders. Ch0n dressed himself as before in full patrol order but this time he had his daypack, horse bow and quivers behind the saddle instead of on his back.   The short sword was sheathed in a scabbard in front of his left knee, the handle sticking straight up.   The tablet was velcroed to his right thigh where he could see it.   He walked around the doe and pulled at her harness, checked the tie-downs on the travois and checked the buck's girth straps.   He decided to take an image of his little caravan for future explorers.   Then he hauled himself into the saddle and touched his heel to the buck's shoulder.

Chapter Ten: Contact

Ch0n had imagined that the journey would be a lot more rapid than it turned out to be. He had had visions of trotting across the wide plains covering miles and miles every day. The reality was much different. The doe was a sturdy beast and was happy to trudge along behind the buck or even walk alongside. The problem was the travois. It was functional and strong but any attempt to travel at more than a walk resulted in the thing bouncing all over the place and once it even overturned. So Ch0n had to be content to walk along at the same pace he could have gone alone. Still, he thought the advantage of the extra weight he could travel with and the extra distance he could cover more than made up for his disappointment. They passed the lake with the lilies. Ch0n pulled one out by the roots and tested it for eating qualities. He was surprised to find it quite edible and nutritious in value and when he tried it, it was quite sweet to eat. He pulled out several of the plants. He had to tether the deer because the buck had tried to wade in to the water to eat the plants. They were content to eat what he provided while he stowed several for later on. Later they passed another enormous bamboo grove near a spring that was feeding a wide, shallow basin covered in green grass and small shrubs. Ch0n decided to give the deer and himself a rest so he removed the travois and hobbled the two animals while he registered the site on the tablet. Nearby on the edge of the green was a small stone rise with a cave in the rock face. Ch0n decided to investigate it as a possible outpost. He liked the feel of the place with the sweet water and grass so close to the bamboo grove. He left the deer to their grazing and started for the rise with Friday at his heels. It took about twenty minutes before they started to climb out of the basin when Friday stopped and sniffed the wind. He growled in his throat and his hackles rose. Ch0n dropped his visor but there was no sign of a dragon. The wolf was pointing at the cave entrance only fifty yards distant. ChOn did a quick weapon check. He had the pulse gun and the rail gun as well as Shiew. He decided to go with the pulse gun because of its marginally longer range. He knew it could kill a dragon at close range if needs be. Without thinking, he turned to his flank and approached the cave from an angle. If something were to charge out, he would be better served on the flank than in its path. He wished he were not alone but that was a pointless feeling. He was alone and he would always be alone. He had to develop tactics that suited lone-wolf fighting.

ChOn was less than ten feet from the cave when Friday froze and growled low in his throat. He lay flat on the ground in a shallow dip and waited for whatever it was to emerge. It didn't take long. The chameleon came out of the cave at a walk. ChOn decided right then it must be the top predator of the planet or it would have been more cautious. It was bigger than the others ChOn had seen but not by much. It was upwind of them and so couldn't smell them but it flicked its tongue and caught the scent of the deer in the distance. Its head turned and then it started to change colour. In less than thirty seconds it was a shimmering green the same colour as the grass at its feet. ChOn watched it through the visor and knew he would have to kill it immediately or risk losing one or both of his deer. They were hobbled and the whole reason for that was so they couldn't run away. He drew the pulse gun and set it to 75% power. The creature had only walked twenty feet when he called to it. It stopped and turned to face him. ChOn stood up and waved. The dragon looked back at the deer and then at ChOn and came towards him. He shot it over the heart, or where he thought the heart should be. It staggered and dropped like a stone. Its eyes were still working but its limbs were jelly. It wasn't dead and ChOn decided to make a run for it and leave the area before the beast recovered. It would be handy to know there was one living here if he wanted to use the place as an escape route or to leave a cache. He thought how secure a cave would be with a dragon guarding his stuff and resolved to return with his most precious stores to bury them here under the eye of this huge chameleon. He took off down the slope at a run and reached the deer in just a few minutes. He looked back at the cave and saw the creature still stunned at the entrance. He took a further few minutes to get the doe harnessed up and then they were all trekking North East on a walk into the unknown. ChOn checked the dragon through his visor and then with the telescope until they left the rim of the basin and followed a straight line towards a high peak on the horizon.

The ground hadn't changed since they left the cave. The entire scape was undulating plains with rocky rises every so often and copses of trees, shallow springs and creek beds, some dry and some running but all difficult to cross with the travois. In the distance ChOn could see a line of craggy hills. He was navigating towards the highest point. He hoped that from there he might be able to see across the plain he was sure existed on the other side of the mountains. He had seen the footage from the mother ship and was confident that that was where the settlement was going to be. He felt a tingle of anticipation course through him. He missed being with people. Passing most of one's life asleep was one thing but his waking hours were full of team training and practice. He was not accustomed to living and working alone and he didn't like it. He realized it only with the prospect of an encounter with sapients. It made him press on harder for the line of hills ahead.

It took them all the rest of the day to arrive at the foothills of the rise. ChOn decided that he should find a camp for the night and tackle the climb the following day. From a distance he had seen a cave which he could defend and which would allow him to stable the deer for the night and leave the wolf at the entrance while he went hunting. By the time he was ready to hunt it was almost dark but all was in order. He took his pulse gun as well as the kinetic pistol and the katana for self-protection, set his helm to heat and starlight modes and set off. The wolf was not happy to be left behind and set up a howling as ChOn trudged off but soon all was quiet again. Within only a few metres he came across a goat-like creature in a copse of trees. This struck ChOn as strange because goats were herd animals. He approached it only to find it had a broken leg. That explained why it was alone. He dispatched it swiftly with the katana and bled it out by hanging it from a branch. It was a simple matter to skin it and gut it and he carried the carcass wrapped in a space blanket back to the camp. Friday was dancing on his chain. The goat was the first fresh kill he had shared for a couple of days apart from a couple of rats and a rabbit. ChOn cut it up with the katana and threw half to the wolf. The rest he cooked over the coals of his fire while he was establishing his perimeter and securing the entrance to the cave. The meat was a welcome change to his recent diet and he gorged himself before throwing the remnants to Friday. He checked the tablet, brought his log up to date and settled in for the night with the minitron playing its default program.

He woke up as the first rays of the sun entered the cave. The deer were restless so he set them free on their hobbles to graze while he checked his perimeter and had breakfast. The wolf ran away as soon as he let it loose and ChOn knew it would be off hunting for an hour or more. He took the time to strip, clean and assemble all his equipment. He was strangely nervous at the thought of what might pass later in the day. He surveyed the photos taken months before of the plain and the village at its edge. He blew it up for the hundredth time looking for a detail he may have missed but found nothing. It was a basic village with semi-permanent structures in a circle. In the centre was a flat area containing a fire and some seats. Surrounding the village were fields of tall grass and goatherds maintaining their flocks. There was a stream on one side of the village.

Nothing more. No defences. No apparent weapons and certainly no security patrols. He could just walk in. Which was exactly what he planned to do and take things from there.

By the time Friday arrived back, ChOn had the deer saddled and set to go. The Doe was so accustomed to the travois that she wandered grazing with it trailing behind. The buck was more skittish and seemed eager to be on his way. ChOn donned his full military rig. Long sleeves. Long trousers. Boots. Weapons belt. Kinetic pistol and short sword in their saddle boots. Pulser in its holster. Shiew was sheathed on his body armour with the handle in reach over his right shoulder. The helm had the visor down to hide his face. He knew it looked like a curved, gold mirror from front on. He was ready. He mounted the buck and attached the lead rope to the saddle. He left nothing in the cave to suggest he had ever been there as he set off for the pass to his west.

The going was rough for the travois. The deer were sure footed enough but the way was rocky and so the pace was slow. Finally, after several hours hard climb, they reached the pass and looked over the plain. It stretched for miles, green and brown with the odd copse of trees and depressions or rocky outcrops. Towards the northern edge, within two hours march, was the village. ChOn felt his heart quicken as he saw it. He used his scope to check for details but there wasn't much to be seen. He did see movement towards the rear of the settlement but it was nothing more than a glimpse of a body lifting a flap and entering a dwelling. It confirmed for ChOn that it was occupied at least so he did a quick check of his armour and weapons and started down the gentle slope towards what, he did not know.

After a while the village dropped from view as ChOn went down into a saucer-shaped depression. There were several trees and a small spring there as well as a man-made corral, constructed by moving thorn bushes into a rough circle. He made a note of the place on his tablet and continued to the rim of the depression. Once there he paused to think. He discovered he was more nervous than he had thought he would be and so decided to wait at the corral behind him and survey the village for the rest of the afternoon and then in the morning venture forth to investigate and record the inhabitants. He rode quietly back the short distance and installed the deer in the corral, which hadn't been used for some time as there was plenty of green pick inside it. He set up his perimeter with his makeshift bed inside the corral tucked into the most protected corner. Then he decided what he would need to man an observation post and took the bare necessities with him to the place he had selected. It was just below the highest point of the rim and was formed by a small scattering of boulders, from which he could observe without being silhouetted from the village. It had taken him more than an hour to get settled and in place. He estimated there were about three hours of reasonable light left for his task. He lowered the visor of his helm and selected the telescope option and connected it to the tablet by BTXV. That way he had the option of watching live, using the screen to blow up the image even further or recording everything. In addition, he had his light pen option, with which he could make notes on the screen or even freehand draw a map of the village as he worked out what everything seemed to be.

The first thing he noted was the apparent lack of movement in the village. This struck him as unusual given the hour. His instinct told him that there should be someone preparing the village for the evening routine of eating and sleeping but to this point there had been the single sighting of 'something' and nothing else.

A further hour passed and he saw movement from outside the village perimeter. The wolf raised his head and looked in the direction of the movement and his ears pricked. Ch0n turned on the screen and recorded his first contact with sapients. There were seventeen of them. Their skin was pale orange like most of the other mammals ChOn had seen. They appeared to be somewhat shorter in stature than humans but otherwise the same at first examination. He assumed the group was made up of males because they looked like human males. They were clean shaven and had longish hair tied back or held in place with a cloth band around the forehead. Their garments were made or sewn to form a tunic to mid-thigh and were sleeveless. A belt of something was tied around the waist to give it form. They were armed with short spears and nothing else. They were herding goats. Dozens of goats. Maybe more than a hundred estimated ChOn when he was finally able to drag his eyes from the humanoids. His peripheral vision was caught by movement from the village. Women and children appeared from somewhere and ran to meet the men. The women were dressed similarly with shiny ornaments hanging from their necks, wrists and ears and they had made more effort with the tunics so they were better fitted. The children were mop-topped miniatures of the adults but what struck ChOn was the form of the reunion. The women were shouting and waving and pointing animatedly away from ChOn's position towards a long line of hills in the middle distance. ChOn could not hear any sound but it was obvious the women were in some distress and the reaction of the men confirmed it. They herded the goats together and pointed to ChOn's position. As one they started towards him, hurrying as much as the goats could be herded. ChOn estimated he had maybe an hour to get organized. He ran down the hill to the camp and saddled the deer. His shelter he bundled up onto the travois and he dressed in his full battle order. He had decided not to allow contact on terms other than his own so he dragged the doe as fast as he could through the trees, over the opposite rim and down the other side. He guessed the villagers were going to use the depression as a shelter for the goats and from whatever they were concerned about. He searched for a place to spend the night and could find nothing suitable so he decided to make a long arc around the depression towards some other trees he had seen from his observation post. There he spent an uncomfortable night with the deer hobbled and tethered and he and the wolf snatching sleep close by. He cursed himself for not having ridden to the village during the previous afternoon. Then he congratulated himself for not having done it. This way he had control. That was what he wanted.

Dawn broke with ChOn already awake and the deer moved to deeper shelter. He watched the rim of the depression but nothing moved. Close to the village, however, there was plenty of action. An organized foot patrol of raiders had encircled the village and was waiting for some sort of signal, it seemed. ChOn dropped the visor and studied the soldiers. They were of similar size and colour to the others but were dressed more formally and were armed to the teeth with short swords and spears. They wore leather tunics in the style of breast armour and leather skirts to mid-thigh over their cloth tunics. Their legs were wrapped or bound with thongs connected to rudimentary sandals. On their heads they wore leather-look helms with studs around the edge. On their backs were round wooden shields. As one, they suddenly started running the short distance to the village. They searched it systematically and met in the central community area. An animated discussion seemed to be taking place and then they formed into a troop and marched away. There were twenty one of them. *Two squads of ten and a commander.* ChOn found himself saying aloud.

Someone must have been watching from the villagers' hiding place because a short time later, the group, some sixrty in all, started to trickle into view over the lip of the depression with the goats walking along in a controlled herd. The motley bunch was three quarters of the way to the village, having passed in front of ChOn's position, when the patrol materialized from the long grass and set upon them. The men were no match for the soldiers and two were cut down in quick succession before the entire village was taken captive. Several of the women were separated from the rest along with more than half the goats. The remainder were herded back towards the village and the captive women and goats pushed away in the direction from which the patrol had come. One small boy ran back from the village group to the captives and was killed by a soldier with a spear.

Up to this point, Ch0n had been a curious onlooker. His instincts and the minitron had made him assume the raiding party was looking for food and women for their own village as had been the custom in many cultures. The remainder would be allowed to continue their lives for some time until a new raid took place. The herders in turn would snatch what women and goats they could when the occasion presented itself. It was nature's way and their own to keep the gene pool from being too small and to reduce inbreeding within villages.

The killing of the small boy shook Ch0n into action. On the mothership, children were precious. They were to be nurtured and raised, educated and trained. They were second in importance only to the soldiers, whose responsibility was to protect the mission at all costs. Ch0n made a conscious decision to intervene and leaving the doe and travois in the trees, he put the buck at a fast trot down the slope to the village, about half a mile away. At first nobody saw him but then he watched as both groups turned and stared at him in amazement. They had no idea what was coming towards them. A beast with four legs and the torso of a man behind the head. A God perhaps? A demon? They were paralysed with fear as he put the beast to a canter and rode into their midst. He unsheathed Shiew as he rode and swung it in a long arc, severing the head of the soldier who had killed the boy. With a backwards swing he took another head and then he was past them and turning. Like good soldiers they rallied quickly and formed to meet him but as Ch0n knew from his military instructions, foot soldiers have never been a match for mounted troops and he rode over them and slashed and slashed. And then they were running from him. He followed them and cut them down left and right, the blood coursing through his veins and pounding in his ears. This was his *raison d'etre*. He was a killer, cloned to be a soldier and trained to kill and kill with no mercy in the defence of the mission. He turned towards the herders, who were crying and screaming at him. Some were on their knees and others holding their women and children. They were terrified at the look of him: a giant beast with a weapon so terrible it sang as it killed. A creature with two heads, only one of which had eyes, the other which had a shiny gold bubble. A demon with four legs and two arms. And now it turned towards them, the green blade dripping with blood and the gold bubble moving from side to side watching them.

Ch0n was exhilarated with the fight. His heart was pounding and his blood was rushing. He looked at the herders through his visor and wondered why they were so terrified. Then he knew. He tried to imagine what he must look like to them. They were short in stature. He was a giant of a man. He was riding a deer, which they surely would have seen before but never with a man astride. He took Shiew, wiped the blade clean on the haunch of the elk and sheathed it. Then he raised the visor and waved. There was a shocked murmur from the group as they saw his yellow skin and green eyes. They supposed his wave was friendly because they waved back. Ch0n dismounted and a cry went up from the onlookers as they realized he was two creatures joined together and not one. He walked towards them, his hands wide and palms up. They backed away except for one man, who stood his ground and pointed a spear at him. Ch0n looked at it. It was an iron-tipped, wooden hafted spear that wouldn't do his armour any harm even if the man were quick enough to stick him with it.

Ch0n waved his left hand high in the air and as the man's eyes left him to follow the movement, Ch0n disarmed him with one swift movement of his right arm and hips. Then to show he meant no harm, he held the spear flat in front of him, his arms extended so the man could take it back.

After that, things went easily. People came up to him and touched him. Ch0n removed the helm and his gloves so they could touch his hands and see his face. He motioned to them all and pointed to the village and shooed them away. Then when they were moving he re-mounted the buck and rode back to the wolf, the doe and the travois. The people watched him go and then watched his return with the other animals. When he arrived in the village they crowded around him and his beasts except for the wolf, until he dismounted again. He was shown to one of the structures, which had a pile of skins, tools and clothes outside the entrance. He looked inside. It was empty. A man who seemed to be the leader was shouting at him and pointing to him and the shelter and Ch0n realized he was being given somewhere to stay. He put his belongings inside and installed the wolf at the entrance. Then he called the villagers into the centre area and set up the minitron with the program set to 'language input'.

There was much singing and dancing around a communal campfire. The story of the fight was being retold and retold among the group. Ch0n opened the virtual mike on the minitron and said the key words, *'battle, stranger, monster, weapon, death capture men women and children'*. He then called a few men to him and started talking to them about the battle complete with mime. They answered him excitedly and he had to stop them and make them understand only one could talk at a time. They told the story from their perspective complete with actions and facial expression so it was pretty clear to Ch0n what they had felt and seen. All the while the minitron was analysing the language by common word usage, intonation, comparison with ChOn's story and theirs to try and work out a translation between the languages. It was a system developed by a boy genius from Brazil in the mid 21st Century and was a mathematical formula based on the analysis of every known language. The study had been undertaken by every major university on the planet and used a mathematical formula which used the known usage rates in order of words from conjunctions and nouns and pronouns to nicknames and slang. All words used fewer than a certain pre-determined percentage of times were discarded. Using this method combined with input key words, the program could come up with a basic dictionary of some 200 words within a few hours and within a day, could produce the vocabulary of a two year old. Beyond that, it was unable to easily proceed but the entire reason for the program was to enable immediate translation at a simple level and then the user would have to expand his or her own knowledge.

ChOn kept the villagers talking about the battle and then he stopped them. He input a different series of keywords and introduced himself and asked the men to do the same and then he made the universal sign for 'talk' and indicated the village and the people. They started again waving and chatting all at once and then he slowed them down again and pointed to each in turn and so the process continued until well into the night. ChOn retired to his shelter with a stomach full of goat meat and some sort of meal made from grains or seeds. He was almost asleep when the wolf growled and the tent flap was raised. A woman made as if to enter but Friday growled deep in his throat and ChOn made no move to invite her in so she left again. ChOn slept with the minitron teaching him the local language such as it had managed to determine at that point. It did so by repetition of words and then sentences and phrases in common use based on the input vocabulary.

"The... *im or em*"

"Man…*eman*"

"Run… *ogorien*"

"*The man ran away….Im eman ogorien*"

"Yes…*eo*"

"No….*deo*"

By morning, ChOn had a vocabulary of more than one hundred words at his disposal. He put them to good use over breakfast.

"Why soldiers come? *Adaga amen ake orre?*"

"*Iqui aget eman ma ekaun. Iqui tamo omog.* They come to steal women and goats. They come every dry unknown word."

"Where they come from?"

"*They come from the sunset. Sometimes we raid their village but it is a big village and we have to be careful for they have soldiers and we are unknown word. But we usually unknown word to steal at least one woman.*"

"Are they the same people as you?"

"*Deo. They are the Buqu'e. We are the Arw'an. We were the same but now we are different. They have the same language. We had the same father of father of father. They don't like herding goats. They want to rule us. But now we have you so we are safe.*"

"I want to see their village. But first I have to learn more of your language."

He pointed at the minitron.

"This can teach me but you have to talk into it. It is a powerful thing." He wanted to say, 'magic' but couldn't so he mimed it as best he could. The men laughed and called to nobody in particular. Out of a shelter on the other side of the village came a man dressed in costume. He had feathers in his headdress and bones hanging from his ankles and carried a gnarled staff with coloured stones decorating the end of it. Around his neck and one shoulder hung a woven bag bulging from the volume of its contents. ChOn guessed he was a shaman and powerful in the eyes of the village because when he approached the group, the men faded into the background.

"WHY ARE YOU HERE? WHERE DO YOU COME FROM? GIVE ME THE BOX!"

ChOn looked at the men and went to one of them.

"Why does he shout at me?" he whispered.

"Because he is afraid of you as are we all. But he is most afraid because he is an itzibermin and you have more power than he has. He wants your power for himself so he can have power over you."

ChOn looked at the shaman. The word 'itzibermin' was new to him but he assumed it meant 'magician' because that was the power shaman of all races used to keep their people in check. The shaman threw some black powder on the ground and struck it with the stone on the end of his staff. A small spark was followed by a whoosh of light and smoke. ChOn jumped back and the shaman looked at him with a sneer.

"SEE MY POWER. GIVE ME THE BOX". He made a move to take the minitron. ChOn waited until he was almost touching it and he shouted.

"DEO!" He drew his pulse gun and wound the power to 'high'. He pointed it at a boulder twenty feet away from the watching crowd and let loose a blast. The invisible cone struck the rock and with a loud crack, split it down the middle. Dust and shards were flung into the air. The shaman looked longingly at the pulse gun. The villagers were struck with terror and amazement. Ch0n handed it to the shaman. The safety mechanism was activated and would only reactivate when Ch0n put his thumbprint against the reader. The shaman laughed and pointed the gun at Ch0n and tried to fire it. He shook it and pressed every button he could find on it to no avail. The villagers started to laugh. Ch0n pulled the kinetic pistol from his belt and fired off the entire magazine at the boulder, sending chips and sparks in all directions. He then pointed it at the shaman.

"Give me my weapon, you who would have killed me with it, for now I will surely kill you if you do not."

The shaman pointed the pulse gun at the minitron and tried to blast it but could not. Ch0n reloaded the pistol and fired a single ball at the ground between the shaman's feet. He jumped back and threw the pulse gun to Ch0n, who caught it, put his thumb against the safety mechanism and loosed another ray at the boulder, which split again.

"This weapon can only be fired by a true magic man. Not a false one such as you. But to show you I am not your enemy I will make a gift to you. He took out an incendiary pencil and pressed the trigger. A small flame shot from the end. The people reacted audibly. Ch0n gave it to the shaman, who managed to light it with the second attempt. He showed it to the villagers. It was a powerful gift, this gift of instant fire. He looked in the bag around his shoulder and pulled out a shiny stone. As soon as the light touched it, it sparkled like the diamond it was. It was as big as a plum and the shaman had chipped and ground it to reveal its facets. He gave it to Ch0n, who took it with delight. On earth it was worth a king's ransom. Here it was worth nothing except face to the giver.

"FIRE FOR FIRE STRANGER". He looked longingly at the minitron before turning away. He shuffled into his shelter and was heard singing in a flat monotone.

"Be wary of him because he is your enemy. He wants the box of words. He would have it at any value. Even now he is summoning his power against you".

All the while the minitron was humming away at its task and that night Ch0n increased his vocabulary to more than six hundred words, although he was unable to recall them all for almost a week, during which time he came to know all the villagers and their relationship to each other. He discovered that the woman who had gone to his tent the first night was a newly made widow from the battle. She had gone to him as his woman because a woman needed a man to provide for her. When he had not accepted her, she had gone to the shelter of a man who already had a wife but was a good provider and was happy to take a second. There was no ill feeling on her part or on the part of the other man's first wife. In fact she was a little relieved because she feared Ch0n was not as other men and would harm her.

The shaman was always just out of Ch0n's direct view but never far away. The wolf was constantly alerting Ch0n to a fleeting shadow or a moving tent flap close by. The minitron was well-hidden in the shelter, in such a place that to look for it would take enough time to alert Ch0n that the shaman or anybody else for that matter was in his shelter.

The villagers were fascinated with his relationship with the two deer and the wolf. The fact Ch0n could ride the deer was of particular interest to them as herders. They were forced to do everything on foot and saw the advantages of herding and being able to maintain a fast link to the village at the same time. Being semi-nomadic by nature, they were also keen to explore the advantage of the deer as beasts of burden. Ch0n's travois was the source of much interest and analysis by the women of the village upon whom the task of moving fell. They had developed simple sleds which they used as cargo vehicles but they had to be pulled by hand and a move of the village was a particularly difficult thing to do. As a result they moved less frequently than they might and the herders had to travel further or keep less livestock so as not to deplete the pickings. The deer would not allow the villagers to approach them too closely at first. They were skittish among such a large group of humans and tended to stay close to the entrance of ChOn's shelter. The wolf was another thing altogether. He was a one man animal and allowed nobody to approach him or the shelter. He was even shy of people getting too close to ChOn and when the talk became loud and animated, he would invariably rise and walk to his master's defence, his lip curled in warning. Just so, the villagers could also see the advantages of domesticating wolves as guards for the village.

ChOn overheard the village elders discussing him quite often. His grasp of the language was far higher than they imagined, despite the fact he conversed with them as often as he could, always with the minitron programmed for the topic of the day. His vocabulary had risen to almost a thousand words by now, half of which he had mastered. The language, he discovered was simple with no complicated verb conjugations or adjectival rules. He learned that they were puzzled by the fact he had not tried to take them as slaves or that he had not taken a woman. They had seen his cold fury in action and according to their customs, he had right of dominion over them but had not exercised it. He had not even demanded special attention from the villagers. They had treated him as best they could and he seemed content. It was a most puzzling state of affairs they had decided and one they would need to monitor. The only problem was the shaman who was nowhere to be seen and so his normal function of seer and magician was missing from their village activities. ChOn had made no indication he wished to assume that role, even though he was obviously a powerful magician in his own right and the magic box was obviously the font of his power. No wonder the shaman had coveted it.

It was during the third week of ChOn's stay at the village when he was brought from his shelter by cries of alarm from the villagers. They had spotted another patrol from the Buq'ue approaching the village. It was still some distance off but larger than the previous week. The shouting villagers feared they would be wiped out as retribution for the previous battle.

It took ChOn less than five minutes to saddle the buck and another five to garb himself in full battle order. His weapons were always ready due to his daily routine of maintenance. The kinetic pistol was fully loaded with a magazine of 300 metalstorm pellets. The pulse gun power was reduced to sixty percent, which was enough to stun a man at forty feet or kill him at twenty. He did not want to start the battle at close quarters so he planned a flank assault with the horse bow, followed by medium range with the kinetic pistol then the pulse gun. He had second thoughts about the discharge level of the pulse gun and reset it at seventy percent to give him an extra twenty feet of killing range. Shiew was down his back with her handle over his right shoulder.

He rode out of the village with his visor down and the telescope mode activated. There were thirty-one soldiers plus the shaman, who had obviously changed sides. The soldiers were armed as before with spears, short swords and shields. ChOn knew the battle would be brief and brutal if he fought it out of spear range, which he planned to do. Skirting around to his right, he outflanked the patrol, which tried to change formation to protect itself from his assault. But it never came. He rode to a position 100 feet to their flank and drew the horse bow. At that range the shafts would go through a man. He nocked a metal-tipped carbon fibre alloy arrow and loosed it at the soldier he thought would be the commander. He was almost lifted off his feet by the impact of the arrow and he lay screaming for several seconds until he died. By the time he had stopped screaming, Ch0n had loosed two more fletches at the stunned soldiers, who were standing stock still looking at their commander. Two more of their number fell before they were galvanized into action. They did what they knew how to do, which was to charge at their enemy to engage him at close range as befitted their weapons. Two more fell to the horse bow before Ch0n stowed it on the pommel and trotted to a position outflanking the charge. At sixty feet he unleashed the kinetic pistol along their line, which faltered and dissolved. He moved again as they regrouped and cut down most of the rest. There were about ten still standing and as one they turned and ran from him. He holstered the kinetic pistol and charged after them unsheathing Shiew as he rode. Like all foot soldiers they stuck together in a knot for protection but they had never encountered mounted opposition before and their small group was easy meat for Ch0n. He put his mount at the middle of the bunch and rode them down. The buck lowered his head and brushed two aside with his giant antlers. Shiew was busy hacking and slashing as he rode past the group. Ch0n felt something strike his back as he wheeled to finish the slaughter. He took no notice but was forced to rethink as the remnant formed a tight square and raised their spears as one. He turned sharply, took out the kinetic pistol again and sprayed them with metal pellets traveling at three thousand feet per second. The soldiers turned to a spray of bloody pulp before his eyes and it was all over. The villagers were already celebrating the great victory near the initial skirmish, taunting and desecrating the bodies. The women were hacking at the genitals of the fallen and holding them aloft in victory.

Ch0n rode to them.

"CEASE THAT VILE WORK!" he shouted. "THERE WILL BE NO MUTILATING OF THE FALLEN WHILE I AM HERE. IT IS

FOR SAVAGES TO DO. THESE MEN WERE SOLDIERS. THEY WILL BE AFFORDED RESPECT IN DEATH AS THEY DESERVE."

And then softly,

"How can we expect them to respect us if we act thus in victory? They will send a bigger and bigger force if we are so. Now. Gather them and put them in the earth or send them to your gods in your own custom. It is over."

He was aware that they were staring at him in awe, some with their mouths open and some now pointing. He returned to his shelter and divested himself of his battle order, to see a short sword buried in the sprayform armour. Had he not been wearing it, it would have been half way through his torso and he may well have been mortally wounded. He pulled it out and started his post battle ritual of cleaning all his weapons and kit. He had used most of his magazines of ball bearings for the kinetic pistol. He resolved to depend more on the pulse gun as its force was generated by the small, false-fusion battery and would never exhaust itself.

It was then that he noticed his belongings had been disturbed. He dived down to find the box. The shaman had entered the camp during the battle and had tried to find the box. He must have left in fright and no doubt was already on his way back to the enemy camp. In seconds Ch0n was donning his battle order and reloading the kinetic pistol. He had not as yet unsaddled the buck. He raced to mount and called the wolf. It was already starting to get dark with the sun dropping like a stone behind the horizon as he sped off in the direction of the Buq'ue camp. He lowered the visor and selected 'heat vision' to supplement the night vision mode and let the deer find his own way forward. It was sure footed and set off at a fast trot.

ChOn did his calculations. He estimated the shaman had at least ten minutes start on him. Travelling at a steady jog that would give him a half-mile start. Maybe more. The buck was trotting along at close to twelve miles an hour so he should catch the shaman inside five minutes. He tried to make the beast go faster but after an initial burst, it settled back into its normal mile eating pace and he let it have its head. After two minutes he started to scan the track ahead. For several seconds he saw nothing and then the green smudge of the shaman was visible ahead. It divided into two briefly and then became one again. ChOn realized he was chasing two people moving in single file. It mattered not to him which of his quarry was leading as he meant to kill them both. In less than a minute he saw the two smudges separate again and one stopped while the second went ahead. ChOn guessed that the stationery person would be a soldier waiting in ambush. He rode to within sixty feet and augmented the heat vision with the scope. He could see a soldier waiting, spear at the ready at the side of the track, obscured he believed by the darkness but as plain as day to ChOn. He stopped the deer and watched the soldier stand up, wondering what had happened to the pursuit. There was now no noise to gauge the distance for him. To ChOn, no such problem existed. He took out the pulse gun, turned it to eighty percent to be sure of the range and fired a single pulse. The soldier was flung off his feet and didn't move. The heat sensor in ChOn's visor glowed bright green as the soldier's body heat increased. ChOn put the buck into a trot again and followed the other smudge, he didn't even look down at the fallen soldier but smelt the result of his work on the breeze as he pushed on. The second smudge was now within range of the pulse gun. He rode closer and closer until he could make out the shaman even without the scope. He was forty feet away and trying to stumble along the track, looking behind him as he ran. ChOn merely rode up to the shaman, who stopped and faced him. ChOn dismounted from the buck and walked towards him.

Gavan Connell

"You have tried to kill me twice and now you try to rob me of my possessions. Your life is forfeit. He took Shiew from the scabbard, listening to it sing as he did so. The Shaman could barely make Ch0n out in the darkness.

"I am not who you think but a decoy. The shaman went via another route for he knew you would prevail and come for him. Do not kill me and I will tell you the whereabouts of the Buq'ue fortress and how to enter it. There soon you would find the shaman and the king who would have your magic box. Another thing. You know not the danger in which you have put those goat herders. The wrath of the king of the Buq'ue will fall on them and also on you. Your magic will not withstand the full force of his army when it comes, for you are but one. You and the goat herders are doomed."

Ch0n swung the katana in a wide arc and the man's eyes glanced around and then adopted a look of horror but it was too late. He was already dead. The head toppled to the ground, the eyes still blinking. The body was still standing. Blood coursed from its neck in spurts, driven by the still-beating heart and then even the heart realized there were no more signals arriving from the brain and it stopped pumping. The corpse fell to the ground and twitched for a few seconds until the last of its life departed.

He rode for an hour at a fast clip towards the Buq'ue village. By that time the glow from many fires was evident in the night sky. It hove into view as he crested the rise. He was surprised at the size of it. The shaman, he decided, would have to be dealt with, however because even as he watched, he imagined the magician at the king's court bragging about how he, the former shaman of the Arw'an had prevailed over the greatest and most powerful creature ever to walk the plains, even if he had not managed to steal the magic box.

ChOn rode back to the Arw'an camp. It took him more than three hours at a walk. The deer was content to pick his way and it gave ChOn the chance to think about his immediate plans. By the time they arrived and ChOn was being welcomed, he had formed the spark of an idea to protect the people of the plains from their cousins.

There was much celebration in the camp as he rode in. A great shout arose from the small crowd as he dismounted and unsaddled the buck. He went to his shelter and removed his battle order. A village elder, whom ChOn knew as Boro, appeared at his entrance and summoned him to the centre of camp. There they knelt before him with their hands in front of their faces, palms facing upwards.

"To you we swear fealty, Lord. You who has twice dispersed our enemies and has shown yourself to be immortal, accept us as your subjects and stay with us. We will provide for you in all ways in exchange for your leadership and protection."

ChOn stood before them and held his two hands facing down, which he thought the right thing to do. Once again a cheer rallied forth and the feasting resumed.

ChOn did not tell them that the shaman had outwitted him. He accepted a huge portion of meat and meal and drank deeply from the communal bowl. He explained to the elders that he had seen the Buq'ue village and that there was much danger for them if they stayed where they were.

"In time," he said, "I will re-unite the two tribes. The best of both of them would lead the united tribe to a future of prosperity."

Meanwhile, he asked, if there were more Arw'an villages nearby. By morning he had convinced them to move camps to join forces with the closest other village. He and Boro would go ahead and arrange things to prevent any misunderstandings. Three hours after daybreak, the camp was on the move. ChOn had gone ahead with the travois, the elder riding behind him on the massive buck. They arrived at the next village on foot, however, leading the beasts, the elder walking stiffly in the lead. There was much consternation and hubbub in the camp at the sight of ChOn and his tame creatures. Friday as usual created the most suspicion apart from ChOn himself, who was able to settle them down to listen after Boro had more or less explained who he was and his exploits against the Buq'ue.

"The Arw'an villages are small and isolated one from the other," ChOn told them. "If we are to defend them against the Buq'ue, we need to unite them and make them more permanent. That will mean the goats will have to be better managed for there will be more pressure on their food. In a few hours, Boro's village will arrive here and you will make a place for the people. If you do not, I will subjugate you by force, which is something I do not wish. Send me your shaman."

The head man was Doni. He summoned the shaman. ChOn addressed him.

"I am not here to steal your magic, or to make a competition with it. You may live here under my protection or you may leave the village before the people of Boro arrive. If you oppose me, I will use your body as a means of showing these, your people, my power and magic. It is your choice. Think well. Meanwhile, observe this. He took a fire pencil from his pocket and held it to the shaman's staff. He pressed the button and a blue and yellow flame emerged, setting the staff alight in just a few seconds. Nobody else had seen this display. It was enough for the shaman, who retreated to his shelter. Sometime later, ChOn saw him leaving camp with his meagre possessions.

By nightfall, the two villages had merged. ChOn learned there were many other villages not too far away but he knew there were limited resources to be had for a nomadic population too large for the surrounds. He took out his tablet and looked at the aerial images taken from the mothership. It took but a few minutes to determine his current location and align the tablet to the terrain. Boro and Doni were fascinated by this new magic. They could not conceive that they were looking at their own territory as viewed from the sky and ChOn didn't try and explain it. As far as they knew he was from a distant part of their land or a different country far more developed than themselves and that was the end of it. His 'immortality' was as yet to be explained.

ChOn explained to them that there were rich plains and lakes in the direction of the rising sun, from where he had come, and that there were places that could support a large village and their goats and could be successfully defended from the Buq'ue.

Boro looked at him.

"Lord, the Buq'ue are but one enemy of the Arw'an. There is an enemy far more powerful which comes when the rains have finished and the goats have dropped their kids. They come and steal whole villages, enslaving the men and women, killing the children too young to work and stealing all our goats. They are called the Matáng and they have been our enemies since the beginning. It is because of them we have separated into family groups. That way we can better hide from them and it makes it less worthwhile for them to come. To once again unite is to invite them."

"Trust me Boro and you also, Doni. We will make such a village that they will not be able to conquer it. You have seen what I can do but I assure you it is nothing against what we can do together. You would have me as your king. Well so be it. I would have subjects who trust and obey me. Now, I wish to unite all the Arw'an villages. It is to be done soon. I will need enough young men to accompany me to the place I have chosen for our stronghold and then to go to the other villages and tell them of me and my plan. In order that the others listen to them, I will show them what some have already seen. You may tell them that I will have their loyalty or I will have their heads, every one."

Ch0n took the pulse gun and wound the power to one hundred percent. He wanted a living thing to shoot at but had nothing suitable. The shaman was still visible in the distance but was too far away to use as a target so he was forced to use another boulder. He fired four rapid pulses and it exploded four times. When the dust settled and the shards of stone had stopped raining down, there was a small pile of small and medium stones where it had stood.

"Tell them of this power of mine and that I would have them under my protection or as my enemies. The choice is theirs. And tell their shaman that I will not have any magician in my fort who is not my subject. Their lives are spared once if they choose not to serve me but they are afterwards forfeit. Tell them. Now. Select the number of men I need and have them ready to leave as soon as the sun rises. We have two day's fast walk ahead of us to the new place. They should be ready for that and then to walk to the villages.

Boro, you I will charge with the care of the female tlaque and my travois. Guard them with your life because that will be the price of your failure to protect them and take them to me."

He looked around. He spotted a burly woman at the front of the group.

"You, woman. How are you called? Sonja? It is a good name. Come here to me. I have need of one woman who can lead the other women and children for the way is long and there will be much complaining. Are you such a woman?"

"I am such a one, My Lord."

"Then listen to this. All of you. Sonja, you are in charge of moving the village to where we are going. Follow us tomorrow as fast as you can because I will not return here unless I have to recover my belongings from Boro's corpse. We will leave a trail easy to follow. On the morrow we are moving camp never to return here. Each woman is to look at her household and take with her only that which has been used in the past two full moons. One personal item per person I exclude from this. Anything else is to stay behind to feed the fire. Only you, Sonja may make any further exception. On your head I place that responsibility for at the new camp I will take stock of everything. Any family who does not listen to you will be left behind. In the new place we will not have need for things which have no useful value. Not yet. That day will come. You have to be able to travel light and fast. Do you understand me, Sonja?"

"Yes, My Lord. As do we all. I speak for them now as I will when we arrive at your new place."

Ch0n looked at them in turn, eye to eye. They nodded at him in turn and he was satisfied.

Ch0n had no need for the shelter that night. He wrapped himself in a space blanket with the deer hobbled nearby and the wolf lying at his side. It wanted to hunt the goats and was sulking. Ch0n had caught him a few times but had managed to call him off in time. That night, the beast was tethered close enough to sleep beside his master. "Just in case you can't help yourself," Ch0n had said to him.

He slept little that night. He was not comfortable sleeping on the hard ground and his sleep was disturbed by voices, despite the ear buds. He had listened intently to them because Boro was telling Doni and the others the story of how Ch0n had just ridden calmly into their camp having slaughtered hundreds of Buq'ue and then stayed on. He told him of the shaman and how Ch0n had bested him in the magic stakes and the shaman had disappeared. Then he told him of the manner that Ch0n had defended their village against several hundred assassins, killed them all, made their bodies disappear and had himself been mortally wounded by a sword to the back but had instantly come back to life and finished the gory job of killing everything in sight. The whole village had been witness to his battle and his return to camp with the sword buried to the hilt in his back. He was immortal and therefore a God. His metals and clothes were like nothing ever seen and his magic box could speak to him and show him pictures as well as teach him any language instantly.

"Do not cross him, cousin, because he has no mercy for the living, only for the dead, whom we have been forbidden to mutilate. Those who are not with him are dead within minutes. We are wise to follow his words and we are lucky he is on our side. We need fear no more the invaders from the sunset for his power is infinite and his wrath unimaginable. He bears a blade he calls by name. It sings to him as it slaughters his enemies. I myself have heard it sing and have seen it cut a man in twain with a single easy sweep. His fire bolts you have seen for yourself. And he is yet to reveal to you his rain of death, which I saw yesterday turn fifty men to raw meat in one heartbeat. Aye he is a God indeed and we will be gods beside him. Tell all this to your people as mine have already seen for themselves. Tell the messengers, for the display they saw today was mere child's play for him. He calls himself Ch0n. It is a strange name and has no meaning in our tongue although it is close to Chon'i the Buq'ue God of the Clouds. Remember that name for soon the mere utterance of it will make strong men weak and our enemies grovel before it.

And beware too the wolf. The Ch0n speaks to it in a strange tongue that only he and the wolf understand and it heeds him. You will see this for yourself. It rarely leaves him and none may approach him without the wolf's permission for he tells it when to calm itself and when to show its teeth. It is a fearsome thing to behold. As is his control over the tlaque. He rides it and guides it only by telepathy. I have seen it in battle sweep aside ten men with one movement of its horns. He led it in to the thickest part of the enemy and let it murder them even as his green blade was sweetly singing its death hymn."

It was the first time ChOn had heard the people talking about him. He smiled because it was doing his status no harm and would make life easier for him in the long term. He was to hear much more in the weeks ahead.

When he finally slept, he did so for the first time in his life without the minitron. He dreamed a wild dream in which he was fighting below the battlements of an enormous stone fortress as a battle raged around him. Shiew was singing her song of death. Troops of mounted cavalry were sweeping through the hordes of soldiers making siege to the fortress. High above him was a magnificent, tall red-headed soldier dressed as ChOn was in sprayform armour and helm. She was controlling the cavalry below with a flag, wielded by an assistant who looked like a woman dressed for battle. In her hand the red-headed soldier held a huge crossbow with which she was wreaking havoc on the enemy soldiers around ChOn.

Gavan Connell

Chapter Eleven: The Planning

The next morning, Ch0n set off with fourteen men. Doni went with him and the woman Sonja stayed behind to supervise the packing up of the camp. Boro with the doe and the remaining men started behind Ch0n's group pushing the now-combined herd of goats ahead of them. The women would have no difficulty finding their trail. It was a hundred yards wide.

They pushed as hard as the men on foot could manage and by night were well advanced towards the place Ch0n had in mind. It was one he had marked on the tablet on his way to the village. It was a bend in the river that doubled back almost on itself around a high rocky hill that blocked its path. The plain in front of it was flat and lush. To one side was a huge stand of the bamboo-like forest Ch0n had walked through and not far to the other side was one of the fruit forests. It had all they would ever need and the best part of it all was that it could be defended because all but a small isthmus of land was difficult to cross because of the river bend. That strip of land would serve as the main approach to the camp, would provide an early place to block the goats from straying and would ultimately become fortified with obstacles to delay the advance of any enemy troops. Ch0n maintained his fast pace throughout the second day, following the arrow on the tablet. In the late afternoon they rose a crest and Ch0n saw their destination before them across the green plain. He looked to his left at the hills in the middle distance, knowing that the dragon was somewhere to be found up there. That was something he would have to deal with as soon as the occasion arose. Having a flesh-eating chameleon the size of a large shelter was no small matter. He lowered the visor of his helm and turned on the heat sensor. Scanning the plain and the hills he saw nothing.

They approached the site and ChOn explained his plan in brief. They would put a temporary fence across the narrowest part of the bend in the river to contain the goats when they arrived. The village would go to the other side of the outcrop between it and the river. It would be semi-permanent because it would take months to set up the perimeter the way ChOn had envisaged. He told thirteen of the men to go to the other villages as they had been instructed to do the previous night by Boro and Doni.

"Make haste," he told them. "We need as many hands here as we can muster in a short time because the Buq'ue will eventually send a large force to meet us or worse, the Matáng will come again. Bring only the supplies that have been used in the last two moons and one other thing as will Sonja with your own villages." He sent them off at a trot and as they drew away from his future fort, they started to separate and go their own ways.

It took another full day before the main body of the village arrived. At their head was Boro leading the doe. He handed the rein to ChOn and grinned.

"My head remains safe for now, My Lord," he said.

The women came next pulling and carrying their household goods. Sonja went to ChOn immediately.

"It is as you ordered My Lord. Shall I have them show you what they have brought to appease you?"

"If you say it is as I ordered, then it is so, Sonja. You have done well but your task is just beginning. Take them to the other side of the hill where you will find some suitable place for them. Go close to the water but beware of the rising water mark. Allow space for all but remember we have thirteen other villages to join us within the week if all goes well. I don't want any fighting over space. This is your next task as village planner. Do you understand me?"

"Yes, My Lord. It will be as you wish. But first I will site the latrine because we will need a large one for so many and each village cannot be permitted to have its own. It will be downstream of the camp and well away from the shelters. It is always the first amenity to be planned as you know."

"No. I did not know. It is not my way to live thus. That is why I have entrusted you with the task. So far you have done well. Keep up the good work. In time you will see the grand plan I have for us all. But for now, you must do as you are bidden without much information. Go now for there is much to be done before dark."

"Boro! Bring the doe to me. I have to go away. I will be gone for two days no more. The other villages will not arrive before I do. Tether a weakling goat out there each morning and night in case the predators arrive. We will give them a gift so we don't have to fight them just yet. Keep the goats safe in their corral. The woman Sonja is organizing the layout of the camp. She will need men to help her with the latrine. It is heavy work and not befitting the women, who will be erecting the shelters. She is also in charge of the setting up of the camp. You and Doni will remain in charge of the routine until I get back. Waste no time. The priority after the latrine is the fence from bank to bank at the entrance. Do you understand me?"

"My Lord, men do not dig latrines. It is unbecoming. It is women's work and always has been. We are herders. They manage the village. It has always been thus."

"Hear me well, Boro. I have in mind a new order of things. First will be that there are no women's tasks and men's tasks. We will do as we will do according to our strengths. Men will dig this latrine. Tell them I will it. Tell them I will have no laziness or insolence. Have it done. Do you understand me yet Boro?"

"Yes My Lord, I do understand you but it will not be easy."

"Would you that I appoint Doni to supervise this task and have you work for him? Nothing will be easy from now on. If we want to be powerful we have to pay the price. That price is efficiency and discipline. There is no other way. I need you to do your part as a village elder. I will do my part as planner and protector. We will each have a role to play and power will be given to many who have never had power before. Hear me and do as I say. Now bring me the doe for I have a long march before my next camp."

Boro stalked off to do as he was tasked but he was not happy. He knew he would have trouble getting the men to dig a latrine and he knew he would be punished by ChOn if he failed to get it done. Timing was important to this plan. The infrastructure had to be in place to receive the other village people when they started to arrive and there would be no place for petty bickering. He returned to ChOn with the doe and the travois. ChOn was with Doni.

"Doni," he was saying. "Yonder is a stand of trees that look like grass. The trunks are straight and full of nothing". He gave Doni a lightweight axe with an edge like a razor. "With this, cut as many as you can cut that can take a man's fist inside the hole. Do not cut them short, but keep them as long as you can. Take them to the river over there and stack them. Guard well this blade for it is special to me and I would not lose it for a man's carelessness. Do you understand the task?"

"I understand, My Lord."

"I will leave my spare things in your care, Boro. Once again, guard them with your life."

In reality there wasn't much that Ch0n left behind other than the rail gun and the tarpaulin, which occupied a lot of space on the travois. To this point, nobody had seen the rail gun but Boro looked at it and knew instinctively it was a weapon more powerful than anything he had seen to date. His first reaction was to realize why Ch0n was putting his life as the price for guarding the things and his second was to wonder how much such a weapon would be worth to the Buq'ue in wealth and power to anyone who delivered it to them. What Boro did not know, was that like all Ch0n's technical weapons, it relied on Ch0n's thumbprint on a receptor before it could be armed and fired. Without that, it was just a complicated piece of junk.

Ch0n took with him food for two days. The travois was empty. It would be full on his return. He rode out of the camp studying the tablet. His first stop would be the first fort he had built and where his stores were stashed. There he would decide what the immediate needs were to build his fortress. The trip was uneventful but still Ch0n found himself getting a little excited and nervous as he approached the familiar rocky outcrop he had called home for months. He lowered the visor on his helm and studied the place for a long time through the heat sensor and the scope. He decided it was safe to proceed and finally he opened the gate and entered the familiar surroundings of his cave. Nothing had been disturbed. The deer went instinctively to their corral when he had tended to them. He went outside and cut some forage for them before opening the map on the tablet that told him where everything was hidden. The wolf was nowhere to be seen as Ch0n started to make the difficult decision on what he would take back with him. The travois was the limiting factor, by size and what the doe could pull without over extending herself, although Ch0n conceded she was a lot stronger than he had first thought. Ch0n decided that at some point he would have to make a pack for her back to supplement or replace the travois. But not yet.

As always, ChOn's first thoughts were for the defence of his new site. That would mean all the metal weapons would have to be taken as well as the remote sensors. And most of the general stores. He looked at his list of stores and started to write what he would take. It took him several hours to make the list, dig up the containers and re-shuffle their contents. Finally he had three canisters to be taken with him and the rest he inventoried, buried, and mapped their location in the cave.

The remainder of the space on the travois would be taken up with things salvaged from the landing craft. It was all in all a taxing exercise and he had removed and added things several times before he was happy with the final result. By the time he had finished, it was time to check his perimeter and settle for the night. The wolf had returned with the remains of a rabbit for ChOn to eat. He declined with grace and ate the rations he had brought from the new base. He slept on his raised platform with the wolf underneath it. Shiew was at his side and the pulser at hand. He programmed the minitron to instruct him on the design of mediaeval castles and closed his eyes. He awoke with a start as the sun was rising, surprised he had slept all night without even changing his position. The wolf was moving within seconds. ChOn took the deer out and hobbled them close by while he checked his perimeter. He checked the sky for clouds and returned inside the cave to start the process of stowing his supplies on the travois. It was still early in the day when he checked the cave to make sure there was no evidence of his supplies. He mounted the huge buck and set off the way he had arrived the afternoon prior. The wolf scouted ahead. ChOn had the visor lowered with the heat vision mode activated. The pulser was sitting in a special holster he had added to the saddle for easy access while mounted. ChOn felt quite at home now as he rode in full battle order towards his newfound 'kingdom' and destiny. It took most of the day before he crested a rise and saw the activity in the new location. Things appeared quite normal and indeed as he drew closer, he was met at the entrance to a freshly erected brush wall by cheers and waving of arms. He led the doe through the opening and nodded to the men, who had been its builders. He rounded the rocky hill and headed for the site of the residential section of the site. To the right he could see a large stack of the bamboo trunks and to the left, orderly rows of shelters had sprung up. Doni and Boro saw him coming and ran to meet him. The woman, Sonja was nowhere to be seen.

Doni reached him first.

"It is done as you required, My Lord. The trunks are stacked yonder by the stream above the camp. Your axe I return to you safely but reluctantly for it is a fine thing. I await further directions regarding the tree trunks. They are obviously for a special purpose."

"Well done, Doni," replied Ch0n. "Yes, I have a plan for the tree trunks, which I will show you shortly but first I wish to hear from Boro. How went your tasks?"

"The latrine is dug, My Lord. It was dug by the men as you ordered but not before one of them beat the woman Sonja. The fence we have almost finished. It needs strengthening in some sections before we can say with surety that the goats will not escape or the wolves enter. The goat we tethered by night returned this morning unharmed."

"Well done, Boro on the completion of your tasks. Now where is the man who beat the woman, Sonja and where is she?"

"He is working at the fence, My Lord and she is abed in her shelter, which is that one with the blue bird on the entrance flap."

"Assemble everybody here around this space. I would speak publicly with the man who beats women. And Boro, find me a boy whom I can trust to be the keeper of the steeds. He needs to be big, strong and willing to work. I would have him as a student and assistant. He will be called a 'squire'. Learn that word. It is of my tongue. We will need such words when none of the Arw'an words can describe a new thing."

ChOn left the doe and the travois and walked the buck to Sonja's dwelling. He called her by name before opening the flap and entering. Sonja was lying on her bed nursing a bloody face. One of her teeth was missing. There was another woman with her. She rose to leave but he detained her with a hand signal.

"Woman, why did the man beat you?" he asked Sonja.

"Because, My Lord, I told him he was not digging the walls straight enough and I was concerned they might collapse. He struck me once here and once here and told me he would do it as he pleased and that no man should do women's work. Nor should a woman do a man's."

ChOn looked at the other woman.

"Did things pass as she has told me?" he asked her.

"They did, My Lord."

"Are you able to go to the area we have set aside for communal gatherings, Sonja?"

"Yes, My Lord, although I am ashamed to be seen with my face like this."

"Be not ashamed of wounds sustained in the course of your duty, woman. Wear them with pride. Henceforth the villagers will know you as the woman who started the revolution between the sexes and their roles in the village and none will ever harm you again. This I promise you."

They made their way to the communal area. ChOn dismounted and moved to a position where he could be seen and heard by all present.

"Hear me all of you. This is a new place and we will have new ways of living and doing things. Here there will be no more men's work or women's work. Work will be allocated by me and the elders to those best able to do it and supervise it. Sometimes there will be men and women working together under a common supervisor. That supervisor may be a woman or a man and those working will obey as if the words came direct from my mouth. To disobey is to disobey me. Do it at your peril for I will have no deviation from my plan until it is completed and only then will we be able to relax somewhat but never without vigilance and discipline."

"Soon the other villages will start arriving. They will be given a space in which to live but there will be no isolation of anybody. We are to become one united tribe and we will then unite the Buq'ue with us and so when the Matáng come, we will make them wish they had not. That is my plan for us. Any who wish not to take part may leave at any time. But there will be no return for such people. Never. We will become strong and efficient but the rules will change and they will be strange. When we are all gathered with the other villages I will speak again at length of the new order. Meanwhile we have a lesson to learn."

"Where is the man who beat this woman? Come forward."

There was a murmuring in the crowd and a shifting of people before a man stepped forward. He was middle aged and well built. He shuffled uncomfortably under the looks of the other villagers and the gaze of Ch0n.

"What is your name, man and why did you strike this woman who was carrying out my orders? Speak carefully, man for your life depends on your answer."

"My Lord, I am Silas and I meant no harm to you. The woman told me my work was not what she wanted. She told me I should make the walls straight up and down. She told me I was lazy and good for nothing. It is not for a woman to speak so to

117

a man. Our customs are deep within us and without thinking I struck her. She will recover. After I struck her, I did indeed straighten the walls I had dug. So you see, I did obey her in the end."

"You did not mean any harm to me, I agree. But you did not obey my orders. You knew they came from her mouth tho' they were my words. She herself showed me the importance of the latrine and I know it to be true. More people have died in war by disease than in combat. In my world there is a holy book called the Q'uran. It says there that people should be thus punished, a life for a life, an eye for an eye, a nose for a nose, an ear for an ear, a tooth for a tooth, and this for wounds is legal retribution. Therefore I allow that the woman take your tooth as you took hers. Furthermore, I appoint you as overseer of camp hygiene. You will answer to the woman Sonja in all things. Her, I charge to treat you with fairness and you I charge to obey her as you would me and to treat those whom you may control with the same fairness with which you are treated. Do this on pain of death for you have failed me once and I will not suffer it from you again."

"Sonja. You I appoint town planner and I charge you to assemble a group of able persons to assist you in your task. They are to include one person from each village and this man, Silas. You will answer to me alone. Until your committee is assembled, you will need help from within this group. Take as few as you need and as many. The plan of the new village I will show to you from the hilltop and you will assign space according to the size of each of the villages."

"Hear me all of you. I will speak again when the remaining villages arrive. Meanwhile I tell you that all you have been in the past we will have to study. The system you have used to subsist on the plains will cease and we will have a new order. To each of you I will assign a role based on your talents. Trust me for it will not come easily to many but it is the new way. It is the way that will make us strong enough against the Buq'ue and the Matáng when they come. And they will come because we have bloodied their noses and they can not suffer such losses without vengeance. They need the goats and the women and they will come as they have always done. But we will prevail. This I promise in return for your trust and loyalty. Let this man Silas be a lesson to all. We can not permit disobedience to the laws I will put in place. They are to protect everybody and everybody will respect them.

Sonja. Take this man's tooth and know you are safe from retribution for it is as the Holy Book says, his tooth for yours."

Sonja picked up a stone from in front of her feet and advanced to Silas. He cowered in front of her before a glare from Ch0n straightened him. Sonja took from her bag a sliver of bone and placed it against the exact tooth she had lost earlier and struck it with the stone. Silas cried out and then spat a tooth on to the ground. Sonja looked at the man with no pity and returned to her place in the circle. Silas wiped the blood from his mouth and looked at Ch0n.

"It is done. It is over. No more will be spoken of it," announced Ch0n. "Now it is time to rest. Tomorrow we have much to do. Doni, Boro, Sonja. With me."

He strode to the place where Sonja had set up his shelter, a little removed from the rest. The doe was waiting there, tied to a tree. The buck was grazing nearby. A youth was positioned beside the doe. He came forward at Boro's signal.

"My Lord, this is the boy, Jez. He is the one I have chosen to be your...squire. He is of my village and my brother's wife's family. He is a herder as are we all and the goats are not afraid of him and go to him when he calls. Your tlaque already know him and fear him not."

"Hola Jez. Are you willing to be my squire because I will not have one who is with me against his will?"

"I am, My Lord. It is my honour and an honour to my family to serve you as your slave. For you are fair to those who obey you."

"You are not my slave. You are my squire, which is a man who serves and learns at the same time. You will care for my beasts and for me. In return I will teach you the things you will need to become a man of power with your own squire. These men are called 'Knights' in my language and now in yours. You will also watch my back and my belongings while I am otherwise occupied. This you will do on pain of death because if you do not die in their protection, you will not have done your duty. Do you understand, Jez?"

"I understand, My Lord but I am a herder and not a warrior to defend your belongings to the death. Perhaps you should select another more suited."

"A good and just answer, Jez. It is what I might have said myself. Be not concerned. I will teach you all you need to learn as part of my duty to you. And as you will defend me to the death, so will I defend you. Now. Take all these things from the travois and place them in the shelter. The female needs to be hobbled or tied. This thing goes around her front ankles and fastens here and here. She can walk but not run. The male will stay with her. Take off the saddle by pulling this and this and place it on a fallen trunk so it maintains its shape. Tomorrow I will show you how to clean it. Do you understand?"

"Yes, My Lord, although the words hobbled and saddle are new to me. This saddle and this hobble are made from a material I have never seen nor felt before. Where do they come from?"

"All in good time boy. Just do as you are told while I speak to the elders and then you may go and get your bedding. Tonight you will sleep in my shelter but tomorrow you will sleep in a shelter to be made for you and the beasts and my belongings."

ChOn took the two men and the woman into his shelter and seated them. They looked around at his array of weapons and battle order. The armour with the great hole in the back was hanging on a string near the entrance. They all looked at it and then at each other. ChOn saw the look that passed between them and opened the meeting with a smile and a shrug of his shoulders.

"For the moment let them think what they think. We few and soon Jez will know the truth of the sword. This garment is called armour and I have the means to make several hundred more like it. I also have a soft version that I wear always under my outer garment. No spear or arrow can pierce it. Soon you will see things that will fill you with wonder. I will tell you what you need to know but the rest must remain unknown for even to know will not make for one to understand the how of it. I come from a place far from here. I am the only one of my kind. I have trained all my life to fight and to lead. I have weapons that will fill an enemy horde with fear at their powers of destruction. I have all the knowledge of my people contained in the box. It is called a 'minitron' and I learn from it and it teaches me all I have ever known and all I will ever know outside of my life here as your ruler. That box is never to fall into enemy hands even tho' none but I can use it. Now here is my plan. I will tell you now so we can start on the morrow and we will be ready for the new villagers when they start arriving in the next days."

"Doni. Your village had the bigger herd of goats so to you I entrust them. I have a plan that will enable us to get rid of many of them and yet have more meat and milk than before. Meanwhile you will take them outside the perimeter each morning to an area near the river where the grass grows greenest and fastest. Each day, move them a little until we have established a system of water points where there is none at the moment. You may have only the boys yet to reach manhood as your herders. The rest of the men will be used here to perform other tasks in building the permanent village, which we will call a castle. It is another of many words in my tongue you will get used to."

"Boro. You will be in charge of the male workers. I will divide them with the help of their elders into village groups with you as their overseer. You will speak with my voice so have no fear of your position. From them we will select soldiers, builders and hunters."

"The women will have their own leaders. Sonja is one. We will need another, selected from one of the new villages. When I see her I will know who it will be. She will lead the cooks, healers and teachers of the children too young to work. The women will also tend their houses as they do now. Sonja, you will plan the village on the ground as I show it to you and Boro will build the structures within it. As I have said, each village will have enough space for its needs but with no central meeting place. There will be but one where we met just now. Their goats will be mixed with the others and so we will have but one herd under the control of Doni and his boy herders. You will have men and women to assist you. You will also speak with my voice. Your missing tooth, and that of the man, Silas will remind all that you are not to be argued with. The first task is to build a permanent shelter for Jez and my beasts. I will show you the place. Next to it I will move my own shelter because we are going to need this space when we move the mountain under which we sit."

The three looked at him and at each other.

It was Sonja who spoke the question on all their lips.

"We are going to move the mountain? But how? And what will we do with it?"

"The means I will provide. We are going to break it into small pieces and with them we are going to build a shelter, a castle to enclose this whole area with a fortress in the middle that no man can enter without risking his whole army. It will take a long time to build and many will be unhappy with the work we have in front of us but the end result will ensure our safety against the Matáng and their entire army should they choose to bring it. Meanwhile, I can tell you only a part of the plan until the other elders arrive. Then I will reveal all I can and we must hope there is time before the Buq'ue or the Matáng arrive in force."

"My Lord. Will we ride the beasts as you do?"

"Not all of you, Doni, but your herders will have beasts and we will have a mounted force of soldiers called cavalry. They will be mounted during battles and trained to sweep our enemies from the flanks as I have done these past days. It is a form of fighting that no foot soldier can withstand."

"And will we have weapons of thunder and metal storms such as you have?"

"No. I have enough for a select group only. The rest will fight with spears and bows like that one or crossbows like that one. Those I can make but the others I can not."

"My Lord, we will be many here. How are we to feed all the goats and the tlaque as well as all the people whilst not moving the village as we are accustomed to do?"

"This I will reveal to all but it can be done, Sonja. People will have to change their ways and think differently. But I will show you the way."

"My Lord, you said that in your world there is a Holy Book. What is a book?"

ChOn realized he had never seen a book in his life. His 'book' was the minitron. He had seen images of books so he knew how to describe one but he felt a sudden pang of ignorance for the first time since he could remember.

"A book is a collection of marks on sheets of thin material. The marks show the spoken word and they are used to learn from and to pass information. They are usually made of paper, which we will make from plants and water."

"Lord, could you show us an image from the box? An image of your world?"

ChOn hesitated and then thought what he might show them. He decided to show them an image of a castle. He turned off the language processor and selected an information thread and said,

"Eilean Donan Castle!"

A series of written articles and images flashed to the screen. He touched an image and it filled the screen.

"This is a castle. We will build something like it here, using the river as a barrier where you see water in the image. With a single entrance such as this one. Easily defended."

They were struck with wonder. ChOn swiped the screen and the image gave way to the options screen. He touched a box and words filled the screen.

"This is called text. It has meaning and I can read it in my own tongue".

He closed the page and said,

"Dictionary planet four!"

In an instant an image appeared. It was the cover of a dictionary in the form of a book.

He opened the first page and showed them the words on it. It was an English/Planet four translation starting with all the words the minitron had established in the past weeks.

About – kaia

Above – atuga

Accept – ogog

And so on, page after page.

"This is your language," he said, reading some of the words and showing them. "I can read the marks for they have sounds to them. The box is listening to you and to me and writing the words for those who may follow."

"Others like you, Lord, with weapons to subjugate us?"

"Have I subjugated you? You asked me to lead you. The others will one day come. Not to subjugate but to take the riches of this place and to leave others like me. They will come in peace as I have. You need not fear them. But they will be a long time coming. They may never come. Now go. Speak nothing of the box for it is to be a secret among us. A thing of trust. In the morning, come to me and we will start our task of building the shelter.

The three left, their heads full of unasked questions.

Jez!"

'I am here, My Lord."

"I am going to introduce you to a thing called a bath, Jez. It means immersing your whole body in water and rubbing yourself with this to clean your skin and hair. Your clothes you can also wash. Do you have any animals that live on your body or in your hair?"

"Just the usual ones that everybody has, My Lord."

"In that case you will select your favourite clothing and we will boil water and soak them on the morrow. What you do not need, we will burn. Your hair will be worn short. That way there is no shelter for fleas or lice. I will dress you in a uniform the same as mine, complete with armour. I will show you how to care for it and so it will last you for longer. Now. If you wish to share my shelter tonight, take this and go to the river. Find Sonja and tell her to find a place where we can make a communal bath. It must be upstream from the latrines but centrally placed. Soon we will make a shelter where we will have water for bathing. Now, take this uniform. You put it on thus and the front will close when this side touches that. The pants you put on first. You will need an undergarment but not until your clothing has been boiled in hot water will you mix your garments with mine or this uniform."

He took a utility belt from the wall and removed a tool from its pouch.

"This tool has many uses. It will cut and hold. It will punch holes and more. This part will cut hair. It has two metal blades which open and close and will cut whatever is between them, including your uniform, the edges of this shelter and light vegetation. I am giving it and the belt to you. The belt you can use to hold your trousers and other things you will get as you earn them. Look after this tool because it is a rare and valuable thing. Now go and bathe yourself, burn those garments, don the uniform and then return. You may sleep inside with me but your belongings remain outside until they are clean. When the new shelter is built for the beasts, you will sleep with them and husband them. Do you understand?"

"Yes, My Lord. I understand but I do not understand why you do not take a woman to look after your needs."

"What needs have I that you cannot fulfil? I have need only of a strong arm and eyes looking after my beasts and my back while I am otherwise occupied. I am accustomed to looking after myself and I see no need for more. You will one day be a powerful man in this village not for your birth, but for your knowledge of the things I will show you. In time you will be called a Knight and ride a tlaque of your own and have a squire of your own. That is the way of things. You will help me and I will teach you. Go now. I am afraid the bugs will jump from your garments or your hair onto my bedding."

Jez went to seek out Sonja and to tell him of Ch0n's strange request. She smiled at him.

"Our Lord is wise in the ways of things. We women bathe ourselves every moon for that is when we bleed. If we do not, we stink and get sick. Until now the men have not been so diligent with their cleanliness but now we will see how they like it. I will instruct Silas to go to the flint maker and have all the men and women shave their heads. We will burn all the hair and all the lice with it. The women will then grow their hair again but the men will wear theirs cut short or shaved in the manner of our lord."

"And what of this boiling of garments and burning of the remainder?" asked Jez.

"I know not why nor how we will do this thing called boiling. But I know we will do it because he has said we will and so we will obey when he shows us the how of it. Come now and we will find a place for you to clean your skin and shave your head."

"But what of his not wanting a woman to serve his needs? I am frightened he may want me to do this for him. He tells me he *has no need of a woman, only of me. I do not want to serve him as does a woman. What will I do if he wishes it?"*

"You will ask him if he will forgive you your ignorance of such things and you will come to me. I know not his ways nor his desires but I am sure we can find a way to serve him if he desires it. We know he has the body of a normal man only bigger and his bodily functions seem as ours are. If he has desires of a sexual nature we do not yet know but we will discover that in time. We know his anatomy is the same as ours so I imagine his kind uses their women as we are used for pleasure and offspring. Leave him to decide but I do not think he is a domagamag. They are usually more effeminate and want to work with women and share their stories of male lovers. This one will want a woman if he wants to take his pleasure and any woman would beg to have him as her lover. Me included."

They came to a place where the river bank had a number of large flat stones leading to the water's edge and more that were partially submerged. Sonja looked about her to see exactly where they were relative to the camp.

"This will do. It could be better placed but it is central enough. And it is hidden from the village by the rise so those who desire to bathe may do so without witnesses, other than those here with them. Would you have me shave your head? I have a flint that will do it fast enough."

Jez proudly took out his multi tool.

"He gave me this. It has a number of tools for which I am sure there is a purpose. The blades are sharp enough to shave with but these cutters will do for my hair. Look at this thing. When you hold it thus and draw it back towards the eye, it makes the object seem larger beneath it. I discovered its purpose when I was playing with it before I came to you. It is magic. Look. If I hold it against your hand and draw it so towards your eye you

can see the sun formed on your hand. But then it becomes smaller."

Sonja pulled back her hand.

"It made my hand burn. Feel it for yourself. When the sun becomes a small point it burns."

Jez tried it and he too pulled his hand back in amazement. Then he pointed at a tuft of dead grass showing from a crack in the rocks. He aimed the point of light at it and was rewarded with smoke. Sonja blew gently and a flicker of flame licked the tuft and it caught.

"What magic is this he has given you? The gift of fire to carry with you always. Guard that tool well because its value is beyond measure. Now, show me how to use the cutters and I will cut your hair and shave your head. Then I will wash you and also myself for I like the scent of this white stone he gave you to clean yourself with and if you desire it, I will pleasure you afterwards."

Gavan Connell

Chapter Twelve: The Buq'ue

The former shaman of the Arw'an village of Boro was once again in the presence of the king of the Buq'ue.

"Your majesty, I fear you are delaying too much. It is now three days since I returned empty handed from the village of Boro the Arw'an herder. Your war patrol of more than thirty men was decimated by this strange foreigner, the ChOn. I myself was lucky to escape thanks to my superior cunning and magic power which rendered me invisible to him. But I implore you yet again. Kill him. If you do not, he will use his weapons against you and steal your kingdom. The Arw'an will rule the Buq'ue and return you to herding goats like your ancestors used to do before they became warriors and hunters. Let me tell your elders what I have told you. Let them know what their enemy, our enemy is capable of. I alone have the power of magic over him and have escaped his clutches twice. I alone have lived to tell the tale after a battle and thanks to my magic, one other man escaped with me. One who was in the forefront of the battle and became invisible through my magic before the ChOn could kill him as he did the rest. Let him speak for his is a tale of horror and blood such as we have not seen since the last Matáng raid."

The king listened patiently because he was troubled by the stories of this strange giant who rode beasts and had weapons no man had ever seen. He was deeply disturbed by the name of this new enemy. 'ChOn'. It was too close to his cloud God, Chon'i, the God of thunder, lightning, rain and abundance to be a co-incidence. He didn't want to upset the most powerful God of many Gods. What if ChOn'i had come down from the sky as some of his soothsayers were telling him? What if he were intent on vengeance for the way the Buq'ue had killed, raped and enslaved the Arw'an for decades under his very rule? He wanted his elders to advise him and his soothsayers to read the signs as they had always done. Most of all he wanted to avoid responsibility for making a decision that might well cost him his kingdom and cause the downfall of the Buq'ue.

"Let the shaman of the village of Boroi speak of this Ch0n!" he roared and silence overtook the gathering of elders. In the distance women could be heard keening a death song for their husbands and sons and brothers.

The shaman rose to his feet and took out the light pen. He adjusted the power of it, clicked it and there was a gasp as the blue and yellow flame hissed into the air almost a foot.

"I am Pik, former shaman and magician of the village of Boro the Arw'an! See my magic. I bear the power of fire in my bag. I have the power of invisibility over my sworn enemies. I have escaped sure death by the hand of this Ch0n by cunning and magic. I saved this soldier three days past by making him also invisible and passing with him from the camp of Boro to the fort of the Buq'ue. Hear me well for there is an enemy close by who has the power to kill and enslave us all unless he is killed."

"He commands the beasts of the earth and they heed him. He rides a tlaque and it kills on his command. I have seen this beast kill half a dozen of our finest soldiers with a single sweep of its head as it charged into battle with the Ch0n astride its back. He bore a bowed weapon that sent missiles from thirty paces into the bodies of your men and when they charged him, he unsheathed a terrible blade of green that sang to him even as it wrought slaughter. Finally he took a machine of metal from his clothing and conjured up an invisible storm of bees that turned to pulp all who were still fighting. He did not even need to use the weapon I once took from him. It is a weapon that breaks rocks without sound. He points it and they break. When I took it from him, it was broken or I would have killed him with

it. Instead I made myself invisible and left the village unmolested. Here I came to tell your king of the first killings and then after almost a moon cycle, he sent me with his war patrol to kill the ChOn and bring back the box that is the seat of his power, knowledge and magic. Without it he is nothing for he consults it before every decision. During the battle I and this man went to his shelter and sought the box but it was well hidden and he came too soon for us to search better. I made myself and this man invisible and returned here even as he hunted for us. He caught two other men who travelled close by and slew them both. I saw this in a vision. When I arrived here to tell our king of the slaughter, he wanted to know more and more. He still wants to know more but I say this. I will be your magician and I alone will show you the manner to defeat this ChOn but we need action and we need it now before he renews his strength for the next battle. He is but one and we are many. Even with his weapons of death we can defeat him if we attack in numbers. That is all. Your majesty I implore you to send a force of hundreds against the village of Boro so we may kill the ChOn, gain the box and have the power he now possesses for ourselves. For you, the king of the Buq'ue. What say you?"

The gathering became animated at this plan of action. The king held up his hand.

"I have heard you more than once. Now the elders have heard you. And the soothsayers. But I have a question for the soldier who accompanied you from the village. Answer me, man. Were you invisible as this Pik claims you were?"

"Yes, My Lord. We were indeed invisible for we walked from the camp unmolested and unchallenged. Later we heard the ChOn hunting for us but he found us not. Instead he found the other two and we heard their cries as he slew them both. My Lord. I have never been invisible before and to me it was as if nothing had changed but if we were not invisible, how could we have walked from the village as we did?"

The king nodded.

"Pik, you will remain here as my chief magician. You the soothsayers will meet and advise me on the morrow of the signs and what I am to do. The remaining elders will stand by to mobilize a force of two hundred men to march on the Boro camp if the soothsayers say it is a favourable time to do so. Leave us now."

The group dispersed. Only the king, Pik and the king's bodyguard remained.

"I do not believe you made yourselves invisible, Pik, for it is impossible in my opinion. If you can do it, do it now."

"But your majesty, I can do it only in the face of my true enemies and here I am among friends. It is a gift of magic, not a sleight of hand to be played out as if on a stage."

"Then tell me more about the Ch0n. Tell me everything you know."

"Well, your majesty, I overheard a villager saying he is immortal. That he took a blade full in the back and rode into the camp with it sticking out. It was then I made us invisible for I wanted to hear what I could hear without fear of discovery. He entered his dwelling seconds after I had left and then ran out again with the sword having been withdrawn and no sign of any wound upon his person. It was then he hunted me for he guessed I had entered his dwelling and disturbed his belongings, of which there were few. Nothing to steal other than the box, which we could not find."

"And tell me magician. What is his weakness? You who have seen him in battle single handed against more than thirty men. If we march on the village of Boro, how do we kill him?"

"Your majesty. It is a simple plan. We attack the village and before he sallies forth in its defence, I will make myself invisible and walk up to him and kill him from behind with a war ax. It is well known that even immortals cannot survive their heads being separated from their bodies. In return for this deed, I would ask nothing more than to be your humble servant and keeper of the magic box. Only a true magician will be able to reveal its secrets for it is surely protected from mere mortals by a powerful spell. I will reveal to you all that I learn and you will have the secret of eternal youth as shall I. We will rule the earth against even the Matáng for they will know nothing of the power we can wield against them. What say you?"

"I say it is a lot to risk on the power of one man to make himself invisible. But I have your word and the word of a soldier that you have this power at your whim so if the soothsayers say the signs are right, we will attack the village of Boroi in the afternoon of tomorrow. Now leave me. Tell the guard to send in my third wife. She knows how to prepare me for battle like no other."

"Your majesty. We are in need of goats, slaves and women for this season the raids have dealt us failure. Might I remind you that your third wife is the second daughter of Boro himself and that he has another even fairer?"

"How quickly have you changed your allegiance, magician. Fail me and you will need more than the gift of invisibility to escape me and then we will certainly know how a body can not survive without its head attached."

Pik retired from the king's chambers, passing on his way out a giant guard with leather tunic and his face covered by a black turban, with only his green eyes showing. He was the tallest man Pik had ever seen apart from Ch0n.

"The king would have you send in his third wife," he told the guard, who merely nodded and turned and left. Pik followed him with his eyes.

"Surely there is the one who could match the ChOn in a fight to the death for he is of the same stature, albeit finer." He thought. *"But he moves like a cat. When I am second only to the king I will have him as my own bodyguard, decked out like the ChOn with all his weapons except the box, which I alone will control. Then none will touch me. And then I will make myself king in my own time and rule the entire world."* He laughed to himself. *"How easy it is to become invisible. Any fool can do it. Invisibility is only the skill of being unseen and un-noticed. It has nothing to do with not being visible".*

The day dawned gloomy. Clouds filled the sky and steady drizzle was falling as the Buq'ue fort stirred. The king awoke refreshed and well satisfied with the ministrations of his third wife who retired to the harem when the king called for the soothsayers and elders. They gathered in the main meeting hall with the townsfolk all awaiting the verdict.

"So what say you, soothsayers? How do you read the signs? Is this a good time to do battle against the ChOn and the village of Boro the Arw'an?"

He soothsayers shuffled collectively and then their spokesman answered.

"Mighty King. We have read the signs and we think this is not a good time to do battle. The ChOn is planning to defend the village with his weapons of mass destruction and is waiting for us even as we speak. The signs tell us to wait until he is off guard and then attack when the villagers are tired of waiting at the ready. It is raining and we think he may have influence over the weather because his name is so close to that of Chon'i or

he may be the incarnation of Ch0n'i himself. Why otherwise would it be raining when yesterday there was no sign of rain?"

Pik jumped to his feet.

"Charlatans!" he cried. *"Charlatans who take the easy road of advice for they can not be proven wrong if we sit here and wait. It matters not that Ch0n has the villagers waiting at the ready. Our force will dispatch the village herders and then we will carry off the stock and the women and whatever children we want. I will personally dispatch the Ch0n. The time is now!"*

The king was relieved. He had no great desire to face the Ch0n if the stories were true. And they must be true because of the thirty men he had dispatched only days ago, only one and the magician had returned. And what if the Ch0n were the incarnation of Chon'i? Better to leave well enough alone.

"These wise man have served me well for many years, magician. Do not be too hasty in calling them charlatans. If they say the signs are not right, they are not right. Now wise ones. When will the time BE right?"

The soothsayers were ready for this question and had argued all night over the answer. They had thought of some improbable sign that would herald the right moment.

"Great King Buki! The time to attack is when we get word from the Arw'an themselves that Ch0n has lost the will to fight. Only then will we attack and we will not fail."

Pik could not believe his ears. These men were indeed wise. They had guaranteed they would never be caught out as he himself had done on many occasions in the past. There was nothing he could do in the knowledge the soothsayers had the king's ear.

"So be it!" roared the king. *"We will await such a sign."*

137

Gavan Connell

Chapter Thirteen: The Gathering

It was on the fourth day that the first two villages arrived at the new site. It was the same day that the shelter for the tlaques and Jez was to be built and the men and boys separated into working groups. Ch0n was kept busy receiving the elders of the villages and soothing their egos as he told them individually of his plans. They were not happy to pool their goats and manpower and some were not happy with the area they had been allocated. Ch0n managed to get them all onside through a combination of good leadership and threats of expulsion. He wanted to give them an awesome display of might and power but also wanted to wait until all the villages were present. He spent the coming days preparing to do just that, digging holes and planting high explosives at regular intervals and tamping the holes with mud. Doni, Boro and Sonja were busy all day with their tasks and Jez was busy in his new shelter organizing storage and fodder for the beasts as well as arranging his own corner of the castle-to-be.

By the sixteenth day, all thirteen villages had arrived and were settled and quartered. Ch0n had identified another woman from the new arrivals to become the head woman. She was another older woman strong of body and will and already a leader in her own large village. She had taken to Ch0n's task with vigour and the women were fast being organized into groups according to their skills. Her name was Kelda. She was a healer and gatherer of plants for food and healing. She decided this was a priority and soon organized a small army of foragers as well as teachers, healers, cleaners and stores people. She and Sonja were wary of each other for the first day or so until Ch0n made it clear there would be no usurping of roles or personnel. All disputes between them were to be settled by agreement or he would intervene. And so they formed their own planning group with others of the women and in two days the camp was humming, clean, had a track system and a system of male and female bathing days introduced. All the hair was burned and all the clothes progressively boiled thanks to ChOn's Fresnel lenses and some small rock pools in the river.

The day after the villages had all assembled, ChOn told them all to move out of the village to a vantage point some distance away. There he told them of his grand plan to build a fortress using the mountain as materials. They would use the stones and the limestone mud to build walls twice the height of a man around the whole camp and then build a fortress within the walls inside which they would be able to fight off an attacking enemy. He told them of his plans to create guilds of trades where each man would have work and that people would eat what they gathered or grew and they would buy or trade for meat, which the herders would provide. Only does which threw twins would be retained and only the biggest and strongest bucks would be allowed to breed. All other male goats would have their testicles removed and be used as meat. An army would be raised and trained and paid. A system of money would be introduced. Money was something that people could accumulate to trade for goods. ChOn would show them all this in the coming days but now he had for them a demonstration of his power. He pointed to the small, rocky 'mountain' that formed the centre of their camp.

"Watch yonder mount. I have prepared it to mine the rocks for the outside wall. This is but the first of many such things you will see as we need more stones to build the village and fortify it."

He pointed a small black box with a wire antenna at the mountain and pressed a sequence of buttons. The explosives detonated in a series of mini explosions that lasted several seconds. The ground shook and the dust and debris flew but did not reach their vantage point. Some of the villagers screamed and hid their faces. Some fainted. Others yelled with excitement. Others sat wide eyed. Children cried and mothers hugged them. When the dust settled, the entire tip of the mountain was a pile of rubble.

"It is safe to return to your shelters. I want every man, woman and child to collect one rock and carry it to the base of the mount. Tomorrow, all of you will be engaged in moving stones to the perimeter wall that Boro and his team will build. The first section will be the entrance where there is currently a fence to keep the goats in. This wall we will build to keep the Buq'ue out."

In the Buq'ue fortress, Pik heard a distant rumble of thunder and looked at the sky. There were no clouds today. What could it mean? As he wondered, he saw a group of men approaching his shelter. He recognized them all. They were the shaman of several of the Arw'an villages. They hurried to him and told him the news that the villagers had left their grazing grounds and had been led by guides to an unknown location because ChOn feared the Buq'ue attacks would decimate them village by village if they didn't unite. They were much taken aback at Pik's roar of laughter.

"It is the sign!" he shouted. *"It is the sign the soothsayers predicted! The hour is here! Come brothers we must tell the king the good news."*

In two weeks the army of men had a wall as high as a man across the bend of the river. It had two sets of double gates of bamboo as high as two men and there were two block houses as high as three men guarding the gates. No one could pass through the second row of gates without passing below the gatehouse, which had holes in the floor for thrusting long bamboo spears and pouring boiling water or raw sewage. The first gates could be dropped from above trapping anyone

141

between the two rows. But the main defensive weapon was the corner gun emplacement where the rail gun was to be mounted with a view along the entire wall through protected slit windows. ChOn had spent hours training a select team to operate it and they had practised firing individual rounds and short and long bursts into lines of mock up targets. The only worry ChOn had was their ability to stay at their posts while under attack. For that reason, he had built the emplacement with a lockable door so none could enter or leave without coming under fire from a fully kitted soldier, Jez, who now had a functioning helm, sprayform armour and kinetic pistol to add to his multi tool. He had proved a good student and a calm one under pressure. Doni had chosen him well, ChOn had thought on many occasions.

"That weapon must not fall into enemy hands. They will not be able to use it without ammunition but we need it as our primary defensive weapon until we have better walls. You are to make sure that nobody enters that emplacement or leaves. Even if you have to risk your own life to do it," had been his instructions to Jez when his role had been explained.

Meanwhile, the small number of 'soldiers' ChOn had at his disposal were being trained to use spears and shields. He did not trust them as yet with weapons that might be lost in the first battle. He would bear the brunt of the fighting along with the rail gun and the archers on the wall. The five horse bows had been allocated to the men who had shown a natural aptitude to shoot them straight. At this early stage it was the best ChOn could do. He had no idea if the Buq'ue were coming that day, the following or not at all.

He fitted the big tlaque with breast armour and side skirts joined with nylon ties. The surprise aspect of his being mounted was now lost and surely they would work out that the beast could be stopped at close range with a spear and ChOn would have to fight dismounted. He decided to change his own tactics and use the kinetic pistol and pulse rather than allow close quarter fighting and even then he thought he might dismount if he had to and fight on foot. He was more accustomed to that anyway. But he would need Jez to keep the buck from wandering or getting captured. It was then that he decided a priority task was to form a cavalry troop.

ChOn spent almost all his time training Jez and the army and inspecting. He had no high hopes for the men at first. All he needed from them was to perform a single role and do it as best they could. And not to lose their weapons. Primarily they trained with short stabbing spears made from the bamboo and fitted with long metal blades made from re-forged short swords captured from the Buq'ue dead. He made their shields out of the wet hides of all the goats they slaughtered and left them in the sun to harden. They were not spear proof but they did allow their bearers to deflect thrusts while their own stabbing spears, much shorter and easier to manage were employed. ChOn had the legendary Zulu warrior chief, Chaka, to thank for this weapon and also the horns of the buffalo tactic, which ChOn knew as the double pincer movement from his own training. In short order he had some hundred Infantry soldiers and the five bowmen who employed the horse bows from ChOn's dead comrades. The war arrows were precious so ChOn had them make training arrows from the reed-like bamboo shoots that grew as straight as if they had been manufactured. They flew true over fifty feet once fletched with waterfowl feathers and lacked the weight to penetrate even a hide vest. But they allowed the archers to train day after day. ChOn decided he would use the clay-like mud from the bottom of the nearby lake to fill the flutes and give them more range and power. He set a group of women to perform that task and to bind a small wedge of metal to the tip for penetrating power. As the days passed, the piles of arrows grew bulkier; the Infantry grew more disciplined and the wall grew higher across the isthmus.

The most important and difficult training was conducted with eight especially selected men from the village. Those Ch0n trained to use the radios and to be able to lead small groups of three fit young men across the countryside. He sent them out half at a time, to three distant hilltop Observation Posts where they could see across the plains. He designated them OP1 and OP2. Every two days they returned after their relief patrols had taken their places. They carried mirrors as backup but their primary means of communication was the radio built in to the helms of Ch0n's dead colleagues. Either Ch0n or Jez always wore a helm to ensure communications were open and in case any warning were sounded. The men on these OP were selected for their ability to run. They carried no weapons and had been instructed not to allow the helms to fall into enemy hands at any cost. Ch0n had shown them how to disable the entire function of the helm. The role of the outposts was to alert the village by radio or signal mirror if any enemy force were seen advancing towards the village and then to run to the village ahead of the advancing force to provide as much information as possible to the defenders.

The weeks passed. The petty squabbles caused by land allocation had long been resolved. The woman, Sonja, was a hard task mistress and would stand no bickering. She was as fair as she was hard, however and once people realized they were actually better off being organized than being left to their own devices, they sought her out to resolve their problems. She and Kelda saw what Ch0n was doing with the men, organizing them into soldiers, herders, artisans and labourers and set to doing the same with the women. They needed tillers of the gardens because Ch0n had told her the secret of food production was to grow it in a fashion that enabled the end users to harvest it close to home. He told her how to use the manure of the goat herd and how to make water conduits from the long, hollow bamboo trunks. Inside a few weeks a garden started to take shape near the river where water was plentiful.

ChOn tried to explain to Kelda that he had seen images of domestic fowl on the minitron but to this point, nobody had seen anything suitable. The waterfowl were too flighty to pen and were at hand in any regard. So there were no domestic creatures in the village apart from the wolf, who continued to both fascinate and terrorize the villagers by his presence. They whispered among themselves that he was a magic creature who could understand ChOn's language for it appeared to be so. He was always calm around ChOn and would suffer the children to approach him but not the adults and nobody dared to enter ChOn's personal dwelling uninvited because the beast would suddenly rise and put his head close to the ground and growl deep in his chest until ChOn calmed him with a word or a gesture.

They also needed men and women to sew, make the arrows, scrape the hides and dispose of the village garbage. ChOn had shown them the value of compost and they incorporated this into their gardens, laying rows of organic matter and keeping them moist and turning them daily. The village started to take on the appearance of order. There was food for all, provided by the women not otherwise engaged, cooking for family groups, their rations of meat and the vegetables ChOn had been able to identify as safe and those the women traditionally gathered. But there was a potential problem with the plants because the village was consuming them faster than they could hope to grow inside the village garden and so foraging parties had to be organized. This took valuable people away from ChOn's primary role of building the wall but it continued to grow and the internal buildings were spit locked into place as the mountain was gradually reduced in size foot by foot and the rocks cemented together with limestone mud and grass.

After two months had passed, Boro and Doni went to ChOn's dwelling and announced the wall, the towers and the main gate were completed across the isthmus to a height of two and a half men and the entire village was now walled to the height of a man with towers on all corners. A secure point had been constructed to allow water gatherers to do their work whilst being defended from two corner towers. ChOn had been overseeing the construction from a distance and had not needed to make too many changes as the wall progressed. He was pleased with the work of the two men and told them to gather the village that night. As usual the tribes gathered in their small groups and as usual ChOn called those forward he wanted to speak to.

"Look upon Boro and Doni, former village heads of two small villages and look yonder at the wall they have built and the goats that are safe within its shelter. And why have they built it so? Because I ordered it and you here in front of me have done the hard work under their direction. And just as they have built the walls, the women Sonja and Kelda have built the village from within, thanks to all the men and women who have worked for them. We have not taken a single day's rest since we arrived but tomorrow we will all rest and feast. Only the soldiers will remain on guard because the defence of the village can never be neglected. Half will be stood down for tomorrow and half the following day but those stood down must remain able under pain of death to mount the defence of the wall. As you can see, the castle within the walls is starting to rise from the ground and we will continue to build both it and the rest of the wall which you see surrounding the entire village. By the next moon the wall will be as high as two men along the river. In two moons it will be as high as two and a half men and the inner castle will start to take form. You have worked well."

"To these four and to all who directly serve me, I will allow as much room inside the castle as can be covered by twenty paces long and twelve paces wide. It is a reward for their work. Some of you who have assisted them will also be granted space or privilege. But all will be cared for and all will get the chance for betterment. The women who are healers will have a central place in which to work. It will be the place best protected from harm so they can do their work in no danger. Now rest and prepare for tomorrow's celebration."

Ch0n bade the four stay with him.

"Well done to you all. So it shall be for those who serve the Arw'an well. Everyone who works will get their reward. And as we expand the rewards will also get bigger but I will have no corruption. As easily as I give, so can I take away. Now go and pace out your allotments close to my own so the builders may spit lock your walls."

Gavan Connell

Chapter Fourteen: The Attack of the Buq'ue

Pik was indeed invisible. After trying desperately to convince the king of the Buq'ue to attack the village of Boro, he had left the Buq'ue village to roam the country. He left behind the trappings of the shaman and travelled instead as an outcast, one who was deemed crazy and useless to a village and so sent away so as not to consume the valuable supplies of the village. As such, they were as invisible as ghosts. Nobody knew them and nobody wanted to know them. They lived off the land and begged for a living. Pik was desperate to get the minitron and so, disguised as an outcast, he went first to the village of Boro to secure it by stealth and cunning. It was two days after the remaining Shaman had arrived in the Buq'ue village telling tales of their villages suddenly moving under directions from a messenger from the Ch0n. He knew there would be nobody at the village but he wanted to try and find where the village had gone to by following the tracks. They led him to another site where a second village had joined them and then it turned towards the morning sun and continued straight. He lost the tracks because an enormous herd of beasts had also moved in the same direction before turning away and Pik lost several days trying to work out which tracks belonged to which group and had had to return several times by tracking the edges of the flattened grass. Then it had rained and he had lost everything. The rain flattened the plains and then the grass sprang up again as though it had never been disturbed. There was no way to find the tracks again so Pik just wandered towards the morning sun looking for something to give him a clue but finding nothing. His meagre supplies were running out when he turned back to the setting sun and made for the Buq'ue fort again. Unknown to him, he had missed the new

Arw'an village by less than a day's walk and had almost reached Ch0n's original fortress when he decided to return. But he knew there was a large village somewhere relatively close but that he would never find it alone. He needed to secure the king's permission to send out a sizeable force with a supply train to conduct a search-and-destroy patrol on a wide frontage. But the king was not keen to engage the Ch0n and his weapons for the sake of a few women and goats. There would have to be another reason. By the time he reached the Buq'ue fort almost a month after he left, he had a plan. Without going to his own dwelling, he went straight to the king's throne room and prostrated himself on the floor.

"Majesty. King Buki. I have spent the past moon searching the flat lands for the Arw'an villagers and have found nothing. Nothing. This can mean but one thing. The Ch0n has united them in one place and is planning to build an army and a fort from which to march on the Buq'ue as we have traditionally marched upon them in their weakness. The Ch0n would have your head on a stick and your throne for himself. One moon and seven days have passed since the Arw'an Shaman came to me to tell me of the messengers from the Ch0n, how they told me he had commanded them to burn their belongings and take up the life of soldiers under his command. If they are united as one and are training themselves for battle, they will be weak for some time yet. The Arw'an are not accustomed to living in large groups and they will need to forage. They will need water and they will need grass for their goats. When they are trained enough and their forage starts to thin, they will have no option but to march on the Buq'ue in force with the Ch0n at their head to conquer thee and usurp all the Buq'ue have here in plenty. It is obvious. You can wait no longer as you value your head and your people."

As he spoke, a low rumble filled the air and the ground trembled slightly.

"Majesty, I have heard these sounds of thunder many times as I travelled and not been able to determine from whence they come. Sometimes they are accompanied by clouds and others not. The sound seems to come from the direction of the morning sun but surrounds the entire plains with its rumbling. Perhaps it is some God telling us that the time to attack has arrived."

King Buki shifted uneasily in his throne. He saw the logic of the shaman. He had heard and felt the occasional rumblings from the direction of the morning sun and had wondered at their origins. His soothsayers had not been forthcoming with any sensible suggestions and yet this shaman had offered the possibility that it was a God. If ChOn'i were the God of rain, might he not be able to create thunder from nothing? But more disturbing was the thought that his tribe might one day be subjugated by the Arw'an and the ChOn, and his own head might adorn a stick at the entrance to the fort. His army chiefs had been waiting patiently for orders to get started so there was no need to delay further. He looked at the entrance to his dwelling and tried to imagine his head stuck on a pole adorning it. It wasn't difficult. He summoned his soothsayers.

"Tell me if the timing is right!" he ordered.

The soothsayers were experts in their king's body language. They had known from the start he was worried about the ChOn's power and how it might affect him but they knew he also thought he was safe if he stayed put. This time they saw he had been swayed by the arguments of the Shaman, Pik, and that the time was right for them even if not for a battle. They cast their bones and sticks and made much of reading how they fell before putting their heads close together and consulting. Finally they rose as one and their spokesman announced the signs were all aligned for a great victory if they could find the Arw'an village before the next moon rose full.

The king nodded his assent to his commanders. Pik was jubilant. He withdrew backwards, grovelling all the way to the door. He stood and turned, only to be confronted by the king's giant bodyguard. The eyes behind the slit in the turban were strangely youthful looking but untrusting.

"*A giant eunuch,*" thought Pik as he stepped past the soldier and went to his humble dwelling. Once there he washed and slept, knowing as he went to his bed that his dream of power was about to be realized.

The following morning there was much hubbub in the fort. Two companies of soldiers were assembled with their commanders before the king's dwelling. The king himself was not going to join the battle. He expected it to be over within the month and didn't want to be living hard in the field when he could be warm and comfortable here with his third wife, waiting for his fourth to be, her sister, to be brought bound to the harem. The king was addressing the commanders to one side. There seemed to Pik to be no urgency in the proceedings and he felt a little uneasy at this. The mood was jovial if anything, like a crowd going along to the wrestling or a footrace. The commanders received the last of their orders and returned to their companies. They shouted a few words of command and the troops moved off in column of route out of the fort and down a track that led towards where the sun had risen some time before. Behind them, a gaggle of porters carrying supplies shuffled along with a few women and last of all, an outcast looking for any scraps he could scrounge from the baggage train. He was beaten off several times before being ignored and the train ventured out on to the open plains in search of the Arw'an.

Based on Pik's information, the column moved towards the rising sun for two whole days before setting up a large bivouac complete with campfires and dancing. The commanders gathered their junior commanders together to formulate a patrol plan that would eventually find the Arw'an camp. The plan was well thought out and involved breaking up into groups of ten soldiers under a 'cabot'. They would fan out to the horizon on fixed bearings and return to a central position to be determined by smoke. The rightmost cabot would be traveling with the company commander who would signal for the remaining nine to move to his position for the night encampment. The other company would do the same and with twenty cabots fanning out and then centralizing, they could cover enormous tracts of land in one day at walking speed. It was a plan destined to succeed. It was a tried and true method used by the Buq'ue to search for remote villages and new hunting grounds.

It was on the seventh day that one of the cabots stumbled upon a dead goat with its ear cut in the style of the Arw'an. Each village cropped or docked part of the ear so they could identify their goats from those of neighbouring villages if the two flocks managed to get mixed up. The cabot sent a runner to the next cabot who sent a runner in turn until the company commander was aware of the discovery. The find resulted in a change of the axis of advance slightly and a new level of intensity among the scouts. Two days later they came to the top of a hill and found signs that people had been using it for some weeks as a camp. What they didn't know was that it was one of the Arw'an Observation posts and that their advance had been noted and reported back to the Arw'an village and to ChOn himself. It was two days after the village feast that his helm squawked into action with the news that a Buq'ue patrol had been sighted by OP1 and that the OP would be withdrawn under cover to observe from a distance the Buq'ue advance. Half a day later, OP2 reported seeing another Buq'ue patrol advancing towards them and they also withdrew.

ChOn took out the tablet and called up his rudimentary map. The two OPs that had seen the advance were more than two miles apart. That meant the Buq'ue force was advancing on a front at least that wide. ChOn tried to calculate the size of the force and came up with two hundred men advancing to contact in squad sized groups (an assumption that proved to be more or less correct) one visual distance apart. He ordered all the OPs in to their secondary posts and stood the village to defensive positions for practice. He told them that in a day or two the Buq'ue patrol would arrive in numbers that would require the soldiers to deploy. The women and children went to the central castle, such as it was and the soldiers deployed at the main wall. The rest of the wall was protected by the river and ChOn kept a small reserve force centrally located to deploy in the event some of the Buq'ue soldiers breached the main wall or tried to cross the river and attack from the rear. He knew it was unlikely because they didn't have the mobility to deploy in any manner that couldn't be countered from within the fort. His only real fear was that his inexperienced men would falter under attack and the wall would be breached.

His plan of defence consisted of deploying a platoon of Infantry outside the wall on the main track in to the village. When the main Buq'ue force arrived, they would charge forward and engage the Buq'ue with throwing spears at maximum range. This platoon had been selected especially for the task and contained only those who could throw a spear more than a hundred feet. Accuracy was not an issue because the Buq'ue force would be concentrated and the aim was to engage the battle with or without enemy casualties in the first volley. When the Buq'ue attacked, the platoon would hastily withdraw towards the wall, making sure they didn't break ranks. They would maintain contact with the enemy until they reached the wall, at which time they would enter through the main gate and the gate would be closed while the archers went to work. ChOn would not be involved at this stage. Jez was to take up his position outside the tower holding the rail gun and only if ChOn gave the order was he to allow the gunners to open fire. The remaining kinetic pistols were deployed strategically along the wall to allow them to be fired as much as possible along the Buq'ue line and not directly into it at right angles. Ch0n would be waiting outside the wall in a shallow depression with five soldiers carrying pulse guns cranked to full power. They would open fire on his command along the ranks of the Buq'ue as they passed. Ch0n would use his advantage as a mounted soldier to outflank the enemy where he was most needed. He planned to engage the Buq'ue from just outside spear throwing range, which was on the limit of the kinetic pistol but still within the capacity of the pulse gun. They rehearsed the manoeuvre several times during the day. The women who had made the arrows were part of the defensive line making sure their bowmen were well supplied. The aim was to defeat the attack on the wall with bows and spears unless the situation became dire, in which case the kinetic pistols would be used and as a final resort, the rail gun would sweep the wall clean from the corner tower. At the end of the day's rehearsals, Ch0n was satisfied. He knew the Buq'ue were bivouacked half a day's march away and as yet there was no evidence they had discovered the camp or even that they knew it was close. Ch0n decided late that afternoon after talking to OP1 that he would conduct a night raid on the outskirts of the Buq'ue camp to lower their morale. He told Jez of his plan and told him to man the defences as the military commander if he should not return. He mounted the tlaque and trotted off to where he knew OP1 was waiting and watching. In two hours he was lying on a small knoll observing the Buq'ue campfires. He calculated that they were perhaps a mile distant and that he could cover that ground in less than twenty minutes on foot or less than five on the stag. He opted for the latter option based on his need to ensure he could break contact easily when the initial contact had been made. He checked his equipment, told the commander of OP1 to change frequencies so only he and Ch0n were on the same net and mounted the steed, visor set to starlight. He could see clearly out to 300 feet in the darkness and he knew the tlaque could see just as well. He started the creature towards the nearest campfire at a trot and drew the pulser.

The beauty of the pulse was that it made no sound as it pushed a conical shockwave towards its target. Nobody would know from where the havoc was being wrought. From the glow of the firelight, ChOn could see in but they could not see out. ChOn's visor allowed automatically for the changing level of light as he charged into the camp. He fired at the sentry, who was too shocked at his appearance to even shout a warning. He fired at the bodies lying asleep around the fire and he finished the raid by lobbing one of his precious grenades into the fire. By the time the explosion rocked the area and flames were shooting skyward, he was fifty yards in the clear and heading for the OP. The tlaque bolted with fright at the explosion and it took ChOn a few nervous moments to settle it down before he guided it into the dead ground behind the knoll. He jumped to the ground and ran to the OP where the cabot was staring wide eyed at him. ChOn set his visor to telescope and watched the results of the ruckus he had caused. He could see men running backwards and forwards looking into the darkness but not daring to venture too far. Where there had been maybe ten fires burning, there was mostly blackness, although the IR function on his visor picked out the green glow of where the fires had been doused or buried. In the distance he could hear men screaming in agony and shouting to quell their fear. He told the commander of the OP to change back to the main frequency and ordered both the Ops to return to the castle at a run as soon as the Buq'ue started to advance. Their work had been done and done well, he told them and now they were needed at the castle to man the battlements and provide ChOn with communications for the fight. He then mounted the buck and trotted back to the camp, well satisfied with his work.

Pik was several fires away from the camp that ChOn had chosen to raid. He knew what was happening as the confusion grew but he was shocked and frightened by the massive noise and flames and sparks that rose in the air and set alight the grass and one of the tents of the company commander.

"What manner of man is this?" he asked himself before deciding it was time to leave the main camp in the early morning and try and follow the tracks of the tlaque to the main camp. He would continue his role as the shunned beggar to gain access to the village and then he would enter ChOn's dwelling during the battle and steal the magic box. He could barely keep himself from laughing as he thought of himself controlling the magic of the box and with it, the kingdom of Buki. He slept fitfully for the rest of the night, disturbed by the running of feet and the shouts of frightened men trying to guess what had caused the noise. At first light he cut through the camp to the spot where the fire had exploded and looked for the tell-tale hoofprints. He found them among the sandal marks of the soldiers and followed them at a walk towards a low knoll in the distance. He reached it to find it had been occupied for at least a day by more than one person. He looked from the knoll to where the Buq'ue army was stirring. He realized they had been watched for at least one day, perhaps more. This place was like the one he had first seen some days before when the third Cabot had discovered it. It was a watching position and he knew then that the entire Buq'ue force had been watched, followed, counted and perhaps even subtly herded towards or away from the Arw'an camp. He looked around and in the distance saw movement. The sun was low but by shielding his eyes he could make out the figures of two men running. They had run to warn ChOn yesterday and last night he had come to see for himself and to do some damage. Well he had succeeded in the latter at least. The morale of the soldiers was at rock bottom after weeks of hard patrolling on short rations and then their first contact with the ChOn had been one to strike fear into their hearts before they had even seen him. He strode confidently from the knoll to where he had seen the men running. Their tracks were easy to follow where they had kicked the dew from the grass. He knew he was close now. For them to be able to run messages back to the village they had to be within half a day's run. Even so, he was surprised when he topped a rise and looked for the first

time at the Arw'an defences. The village was nestled into a tear-drop shaped bend in the river so it could be approached from just one side. That side had been sealed off with a stone wall that stood higher than two men one upon the other. There was a wooden gate under a stone battlement and the wall had towers at each end. Pik was astounded at what he saw and wondered immediately if the village had been there for some time, years even, and was being defended by several men like Ch0n. He adopted the posture of an outcast and walked boldly to the main gate. He was challenged there by an armed guard. The walls were thick with other armed men and he knew the task of the Buq'ue would be a formidable one to overcome the defences. He wondered briefly if he should change sides but then realized he had tried to kill the Ch0n once and that he would have to forever hide from the public gaze lest he be recognized. After a short interrogation, he was told he could pass through but that he would be sent away again that night as was the custom with the crazy ones. He worked his way to the back of the village where a formidable woman shooed him from the kitchens to what looked like a central eating area. He suddenly felt hungry and when he was thrown some burnt cake, he ate it as though he really were an outcast. Nobody paid him any attention after he left the food area. He was as invisible as he could be, although he was in plain sight of half the village. In the centre of the village or was it a fort, Pik found what he was looking for; Ch0n's dwelling. It was bigger than any other dwelling and far grander, it being built of the same stones that had been used on the wall. Pik wondered from where they had gathered the stones because there was no evidence that there were loose stones in sufficient abundance as to build what he could see. He slunk into a dark shadow and watched Ch0n's dwelling. A man came out of a door wearing the same armour as the Ch0n down to the belt and carrying a sword like the one that sang as it slew. He was a full head shorter than the Ch0n but he was leading one of the beasts, the tlaque so surely he was a man like the Ch0n. A warrior with no mercy and fire at his disposal. Pik decided that the Buq'ue would not be able to take the village but he didn't really mind as long as the Ch0n was distracted long enough for Pik to find the box and take it to the Buq'ue fort. He would have to hide it under his robe and then melt into the crowd for some time because there was no escape from the walled village, only the gates he had entered by.

The Buq'ue advance party topped the rise and looked down on the same sight that had greeted Pik. The commanders were summoned to see what the position looked like and to formulate their plan of attack. The wall appeared to be too tall to go over without assistance so a human ladder would have to be made with men running up the backs of those braced against the wall. The gate was open and made of wood so it could be breached. The towers were too far from the main gate to do any real damage. They decided to just march up and storm the wall at one end while breaching the gate at the same time. They formed up their troops, gave their orders and when the green flag was dropped, they marched towards the gate, a formidable force by any reckoning, thought the commander. As if by an unseen order, a platoon, no a company of soldiers, appeared between them and the gate. They had obviously been lying in the grass or in a dip in the ground. The vanguard barely paused as the two forces drew closer. And then all as one, the Arw'an soldiers loosed their spears at the Buq'ue. It took the Buq'ue by surprise because the range was more than most of their spearmen could throw. They raised their shields as the spears landed amongst them. Some of their men went down with spears through their heads and faces or shoulders. The bulk of the spears fell harmlessly, however and the Buq'ue advanced to the traditional spear throwing range. As they approached, the Arw'an pulled back so the Buq'ue didn't throw their spears until finally the Arw'an melted back through the wall and the gate closed behind them. The Buq'ue line continued. Then it split as one half went to the wall and the other to the gate. Before they were even close, they were met with small volleys of arrows that continued unchecked as they marched. Their front rank was being cut to shreds four or five at a time and they were helpless. When they reached the wall they tried to form a human ladder but were pushed and prodded and killed and maimed by the defenders from above who were stabbing at them from between the castellations on the wall. From below, the defenders were unseen. The second rank and the third arrived on the scene and watched helplessly as those in front were cut down. The arrows were coming from the towers now and being fired along the wall. Confusion reigned and then the pulse guns opened up, unheard from the flank. Nobody was even aware of the pulses as they hit those on the extremities of the attack. Nobody knew why people were being thrown to the ground with bits missing from their persons. Then the pulses stopped and the arrows started afresh. At the main gate the carnage was even more intense because the attacking force had allowed itself to compress as it approached what was a narrow opening. Boiling water poured down on those below the first gate and then almost as if it had been ordered, the gate swung open and attackers poured through into the confined space under the guard tower. They were massacred from above by long spears and boiling water while raw sewage filled the wounds of the living. But there was no turning back. Within half an hour on Ch0n's watch, the Buq'ue had lost more than half their troops. He ordered another volley of fire by the flanking defenders and a further wave of the Buq'ue soldiers fell without ever hearing what had killed them. Then Ch0n rode from his position and cantered to the rear of the Buq'ue force to where the commanders were trying to direct the battle with flags. When they saw him they threw down their weapons and flags and prostrated themselves before him. He was still more than thirty feet from them when the noise of battle ceased. He had spoken into his helm and ordered a ceasefire. Those on the wall pointed in his direction and those below followed their stare. The Buq'ue realized their commanders had surrendered and they threw down their spears. The defenders gave an almighty cheer and spewed out of the gate to subdue their prisoners. Their commanders had been given strict instructions there was to be no killing of the surrendered or maiming the bodies of the dead. For the most part this was well policed until, late in the afternoon, ChOn entered the gate on the tlaque and went directly to the central meeting area. The prisoners, numbering eighty-two were knelt before him. Their commanders were with them, kneeling in a single line in front of their men. ChOn called for them to stand and be brought forward.

"You came here to kill us and subdue this village so the king of the Buq'ue could rule over all. He might have sent double the number and you still would have failed. Listen to me well, you who command the Buq'ue. I am ChOn and I have been chosen by these Arw'an to lead them and protect them from such as you. But I am not a cruel man and there are already enough Buq'ue widows for one day. I am in need of an army to defend my people. One day the Matáng will sweep from the setting sun and we Arw'an and Buq'ue will need to unite to defend ourselves. And one day men will come who would steal the very earth we walk on for their own use. Swear fealty to me and I will not only spare you, I will return your weapons and take you into the bosom of the Arw'an village and its army. What say you? You have the choice, such as it is. Life, loyalty and a soldiers' lot or death. Choose one or I will choose on your behalf."

ChOn drew Shiew from her scabbard. The blade sang as he freed it. There was a pause and ChOn moved swiftly. People later said that he had moved so fast that the eye could not see what happened next. He stood before the two commanders with the blade vertical. Somehow, the blade had become bloody. Then the body of one of the commanders toppled forward and the head rolled to ChOn's feet.

Gavan Connell

"Too slow. Choose or die."

The second commander shouted at once.

"Faith. I swear allegiance and I will command as many of my men as will follow me into your army, Lord. He rose to his feet and turned to face the Buq'ue soldiers. "We are cousins of the Arw'an. There is no shame here if we swear loyalty to their king instead of death."

The Buq'ue men shouted as one and Ch0n signalled for them to rise.

"Take your weapons and use them in the defence of the Arw'an, even though you may fight your brother. You have sworn before me and any treason will be rewarded with this."

He held up the lifeless head for all to see.

"Let there be no misunderstanding. What is your name, man?"

"I am called Izaki, My Lord."

"Then go with your men, Izaki of the Arw'an."

The crowd dispersed. Ch0n called Sonja.

"Those men will need shelters. Tonight they may sleep in the big meeting room but tomorrow they will need a space. They will need chattels. Some will need women if there are any without men to provide for them. Over there we will construct a building for soldiers who have no women. It needs to house two hundred at a time. Sleeping quarters only. The central eating area they will share and the other communal facilities. Do you understand me?"

"Yes My Lord but I do not pretend to understand why they are not being enslaved. It is our way."

"We need to unite the Arw'an and the Buq'ue. When it is done, these men can return to their village. I will try and achieve this very soon but until then, we need communal housing. There will be no more slaves while I rule."

ChOn turned to look for Jez. As if by telepathy the boy appeared.

"How do you do that, boy? You appear just as I am about to summon you. I swear it is a gift of magic. Take the tlaque and house him. I am tired after all that being king. Wake me in the morning when the sun is showing its whole orb."

"Yes My Lord," replied the squire. *"The battle went well I thought and we still haven't shown the rail gun to the Buq'ue."*

"I hope that day never comes. Tomorrow ready the tlaque. I am going to ride with all speed to the Buq'ue fort and kill their king. That should put an end to the fighting. If I can get in and out before I am seen, I should not have any difficulty. Then we will ride against the outposts and subdue them one by one until there is nothing but the central fort with no king for a while. Once we have their outposts sworn to us we will have the ability to bring the main fort under control and there will be no more wars between cousins."

ChOn whistled the wolf. He did not appear. ChOn was perplexed. The wolf never ignored him and he was surely still in the castle. Perhaps he had managed to lock himself up. Just so, ChOn went to his dwelling at a fast walk. He rounded a corner and saw the beast standing over the unmoving form of a beggar. As he approached, he thought the man looked familiar and then the truth dawned on him. It was the former Shaman of Boro's village. ChOn stood next to the wolf and told him to stand down. The Shaman was blubbering with fear.

"You came to steal that which you have coveted since you first saw it, Shaman. How are you called?"

163

Gavan Connell

"I am Pik, first among the Shaman of the Arw'an and the Buq'ue."

"So, Pik, would you like to see the box you came for? I will show it to you and I will reveal all to you in return for your silence. Do you agree to the terms?"

"I do agree."

"So come with me and be amazed. You will believe nothing you see because it is beyond your dreams. Watch your head, now. Be seated there. Don't be alarmed. The wolf will sit with you."

Ch0n took the minitron from its place and booted it. He sat next to the Shaman and started to speak quietly.

"I come from another world where there are people in great numbers like there are stars in the sky. I flew here in a ship of shiny metal but became stranded here many moons ago. The weapons I carry are from that other world and they are powered by a force that is so strong it can never be exhausted. If I had the means I could throw light over the entire village. Every dwelling could have its own light. I could destroy every living creature on this world and still have power to spare. I see you don't believe me. Well that's to be expected. Look at these images and you will know it to be true. Here is a city of ten million people. Look how they travel in wheeled vehicles. Look at this. It is called a helicopter and it can be used for transport or cargo and here are horses being raced for fun and financial gain. Soldiers. Black warriors from a distant past who taught me how to fight this battle. And here is an ocean with waves that people can ride for enjoyment and gain. Here is a ship that sails those seas with cargo and passengers. Look at the images of the creatures that walk and fly on my world. This one with the long nose is as big as a dwelling. And this one with the long neck is as tall as a tree. This is a colourful bird that talks like a human. Listen to it. Here is a bomb that could kill every soul on this world in one loud explosion, like the small one I made last night. And here is a castle in a small country. I am going to build one just like it. And look at this. Thousands of men opposing each other in a war that engulfed almost a whole world and was ended with the bomb I mentioned, that did this to a whole city. And here is a rocket that took my species off their world and led to the soldier that I am and why I am here and what I am made to do. Are you not amazed and shocked at these images?"

The shaman nodded his head. He was indeed awestruck and his head was spinning with the magic of the box. More than ever he coveted it, not knowing that its secrets were locked securely away with Ch0n holding the only means of accessing them.

"I would see more of this world if I may for it is truly a wondrous place from whence you come."

"No you may not for it is late and I need to sleep. I swore you to silence and you agreed to the terms did you not?"

The shaman nodded and stood to leave. He bowed to Ch0n and walked to the door. He was smiling to himself. He wanted to ask Ch0n if he might return in the morning and turned to face him just as Shiew separated his head from his body, guaranteeing the silence he had promised.

"Jez! I have some mess for you to clean up for me. This is the former shaman of Boro's village. He would have stolen the minitron had it not been for the beast, Friday. Now I will sleep. I have a long few days ahead. Put the head on a stick with that of the other I slew. Display them by the main gate for seven suns for all those who would oppose us to see. Then put them on an ants nest for I would have them cleaned and set to one side for those who may follow me."

Chapter Fifteen: A Family Reunion

Ch0n woke with a start when the wolf stirred beside him. The beast raised his head and looked at the entrance to the dwelling. A low rumbling sounded somewhere in his chest. It was a sound reserved for Jez. He knew Jez was allowed into the dwelling but still demanded he seek permission when Ch0n was within. It also allowed Ch0n to relax in the knowledge it was only Jez approaching.

"My Lord, I have your breakfast. Today is your bathing day. The woman Sonja is waiting at the baths to shave you. When you return the tlaque will be ready for you. Will you be requiring the female tlaque to bear your shelter?"

"No. I will be travelling swiftly and will camp where I find shelter. Make sure my battle order is complete. I would travel fully armed. I will need porridge for two days. By then I will have reached the Buq'ue fort and will either prevail or perish. If I do not return within five days, assume I am dead. Summon the four. I would speak with you and them before I leave. Allow me time to bathe before they come."

Ch0n wolfed down his breakfast of porridge and milk. It was a staple breakfast of the plains folk, made from seeds roughly ground and goats milk. He found it very satisfying. A bag of the dry seeds could be mixed with water and would stick to his ribs all day on the trail. He strode through the village clad only in his tunic to the public baths. It was men's day. Sonja was waiting for him at the entrance. She was not permitted to enter so she shaved Ch0n's beard and head as she did every two days. It was a task she would allow no other to perform because it involved passing a razor sharp blade over her lord's throat and head. He had elevated her to royalty and protected her from harm and she was his devoted servant to the death.

She was a little older than ChOn and had borne two children to her husband. The children had not survived childhood and her husband had drowned trying to rescue a goat from the river some time before. Unlike most women, she had managed to survive spinsterhood for she was a strong person and needed no man to provide her daily sustenance. When she needed sexual pleasure, she either pleasured herself or offered herself to one of the young men of the village. They were only too pleased to learn from her in turn. She harboured carnal desires for ChOn but had never offered herself to him. She had no idea if he needed sexual relief. Jez had never mentioned it to her following their discussion of some time before so she just let it be. Every second day she shaved ChOn and felt his smooth skin against her as she fussed about him and every second day she wondered what it would be like pleasuring him. He dominated her in height and bulk. She barely reached his chest in height and would have been a doll in his embrace. But every second day when she left him, she called on Jez and used him to calm her desires as he used her to relieve his own. Today ChOn wanted to talk to the four so when he went to bathe, Sonja had to hurry to Jez's dwelling above the stables. He was busy readying ChOn's battle order and the tlaque when she entered. She went straight to him, leaned against a rail and raised her skirt. Jez needed no further prompting and lifted his own tunic. They mated like animals while the tlaque chewed cud by their side. When it was over, they both simply straightened their garments and separated with not a word having been spoken. But a smirk passed between them as she left the stable. *"Two days and I'll be back for more,"* said Sonja's. *"I'll be ready,"* said Jez's.

ChOn left the camp some time later having given instructions to the four and Jez. They were all present so there could be no doubt. Boro was in command but could make no policy decisions nor task Jez in any way. He was to continue building the perimeter wall. Doni was to build a large corral outside the main wall but immediately adjacent to it. It was to have three bamboo rails, the highest as high as the top of ChOn's head. The gate would be against the wall so that they could herd the wild tlaque into it and seal it off. Sonja was to maintain her duties as town mayor and Kelda would provide her usual administrative services to the village and tend to the wounded from the battle. She already knew of the need to stop infection and to boil any cutting instruments and wash hands before treating any wounds. Jez was to command the army and oversee their continued training. The OPs were to be re-deployed and would report to Jez. All the weapons were to be cleaned and stored in skins against the air. The fletchers were to continue with the production of arrows, both for training and for battle.

It took ChOn two days to reach the Buq'ue fort. He paused on a small rise to survey it. There was no security outside the perimeter. The main gate was guarded by a small detachment of soldiers. Smoke from cooking fires filled the air above it. The king's dwelling dominated the skyline. It was located deep inside the perimeter but there was a straight track leading from the gate to the entrance. He decided to do his work on foot in the early morning. That way he could subdue the guard without alerting them by galloping across the plain. Then he would steal to the king's dwelling and have done with him and anybody else who opposed him. He knew there was some risk involved in fighting on the ground against multiple opponents but he was well trained and well skilled and had weapons that would give him a distinct advantage. When night fell he was asleep in his hide with the tlaque hobbled in dead ground and the wolf at his side, asleep but with all his senses at work.

ChOn stirred and roused himself in the early, still-darkish part of the morning. He set a water skin into a hole in the ground and the two beasts drank from it. He tethered the wolf and checked the hobbles on the tlaque. The moon was low in the sky and clouds drifted across the sky, driven by a light wind. The grass waved and danced in the wan light as did the myriad of small bushes and trees between ChOn and the fort. It couldn't have been better conditions if ChOn had ordered them personally. He had the added advantage of the night vision enhanced with thermal imaging or passive infra-red, which was ancient technology but still handy in the open. He had decided not to use Shiew to gain access because of her habit of 'singing' when she was drawn. He kept the katana sheathed over his right shoulder and readied his short sword in its sheath over his left shoulder. It was in fact equally named a long knife. It had a blade 20 inches long and three sixteenths of an inch thick. The handle was similar in size and design to the katana, being of bound synthetic, non-slip fibre with a square hilt. It could be used two handed or one. The blade was almost straight, matte black, razor sharp on the cutting side and finished with the lethal tanto point. It had been designed for one purpose only. He also had with him his sais, one in each boot and his pulse gun and kinetic pistol. He felt less confident without his bow but he knew if he had to stand and fight once the alarm were raised, he would have to fight with cold steel and a bow or crossbow would be left behind and that was not something he was prepared to suffer. He set off at a slow but steady pace, using the scrubby bushes as screens as much as possible. He cut to the right side of the main gate because the wind was blowing from the left side and he could use it to mask any sound he may make. The two guards were standing, talking on the left side using the wall to stay out of the wind. They were awake but not alert and by the time they reacted to the black-clad figure running across the gap in the wall, they were already dead. They had not made a sound apart from that which they made as they dropped to the ground. ChOn pulled them hurriedly into the shadows and ran towards the king's dwelling through the shadows cast by the dwellings on the side of the track. He might as well have strolled down the middle of the track because not a soul was stirring.

"Poor discipline. Especially in time of war, such as it is," thought Ch0n.

He reached the king's dwelling and entered via the main flap. He had expected there to be resistance and he wasn't disappointed. There were five guards in the ante-chamber, playing some sort of table game and they sprang to their feet as he bolted towards them, drawing Shiew. There was no point in trying to stop her from singing now and he needed the long blade to beat five soldiers. He slew two before they had even risen and the third followed his colleagues a second later. One of them shouted out for assistance before a backhand cut silenced his shouts as well as those of his remaining colleague. By now the king himself was awake. Ch0n swung the curtain aside and found him trying to hide but he was no coward. Rather he was naked. When Ch0n spotted him, he drew a sword and stood to defend himself.

"You are the one they call the Ch0n. Would you fight a man before giving him the time to dress for battle?"

"From what I see, you need not fear tripping over that thing," replied Ch0n. "It will not swing you off balance either."

"So be it. But first, what became of the army I sent to the Arw'an village? Are they all dead?"

Ch0n walked calmly into range and the fight was engaged. The king, for all his apparent lack of courage when it came to sending his armies to fight, was just as keen as any of his subjects when it came to self-defence. He was agile for his size despite years of easy living but able with the sword and obviously well practised with it. Hand to hand they went, katana against broadsword. Before long the king, lacking Ch0n's fitness level, tired and finally dropped his guard. Shiew sang her death song. Ch0n found himself on one knee in front of the king, Shiew in a backhanded grip, the blade horizontal. The headless body of the king slumped forward to the ground in front of him. The sound of people running and shouting came to his ears and he quickly surveyed his surroundings. There was no exit so he would have to cut one. He sliced the hide and stepped through the opening to find himself surrounded by soldiers and shouting villagers. He re-entered the dwelling to find the entrance filled with soldiers. He drew the kinetic pistol and sprayed the forward rank, which dissolved in a mass of blood and spray. The others managed to withdraw against the pressure of those behind. He turned to face the opening he had just made and fired through it. Screams from outside told him he had hit plenty of targets. But at the same time he knew that fighting his way out on foot would be hard. He would have to kill dozens, if not scores of people. He took the pulse gun from its holster and reloaded the kinetic pistol. He was about to charge through the door with both weapons blazing when a voice from outside stopped him.

"I would speak with the Ch0n."

It was the voice of a boy. Ch0n hesitated before answering.

"Enter! But you alone and know your life is mine if you are playing false."

The entrance flap swung back and a tall soldier entered the room. He was at least a head taller than any of the humanoids Ch0n had seen. He was easily more than six feet tall and only a few inches shorter than Ch0n himself. Ch0n was immediately on the defensive. The soldier wore a leather breastplate over a wool tunic, and around his head was wrapped a turban of black wool. Only his eyes were visible. He carried a long-handled ax with a hide loop around his right wrist and a short sword was tucked into his kamarband. A sling with a hide pouch hung from his neck and Ch0n looked for and found the pouch that would hold the stones. It was under the soldier's tunic on the left side where a pocket would be found.

"Right handed," thought Ch0n automatically.

"Speak now or die Buq'ue," growled Ch0n. He had holstered the kinetic pistol and was standing easily with the katana in his right hand, point resting on the ground slightly behind him and a foot from his side. He could cut upwards with a flick of his wrist whilst adopting an attacking stance in less than a second, much less than the two and a half seconds it would take his 'guest' to get within ax range. He couldn't throw the ax any faster and he would give himself away in any event by slipping the wrist thong first.

The soldier looked at the dead king at Ch0n's feet. The head was some feet further away. He looked at the katana and nodded.

"In our culture, he who slays the king in fair combat has the right to declare himself king." The voice was measured and soft. Certainly not that of a wizened old soldier of the king's bodyguard but more like that of a boy who might be his teenaged son. *"I know you not, but I know you possess the means to leave this place and kill every man and woman who opposes you. I would save my people by declaring you king by right of combat. It is obvious from what I see that you entered with intent to kill him and that you slew five men before you slew him. Had you killed him with one of your devil weapons, it would not have been deemed a suitable combat to claim the crown but as I see, you slew him with the sword even as you are poised to slay me with a single upward stroke from the wrist. What say you? Would you be king of the Buq'ue and prevent the slaughter of my people?"*

"What claim do you have to call them 'your' people? Are you the king's son? Would you slay me and claim the throne you thought would be yours by birthright?"

The boy laughed.

"Nay. I am not the king's son. I was part of his bodyguard but I was off duty when you called or perhaps we would have known each other better. Not for long, of course for that is the way of a soldier. But perhaps better. Answer me now for the people outside are impatient for my return. They fancy you will go down by sheer weight of numbers. Only you and I know better. It has long been my plan to unite the Arw'an and the Buq'ue. We will need to unite if we are to survive the attack of the Matáng, which comes from time to time. It has been many winters since they last came and almost were repelled. They took half of us as slaves and stole all the livestock they could find. This time they will come in larger numbers and we will be slaughtered or enslaved. In you I see a way to unite us. I will be the first to swear fealty if you wish it so."

"I too wish to unite the tribes. That is why I came to kill the king. I thought to kill him and then the Buq'ue would not send more armies against us for some time. By then they would discover we are unable to be beaten. At that point I thought to have bargaining power. If my plan can be accomplished without bloodshed, I will do whatever it takes but I warn you, boy, yours will be the first head I will take if treachery is afoot. Swear your fealty but do not swear with your fingers crossed because I will show you no more mercy than I did to your king."

The boy nodded and turned to leave.

"So be it, My Lord. I will go and appease the people before returning with the village elders. Then I will swear before you and them. With or without them I will swear for we have the same plan and I will help you as you will help me."

He turned on his heel and brushed under the flap of the dwelling. Ch0n looked at the carnage around him. The front wall of the dwelling was splashed with the gore from the kinetic pistol and he conceded he may have held the firing button a little longer than was necessary. The six headless corpses adorned the floor and the hides were soaked with blood. At one end of the large chamber was a seat. It looked throne-like to ChOn so he went and sat in it. He removed his helm but kept it in reach. He put the kinetic pistol on his lap and the katana, Shiew nestled against his back with the handle over his right shoulder. The pulser was humming at his left side, armed and ready. ChOn tried to look kingly but in the end just sat and waited. Some time passed before he heard the boy at the flap.

"I have returned with the elders, My Lord. We are six. We would enter."

"You first, boy and then the others one by one when I give the word. Remember my words. If you are playing false you will not leave this place alive."

The soldier entered and ChOn pointed to a place off to one side.

"Stand there," he ordered. "Enter the next of you!"

In turn he directed them where to stand. He determined this by their size and apparent ability to move easily. Those who looked like they might be able to fight, including the boy, he put on the left of him. The kinetic pistol was in his hand in his lap facing that side. He only had to raise it slightly and he could send all those on that side to their God in less than one second.

"Say what you have come to say, boy," he ordered. "Choose carefully your words because they may be the last you utter."

"Might I approach thee, My Lord?"

"You may do so but only you and only to where the king's head lies."

The soldier moved to a position in front of ChOn and some ten feet distant.

Gavan Connell

"My Lord, I have spoken to these elders of the village. I have told them you entered the king's chambers and slew him and his bodyguard and that you claim the crown by right of combat. They can see with their own eyes that the king was slain with a sword and not a devil weapon. They are content that you slew him in fair combat as is our custom. Those present are five of the six elders. The other does not accept that you have a right to the crown as you are not of us. He has a son who would be king. Even as we speak he is waiting outside to challenge your right by combat. If you are to be king, you must slay him or he you. If you choose not to do so, there can be no peace in the village for there are those who lost their men tonight in this skirmish. Would you accept the challenge?"

"With what weapons will this challenge be fought?"

"With swords or daggers. As you are the one being challenged, you have the right to choose."

"Then I choose swords."

"So be it."

The six left the chamber and Ch0n followed. He had donned his helm, more in case he was attacked at the entrance to the dwelling as he left. The kinetic pistol was in one hand and the pulser in the other as he stooped, looked around and then exited. The entire village, it seemed was in attendance and when he stood to his full height, a murmur passed through the crowd. They fell back a few steps in awe. They saw before them a giant with a gold face. His gloved hands held the devil weapons. He strode to the centre of the circle of people.

"Who would challenge my right to the throne of the Buq'ue?" he roared. "Have I not slain the king in single combat? Has not a member of his bodyguard sworn that I slew him fairly? I claim the crown. Let any and all challengers come forward. Let this be settled. But know this. If I win this fight, any man or woman who opposes me thereafter will be sold into slavery to the Matáng. I will drive them to the border of the Matáng country like goats and leave them there. So let all who are against me declare themselves now or forever be silent."

A man stepped forward. He was obviously a soldier. He wore his breastplate and tunic like a soldier. He carried a broadsword and a shield of cured hide. He wore a leather helmet over a shaved head.

"I am Pek, son of the elder, Arok. You are not Buq'ue. As such you have no right to the throne in my eyes and I intend to claim it for myself and for the honour of my family and of all the families whose men you slew tonight. You have chosen swords in preference to daggers. Here is mine in plain view. You bear the devil weapons still. If you slay me with those you forego your claim. You will never leave this circle alive for you will be borne down under the weight of all the villagers present and your head will adorn the entrance of the king's dwelling. Know you that I have fought many times in battles against the Arw'an herders and my sword has sent many of them to their Gods. It is blooded and ready. As am I."

ChOn holstered the two guns and walked towards Pek.

"I accept your challenge, Pek. I am ChOn of the Arw'an. We are cousins of the Buq'ue and so it is by that right that I claim the throne. You may lay down your sword and swear fealty to me and your life will be spared. You do not have to die for foolish pride. For foolish it is. Your sword has been blooded I am certain but this very night I slew five of the king's bodyguard in one single skirmish and then slew the king afterwards. I doubt not your courage but you still have the chance to live a long life if you so choose."

In reply, Pek spat on the ground. It was not something ChOn had ever seen but there was no doubting its meaning. He took a step back and unsheathed Shiew. As she cleared the edge of the scabbard, the vibration of the unsheathing made her hummm. Pek saw it and heard it. ChOn watched his eyes for a reaction and saw naked fear but it was too late for surrender now. ChOn took up the classic side on horse stance with the katana held one handed over his head, the other hand holding the blade between finger and thumb, the other fingers spread, the point facing Pek. He stood absolutely still and waited for the charge. When it came he moved the katana just once in a long, two handed circle and stood up. Pek lay twitching at his feet in two pieces, having been cut from the left shoulder through to his right hip. The crowd was as silent as though they were still waiting for the fight to begin. Then the noise level increased to a hum and then a roar. ChOn sheathed Shiew and drew both pistols.

"It is done. If there remains any among you who would challenge, step forward now. And I mean right now." He looked around the circle. Most people were looking at the body of Pek, which was still moving.

"So be it. I claim the crown. Now swear your fealty as is my right by combat."

The boy-soldier was the first to step forward. He went to ChOn and knelt on both knees and put his forehead on the ground.

"I, Karín, member of the king's bodyguard swear fealty to thee, ChOn, My Lord, King."

He stood up and turned to go.

"Karín. You have sworn fealty to me but you hide your face from me. I would see your face."

The boy unwound the turban from around his face and head. He shook his head and revealed long, red hair that hung to the middle of his back. ChOn looked at him and his heart missed a beat. It was a woman. A tall, red-headed woman. He had seen her face before in a dream, standing beside him in the battlements dressed in armour while the hordes fought below.

"Are you shocked, my King? You look as though you have seen a ghost."

"I know you, woman. I have seen you in a dream. We fought together against the Matáng. I swear it."

"Then it seems our dream to unite the tribes will be fulfilled, my King."

The village elders followed in turn, led by Pek's father. It was a show of acceptance by him and one that ChOn knew was purely to display to the villagers that he had changed sides. When the six of them had sworn, one of them called on the entire village to show their acceptance and a roar ensued that left ChOn in no doubt. He was King and the Buq'ue and the Arw'an would be united peacefully.

ChOn passed the next day with the elders. Karín, it seemed was deemed to be a freak of nature and bewitched. The previous king had had her on his bodyguard because nobody else would have her. She had no man to look after her because she could defeat any of them in single combat and had done so many times since her youth. People were frightened of her so she lived at the king's side except when she was bleeding. It was rumoured that she was the king's lover as well as his bodyguard but nobody had ever tried to prove or disprove the theory. She was accepted by the elders because of her position in the king's hierarchy but now with a new king, she was on the outside immediately. ChOn saw this and moved to reinstate her.

"As she was the previous king's personal bodyguard, so shall she be mine," he told them after listening mostly patiently to their complaints about women holding positions of power.

"Furthermore, she will be my squire. A squire is a soldier under the personal care and tuition of a Knight, who is a soldier of the king's court. I have no Knights among the Buq'ue. One day I shall. Now I need to know who among you will run the village in my absence. I need to return to the Arw'an but I will be back soon to arrange the new order of things. I will need someone to take charge of day to day matters and someone to command the garrison troops. Find me that person first because I would have him know my plans for training."

The elder called Ikan was deemed to be the person best suited to be the town mayor in Ch0n's absence. He in turn suggested a middle aged officer of the guard to be the garrison commander. Ch0n spent a long time explaining the concept of Infantry and bowmen. He told the commander, Ronik to select soldiers who were the fastest, the strongest, the most agile and the most intelligent and to divide them into groups according to their skills. They would be trained to enhance those skills so that the fastest would be trained to run, the strongest to bear loads and the most agile to counter obstacles and spear thrusts. The most intelligent were to be placed in each group and trained to make plans and to obey them.

"Do you understand my orders, Ronik?"

"I do My Lord."

"Then do not fail me. I will return within two full moons to check your progress."

He set the elders to organize rubbish disposal, to dig latrines and to organize bath days. He instructed them to shave their heads and wash their clothes and their bedding. Then he announced he would be leaving that night. He had been one night and one whole day in the village and had slept no more than a few hours by his clock. He began to plan his return. The tlaque was still hobbled in the distance and would be looking for water. Ch0n felt a moment of anxiety for it and the wolf. At least they had shade. He asked for two days' worth of porridge and a canteen of water and at last light he left the king's dwelling, passed through the gates with their new guards and new routine and set off for the mound where his creatures would be waiting. Before long he became aware that he was being followed so he dropped to the ground and waited. Through the visor he picked up the woman, Karín following his tracks in the pale green light. Ch0n was impressed. He watched her pause and listen. He knew she was waiting for a sound to tell her which direction he was taking. He remained still, watching her greenish form searching for him. She cocked her head, she sniffed the air. At last she moved towards where he was lying. When she was twenty feet from him, she stopped.

"My King, I know you are here lying in wait for me. I see you not. I hear you not but I know you can't be more than ten men's height from where I am because you have been stopped for only enough time for that to be the case. Declare yourself. I am not here to try and harm you. I am your bodyguard. Where you go, I go."

Ch0n stood up and at the first movement, her head turned to face the almost imperceptible sound.

"Aaah. You were a little closer than I thought." She moved quickly to his side.

He led her to the knoll and heard the wolf calling him softly. He answered in a tongue the woman did not recognize but she did recognize the scent of the wolf and had her sword out in an instant. Ch0n steadied her hand.

"He is my other bodyguard. One you will come to know well. And I have another beast nearby waiting for me. Can you hear him moving over there?" He pointed.

181

"Yes, I can hear something big moving as though it is hurt. Its gait is uneven."

"It is tied so it can't wander too far. It stays with the wolf when it is frightened or by itself because it cannot run." He whistled softly and the tlaque came to meet them. The woman was terrified of it.

"Now I will remove these hobbles and we will mount it and ride back to the Arw'an village."

"Mount it? You mean climb on it? Ride it? My King! Is it safe for you to do this?"

Ch0n took the canteen of water and emptied it into the skin. The wolf drank a little and the tlaque sucked at it quickly.

"We will need to get the beast a decent drink soon. There is a small creek not far from here." He took the tablet from its pouch and set it to 'home'. An arrow appeared on the screen. The woman was fascinated.

"What is this magic? It has a light that lacks heat and it feels like nothing I have ever touched. What is the meaning of this little spear?"

"It tells me the direction to the Arw'an village. During the day I have no need of it but at night I need it to take me to the water which is on the way. I do not know the land well enough yet but one day I will not need this thing at all."

"Is this the magic box the Shaman, Pik, spoke of to the king? The one that is so powerful it can bestow wealth and power unlimited on he who owns it?"

"No. That is safe in my dwelling. When we get there I will show it to you. Only I may use it. It is programmed to know me and to obey only my commands."

"Programmed? What is this word and what does it mean?"

"It means like the wolf. He knows me and my scent. He obeys no other but me. He may be fed and sheltered by another but he will obey only me. He is programmed by me to obey."

"Oh..."

ChOn heaved himself onto the beast and put a hand down for the woman. She took it and he heaved her upwards until she sat astride it.

"Hold me by the waist or you will fall off," he told her. She did so and ChOn urged the buck into a trot. It was glad to be unfettered by the hobbles and set off at a good pace. ChOn guided it towards the water he knew was some distance ahead. The wolf loped along beside them and in front of them but always close. The woman clung to ChOn at first and then as the yards unfolded she relaxed. She took her arms from ChOn's waist and held them out at her sides like the wings of a plane. She flapped them like a bird. Even when the tlaque stumbled once, she didn't shift her seat.

"I feel like I am flying," she shouted in ChOn's ear. *"I will have one of these for my own use when we get to the village. It is fitting that the king's bodyguard ride one of these beasts at his side. Is that not so, my King?"*

ChOn was one step ahead of her. He had wanted a troop of cavalry and the woman rode like she was part of the creature.

"You will have sixty of these beasts, woman. You will be commander of the household cavalry. You will select the soldiers personally."

"Cavalry, my King? What is that? And what is a household?"

ChOn sighed.

Gavan Connell

"A household is a group of people connected to a dwelling. In this case, my dwelling. It is called a house in my tongue. My house. Cavalry is made up of mounted soldiers. Their task is to surround the enemy and strike at him from behind or the flanks. This is easy for mounted soldiers because their tlaque can move to position faster than foot soldiers can adjust their positions to defend their rear."

"I like the sound of cavalry. I shall command it well, my King because I can see its worth even in the darkness. I have much to learn of the Arw'an ways."

"Be quiet, woman. We are almost at the water. I have to make sure it is safe from wild beasts."

"And how can you do that in the darkness, my King?"

"Be quiet, I said. You have more questions than I have answers."

ChOn surveyed the stream with the thermal imager and the starlight scope combined. There were a few small creatures at the water's edge but no green images lurking in the shadows of the scrubby bushes.

"It is clear to approach the water. We will allow the tlaque to drink his fill, we will rest while it quenches him and then we will ride until morning."

"What magic do you use to see in the darkness, my King? I knew back there while I was seeking you that you were watching me from afar. If not, you would never have stopped because I was making no sound that would carry against the breeze."

ChOn removed the helm and placed it on her head. He changed the mode from starlight scope to passive infra-red and back again. He zoomed in and out and switched the thermal imaging off and on again.

"It is called an integrated night vision array. We call it an INVA. It enables one to see in partial light to total darkness depending on which mode you are using. The red is from body heat. The pale green is amplified light and the green blobs are heat signals. There is a digital telescope built in to the visor to see things closer than they are."

"Oh... I have much to learn about the Arw'an ways. Much more than I thought."

"These are not the ways of the Arw'an. They are the ways of my people. When we arrive I will show you from whence I come and although you will not understand, you will see why these things are possible. Meanwhile you will learn to use them even if you do not understand why they are possible. It matters not."

He eased the tlaque towards the stream. They dismounted and let it drink deeply. The wolf jumped in the water and shook itself violently.

"I would know more of your weapons. The sword I have seen doing its work but I do not understand why it sings meanwhile. Does it enjoy the taking of life? It seems to me to be a living weapon. It is a thing of beauty in its appearance and in its work. Are there more of them where we are going?"

"It is the only one of its kind. It sings because the movement of the blade against the scabbard sets it to vibrate like the skin of a drum. Then the passage of air across its edge makes it sing. It is made of a metal so hard that it can not be broken. It may only be sharpened by producing a specific sound so the edge is not so hard. There are others of the same form but made of a different metal. I will give you one as a gift when we arrive and

I will teach you how to use it for it is a skill that needs to be learned."

"Then I will learn it well, my King and you will personally see to my training for I will have no other but you. And what of the devil weapons?"

They are called pistols or guns and none can use them but me unless they are programmed for they are linked to one person. It is a secret known to only three persons. They are you, my squire, Jez and myself. No other may know because I may need to use them as a bargaining tool at some point and I do not want it known that they are impotent in the hands of another."

"Oh... I had hoped to use them or at least try them. Can you show me how they work? I have heard of them and seen what they can do but I have never seen them at their work."

"Tomorrow I will show you. You will have one. Now it is time to mount the beast and move. I do not like to be still at night without a cave for shelter or at least a stone at my back."

"My King. You have me at your back and I am more reliable than any stone. That you must believe. None will approach you uninvited while I live. My oath of fealty was a jumble of words for the village. My loyalty goes further than any words can speak. You are my King. My Lord. I would have none but you."

They mounted the tlaque and trotted towards the Arw'an castle. The woman wanted to wear the helm so ChOn put her at the front and he rode behind her. She took the reins of the tlaque and by morning she had it completely under control. ChOn knew he had made the right decision to appoint her as commander of what would be his cavalry and decided to increase the size of the force to one hundred riders when he could, divided into two troops. He knew already she would be an excellent leader of men and that she would select two able troop commanders.

They rested in a copse of fruit trees until mid-morning and then started again. Karín mounted the tlaque by leaping nimbly on to its back and taking the front position. She was obviously very supple because she did not suffer at all from stiffness in the thighs. Ch0n was both pleased and peeved at her impudence but said nothing.

"Show me the magic spear so I may guide the beast to the Arw'an village, my King."

"During the day we have no need of it. The way lies yonder by that rocky outcrop. We will pass to the right side of it where there is a cave. We will rest there tonight and tomorrow we will arrive at the castle."

"So be it, my King. We will make good time today for I have learned the strength of the beast. It can move faster than we have been travelling without tiring for it is lazy. You have been soft with it I fear. It is your master on the trail and not you the master of it. You allow it to make its own pace. I will push it harder and you will see."

She touched the creature on the shoulder with the flat of her sword and dug her heels into its sides. The buck gave a snort of disgust at being treated like a beast of burden and trotted towards the rocks in the distance. Ch0n noted the woman was urging the creature with her heels and that the beast had lengthened its stride by no more than a foot but they were travelling noticeably faster than before.

"Tell me of yourself," ordered Ch0n.

"There is not much to tell, my King. I was born in the Buq'ue village to a servant of the previous king. Nobody knows why I am so tall or why my hair is a different colour to the rest of the

villagers. My mother was taken from the Matáng camp followers during a battle and so I suppose I am Matáng. They are a taller people. Taller than all of us but I am different even from them. Just so, I suspect I am of their blood but my mother never told me if she had been with one of them. From early childhood I was different and was shunned by the children of the village. I took up a wooden sword and the sling at an early age to fight my way out of my situation. By the time I first bled I was already able to best every man in the village in hand to hand combat and other games of strength and ability. Because of that, I was never taken as a wife. The family of the previous king was the only caring I ever had. When he won the crown by right of combat, he took me as his first bodyguard. I have been with him every day and every night since apart from three days every moon when I bleed. For it is unclean for a woman to be in the same dwelling as a man at that time."

Ch0n stopped her.

"What is this bleeding you speak of? I know nothing of it."

"My King! Do not the women of your village bleed? It is part of being a woman. Every moon we bleed. Some say it is so we can bear children because those not yet bleeding have never borne a child and those old women who no longer bleed don't have children either."

"I know nothing of this but I will seek information from Sonja and the minitron, the magic box that teaches me. It is a strange thing, this bleeding. Continue."

"I have been in the king's 'household', did I use the word correctly? for all my life, really."

"Yes, you did."

"I had a dream to unite the tribes as I told you. You have given me the means to do it. I wanted to be queen of the two tribes

and would have sought the crown by right of combat when the old king was deposed. But he was deposed by you and I knew I could probably not defeat you so I am your squire instead and your bodyguard and perchance your woman. For I would have no other but you."

They rode in silence and then ChOn told her the improbable story of his coming to the planet and the events leading to the present time. Karín was both thrilled and dubious. She did not say as much but in her imagination she had ChOn arriving in some sort of rainbow from the clouds. From the stars? Not likely? She thought of ChOn'i.

They arrived at the cave much earlier than ChOn had calculated. The tlaque was blowing more than usual but after a drink and a feed of brush, he recovered quickly.

"He is unfit" declared Karín. *"He will get fitter with proper work."*

The wolf was hesitant to approach the woman but when he lay next to ChOn, the woman placed herself next to him and he would not move from ChOn's side. A low growl started in his chest but ChOn calmed him with a word and he went immediately to sleep but his ears kept rotating and his nose never stopped twitching. ChOn slept next to him and the woman took up a position at the entrance to the cave and slept sitting up. When the first rays of the sun appeared on the horizon, she woke. The wolf was sitting close by her watching the plains in front of the cave. The woman patted the ground next to her.

"Come here wolf. We are two, you and I, living a life apart from others and both guarding the back of our master. We have to learn to work together or we will get in each other's way. You will have to learn to let me close to him for I mean to stay as close as possible until our dream is fulfilled and our destiny, whatever that may bring. And I will tell you a secret. I will have

him as my man. I would have no other but he and you will have to get used to that as well. Come. Come my pretty."

The wolf looked at her and then looked away and trotted out the door.

"As you wish, wolf but we will be friends in your good time."

Ch0n woke some time afterwards. The woman was moving about the entrance to the cave and the wolf was gnawing on the remains of something furry.

"You left in a hurry and we have no more porridge, my King. The wolf has hunted for himself but we have nothing to eat. It is usually a man's task to provide food for his household but as you are a king and a foreigner, I will provide for us."

"Is that so? You presume much, woman. Come with me and we will hunt together. I will show you how the pistols work."

They tethered the wolf and set off down the slope towards a small pond in a copse of trees. Ch0n was as usual dressed in his full battle order. He was always prepared for the unexpected in that regard. The woman wore her woollen tunic and carried the sling and her pouch of round river stones. She moved easily over the ground. She was the first to spot the rabbit munching sweet grass by the edge of the pond and she signalled for Ch0n to wait. She took a stone and fitted it to the sling, twirled it about her head a few times and let the stone fly. It hit the rabbit behind the ear and it dropped immediately. The woman grinned at Ch0n.

"That is how you hunt rabbit, my King."

Ch0n was impressed again. He moved towards the pond to look for more game when he saw a heat signal in the periphery of his visor. Standing near a tree watching them, not moving or even twitching, was a chameleon dragon. The woman saw him pause and looked where he was looking. She could see nothing in the mottled sunlight. Ch0n took the pulse from his holster and set the pulse to 70%. He did not want to kill the creature. Nor did he want to be breakfast for it. He aimed for the centre of the body and pressed the button.

The false-fusion battery sent the conical pulse towards the chameleon at just under the speed of sound. The pistol itself made no noise when it pulsed but a green light flashed in the screen followed briefly by a red one telling Ch0n it was charged and ready to fire again. Sixty feet away, the dragon just collapsed where it stood. Karín saw the movement of the bush and the flattening of the grass and knew what she was seeing. Few of the Buq'ue had seen a dragon and lived to tell the tale but there were legends aplenty and some survivors to tell their accounts. She rushed over to it and waited for the colour to fade. When it did, she surveyed the pale orange reptile at close range.

"Can we skin it? They say that if you can skin a dragon before it dies, you will have a suit of armour that renders you invisible."

"We have no knives and I have no desire to kill this animal to test a theory. You will have your armour. It will be the same as my own. Meanwhile, we will have to share this rabbit because we have quite disturbed the scene and there will be no more rabbits taken today. Now let us return to the cave and eat. I want to be at the castle before the sun is at its highest point."

"That is the second time you have used that word, my King. What is a castle?"

"A castle is a dwelling made of stone. It has a wall of stone surrounding it and a second wall within the first. The main building is a fortress that no invading force can easily conquer. Later today you will see one in progress."

Gavan Connell

Chapter Sixteen: The Homecoming

They topped the rise just as the sun reached its zenith. The woman pulled the tlaque to a halt and sat admiring the view. In the five days since ChOn had left, the corral had been built. The castle walls seemed a little higher and the level of activity was high. ChOn was pleased. He turned on the radio, which until now he had kept switched off. One reason was that he didn't need to talk to anybody, the other reason was that the woman, Karín, had barely stopped asking questions since they had teamed up.

"Jez, are you listening?"

"I am, My Lord. We have been expecting you for the last while. OP1 reported sighting you and the woman mid-morning."

Have the four waiting for us in my dwelling. Also have the former Buq'ue commander with them and you of course. We have much news. And tell Kelda we are hungry for meat and vegetables."

"As you wish, My Lord."

The woman had listened to the exchange.

"What manner of magic is this? What manner of man are you and what manner of people are the Arw'an? How is it that we Buq'ue have been able to dominate you for years and yet you possess these things?"

"All will be revealed to you, Karín. All these wondrous things I brought with me. As I told you, we were six. Of the six, only I survived and so I have six of everything. Six swords. Six helms, six pistols, six bows. My companions have provided me with all I need to keep a kingdom safe from harm. This you have just heard comes from the other five helms. It is called a radio. It can send a voice for as far as a man can see in a straight line and less over the hills. We have a system of early warning. That is how we knew the Buq'ue Army was approaching and from which direction. It is all part of the defence of the Arw'an from our enemies and now the Buq'ue will share all we have. Now urge the tlaque forward because we have much to do and the first thing is to eat."

They passed through the main gate, under the guard house and through the second gate. Karín was all eyes as the castle unfolded before her. She knew that had the Buq'ue sent their entire army, they would have been defeated at the wall. Ch0n pointed her to where Jez was waiting. The squire nodded to Karín as their eyes met and then he greeted Ch0n.

"Well come My Lord. I will tend the beasts while you and the woman eat. The four plus the former Buq'ue commander will be in your dwelling by the time you have finished."

"Karín, this is Jez. Jez, this is Karín. Karín, Jez is my squire and garrison commander. To him I trust the training of the army and the security of my belongings. He husbands my beasts. One day he will be a Knight and ride a tlaque into battle at my side. He has access to my chamber at all times. Jez, this is Karín. She is my squire and bodyguard. She will be the commander of the cavalry and will answer to me alone as commander in chief. She will have access to my chamber at all times. You two need to get to know each other. Jez, make a space for Karín above the stable. She will keep her belongings there and will lodge there with you. Do you both understand?

"Yes, My Lord," replied Jez. *"It will be as you say."*

"Yes, my King, but there is one thing I wish to say. I will keep my belongings above the stable as you have directed but I will sleep at the entrance to your dwelling. You would not have the

wolf sleep in the stable and nor will I. My place is with you and I will not be separated from you. Not even if you command it." She looked at Jez and then at Ch0n. *"I can not guard you from afar. Had I not been in the last day of my bleeding at the time of your entrance to the king's chambers, I would have been asleep at the foot of his bed, or perchance at his side but I would have killed you or died protecting him. I will not make that mistake again. Even when I am bleeding I will find a way."*

Ch0n looked at Jez and shrugged. It was decided.

When the four arrived, they were presented in turn to Karín and their roles explained. After them came Izaki, the former commander of the Buq'ue raiding party. He saw Karín and started.

"You!" he said. *"What brings the king's personal bodyguard to the Arw'an Castle?"*

"Greetings Izaki. It is not for me to say why I am here but for the king of the Buq'ue himself."

"The king? But where is he? I see no king here."

"I am the new king of the Buq'ue, Izaki. I slew him and claimed the right to the crown by right of battle. I slew Pek the challenger and the entire Buq'ue village has sworn fealty to me even as you have. The Buq'ue and the Arw'an are united under one ruler. Together we will grow strong and modern in our approach to things and when the Matáng arrive as one day we know they will, we will not be defeated at their hands, though they bring a host to conquer and enslave us."

"It matters nought to me, My Lord that you are the king of the Buq'ue for I have sworn fealty to you here in the Arw'an castle and you would have been My Lord and King regardless. You may count on me as before for in my eyes you were already My Lord. I see you have inherited the bodyguard that accompanies

the position of King. You have chosen wisely to keep her at your side for she has not been bested in games or challenges in my memory and we grew up together so my memory is a long one." He bowed to Karín and unconsciously rubbed a spot on the side of his head where Karín had once hit him with the wooden sword. She repressed a smile and instead nodded formally in his direction.

ChOn told the extended version of his few days away and those present listened in wonder and awe. Karín interrupted when he missed a detail and the four looked at each other when this happened and wondered at her impertinence. After the tale of conquest and tribes united, ChOn called for a report.

Boro reported that the progress of the walls was going as planned and that they had managed an entire row of stones around the perimeter in the five days. The main castle wall had risen one row also.

Doni reported that the corral had been completed and that more rails had been cut and were drying outside the main wall. The male goats had been separated from the females and were waiting for ChOn to look at them. The females were due to start dropping their kids in just a few days in accordance with the rising of the moon.

Sonja had managed to house the new arrivals, some with single women, some with widows and the rest in a temporary dwelling. The site for the single quarters had been spit locked out and was waiting for Boro to allocate a works priority to it.

Kelda's administrative team was suffering from a lack of trained people and that situation was not going to improve until some sort of program was set up. ChOn made a mental note to make the work more attractive.

Jez had the army training as usual. The new Buq'ue recruits he had kept in one platoon under their own commander but he had inserted a few cabots in the ranks to make sure training was in accordance with the Arw'an tactics. Izaki nodded agreement at ChOn when Jez's report was finalized.

"Tomorrow we will have a day of feasting," declared ChOn. It will be to celebrate the new alliance between the Arw'an and the Buq'ue under one leader. In reality it is the start of the reuniting of two families. Doni, I will come with you and oversee the selection of the goats for slaughter. Kelda, your cooks will be busy tonight but they will get their reward when the food is enjoyed and they are recognized for their work. It will be part of getting more people in those jobs.

Sonja, is it men's day or women's day at the baths?"

"It is men's day, My Lord. I will ready your bath and attend to your shave. Allow me time to heat the water and I will send for you." She looked at Karín. *"If you are to sleep in the chamber of our Lord, ChOn, you must bathe and cut your hair off. It is the only way to kill the lice. We have all done it. Your hair will grow back. You will also have to boil your clothes. Meanwhile you may borrow a tunic from our Lord, ChOn, for nobody else is tall enough to fit you with one."*

Karín was about to protest but ChOn cut in first.

"The woman Karín answers to none but me. Let that be known. She will shave her head and boil her clothes but by my direction in accordance with the village laws for all newcomers. We will not allow the lice to gain a hold in the castle. She will come to the bath with me. Sonja will shave Karín before me while I am looking to the goats. She will bathe just this once on men's day. Then she will fall in to the sequence of things. Jez, fetch a spare tunic and kamarband for Karín if you would. Karín will boil her tunic and the turban she carries with her. That is all for today. Tomorrow, we feast".

ChOn went with Doni to the pen where the male goats were being held.

"Here they are as you instructed, My Lord. They number two hundred and sixty in all. We will need twenty for tomorrow's feast. There is a nice big, fat one just asking to be eaten. That one with the one crooked horn."

"We are going to kill thirty and not twenty, Doni and I will explain why. We can ill afford to keep so many goats on such restricted pasture. The pasture we will improve by recycling the dung of the goats and moving water to the fields but we will need to reduce the size of the herd. We do not need a hundred male goats. We need three and no more. The others are just eating grass. We need fewer males and more females. I know we have so many males because each family has its own male for breeding with their females but look at that one, for instance. It is small and skinny and so will have small and skinny offspring. With three big, fat, woolly males we can have ninety more females. But not only that, we will keep only those big, fat females which throw woolly twins or triplets. All the male offspring will have their balls cut off so they grow faster but do not breed with the females. When we need more males we will keep the biggest, fattest, woolliest offspring and let them grow their balls to adulthood. In no time we will have a smaller herd of bigger, fatter, healthier animals. They will give more meat. The females will give more milk and the entire herd will give more wool and hair. That is the way to manage stock."

"But My Lord, how will I sort out the squabbles of the people whose animals are being killed and who will get no payment for them? Already some families have no goats at all because they have all been killed for their meat. The biggest and fattest of them apart from a few."

"Are they still eating? Does anybody in the village lack food? Do those with no goats and no women to forage still eat? Do those with goats live behind the protection of the wall which has been built by people whose goats have been put in with all the rest?"

Doni smiled.

"So we all have goats. We all have a wall. We all eat from the same kitchen. We all bathe in the same baths and we all enjoy the protection of the same army and the same wall."

"That is correct. I have no goats but I eat meat. I have no bath but I bathe well. I have no garden but I eat vegetables and seeds. I am the one with the weapons but we all live under their protection. That is the way. When we have a way of payment for services, people can buy a goat for their garden. A neutered male goat or a pregnant female. No whole males allowed as house goats. Just females for milk and manure for the garden. That is how things will work. Now. Show me the biggest, fattest, woolliest three males and we will set them apart. The rest we will set for slaughter but while they are waiting we will feed them well to fatten them."

ChOn arrived as Karín was having her head shaved. She was in a foul mood. When he approached, she calmed down and Sonja finished her work in peace. Karín was wrapped in a spare tunic of ChOn's that was about the right length but otherwise she looked like a sack tied in the middle. Her head was bare and sported a few nicks that were bleeding. She glared at ChOn but said nothing. He felt the need to appease her.

"Woman, this thing is done for all our good. The creatures that live in our hair and clothes suck our blood and lay their eggs in our hair and live in our bedding. Shaving, washing and then boiling your clothes kills them all and they can not spread to the next person. Remember the first time I saw you, you were wearing the turban and your hair was not to be seen.

Tomorrow your turban will be clean and ready to wear and you will be able to wear it again. Your hair will grow back if you wish it but I think you will find that to wear it short or even shaved will be cooler and more sensible under a helm, which will soon be your daily head dress."

"Does my King order that I shave the hair from my ibuw as well?"

Ch0n looked at Sonja, who was enjoying herself very much. She pointed at her own groin and nodded 'yes' to Ch0n and grinned widely.

Ch0n nodded his assent.

"I think it is best. Sonja will do it here or you may do it yourself in the bath where the water is hot and it is more private."

"I would have you do it, my King, if it pleases you."

"No. It is not something I am used to and I might cut you badly. Either Sonja or yourself should do it."

"I think Jez would like to do it, my King. I will ask him to help me for it is a hard place to reach alone and Sonja will be busy with you."

"As you wish." He called to a man passing by the wall of the bath. "Hey, you! Please send for my squire and have him come to the baths. He is needed here."

Sonja was less pleased with this turn of events than she had been just moments before. She looked at the amazon sitting on the stone in front of her and then looked at herself. Today was her day to shave Ch0n and have Jez mount her in the stables. She wasn't happy that he might get to mount the filly in preference to the mare. She told Karín she had finished.

"Go to the bath where you will find hot water running from a tube. Use this on yourself. It is a gift from our Lord, Ch0n and is used to clean your body and improve your smell. There are few of these… soaps so do not waste it. Jez has a tool that you can use to cut your pubic hair. You can easily do it yourself unless you want Jez to do it. I am sure he will be willing."

Jez arrived at the run.

"Karín would have you shave her pubic hair," said Ch0n using the new word. He took Karín's place on the flat stone in front of Sonja. Sonja put a scalding woollen cloth on his face and started to massage it. She leaned into him as he leaned back. She saw the look of pure jealousy on Karín's face and knew this was the last time she would ever shave Ch0n. Karín went into the baths with Jez, who reappeared in seconds, blushing and without his multi-tool. Under the cloth, Ch0n smiled and Sonja laughed.

"You have a strange sense of humour, My Lord. That one has a temper and a half and you have tested it today."

A thought occurred to Ch0n.

"Sonja, do the Arw'an women bleed?"

"My Lord, that is a topic usually not discussed between a man and a woman. It is forbidden."

"So they do, then. Why?"

"My Lord. This is most improper but I will explain. It is part of the cycle of reproduction. The women bleed once every moon to let the woman know if she is with child or not. If she bleeds, she is not but if she stops bleeding, she will have a child within ten moons. It is part of a young girl's entry to womanhood, this bleeding and the first time she bleeds, she is taken to a secret *place and shown the things a woman must know to get by in this world."*

"Oh... Well that's all I needed to know. I will seek more information on the minitron. I know not if earth women bleed. If they do, I suppose we are closer to the same than even it appears."

Sonja shaved his face and his head and massaged his scalp as she always did. The feel of him aroused her as always and when he stood to enter the bath, she walked with unnecessary haste to the stables where Jez was waiting for her.

ChOn entered the bath as Karín was leaving. She was wet under the tunic and her bald head was almost yellow from lack of exposure to the sun. She glared at ChOn as she passed him but had time for one more comment.

"It is done, my King. Would you like to check? I found no bugs or eggs or anything else, but I believe there is an animal living there for I found its burrow."

ChOn was surprised at this last comment. He was a clone. He had never had a mother or a father. There were no females on the ship and any reference to the manner of reproduction had been locked out of the minitron's loop. In other words, he had no idea about a woman's anatomy.

"Show me."

Karín was only too happy to show him. She looked around and there was nobody in sight. She could imagine herself coupled with the ChOn if they were compatible and she believed they were because on the trail she had watched him relieving himself in the same manner as the Buq'ue men, standing up and holding their manhood. She lifted her tunic and showed ChOn her neatly clipped hair. He saw the slit beneath it and wondered why it was different. But he said nothing because he knew he would look foolish as he had felt when he didn't know about the bleeding.   He knew about male and female goats because he had read about animal husbandry before talking to Doni and now he saw the connection.   A man had to join a woman to breed a baby.   The women would bleed unless she was carrying one.   Of course ChOn had no need of a baby so he just nodded at the woman and continued to his bath.

Karín's mood went from black to blacker.

"My King.   What service would you have me perform for you now?   I could bathe you if you like."

"Thank you, Karín but I am quite capable of bathing myself.   Go to the stable and see if your tunic is dry.   I had Jez hang it by a fire.   And your turban."

That night, ChOn slept the sleep of the dead.   He was exhausted from his past five days.   He had missed two nights' sleep and had slept hard on the trail.   During the night he dreamed his dream.   He was standing on the battlements looking down at a raging battle.   Beside him stood the woman, her hair streaming behind her in the wind.   She was directing the cavalry below by the use of flags.   A war machine was pounding the walls of the castle with stones and teams of sappers were digging trenches ever closer to the main perimeter.   He had another dream.   The woman was sitting, holding his head in her hands and she looked to be crying.   He woke in the morning to see her asleep at his door.   She was lying on a paillasse with a skin thrown on top of it.   When he moved, she woke up in an instant.   She saw him watching her. She scowled at him and went back to sleep.

He looked at her sleeping form and tried to reconcile it with the images he had found on the minitron. He had asked for human reproduction and had found only a narration graphically illustrated.   ChOn had seen the goats mounted occasionally but it seemed so matter of fact. The human act as portrayed in the narration seemed much more intense. At least he knew now how it happened. He had found it mildly curious but the drawings of the naked woman and the pointer had not done anything more than educate him anatomically. There had been no suggestion that humans did it for pleasure. The entire narration was based on reproduction and the act necessary to produce a baby. He took out his tablet and made an image of the sleeping woman. In the caption he wrote:

Female specimen, non-typical. Red hair. Taller by almost a foot than her sisters. Taller by half that than her brothers. It is reported that a taller race called the Matáng lives further west.

The feast officially started at mid-day but unofficially started as soon as people stirred. There had not been many days of leisure in the new location and this, the second, was being treated as a super special occasion. ChOn had declared that the Arw'an and the Buq'ue were united under his rule. That meant no more petty raids and women being stolen and goats herded away. It meant perhaps a reuniting of families where the women from both sides had been stolen never to return to their villages. By the official start time, most of the men were drunk and most of the women were dancing semi-naked around the central fire.

One group, however, was very alert. On feast days such as this, games of skill and endurance were the norm and prizes were handed out to the winner. Points were scored for each event and the overall winner was declared and lauded until the next feast when he would have to earn his laurels again. Prizes were usually trinkets or flowers but this time, ChOn had declared that the winner would receive a weapon of war. As most of the contenders were already soldiers and quite fit, they all expected to win. Each of the combatants had a particular skill that would ensure him a top finish in that event and the best all round competitor would be a worthy winner.

Boro and Doni listed the events that were traditionally held. There were five in all. Ch0n wrote the list on his tablet in order of competition:

Spear throwing – distance and accuracy at twenty paces

Standing high jump

Foot race over a distance of two thousand paces

Swordplay with shields and wooden swords

Freestyle wrestling

The first event took place after a ceremony of thanks to the Gods and to Ch0n. There were about twenty hopefuls and a couple of drunks who were whisked away before they could accidentally spear anybody in the assembled crowd. There were the usual crowd favourites and villains but one competitor stood out for two reasons. She was a woman and she was by far the tallest of the competitors.

They drew lots for turns and the competition started. Most of the throwers could throw a spear out to a distance of twenty five yards but two went close to thirty before Karín took up her position on the course and ran to the line. She passed the thirty yard mark by a good two feet and from then it was catch me if you can. One particularly robust soldier bettered her by a foot and she finished second, much to her chagrin, but she was gracious and shook the winner's hand afterwards.

The accuracy throw went better for all. This was their bread and butter and most of the competitors struck the target, which was a goat skin stretched between two bamboo poles. Karín was one who barely hit the target and so finished well down the field but as she was not a soldier, she didn't mind.

The standing high jump was a foregone conclusion. Karín scratched her mark a good foot above the next competitor.

The footrace was a favourite with the crowd because it involved an out and back run previously measured off by one of the elders. It was one thousand paces straight towards the knoll overlooking the gate, around a judge and straight back. There was to be no contact between competitors that would cause one of them to fall. They set off at a gallop with Karín in the mix and when they turned for home a roar went up. The crowd favourite, Bezel was in the lead with Karín loping along not far behind. Bezel was making hard work of it, his head bobbing up and down while Karín was taking long strides and reeling him in with every step. When they crossed the line, Bezel had won by less than three paces and Karín was another ten in front of third. They all sucked in the air as the next event was to start immediately.

The swordplay was by knockout competition. Every loser would be eliminated and every winner would proceed to the next round. The elders had drawn straws to pair each contestant with another. They were given wooden swords and were able to use their own shields. Karín had borrowed one from Jez. She was paired first with a brute of a man who was no match for her agility. She worked her way through until there remained only two. She won the final bout quickly and so at the start of the last event, went in ahead of the rest on points won.

The wrestling was usually conducted with the combatants naked from the waist up to prevent holds on clothing. Karín decided to go with the flow and stripped to a short skirt along with the men. The villagers were enthralled at the sight of her standing semi-naked waiting for her bout but she was undeterred by their stares. ChOn eyed her closely. He compared her body with that of the narration he had viewed the previous evening and decided a naked woman looked more inviting in real life than sketched on the flat screen.

The bouts were conducted as for the sword play. Combatants were paired off by ballot. Karín's first opponent was a lithe young man who was put off by the lewd shouts from the onlookers. Karín pinned him easily with her height and weight advantage. Her second bout wasn't so easy and she had to fight strongly before managing to get her opponent in a choke hold and having him submit. There remained five of the original twenty. They compared points to see who would stand out until the final bout and it fell to Karín. She was able to watch the other four and then the final two before she was matched with the winner. He was a strong and agile man who had concentrated on close quarter holds and had won one bout with a bear hug that prevented his opponent from breathing. He had sufficient points so that if he won, he would be the overall winner and of course Karín was the leader before the event so if she won she would also win the tournament. When the bout began, she sized up her man. He was a head shorter than her but weighed half her weight again and was probably several times more powerful. Karín had to keep away from the massive arms. He crouched low and rushed at her but she jumped in the air and caught him on the chin with her knee. He stumbled but did not fall. Karín turned quickly while he was recovering and kicked him between the legs an almighty blow that had the crowd howling and the elders discussing the legality of the blow. While her opponent was doubled over in agony, Karín walked around him and lifted her knee into his face with all her strength. He went down as if poleaxed. The elders had no choice but to award the fight to her. As one explained as he lifted her hand in victory, free wrestling implied there were no rules on how the bout must be fought.

Karín went to Ch0n and knelt before him. She was still half naked and her chest rose and fell with her breathing. Her eyes were alight with the adrenalin rush as Ch0n declared her the village champion. He offered her the choice of a katana or a pair of sais as her prize and she took the katana and held it out to him.

"My King," she shouted for all to hear, *"I take this sword and pledge upon it, my unswerving service to you, all the days of my life."*

The throng went wild and ChOn tilted his head in acknowledgement. The crowd dispersed to the feast and ChOn retired to his chambers to plan the next day. Later in the afternoon he summoned Doni and told him of his plan. ChOn was going to ride over to where he had seen the herd of tlaque some months before. If they weren't migratory, they would probably still be there because of the sweet pickings and the water. He would drive them towards the castle and at a point nearby, the villagers would form two lines and the tlaque would be herded into the corral. Once there they would be divided into males and females and those not needed would be released back into the wild. Initially ChOn wanted one hundred mounts but he knew that realistically, that number would have to be gradually obtained and if he could get more than fifty in the initial roundup it would be a huge gain for him. Doni nodded approvingly at the idea and left ChOn to his own devices while he went to tell his herders the plan.

Despite the noise outside his dwelling, ChOn slept well. When he awoke the woman was asleep on her paillasse with the katana. The wolf was lying beside her. ChOn tried to get up without disturbing her but as soon as he moved, she awoke.

"You sleep lightly, Karín. I had thought to go for my shave. It is men's day at the baths and I have a long day ahead."

"I will shave you from this day on, my King. The woman Sonja has other things to occupy her time and I have nought to do but serve you. I will be careful with the blade. Even though it is my first attempt, I will be thorough."

"As you wish, Karín but there is one thing I wish to say to you before we leave the tent. I find all this 'my King' and 'My Lord' very taxing. When we are alone and when it is not required, please just call me by my name. It would please me greatly to hear my name spoken more often."

"Yes, my King. I will do as you wish but it is not easy for me. I will try and remember. Now. Where is the blade you shave with and how do I heat the water?"

"Perhaps Sonja could show you just this once. There is no shame in not knowing. She knows these things and she will teach you gladly."

It was an ordeal at first with the two women trying to show and learn and both wanting to shave their Lord. In the end, ChOn told Sonja to shave his beard while Karín watched and then for Karín to shave his head under instructions from Sonja. Karín studied Sonja's technique, noting especially how she managed to get ChOn to relax into her bosom and how she managed to frot herself against him at the slightest opportunity. When it was her turn to do the shaving, she made sure that ChOn had every chance to feel her against him. It was so comical that later, when he was alone in the bath, the two women laughed together and went together to the stables. There, Karín went to her lodgings and Sonja went to Jez. Karín listened to them coupling and imagined herself joined to ChOn as she had joined his predecessor from time to time when she had been summoned to his bed.

She heard Sonja leave Jez's chamber and soon Sonja's voice whispered at her entry.

"Karín. I know you are burning for your Lord. While you wait for him, you could do worse than to use Jez to douse your fires as I have done these past moons."

"Hush, woman. I want no other and will have none but him. I will wait until he is ready or I can hold back no longer but I WILL have him and not just as a lover. He will be my man and I will

be his woman. Nature has made me for him. Of that I am certain. My life of torment and loneliness for being a freak were for a purpose. He will need a women like me to take his manhood without pain and to bear his children without tearing. I have done with boys. I will have none but him."

When Ch0n returned to his chambers, Karín was at her post at the entrance as usual.

"Is there anything I can do for you, my King?"

"Yes, Karín. Tell Jez to ready the tlaque. I will ride out as soon as I am dressed. But first, take this." He threw her an olive drab flying suit, designed to be worn either inside a spacecraft or as a lightweight fighting uniform. "It should fit you well. It belonged to a compatriot of mine who was almost exactly your size. And take this as well. You will need it for a while until your hair grows back a little." He tossed her a silk beanie. "And while I'm at it, you'll be needing a weapon belt. Have Jez get one from the storage area. And if you see something else you need, bring it to me and I will tell you if you may keep it."

"Am I to go with you today, my King, Ch0n? I would ride the tlaque to see the herd that will make up my mounts."

"Yes. You will travel with me always. Do not ask again for now you have the answer."

Karín smiled at him.

"As you wish, Ch0n, My Lord. Now I wish to try on this wonderful soft garment." She stripped naked and tried to work out how to don the flying suit. Ch0n laughed. He went to her and showed her how to open the Velcro fastening that ran the full length of the front. She stepped into the legs and put her arms into the sleeves and shrugged the suit on. It fitted perfectly. She looked a little silly with no boots so Ch0n told her to get Jez to find a pair that fit. She was like a child at

Christmas. She pulled the silk beanie over her head and ran for the stables.

ChOn dressed in his traditional two piece uniform. He went out to the stable in full battle order as usual. Jez had the tlaque ready and Karín was standing at his side with her flying suit pant cuffs rolled around her new boots, ChOn's helm on her head and the katana sheathed with the handle over her right shoulder the same way ChOn carried Shiew. He noted the sai, one in each boot and the sling around her neck. Her weapon belt held a water canteen and a tonfa. She was ready for battle. She looked in no way comical. She was every inch the storm trooper to look at. ChOn looked her up and down and nodded his approval. She took the reins from Jez and looked at ChOn. ChOn felt lost without his helm so he called for Jez to get him the remaining spare from the storage bin. He tapped Karín on the helm and told her to remove it. He gave her the newer one.

"This is mine. I have worn it in and I would keep it for my own use. You can take this one but if we need it, you will have to give it up."

She nodded at him.

ChOn looked at Jez.

"Tell Doni we will call in when we have the tlaque on the move and when we need the villagers to form the tunnel," he ordered. "We should be back by nightfall at the latest."

ChOn selected a frequency that he and Karín could share.

"When we two need to talk privately, select this button here and at the same time press this one here and some moving marks will appear on this display. When you come to the one that looks like two lines, stop. Like this. Now you do it."

Karín did as she had been told and selected the frequency band 11.

"Good. Now do it on mine."

She did.

"Good. Now only we can hear each other. When we need to talk to the whole group, we select the band that has just one of these scratches. It is called, 'one.' Say it."

"Wun,"

"Good. Our private band is called 'eleven'. Say it."

"Eleven."

"Good. Now if we are on band 'one' and I say to you, meet me on 'eleven', you would change to our private band. Nobody else may ever hear that word, 'eleven.' Do you understand me? Nobody. Not even Jez. He and I have our own band which we three will share. I will show you that scratch later. Now. When you wish to speak, just speak normally. Inside the helm there is a box that sends your voice to me. When you talk, it does it automatically and when I talk my box will send my voice to you. There is one rule. Only one can talk at a time because the box can process only one voice at a time. Do you understand? Good. Now. Meet me on eleven."

"Eleven." She nodded.

Karín quickly changed the frequency band to '11' and they both put on their helms. "Mount up," ordered ChOn, signalling at the same time towards the tlaque.

"Mount up."

"You don't have to repeat everything I say, woman."

"I know that My Lord, Ch0n but I am learning the magic and I must practise. No?"

Ch0n laughed and the sound travelled like music to the woman's ears.

"Yes, you must."

The woman jumped nimbly up on to the saddle and pointed to the spot behind her.

"Mount up."

Ch0n smiled and heaved himself on to the tlaque. He looked around for the wolf. It was sitting in the entrance to Ch0n's dwelling. He clicked his fingers and the creature bounded over to him and Karín dug her heels into the tlaque.

They had not gone more than a mile when the earpiece in Ch0n's helm crackled into life.

"What means, 'wun'?"

"It is the number in my tongue that you call, 'aiken'. 'Eleven' is the number you call, 'ata ma aiken'. Ten and one."

"Will you teach me to know the scratches?"

"If we have time. But I will teach you to read some of them. Some words like my name and yours and Jez's. Words like 'get' and 'tlaque' and others of the important words. There is a thing we call the alphabet. That I will teach you because each of the letters has a sound of its own that makes up the scratches. The scratches we call writing."

"Raiting. Teach me the alphabet."

Ch0n sighed. He did used to enjoy these long rides by himself. His escape from responsibility, just he and his creatures wandering on the plains mapping the land.

Gavan Connell

"OK. In my tongue there are twenty seven letters. Five of them are called sounds. The others are called consonants but the most important of them are the five sounds for they tell you how to say the word. The consonants are there to form hard corners if you like in the words."

"What means okay?"

ChOn sighed again. It was going to be a long day.

"OK is not really a word but we use it as a word to mean 'all right' or 'I agree' or even 'ready'. It has its origins in one of the great wars we fought between nations on my world. I will try not to use too many words that are not real words. It will make it easier for everybody."

"It's okay. I am a quick learner as you will soon see."

"The five sounds are 'a', 'e', 'i', 'o', 'u'. In times gone by, they had many different sounds each one but in modern times they have been simplified by using an ancient language used by the Romans, whose military tactics I am teaching our army, so they now all sound the same. Now repeat them. 'a', 'e', 'i', 'o', 'u'"

"'a', 'e', 'i', 'o', 'u'. We have those sounds and more."

"Good. Yes, I know but we are learning to read and the other sounds may be formed by grouping the basic ones."

"'a', 'e', 'i', 'o', 'u', 'a', 'e', 'i', 'o', 'u', 'a', 'e', 'i', 'o', 'u' 'a', 'e', 'i', 'o', 'u' 'a', 'e', 'i', 'o', 'u' 'a', 'e', 'i', 'o', 'u' 'a', 'e', 'i', 'o'..."

"Enough!"

"But My Lord, ChOn, I must practise."

"Practise all you wish but take off the helm or when you are alone. I will show you how to write those sounds. Now. The alphabet is taught to children in a song. It goes like this…"

For the entire morning, the two sang the alphabet song with ever more extravagant endings. The wolf joined in at the end and the tlaque trotted along at his extended pace for Karín might have been singing but she wasn't about to let the tlaque slacken his effort.

They passed the small lake where ChOn had seen the herd of tlaque the first time. He was tempted to take Karín to his cave by the landing site but there was no time for tourism just yet. He decided to return as soon as possible because it was time to transfer the entire cache to the castle where it would be safer. He remembered the radio in the tree with its antenna searching the sky for signals and decided it would be better used as a base station at the castle, freeing up Jez's helm and extending the range of communications, perhaps as far as the Buq'ue fort. While he was considering all of this, they topped a small rise and saw the herd stretched out before them. There were hundreds of the creatures of various ages all grazing contentedly. Their mount sniffed the air and charged down the slope towards them, roaring his presence. A single male separated itself from the herd and ran out to meet the challenge. ChOn and the woman had no idea what was about to happen but the two mature males confronted each other with antlers down, their hooves pawing the earth.

"They are going to fight!" shouted ChOn. "Get off. Now!"

They both jumped down. ChOn drew the pulse and waited. He could not risk his tlaque in a fight. He was still young and inexperienced. The probability of his defeating the monster in front of him was almost zero. ChOn set the pulse to maximum and took aim at the herd-leader. As the two charged at each other, ChOn discharged a pulse that took the beast full in the chest and stopped him dead in his tracks, literally just before impact. Their own tlaque continued his charge and lifted the herd leader off the ground. It was still twitching when it landed but there was no doubt who had won the day. Ch0n's tlaque lifted his muzzle to the air and trumpeted his victory. The rest of the herd simply walked over to him. He sniffed each of the senior does in turn and then allowed Ch0n to grab the reins.

"I will see if he is still quiet enough to mount," he said to Karín. "He may not want to let us ride him now he is a king in his own right."

"Just like the master", thought Karín, *"but I will ride the master when he is tame enough."*

"Steady, boy," whispered Ch0n into the big ear of the tlaque. "I'm going to sit on you." He heaved himself into the saddle and called to Karín. "Mount up."

She jumped onto the beast's rump and Ch0n rode through the herd and out the other side. They followed their new leader like the herd animals they were.

"This is easier than I thought," said Ch0n. "I will try and make them follow at the trot, otherwise we will have to walk all the way." He urged the beast into a slow trot. The tlaque knew Ch0n was guiding him and not the one who made him run too fast. The tlaque immediately behind him quickened their pace and trotted after him until finally the hundreds of creatures were all trotting behind in a long ragged group. When night fell, Ch0n ran them into the corral unassisted and Doni closed the gate.

"Meet me on one," said Ch0n and felt Karín's hand move behind him.

"Jez, we will leave the tlaque here with the herd tonight. I need you to come and help us with the saddle and to rub him down."

"As you wish, My Lord."

"I am filthy. It is men's day at the bath but if there are no men present you should also clean yourself. You look like a walking dust bowl and your face is wet with mud and sweat."

"My Lord, ChOn. Yesterday at the games I wrestled naked in front of the entire village. I have no fear of bathing on men's day."

"But it is not for you to decide. The men may not want to bathe in front of a woman."

"I have seen what a man has. It holds no surprises for me."

They went to the baths. It was dark and nobody else was present. ChOn stripped naked and entered the warm water and called Karín. She did the same. She had fine lines and pale skin, almost the same colour as ChOn's own Asiatic colour. He washed himself vigorously and left the water to where his clean tunic was waiting. Karín's eyes followed him, studying every inch of him. She had coupled on numerous occasions with the former king of the Buq'ue since she first bled. He had not been a big man like ChOn and his manhood had been in keeping with his size but ChOn was another matter. She was relieved to see that ChOn's anatomy was as she had guessed, the same as her people. She had worried that he might have been somewhat similar but incompatible with her own body but now she was certain.

"It seems I was wrong, My Lord, ChOn", she thought. *"Perhaps there are surprises yet in store for me. I would know your manhood. But I am patient. For now".*

The next day ChOn and Doni surveyed the herd of tlaque. Karín was at ChOn's side chattering away as usual and occasionally breaking into the alphabet song.

"My King, from these tlaque we will select the beasts for the cavalry. No?"

"Yes. The males we will neuter and the females we will keep for breeding stock and beasts of burden. The young males we will also neuter for meat and for future mounts. This will be a difficult process for we have no yards to control them. I fear we will have to release my beast to keep the herd here in the beginning but we will keep one almost mature male so that when we allow the herd to go back to its usual feeding grounds they will have a dominant male. With just those we need here, we can build stables for the mounts and my beast can return to my own stable. When we need him for breeding he can run free with the females."

"And what of me, My Lord, ChOn. When I need breeding will you run free with me"? she thought.

"Doni. We need to separate the males from the females. Have Kelda bring a water vessel here and boil some water. Jez, fetch my hunting knife and the sharpening stone. And my sewing kit and the torn uniform. We will stun each beast with the pistol, wash them with hot water and cut their balls from the bag. Then we will sew up the bag to stop dirt entering and that way we should not lose the beasts to sickness. Karín, as the commander of the household cavalry, I will give you the choice of all the males as a mount. Then you will select thirty-two more. They will be mounts for the first troop with two spare mounts. Here is a paint marker. Take care moving among them. Mark those you want with the paint. Thirty three in all. Yours first."

"I chose mine within moments of arriving here, my King. It is the one who sniffs the air in curiosity. That is the intelligent one. And it has a distinctive white backside. I will paint it first."

"Will you name it?"

"Of course! It will be called, 'Oeta' which means 'flight' for on him I will fly like a bird. Now watch me paint him and talk to him."

She walked around the edge of the herd and delved into it until she was in front of Oeta. She held out her hand and gave the beast something, which it ate. Then she drew a mark on his flank. It was an eye. She walked to the beast's head and looked into its eye and whispered into its ear. Then she took a handful of mane and before ChOn could shout a warning, jumped nimbly onto its back. It stood, puzzled but did not protest. The woman urged it forward with her knees and it moved through the herd. She shifted her position and it turned towards ChOn and stopped at the rail in front of him.

"This is the one I was talking about, my King. The one with the white backside."

She swung her leg over the beast's withers and slid to the ground.

"Doni, this is my mount. It will be the last to be cut. I do not want any experiments with the pulse, the knife or the needle on this one. Do you understand me?"

"I answer to the Lord, ChOn and not to you, woman. You have no authority here."

"Doni is correct, Karín. As yet, you have no authority here but I am about to give it to you. Doni, you were right to chide her for she was impatient. I have promised her the position of Commander of the household cavalry because she has a way with the beasts and she can fight as we all saw yesterday. As such, she has total authority under me over all things that pertain to her position. On that and that alone, she speaks with my voice. Do you understand me?"

"Yes, My Lord."

"Karín, you have been given your command as of this moment. You may direct all but me when it comes to the Cavalry but not for anything else. Your power of command starts and ends with the Cavalry. Do you understand me?"

"Yes, my King."

"Good. That's all settled. Pick your thirty-two while Doni is arranging to divide the corral. Kelda will soon have the water boiling. I will consult the minitron on how we will cut the beasts and we will begin. Karín. What did you feed the beast before you rode him?"

"It is a potion we women use sometimes when our men want to couple with one of the other women in the village. While we may not have laws regarding one husband and one wife or one lover, we do have feelings and so when we do not wish the coupling to take place, we feed our men the sweetest of juices from a root called 'yoni' that grows plentifully here. We mix it with the porridge and it dulls their senses. They can function more or less normally but their desire for physical activity is affected. The tlaque simply did not want to run because his brain was numb. He was able to walk and even run but the medicine is powerful."

"I do not understand why a man would want to have a child with a woman other than his wife. Do the children of such couplings become part of the family of the woman or the man?"

"Aaah! Now I understand, My Lord, ChOn," Karín thought silently. *"You are a baby when it comes to the act of coupling. You had never seen a woman until now. You have seen the beasts couple to produce offspring and thought that was the only reason to couple. You have never lain with a woman and felt her flesh suckling your manhood. Oh! To think I am to be your teacher as you are mine."*

"Children do not always result from couplings my King," she told him. *"I will explain this to you later. Here are Jez and Kelda with the water. I must start the selection process. I have a pouch of the yoni so we can lead them easily to where they may be stunned."*

Ch0n tried to guess the weight of the beasts. He asked all present to guess how many men it would take to weigh as much as a tlaque and then averaged out all the guesses. The minitron told him a fully grown elk male would weigh more than 700 pounds but these tlaque were much bigger. An elk was only eight feet long and these almost-adult males were nine and ten feet long. He decided that using the guesses and the minitron as well as the fact the stags were still not fully grown, that 900 pounds would have to do as the first guess. He set the pulse at forty percent. Karín rode the first of the males to the corner of the corral where the water had been set up for washing. She slid from the beast's back and Ch0n released the pulse. The beast dropped to its knees and rolled on to its side. It was still breathing. Two herders opened its back legs, a third washed the area with soapy water and then Ch0n directed Doni's grizzly work using an image from the minitron. Finally, Kelda sewed the slits and covered them with cold ash from the fire, a trick the women used to keep insects from laying eggs in a raw wound, and the job was done. Now it was a matter of waiting to see if the beast would wake up. It took another twenty minutes on Ch0n's watch before it revived. It struggled to its feet and wandered a little unsteadily into the new section of the corral as if nothing had happened. The small crowd cheered. Ch0n reset the pulse to thirty seven percent and Karín presented the next beast. By the time Oeta was led to be done, they had changed the water several times and Ch0n had lowered the pulse to thirty six percent, which meant the beasts were waking up within minutes of their surgery. Not one had suffered any instant ill effects but the proof was to be in the coming day when they would know if the wounds were going to fester.

Oeta's gelding went smoothly. He woke up and strolled to the others.

"Doni, select the best remaining male and paint him. Geld another ten. Separate all the other males and pen them ready for gelding in the next few days. We will select them or slaughter them as they are needed. Take thirty females that appear to be pregnant and separate them and pen them. When that is done, release the rest, including the male you have marked. They should return to their traditional grazing grounds alone once they have a new dominant male. If they choose to stay close, we will have beasts to hunt. Karín, you will need stables for the beasts. I will show Boro how to build them from bamboo. The spot should be inside the walls but away from the houses. Each mount will have its own stable. Oeta will live with my beast in your lodge. Each member of your troop will select his own mount in turn after drawing lots to decide the order. They will then be responsible to make a saddle and bridle and to care for their own beast. They need to understand that the beast will save their life in battle if it is well cared for or may falter if not. A good cavalry soldier looks first after his mount and then after himself. Tell Sonja I wish her to provide water conduits to the stables so the beasts may be washed. Also, I need to know if there is a plant you use to clean yourselves of internal parasites. It is something I had not thought of before but it is important. You have enough to keep you busy for a few days. After that we will ride to the Buq'ue village to see how things are progressing."

"Her own mount, My Lord, ChOn."

"Her own mount? What do you mean?"

"I mean, My Lord and King that your household cavalry will be made up of women. Not men."

"But that is absurd! I forbid it. Absolutely not. Women are not cut out to fight. No. The very idea that women could do this is against everything I have ever read or heard of."

"Did I not win the games yesterday, my King? Did I not outrun, out-jump, out-fight and out-wrestle twenty men?"

"Yes. But you are different."

"Yes, My Lord, Ch0n I am different. You are right. Good it is settled then. I have already selected six of the thirty. They are all very intelligent and strong. I will need such as they for the beasts will not respond to a weak person. Also, they are young and have no men. That is also good for when a woman has a man, she becomes useless because her heart becomes sick with the thought of leaving him."

"Karín, I said 'no'. You have twisted my words."

"My Lord and King. Have you ever seen what happens to the prisoners after a fight between villages? You forbade it once I have been told. What usually happens is that they are turned over to the newly-created widows. The prisoners are usually gelded first, but without the aid of the sweet roots or the pulse. Then they are usually skinned. If they survive that, they are usually tied to stakes and left to the mercy of an ant colony. Or thrown into a fire. Or stoned to death. My Lord, women were made to defend their families. Does not the meekest of the she-goats become a raging beast in the face of a wolf? Do not mistake us for weak because we are women. I promise you I will select only those who can ride swiftly and handle a lance almost as well as I. All who fail this test will be returned to the village sewing circle but I assure you, they will not fail because you will train me and as you train me, so shall I train them."

"Be it on your own head, then. If you fail me in this, I will restrict your duties to my personal bodyguard and nothing else. You will lose your command and spend the rest of your days watching my back. Do you understand, woman?"

"My Lord, my King. Do not place such temptation in my path. I wish to succeed as Commander of your elite troops. If failure means I am to spend the rest of my life in your personal service, I would fail gladly. Rather, my ChOn, should I fail you in this, you should punish me by placing me in the service of Kelda, where I can see you every day but know you shun me for my failures."

"I know you will not fail. I have had a dream. Twice have I dreamed it. I am standing in the tower of the castle with a red-haired woman at my side as a battle rages below. That woman is you. When you revealed your features to me in the Buq'ue village I recognized you instantly. And I have had another dream. In this dream I am lying in your arms and you are crying. I know not the meaning of this dream but I think in it I am dying."

"When you die, my King, it will be because I have died first in your defence. Nothing will touch you while I live. That is what a bodyguard is for. Even when I am bleeding I will stay closer to you than decency permits for not having done that cost the life of my former king. But now I have three days' work to complete. At the end of every day I will bathe myself and place myself at your service. Meanwhile I will wear the helm. Just say the word, 'eleven' in any context other than, 'meet me on eleven' and I will come to you."

ChOn nodded. Karín knelt at his feet and put her forehead on his boots for all present to see.

"My King, you have honoured me beyond your understanding with this thing. I am going to change the status of women in

this tribe by training them to a condition of excellence in a world of men. It is but another reason we serve you as a people. I have seen two kings before you and they were proud and greedy. They took what they wanted and people were happy for them to do it. You are the same in that regard but they never gave anything back. You take goats and land and power and in return you give pride and purpose. Nobody has suffered by your hand who served you honestly. And though I kneel before you in fealty I know you treat me not as a subject, not even as a woman but as the Commander of your Household Cavalry. Thrice I have knelt before you and sworn fealty and no more will I do it but I do it here where few may see me but you. So you know it to be true. I am your willing subject, your slave if you will it. I desire nothing more than to serve you in every way and to be beside you when your dream becomes a reality. Your second dream I do not understand either but it will be revealed to you. Or to me." She stood up. *"In three days I will ride with you to the Buq'ue village."*

Ch0n watched her as she left. He had formed a special bond with her. It was more than master and subject. More than the comradeship he had shared with his squad. More like a friendship he had never had. He felt uncomfortable that she had kowtowed to him. He knew it was her way but it was certainly not his. He returned to where Doni was about to start gelding the next ten tlaque and drew the pulse gun. Doni, stunned by what he had just witnessed, shook himself into action and shouted at the others to do the same.

Gavan Connell

Chapter Seventeen: Betrayal and Consolidation

Three days after the herding and sorting of the tlaque, Ch0n set off for the Buq'ue fort. Jez had already dispatched a platoon of soldiers on foot and told them they had four days to force-march to the fort so they would arrive at the same time as himself. The tlaque could easily reach the village in less than two days at a forced trot with the woman up front. She had wanted to ride her own beast and make a triumphant return but Ch0n had forbidden it on the basis that it would need at least another ten days for the wounds to be fully healed. So Jez had been tasked to look after it in Ch0n's private stable. His orders from Karín had been more detailed than the orders from Ch0n for the care of the entire garrison and had ended with an implied threat that had chilled Jez to the bone. The rest of the tlaque were stabled in individual stables which Boro had built as a priority. Ch0n had told him the cavalry was so important to the defence of the castle that the wall could wait for the few days it would take to build a bamboo shelter. The roof was made waterproof thanks to a layer of the sloppy droppings of the same tlaque, which, mixed with the limestone mud and dry grass, set like cement. A separate group from Kelda's administrative workforce was then tasked to gather the manure each evening and take it to the gardens where it was mixed with the sandy soil and allowed to compost itself. The beasts in the stables and the corral were fed the bamboo tops and cuttings from a legume tree daily at the same hour. Just before feeding time, a hollow log was played like a drum. In time, that signal would be used to tell the tlaque to return to their corral.

227

Boro had been tasked to provide a shaded area in one corner of the corral where the beasts could sleep or just seek protection from the sun.

"What think you of your Household Cavalry, My Lord, ChOn?"

They had been travelling for less than an hour when Karín asked the question.

"Well, they are well housed. They seem to be well cared for and so far we have not had any riding accidents."

"You know well that we have been forbidden to ride the beasts for another ten days. No wonder there have been no accidents. But they have done well with what they have, no?"

"Yes, commander, they have done well. I have seen that all the beasts have a blanket of wool the same colour and that the saddles are almost completed. Using rolled hides was a good idea. They will mould themselves to the beasts' backs as well as to the troopers' backsides."

"Yes, it was a good idea. One of my troopers thought of it. She used to make chairs for her sick father and most of the materials were too hard or too soft so by trial and error she came up with this. The sewing pattern is the trick to them holding their form. As for our backsides, they will soon be firm and muscular. That is an advantage we didn't consider. There is nothing worse to the eye than a woman with a backside wider than her shoulders. I like the stables. Boro's idea to put the sleeping quarters above the beasts has saved us a lot of space inside the outer wall. Did you bring the minitron this time?"

"No. I do not like to travel with it. It may fall into water or be crushed by a hoof. It is safer at home."

"Home, my ChOn? That is an interesting word for one such as yourself to use."

"I use it with pride. I have spent all my life before this place living inside a metal tube. Most of my life was spent asleep with tubes poked into my body from all sides. This is more of a home than I could have hoped for a year ago."

"What is a year?"

"A year is the time it takes for this world to make a complete circle around the sun. It is marked by the passing of the seasons from hot to cool to cold to cool to hot again. Four seasons in one year. On my world a year takes much longer. I think that is because the world is bigger and so is further from the sun when it makes its circle. I think a year has passed since I arrived. I still use my earth watch to measure time but the seasons are decided by the distance we are from the sun."

"Oh...."

ChOn had been on the planet for three hundred earth days, according to his chronometer. It had passed quickly for him. Ten months. Where would the ship be now? Probably trapped in some worm on the way to the next one, thus following the space highways that allowed FTL travel. No stray asteroids flew in the worms. Everything went at the same speed and in the same direction until they shot out the end and were navigated to the next entrance by the few humans on the bridge. Unbeknown to ChOn, the droids in charge of the humans were at that very moment 'injecting' every male over the age of fifteen with a chemical that was designed to supress any sexual function. Every ten earth months, the same drug was injected into the tubes that fed the almost lifeless bodies. In a place with no women and no need to reproduce thanks to the cloning program, controlling testosterone levels was most important. After twelve months the drug wore off so it was re-administered every ten months. ChOn was about to have a hormone, hitherto supressed, circulating through his body and gradually increasing in strength and influence on his being from now on.

"So sing me the alphabet song for a while."

They passed the night in the cave that was to become in future trips a way station for all travellers between the two main forts. The dragon was nowhere to be seen. Early the following morning they set off again this time following in the tracks of the platoon Jez had dispatched three days earlier. After a couple of hours they caught sight of it in the distance and another hour later they drew alongside the platoon commander. Ch0n recognized him as Izaki, the former Buq'ue commander and his stomach lurched. He had not realized that Jez had dispatched the Buq'ue platoon ahead. Ch0n immediately went on the defensive and rode off to a flank and behind the platoon. He drew both pistols and checked their status for the second time that day. If things turned bad, he would simply shoot and scoot before he was in range of the spears.

They topped the rise of the knoll where ten days before, Ch0n had left the beasts. The fort lay ahead a short distance. Ch0n continued to ride behind the platoon at walking pace. The approached the gate and Ch0n immediately noted the absence of sentries. He called to Izaki.

"Izaki. Halt the men and come here. I need to speak with you." Izaki obeyed. Ch0n stayed mounted. While Izaki was approaching, he whispered into the microphone,

"There is treachery afoot here. I can smell it. There are no sentries. I have drawn the kinetic pistol. If I discharge it, the beast will jump. I will warn you by saying the number eleven just before I do it. Hold the beast when it jumps and then turn and ride for the castle. Do not say or do anything unless I speak directly to you. Do you understand?"

"I do, My Lord. I too sensed it and was about to warn you."

"Izaki! What strikes you as being strange about the fort?"

"There are no sentries at the gate, Lord. I was about to halt the troops when you spoke. I like it not. There is only one entrance on this side of the fort and if we pass through we will be able to be ambushed."

"Divide your force into two open files but keep them together. Squad one will pass through the gate and face left. Squad two will pass through and face right. They will march twenty paces sideways into the fort and form the square. I will follow at a short distance. If there is any treachery I will intervene with the kinetic pistol. I promise you none will survive. This is a test of your loyalty, Izaki. Fail me not."

"My Lord. We swore to you. You need not worry. If there is an issue here it will be because a small group is not happy with you as king. They have not had time to organize more than a few men in whom they have confidence. We will resolve this and the rest of the Buq'ue will remain loyal." He bowed stiffly at the neck and turned on his heel.

Ch0n watched him talk to his two cabots and then the platoon marched towards the gate. The left of the platoon passed through the gatehouse and did a smart turn on the move that had them halted facing left. The rear group did an equally smart right turn that saw them facing the right. Before they could start marching sideways down the entrance road, they were sprayed with spears. But they had been prepared and only one fell. The rest fended the spears aside and then on an order from the commander, the two squads attacked an unseen force that had gathered on both sides of the gatehouse. It was a short skirmish and Izaki signalled to Ch0n that it was safe to approach.

Ch0n was uneasy. He still had to negotiate the gatehouse and once inside, he and the woman would be vulnerable if his platoon had turned treacherous. As they walked towards the gate, he whispered again,

"When we get half way through, urge the beast into a gallop until we are more than a spear throw from the gatehouse."

By way of reply, Karín threw her leg over the tlaque's mane and slid to the ground. She drew the katana while she was running. ChOn eased himself into the saddle and urged the beast forward. Karín arrived at the gate and ran straight through. She stopped just past the last of Izaki's troops and looked back. In front of her were several dead Buq'ue troops and several more who had been taken prisoner, including the officer, ChOn had appointed Garrison Commander. She looked a fearsome sight in her full battle rig, sprayform armour fitted closely to her curves, the katana at the ready and the visor of the helm shining gold in the sun.

"The path is clear, my King,"

ChOn rode through the gatehouse at a slow walk. He did not look left or right as he passed the scene but continued to his royal chambers. On route he told Karín to tell Izaki to bring the prisoners to the central square and call the villagers together. He dismounted, entered his quarters and looked around. Somebody had been living there in his absence. He walked to the square where Izaki had the prisoners lined up, kneeling on the ground. The woman, Karín was pacing along in front of them talking. ChOn couldn't hear her because she had removed the helm so they could see who she was. Her hair was less than half an inch long but they knew her well and what she had been to the previous king. Fear showed on their faces as she spoke individually to them.

ChOn went to the seat reserved for the king and sat. He removed his own helm and waited for the villagers to gather. At last they all seemed to be present and he stood to speak but before he had the chance, the woman started to shout.

"People! Listen to me and heed my words. Twenty days ago in this very place the ChOn claimed the throne by right of combat and we swore fealty to him. He who had the courage to challenge did so and died bravely but futilely. Those who were cowards hid behind the generosity of the King and schemed behind his back and involved their confidantes. They tried to kill the king by lying in ambush and had it not been for the keen eyes of the commander Izaki and the loyalty shown to the ChOn by the former Buq'ue troops, we would have had a murderer and coward as the king. Instead, there are new widows here in the fort. Widows who will be well relieved of the lizards they had for husbands.

Those kneeling before me, you have shown by your actions in the king's absence that you are guilty of treason. The penalty for treason is death. Those who remain at the gate have already paid their penalty and now you will pay yours. I, Karín, Commander of the King's Household Cavalry and personal bodyguard sentence you to death."

She drew the katana and adopted a posture ChOn had taught her. She was placed in front of the first in the line of six men. The katana was almost vertical, held in a two-handed grip with the handle just outside her right armpit. In a slashing downwards arc, she took the head of the soldier cleanly off his shoulders. The body did not move for a full second. Then it started to twitch and finally fell forwards on to the sand. She stood and walked three paces to her left and adopted the same stance. The soldier started to say something and raised his hand in protest and when the katana swept through its arc, his hand and head were severed almost simultaneously.

The third man evacuated his bowels as she squatted in the deep stance before him. The fourth was dispatched in turn. And the fifth.

The last in the line was the ringleader. She had deliberately left him to see what was happening to his men. She wanted to prolong the anticipation.

She stood before him and saw resignation in his eyes. She wiped the blood of his comrades from the terrible blade on to his tunic and sheathed it.

"Let the widows of these men and those who fell at the gate come forward!"

She was looking at him as she shouted and saw his expression change even as the words came from her lips.

"Noooooooo!" he screamed. "Kill me now. Take my head. Do what you will but not this."

Karín smiled at him. It was a sweet smile but it would have frozen a volcano. She leaned closer to him and spoke so only he could hear her.

"Die well, Ronik and when they take hold of your manhood to tear it from your belly, remember the time you stuck it into me against my will before I was even bleeding. I have waited for years for this chance and now vengeance will be mine. And theirs." She turned to the women and resumed her dialogue to them. "If he is still alive when the sun goes down I will give each of you a comb made from the antler of a tlaque. If he dies too soon, you will spend the rest of your days with your heads shaved as a reminder of your lack of skill."

She turned to the rest of the onlookers.

"Let this be a lesson to all those who swear fealty and then betray their oath. Let anybody who does not wish to serve my King, declare himself or herself now. You may leave the fort alive and unharmed but all those who stay to enjoy his protection know that disloyalty is treason and death for you and all those who stand with you. Now! Go or kneel."

The entire village knelt before Ch0n except for the woman. She stood before them all, proud and savage. She turned to Ch0n.

"Look upon your loyal subjects my King. You will be betrayed no more in this place. I have arranged this demonstration for you so you have no doubt as to the capacity of women to engage in battle; for death is to us as life. We bear children and watch some die young. We know how to give life and we know how to take it. This traitor will know the slow way. It serves as a good deterrent to those who would betray you. "

Ch0n was in a state of disbelief at the brutality he had seen from her and would soon see from the others. The ringleader of the ambush was screaming in agony as the twelve widows shredded his clothing and skin with flint and iron blades. Karín was as calm as if she had just ordered the man to be oiled and dressed for a wedding.

The crowd dispersed apart from a few onlookers and some young women keen to learn the art of flaying a living being. Ch0n called to the platoon commander.

"Izaki. You and your men have shown loyalty in the heat of battle. You are appointed the garrison commander with all the rights that accompany the position, including direct access to me. You will move into the quarters near the gate house and assume training of the army. Your Cabots are promoted to platoon commanders and your soldiers are to be rewarded with suitable posts in the army. Fetch me all the elders of the village. I would set up a village council in the form of the one we have at the castle. We need to find two women to perform the tasks that Sonja and Kelda are performing there."

"Thank you Lord Ch0n. I will serve you well as Garrison Commander. My men are loyal to me and to you. We will have no more problems here but the Buq'ue have many villages like the Arw'an had. We will need to bring them all under your guidance. Many of them will not know the old king is dead and many will not know we are changing direction. We have outposts almost to the Matáng lands and they are isolated and vulnerable."

"Izaki. If we are to defeat the Matáng and prosper into the future, we need to concentrate our forces in a smaller number of places. They will raid our outposts for slaves and stock whenever they feel like it. They have not tried to conquer us because they can not survive with their forces stretched across the entire land mass. Neither can we. Before we can do that we need to have a system of mobile defences and they will take too long. We will pull back the distant villages to stretch the Matáng supply lines and make it more difficult for them to raid with small parties. They can do it at the moment because they take slaves and goats and provisions for the return trip and leave enough Buq'ue to rebuild their village until the next raid. If we withdraw to a more central position with more forces, it will create two problems for the Matáng. They will arrive at first and there will be no village to plunder. They will have to return with short rations and no slaves or stock. If they want to replenish their stock of either, they will have to advance with a larger force with its larger supply train and they will not know where they are looking. It will be a slow process and costly because we will soon have cavalry to pick off their patrols and harass their supplies so they will have a bigger problem than before. In the end we will be provoking an all-out war with an invading force on ground of our own choosing or they will have to leave us alone forever. Either way we will win because we have the advantage of being ready and with short supply lines. We can also move our force faster than they can using our communications system and the tlaque. Until they have cavalry, we will cut them to shreds. Set up your firm base here. It is close enough to the castle to provide support one for the other. The wooden walls need to be doubled in height and thickness. It would be better to have a hill to provide stone but we will have to work with what we have. The river is a natural barrier on one side. We will use it to build a moat of water around two sides and then there will be only one land approach. The moat on the downriver side will also provide water for baths. We will speak more of these plans with the elders. Go now and promote your Cabots. Bury the bodies of the dead and put their heads on sticks at the gate for seven days but before you go I will tell you face to face that I doubted you when we approached the gate and you proved yourself loyal. For that you have your head and my trust."

"I saw it, My Lord. I saw how you positioned the tlaque behind and to one side outside spear-throwing range. I have been a soldier for a long time and I can see these things. Because of that I am still alive. It pleases me to know you are a tactical and strategic thinker for I respect not a leader who is all bluff and no knowledge. We will make a formidable team, you and I. The fact you revealed to me that which I already knew tells me more about you than you may realize. I have sworn loyalty to you and now I have fought against my own villagers to prove that my word is good. Know that henceforth you may fight with your back to me and it will be safe." He nodded to Ch0n, less stiffly than previously and turned on his heel. He paused and turned again to face Ch0n.

"Oh! I almost forgot. I note you pay the woman no heed. She has decided she will have no other but you. She would make a good match for you. I have known her since we were children. She has not had an easy life. Ronik, whom you hear screaming yonder, took her by force when she was still a girl. She was the old king's favourite and she was loyal to him but I see in her eyes that you are more to her than he was. I know not your ways and so I am telling you this from one man to another in case you do not see the signs. She would gladly give her life in your defence as your bodyguard but she hungers to give you her life as a woman."

Ch0n nodded and Izaki left.

"Why would she want to give me her life as a woman?" thought Ch0n aloud. "She has all she needs. She is safe and secure. She has power and is able to think freely. Maybe she would like a baby at some stage and she would have me service her. I will ask her if that is what she seeks but after she has the cavalry organized.   Until then she will have to concentrate on being the commander.   I have seen the pregnant women and those with young children. They are useless at everything else but being a mother and that is of no use to me with Karín."

The meeting with the elders was a raucous event. First, they were not happy with the summary executions ordered by someone who didn't have the authority and carried out by someone who didn't allow any time for explanations or appeals. Karín suggested they were defying the authority of Ch0n and as such were guilty of treason themselves, which made them shift uncomfortably in their seats. Ch0n had to calm everybody down by conceding that things may have seemed hasty and brutal but that had the perpetrators been successful, the elders my well have been replaced by some sort of coup because they were sworn to Ch0n. He explained the concept of an eye for an eye and a tooth for a tooth and how foul attempted murder by ambush should indeed be punished by death. And that it would be in future as well. A system of justice for all would follow but in the meantime, the garrison commander would have judicial power over all including the elders and that he in turn would answer directly to Ch0n.

The next argument concerned the promotion of women to the elders' council. Ch0n explained that the elders' council was now the King's council and that women would be invited to attend so they could arrange those things that women were better at than men. Such as town planning and logistics. The elders huffed at this statement until Ch0n allocated one of them the responsibility for locating and digging the community latrine and baths, and laying out the space within the fort so the women from the outposts could set up their families.

"And which among you is the expert on cooking and laundry?" he added. "And health issues and foraging. And teaching children? Women do these things and get no recognition of their responsibility. This woman is my personal bodyguard and Commander of my entire Household Cavalry, which as we speak has thirty-three mounted Lancers, all women."

At this news there was an audible intake of breath from the elders.

"To you elders I allocate the most important task of all. That is this. I need you to go to all the outposts and tell the villagers there to move their village. They need to be moved to a suitable place no more than five days easy walk from here. Those villagers who want to come here to the fort may do so but if the numbers who remain do not constitute a viable village, you are to instruct them to move the entire village here. It will be hard work but if we do not succeed, we will not be concentrated enough to fight off the Matáng when they come.

Before you go, I want you all to go to the Arw'an castle. What is a castle, I see you wondering? Well you will see. Some soldiers from Izaki's former platoon will accompany you to show you the way. The two women council members will go as well. You will leave tomorrow before mid-day. I will follow on the tlaque and will overtake you on the trail. After you see how we are organizing the castle you will return here with the two women, leave them to their work and will disperse to the Buq'ue outposts with your message and convince them that there is no other way to protect themselves in the near future. The details of who goes where you can work out for yourselves. Now how are we going to select the two women for the council?"

"I have one in mind, my King," announced Karín. "She is at this moment flaying the soldier, Ronik. She is the widow of one who was killed at the gate. I know her well. She is very similar to Sonja. Her name is Eloi. What say the elders of her?"

There was much murmuring and nodding of heads and the elders agreed that she would be a good choice. They then came up with a second name, Froncy. Ch0n looked at Karín, who nodded imperceptibly.

"OK," he said. "It is done. Fetch them to the council."

Karín looked at the others present.

"'Okay' is a word in the tongue of the king. It means many things, one of which is 'all right'." She looked at Ch0n. "My Lord, King, Eloi will be busy until sunset with Ronik. Can it not wait until then?"

"I think the others can manage to flay Ronik with one woman less," he replied. "As it is, she will have to clean herself up before she can come to the meeting. Izaki, have one of your men fetch them both if you would."

Froncy arrived first and some short while later, Eloi, who had a wild look still in her eyes. Ch0n went through the thought process that had led them to their new positions of prestige and power and informed them that in his absence, they would answer to Izaki. They both nodded seriously at him and Eloi gave Karín a look of gratitude.

"And when we return from the outposts, what tasks will we perform in the fort, my King?" asked one of the elders.

"Why, you will do what you have always done," replied Ch0n.

"But my King, we didn't really do anything."

"And you will continue just that. It is a very important part of a king's court to have people who are deep thinkers and law makers and advisers. Project managers, I will call them. They don't get their hands dirty because they are too important for that. Instead they wait for the king to allocate them a task and they resolve it. Like the outposts. Like the judicial system. Like errr, holiday planning. As time passes you will prove your worth to me and the fort.

Izaki, are you comfortable that you know your role here? That you are my commander in absence and that all decisions will fall to you? That I will be happy for you to make any decisions that do not involve policy. Such as, changing the position of the moat once it has been planned and is in motion. If you are in doubt, do not start any big projects. Do you understand? Do you all understand the order of command here? Let me spell it out one more time. After the King, is Izaki, who controls the members of the council. Those council members may not change anything without his approval and he may not change policy without my approval. The woman, Karín, has no executive function on the council and answers only to me and none of you will answer to her unless it is a direct message from me to her to you."

There was a chorus of nodding and mumbled agreement.

"Where are the baths?" asked Ch0n. "I need to clean myself and shave. I haven't done either for three days."

"The women usually bathe in the river when they need it," spoke Eloi. "I assume from your orders for a public bath with hot water, things will change and the men will also bathe?"

"They will. Firstly we will place and start building the baths tomorrow. Izaki knows what they need to have. They should be finished before you return and by then Sonja will have shown you the way I want things to happen, from the shaving of heads to the washing of clothing and bedding. If there are no baths, I would bathe in my quarters. Froncy, please organize hot water. That is in your area of responsibility. Administration and logistics."

Chapter Eighteen: The Revelation

Ch0n sat quietly on a stool while Karín shaved his head and face. She was quite the expert at it already after just a few attempts. He was thinking about the problems associated with trying to run a tight kingdom with various Buq'ue outposts as well as the castle. It must have been fairly reasonable for the Romans to have done it all across Europe for four hundred years but in the end that too collapsed as the outposts became more and more autonomous and local rulers kept more and more of the power.

"How can I make sure the two tribes are truly united and not just paying lip service to my rule when I am not here or there?" he asked the woman. "You are of their culture and I am not. I have never lived outside a flying vessel in my entire life and these distances are vast if we have to travel on foot or even by tlaque. I know the Buq'ue and Arw'an were once a single tribe until some were splintered off from the main group because they were tired of living in goat-skin shelters and travelling on every few moons but there has passed so much since then that they are going to be hard to unite and rule as one tribe. One people. It worries me that we may put plans in place to protect us against the regular raids by the Matáng only to find that in the end we will not defend ourselves with one common purpose."

Karín pulled the blade across his cheek as she answered him.

"For generations the Arw'an have lived the nomad life. All their efforts were taken in finding grass for their scrawny goats. They had to move and move but even when they found a good place they had to leave again for they knew that the Buq'ue would eventually find them and attack them. The Buq'ue on the other hand have lived an easier life in villages like this one with

243

permanent water and fortifications for we are at the frontier of the Matáng lands and they have hunted us as we have hunted the Arw'an. When the Matáng stole our women and goats, we raided the Arw'an to get them back. There are many women here who were taken from an Arw'an village and brought here to be the wives of men who had lost wives to the Matáng. The same on the outposts. They came here and we raided the various Arw'an villages and divided up the spoils. The secret lies partly in your plan of centralizing the outposts so the Matáng will not be able to reach them without a supply train and partly in a peaceful interchange of people and trade. Inter-mating and trade, including an exchange of leaders. What would we achieve here in the Buq'ue fort if we had someone from the Arw'an system controlling part of their fort and someone from here over there? It would be hard because families would have to be uprooted and come to live away from their extended family but they were being forced to do that anyway in some cases when they were abducted. I, myself have moved to the castle for there lies my duty. It wasn't so hard for me as I have no man and no children. Perhaps that is the secret. Move single men and women if they have a role to play. And the best way to do that is with the Army, is it not? That way you have men from both tribes defending all the villages and forts as well as the castle. My cavalry troop from the castle could easily be stationed here. They are all young women, fit and strong who could just as easily live in the garrison here while the women from here could move to the castle initially for training and then as a member of the castle troop. It would lead to inter-mating and long term loyalties borne from a truly blended tribe. We could set up a cavalry school at the castle and a military training school here. It would lead to a floating population between the two tribes and your kingdom would be truly united under one tribe."

She finished his shave with a flourish.

"There. I have taken away your hair and your problems at the same time."

"You are right of course. It doesn't solve the problems of distance but they are going to be reduced when we call in the outposts and one day when every village will have a few mounted messengers, that distance will seem a lot shorter. What was that scream?"

"The sun is setting, my Ch0n. The women have just torn the living manhood from Ronik. He will bleed to death in minutes and be glad of it. Now you know your household cavalry can kill without mercy from the backs of the tlaques where their physical weakness is no impediment to their skills as Lancers."

"OK, so let us think this through while I bathe." He stripped naked and stepped into a terracotta urn without thinking and into the warm water. Karín watched his every move hungrily as he lowered himself into the water and started to wash himself.

"We will need to put a priority here on the stables using the same design as the one Boro used at the castle. The priority over there will be the training of the Lancers to a standard such that next time we come to the fort we will come with a mounted escort to impress the locals and they will stay here under command of the garrison in your absence. You will need to appoint a troop commander of course. I suggest a skills competition to determine that."

Ch0n kept talking and planning the two garrisons while Karín listened. She hung on every word as though he were reading from the holy book itself and when he finished, she spoke again at length.

"It will be as you say, my King, Ch0n. Many of the things you have ordered have already started to be put in place, such as appointing a troop leader and the moving of the troop here to the fort. The women all knew they may be uprooted from the

castle and brought here to keep the peace if needed. I have already had the young women here talking of the great adventure that I have in store for them at the castle. You see, my Ch0n, I am not only your bodyguard and personal shaver, I am also your fortune teller and future planner. I have had this dream much longer than you. I had not the means to implement it until you gave me command of your cavalry and then it became obvious to me how we would do it. I was simply waiting for the moment when you would give me licence to speak my mind. And I knew you would for you are a hard man but a fair one and give everybody the chance to prove his worth. Even one as humble as Froncy. I knew my turn would come. You have far too much going on to think of everything and you are the first to know that. You will be a great king of the Buq'ue and Arw'an for you were a great man before you were ever a king."

"You never cease but to surprise me, woman. You have been leading me to this point for some time I suspect. I can but wonder what other surprises you have in store for me as time passes."

"I can promise you, My Lord, Ch0n that you have no idea what I have in store for you. Now are you going to sit in that bath all night? I can hear the sounds of a celebration out in the square. Goodness knows what they are celebrating but we will soon discover."

She watched Ch0n emerge from the water and handed him a clean tunic and undergarment. She watched him dress and she watched him buckle on his weapon belt and sandals. It was as informal as he ever got. She ushered him to the door and watched him bend down and leave.

Her mind was talking to her. *"I will make a perfect bodyguard for you my Ch0n for I can not take my eyes off you."*

They walked to the square where the grizzly corpse of Ronik was still on display. The woman signalled for it to be removed and then asked the reason for the merriment.

"The women Eloi and Froncy are celebrating the freedom of women under the Ch0n. They are saying he has elevated women to the King's Troop council and so we women are going to celebrate. When have we needed a reason and when have we had a better one?"

"Look at what you have done, Lord, Ch0n," said Karín proudly. *"This is your work. You have instantly won the women to your side, no matter what the elders or their men may think. They have worked all their lives for their men and had precious little thanks for it. Some will relish the chance to be more independent. Look over there. There is my cavalry troop waiting to be recruited. Would you help or would you have me do it alone?"*

"I would see how you do it. They are already prepared yet I did not see you tell anybody of your plans."

"My Lord, you look at me but you do not see me. Furthermore, I am not always in your sight tho' you are always in mine, even if we are apart. I told Izaki of your plans to have a troop here before we left the castle. His men have been busy while the council was in session. They have pre-selected the fastest, strongest and ablest of the single young women. Izaki told them to select only those they would take as mates if they were offered. Men are so predictable. They added 'the prettiest' to my list but I made them remove it for pretty women do not always make the best mates for a man. You are lucky. Your mate will be the prettiest of all. For I have seen her and she is both pretty and able. Not all are so lucky."

"And is she in this group you will choose from?"

"The woman you take as a mate, should you accept her, is indeed a member of your household Cavalry my King. I would have it no other way for these are the pick of the Arw'an and Buq'ue women and you deserve only the best of them. She already has eyes for you."

"And do I know this woman?"

"You know her but not as you will know her, and once knowing her you will have no other before her."

She looked at the group of women they had approached.

"Look upon your King. He is looking for fifty among you who would serve him as soldiers who ride the tlaque into battle. You will have to walk five days to the Arw'an camp and undergo several moons of fierce training after which time I will select thirty three of you to stay at the Arw'an village in the Kings Troop as will be named the resident troop. The remainder will stay as squires and trainers in the school of cavalry as we will call the place where we teach those who will follow, for there will be more troops and more recruits needed to fill the places that come available as we are moved, get with child or die in battle. You know me. Many of you have grown up knowing me as the King's favourite. Well I tell you this. I am the Commander of the Household Cavalry and answer only to the King. All who would join me must know in their hearts that they would follow the king to their death. Look upon him. Would you follow him into battle tho' it cost you your life?"

A ripple of laughter started at the back of the group and found the ears of the woman and Ch0n. Karín also laughed, even though she had not heard the comment that started it all.

"Your skills with the sword are well known to us all, Malek. But this sword is destined have one sheath only. More's the pity for most of you who would covet it. Now, who wishes to continue the selection process? We need to hasten for I hear the party

starting and we women should not be absent for a party in our own honour. It is simple. The first fifty of you to run to the gate and return will be selected. There is no fixed route and there are no rules to the race. Out and back to this circle. Now. GO!"

ChOn saw the logic of Karín's selection process. The fastest would have an advantage in a straight line race but this was an obstacle race and some of the obstacles were their competitors. Those towards the rear of the group would have to fight to stay in contention.

"So what were they laughing about back then?" he asked.

"She would follow you to hell but lead you to heaven Malek whispered, I imagine. It was a compliment to you as her King but said in a way to create levity."

"And what was all that about swords and sheaths?"

"I think they all want a katana like the one I have. It is longer and more majestic than the swords they have seen but I told them there was only one and it was mine."

"Oh… But I have four more just like yours. Perhaps they will be able to earn one, one day."

"I think it best that you keep those for the men, my King. My sword is my sword. I would keep it just for myself. The others do not have the height to manage a longer sword than they are used to. It may affect their ability to handle it easily."

"Yes. Perhaps that is the case. Anyway, they will be Lancers and will have no need for swords in battle. Perhaps they didn't realize that."

"Surely not, my ChOn." And then to herself, she thought, *"How childlike you are in the ways of men and women, my ChOn. I can not believe you know so little but that will change and if you*

think the one you call 'Shiew' enjoys her work, you are in for a big surprise when you sheath your own sword for the first time."

They waited for a few minutes and the first of the women started to come into view. Karín counted them into the circle as they arrived; after forty, they started to appear bloodied and scratched and one was sporting a swollen eye. She counted the fiftieth and then a further ten.

"You who are on this side of the line will march to the Arw'an camp with us tomorrow to join us in the training school. You ten will also march with us but at the end of the training you will return here to join the troop which will already be resident here. You will assist them as grooms and reinforcements. There is no shame in this thing. It is just that you finished outside the fifty. The rest of you, thank you for coming. The women Eloi and Froncy will need able men and women such as you in their teams and their work is no less important, just a little less exciting. Now go and enjoy the party but remember that you have a five day walk in front of you on the morrow."

"My King, we will need an escort for so many women and the elders. Might Izaki send a platoon back with them?"

"It is arranged, my fair commander, for you are not the only one who can think ahead. That girl who finished first in the selection race is quite tall. Perhaps she could handle a katana as ably as you."

"That is the woman Malek who made the comment and she is indeed accomplished with the short sword we have here but we need to train her as you say, in the lance."

The party went on all night and there was much laughing and crying in the village as families celebrated the success of their daughters and sisters. ChOn stayed as long as was royally polite and left them to their festivities, which, as soon as he left took on a more raucous and carnal atmosphere. Karín accompanied him to his chambers and sat at the entrance as was her custom.

"My Ch0n, one thing has puzzled me ever since you told me you had never seen a woman. How is it that you were born if there were no women in your world? This is beyond my understanding. Are not babies born to females everywhere? In your world do the males somehow give birth?"

"Before I tell you this, you will have to free your mind of all things you know and hold to be true. You must believe everything I tell you for it is the truth as I know it. I will tell you the story of my life. I will leave nothing out. It will take some time." He moved a cushion close to where she was sitting and started.

"In my world, images of which you have seen, we are many. More than the birds in the sky and more than all the stars you can see. We were so many we had to look somewhere else for spaces to colonize and to garner treasures from their earth for our use. The technology came available about seven lifetimes ago, we would say, four hundred years, when a means was discovered that would give us infinite energy without heat. It had been fabled that hundreds of years before, two men had discovered this and called it 'cold fusion' but it was a hoax. A lie. But suddenly those who had been seeking it came upon its secret. I will give you its name just so it has one if I need to talk about it again. It is called, 'false fusion'. Do not worry how it works for I can not tell you.

Anyway, with this false fusion to fuel flying ships and the knowledge of the stars, the universe and things we called 'worms', we discovered that we could send out missions for fifty to a hundred years or more to gather information and send it back by radio transmission. Now fifty years is the length of a person's useful life, they estimated. Each one of those missions had a whole team on board to gather information and to provide the safety of the ship because if the ship were to be captured, or the information lost, the entire mission of more than fifty years would have been in vain. Most of that time, the humans, like me, were asleep in metal cocoons, with our blood cold and our sustenance given internally. Our bodily waste was collected in tubes and processed and used to fertilize small nurseries where plants could be grown, harvested and fed back to us in liquid form or compressed into food capsules for the times we were awake. We were attended to by metal slaves, droids. They were machines. Complicated like the pulser but in the form of humans almost. They didn't need to sleep for they were machines. Every time the ship entered a solar system, or sun system and 'saw' a planet that was suitable, we were woken up and spent days awake, training for our roles. I was a soldier in a group of soldiers designed to go first to the new world and make it safe for the people who were collectors of information. We had a small ship that could come and go to the main ship. We used to have two but one became unusable so we took parts from it to keep the second going. On this trip to your world, the second ship crashed and only I survived. There were five more exactly like me. Almost anyway, to look at. I found myself here alone with no way of returning to my ship. They sent me some tubes of supplies and returned to earth, my world because they had no reason to stay in space with no landing ship. They told me to gather as much information about the world and log it here on this tablet for when they return. They should take them at least seven earth years. Eight or nine of our years. That is the time it takes a child to become independent here.

Now. Every time we were woken up, there would be those who didn't awake because they had died instead of sleeping. But they had to be replaced and that is where I came in and others like me. From earth they had brought hundreds of frozen embryos taken from especially bred people. Some were soldiers, others were not. The soldiers were all big, like me and the others were all from the most intelligent people on earth but short in stature because they had to work inside the ship most of the time and space was important. When they needed a new soldier, they took a number of frozen embryos and thawed them. These embryos were never sent to sleep like the rest of us because they had to grow after they were born. So there was a small nursery tended by humans and droids to look after babies and children and finally teenagers. The entire time they were awake they wore things in their ears that fed them information they would need to learn as adults. I remember growing up always knowing I would be a soldier and watching endless movies of weapons systems, combat techniques and so on. And then suddenly I was grown up and they put me in a tube and put me to sleep with a minitron connected to my head to teach my sleeping body. I have been woken up five times since then and have been to four worlds where our scientists gathered the information they needed. On two of those worlds we had to deploy the second squad because we were fighting against sapients who saw us as the invaders we were. I managed to escape alive but some didn't and so their places were taken by younger soldiers who were replaced by the teenagers who were replaced by the children who were replaced by clones, as we are called. My name, Ch0n is not really a name. It is a serial number. It means, Clone: Marque H: Serial ten: Batch N. I was lucky to have a serial that could be turned in to a name."

"So you have truly never seen a woman in all your life until you came to this place?"

"No. I do know, though, that on earth, men and women mate and have babies. I looked up the image on the minitron and saw that they mate like the beasts when they want offspring. I know the mechanics of how it works and so I suppose if I one day wish to have an offspring I shall mate with a woman who wishes one at the same time. Izaki thinks you and I would have suitable offspring because we are matched in size but I have no need of an offspring at this time and I need you to command the cavalry so even if I did want one, it is not timely for you to get with child. I have seen the village women with their bellies swollen. They are good for nothing until their offspring have started walking or can be carried in the pouches."

"And your friends who were killed with you? Where do they lie?"

"Friends? I have no friends. They were my companions. They woke up or died. They went to a planet and fought and lived or died. This time they all died. It might just as easily have been me with one of the others sitting here. They are buried in a place I have yet to show you."

"So you have no feelings for anyone?'

"Feelings? Describe them to me and I will tell you."

"It is when you care for something or someone because it matters to you what happens to them. It is something you feel in your heart."

"Yes, if that is what they are, yes, I have them. I care for the wolf and he for me. If he were to die I would miss his presence. There is something comforting about having him sit by my side so I can rub his ears. Yes, I have feelings for him. And I have feelings for you. If you were to leave I would miss your presence as well. You have been kind and loyal and you make me smile when I feel a little grumpy. It would not be easy to find someone as able as you and one with whom I can speak so openly, easily and comfortably. I like the way your hands feel on my face when you shave my beard. You are more tender than the woman Sonja, although she was also quite good at it. I prefer you to do it even though you have cut me more times than she."

"Those are feelings, my Ch0n. They go deeper than that, though when you let someone close to you. You like my hands on you because you allow me to put them on you. You like my presence because you allow me into your personal space and you like to talk to me because I like to talk to you." She swallowed hard before continuing. *"And Izaki was right. We would have good offspring because we are the same size. And because we are so much together and I would like to have a baby with you in the way of the beasts when you are ready for it. I live to serve you and I have been ready for you to summon me but you never do. I did not understand why because it is foreign to me but I do not worry because you have summoned no other either, although Sonja wold have willingly gone with you. And the entire Household Cavalry of two villages, and at the head of them all its commander and then probably Malek. I think you will come to understand these things called 'feelings' as you are more exposed to people whom you trust. They will become your friends and come to mean much more to you than just your squire or your garrison commander or your bodyguard. Now I know your story better, tho' I have no understanding of most of it, I will tell you something you should know."*

"There is a thing between a man and a woman that binds them closer than the fear of death. It is called 'ébon'. The feeling of ébon a man has for his woman and a woman for her man makes them want to be together forever in life and in death. If you look around the village you will see that there are men and women together all the time. They live together and feast together and do everything together because they hate to be separated. Like the wolf is with you. Even now he is asleep less than an arm's length from you as he always is. At night they sleep together and they couple together. They do not couple to have offspring, although offspring sometimes result from the coupling. We call it 'íjon' where the woman is under the man or rides him from above. It is a word not used in polite company because of what it implies but it is the word we use.

They engage in íjon for the pleasure of it. I tell you this because you do not seem to know that a man and a woman can engage in íjon without wanting a baby. Usually a woman such as I would never tell a man she wishes to lie down with him for the purpose of íjon but if I do not tell you, you may never know. I know your manhood is similar to those of the men I have known, only much stronger in size but that matters not. I am built for you. I was made for you because I am the only one in the village who could accommodate your dewen without pain. Well, maybe Malek, for as you noted, she is taller than the rest. But I would kill her first."

"So this thing between men and women they do for enjoyment?"

"I can not believe you do not know this. It has been hidden from you all your life by the minitron. Did you never feel your dewen harden? Is it not a natural thing? I noted that it did not when you checked to make sure I had shaved the hair on my ibuw. I thought you were playing with me in preparation for íjon and then it surprised me for normally the sight of a woman's ibuw would make a man's dewen harden at once."

"I do not recall it ever happening. Perhaps it is something that is not natural for us. I will look it up on the minitron when we get back. I do know that it happens for the purpose of making offspring during the mating procedure."

"There is an easier way to find out, Ch0n, if you would allow me. I can see if your dewen will harden under my touch. I know not much about these things but if your mind has never known a woman and your body has never known a woman, perhaps the sight of a woman is not enough to stimulate your brain into telling your dewen that an ibuw is waiting to receive it. But first I will use the water from your bath to clean myself. I have not bathed for three days either and while that would once not have worried me, I like the feeling of being clean, especially

if we are going to try the ijon. But I have a favour to ask. Just as I have shaved you, I would have you clean me. I want to feel your hands on me. Perhaps it will kindle your fires."

Ch0n watched the woman shuck her tunic. She was naked underneath in the way of her people. She stepped over the terracotta edge and lowered herself into the now-tepid water. She handed Ch0n a cloth and the soap and said nothing. Ch0n started at the top of her head and worked down her back. She was a pale yellow-orange, like everything else on this planet. Paler than the other women. She was as smooth as glass except for where the bones of her spine could be felt. Her arms were long and supple, but strong. Ch0n was an expert on muscles and had studied them at length as part of his training. Bones, too. He knew where the weak point of every bone could be found with the tonfa. As he washed her, he mentally noted them all.

Pressure point behind earlobe, clavicle, downward breaking stroke, shoulder, outside twist to dislocate, upper arm, hard to break but pressure point behind the bicep, elbow, outside sweep with stabilizing hand to enable a break or dislocation, wrist, thumb under palms and fingers behind to disable. Fingers, break, spread, handlebar grip. Almost endless possibilities.

Then he started on the face. "Eyes, sweep or poke, Nose, upwards strike with the heel of the hand, mouth and jaw, too many to mention, throat, chop, squeeze or poke. Thorax, punch, breasts, soft and slippery. Hard buttons on the end. Could be gripped and twisted. Belly, punch, knee, groin, nothing there but a slit. Middle finger inside and pull upwards, thigh, hard to break but bruises easily from an outside knee."

His thought process was broken by the woman's voice.

"My Lord, I can feel your hands all over me but they are not cleaning me. They are probing my weak points. You must stop thinking like a soldier for even a short time if you are to do this. Now. A few seconds ago you were about to rip my ibuw upwards with your middle finger and cause me a grievous wound. If you were to return to that place and explore it a little you will find it is like nothing you have ever felt before."

Ch0n leaned over her and stiffened.

"Where did this urn come from? This one you are sitting in! It is made from clay. I have not seen any clay since I arrived here and I have been searching for it everywhere. Oh, my! This is a find for the age. Clay. Quick! Summon the elders! I must know the source of this clay."

"But My Lord, we were about to…. Oh! Never mind you big baby. I have waited such a time, I can wait a few more hours."

She dressed and flew out of the tent. Ch0n was excited. He touched the urn and banged it with his knuckles. Clay. Bricks. Tiles. Ovens. Oh Goodness. Ovens for food and firing bricks and forging metal. Oh clay! In his excitement he failed to notice that he was half erect. Many tens of thousands of miles away, the comatose forms of his former colleagues had recently received the injections of hormones that would prevent such a thing from happening to them.

The elders were peeved at being roused at the late hour, even by the king. They arrived grumpy and not as co-operative as they may have been. Questions about the urn were deflected with blank looks and grumbled talk of sleep and warm women. Ch0n soon grew tired of it.

"Very well. I see we shall have to refresh your memories and animate you a little more. If you wish to remain on the king's council, raise your hand quickly now. If not, you are relieved.

You may go back to your house now and report tomorrow morning to the woman Eloi for latrine digging duties."

He gave them two seconds to respond.

"Too slow. Get out all of you. I will have a new council before morning. You have hereby lost all your rank and privileges. You have the option of remaining in the fort as Eloi's diggers and living with the rest of the labourers or being exiled to the plains like the beggars. If I want men and women of action on the council, I expect them to be available to me day and night. Now get out."

They looked at each other uncertainly. Ch0n unsheathed Shiew and they heard the faint hum of the blade as it cleared the brass opening.

"Who will be first to openly disobey me? Is it you? Has there not been enough killing done here of late? Would you add your head to those on sticks at the gate? I gave you every opportunity to be important members of the council based on your previous positions but as I suspected, you are lazy parasites. You have sucked your living and your wealth from the villagers all these years but now it ends. You will earn your keep like everybody else or you will leave." He looked at the closest and went into the horse stance, the blade almost vertical but before he was in position, the elders started scurrying out of the chamber.

"You can not treat us like this!" shouted the one called Arok. *"You are not one of us and you have no right to be king! You will regret...."* His final word was cut off, literally by Karín's black blade. She stood by the body and glared after the other four elders.

"You dare to play silly elder games with my King? He may have given you the option but I will not. If I find any of you in the fort at sunrise, I will kill him and his woman and his family and burn

259

the bodies and scatter the ashes under the stables for the tlaque to shit on for the rest of future history. You had no idea the plans you might have shared. He included you in his vision but you were too sullen to attend the council late at night. Now you can wander the plains from village to village looking for scraps or you can go to the Matáng and look for mercy among them. I care not. If your women and children wish to stay without you, they may keep their belongings, their houses and their lives. It is not their fault you are leaving."

Karín walked the village and found Izaki, Eloi and Froncy. She asked all three if they could suggest five men for the king's council. They came up with nine names among them, of which two were common to all.

"Fetch those two and none other. Tell them the king awaits them in council if they wish to attend him. This is an invitation. If they choose to attend in the future it will be a summons."

Ch0n sat quietly in his chambers. Karín arrived to find him looking somewhat defeated for the first time. She went to him and stood in front of him.

"Ch0n! Lift up your head and look at me. You did not select those people. They have lived the soft life for years, doing nothing but attending the king and telling him what he wanted to hear. They were soothsayers as well as tribal elders and manipulated the circumstances to their own ends. I knew they would not last long, even though I hoped they would. They are very intelligent men in their way but now they are outcast. By morning none will remain in the fort. Outside await those of your choosing and their chosen two. We had a selection for new councillors in the square and I am hoping the two we selected will accept. If not we will find two who will. But you need to look the part of king and not just be the king. You have the look of a beaten man at the moment and we can ill afford it."

"You would be my adviser as well as my bodyguard and Commander of my Household Cavalry, woman?"

"That and more, my King. I would be everything you ever need but right now that matters not. They are here."

"Bring them in then," said ChOn straightening up his tunic. Izaki entered followed by the women, Eloi and Froncy and then two men ChOn had seen at the earlier executions. They presented themselves with their foreheads on the carpet in front of ChOn's feet.

"So well come, Makin and Cyris. I am glad you want to help rule the kingdom. Let us begin by discussing this find I have been tripping over for weeks without ever seeing. This urn."

The urn, it turned out, had been stolen from an Arw'an village years before. Nobody was sure which one even. It had been stolen because some smart Buq'ue platoon commander saw that it was being used to hold water.

"Then someone among the Arw'an must know where it originated or must have made it. We have to find out because it is made from a type of earth much prized for its ability to be shaped and moulded and then heated up so it holds water and fire alike. Also, it can be used to make bricks, which are stones shaped so they can be stacked high one on top of other and held in place with the powder from the limestone we have everywhere. It is a find of great importance. Now, Makin, what are your skills? We need a designer and builder and we need a chief herder and breeder."

"My Lord, You are looking at the breeder," laughed Karín. *"He has three women in his dwelling and seven fat children and at least one on the way."*

Makin blushed and shrugged.

Gavan Connell

"What is there to say, My Lord?"

"Then you shall be the beast manager and you, Cyris, have you experience building?"

"No, King. I am a member of the former king's family and well educated in the ways of thinking. I could not build but I could design and have others build. And I can also plan. Not just buildings but strategies and far reaching outcomes. That is my strength."

"So you will plan to build me a stable after the manner you will see in the Arw'an camp. Tomorrow after mid day you will join the caravan to the Arw'an village to learn what we are doing there. When you arrive I will already be there to show you all your tasks back here. You, Cyris, will be the strategic planner for the movement of the outposts closer to the fort. I will explain it further in the morning. I thank the members of the council for attending. This will not be the normal way we do things but as we are separating tomorrow, I thought it important."

They filed out. Only Karín remained.

"That was most enlightening. We have to hasten back to the castle and determine the origins of the clay. It is of strategic importance. I was going to stay here a few days more but now I think we will leave when the others do. I will tell Izaki of our plans in the morning but now I have to sleep. I feel as though I haven't slept for days. Goodnight. You have had a busy day too killing off all my treasonous subjects."

"I hope the elders have all left by sunrise. My ChOn or there will be more killing to be done on the morrow. Would you like me to serve you further tonight?"

"No. Thank you. You have done more than enough for one day and you need to sleep if you are going to search the village at sunup."

262

Karín sighed, thinking. *"I need more than sleep, ChOn, after you set my juices running tonight."*

She lay down on a rug in the doorway and the wolf lay at her side. She slept the sleep of the dead until there was a sudden movement of fur beside her, followed by fearful screaming and snarling from ChOn's chambers. She arrived with her sword drawn to find Arok on the floor by a slit in the wall, a dagger in his hand and his throat ripped out. ChOn was standing by, a sai in each hand. The wolf was chewing on something grisly. Blood and spume sprayed from the man's windpipe as he breathed. His eyes were staring wildly and his mouth was screaming soundlessly. Then everything about him went slack. Karín shook her head.

"That's it. I'm sharing your bed from here on. Even five paces away you are not safe."

They dragged the bloody corpse to the entrance and out into the path. They returned to ChOn's bed and he climbed in. The woman followed him and lay down at his back. The adrenalin was rushing through her veins but ChOn was already asleep. She got up and went around to the other side of him and crawled into the crook of his body. He stirred and threw his arm across her. She pushed back into him and lay awake with the feel of him against her whole self. She smiled. The wolf had not challenged her. It was something she had worried about. He went back to the entrance and disappeared outside and the last thing Karín heard before she slept was the crunching of bones.

It was still dark when she woke. ChOn was not in the bed. She heard him moving about and then he was urinating in the pot provided for the purpose. He stumbled back to the bed and lay down. She turned to face him.

"Ch0n, I would show you the way of the íjon. I am awake and my blood is boiling for your touch on me. It is time for you to learn. First I have to know if your dewen will rise when I touch it for if that does not happen, nothing else will be possible. You have said you have never felt it rise, well in a moment we will know if that is going to change. Just lie on your back and close your eyes. I want you to close out all thoughts of clay pots and household cavalry. Just concentrate on my fingers and where they touch you."

She thought back to the last time she had done this. It had been in this very bed when the king had called for her. He was a skilled lover and had taught her the eleven ways to please a man. She started with the most basic. She ran her hands from Ch0n's chest past his belly to where she knew she would find his manhood. Boldly she stroked it, feeling Ch0n jump at the first touch. She smiled to herself when she felt the object of her desire grow in her hand and from then on it was just a matter of things taking their natural course. She moved above him when she had oiled herself and then he was in her and she felt him fill her. She looked down at his face. It was filled with wonder.

"Well, My Lord, at least we know everything is in working order. Now all we need to do is get some practice into you so you can spend some time making us both enjoy it. Meanwhile I have something I would like you to explore for a while. I'll show you how it works and then I will see what sort of a student you have been."

Some time later, Karín bit into a pillow to stifle a scream. Then she spooned up to her lover and slept again. Ch0n, on the other hand was wide awake. His thoughts never strayed from that first delicious moment. He ran it over and over in his mind until he felt himself stirring. For the first time in his life as far as he could remember, he had an erection generated by his thought process. He was as other men.

Chapter Nineteen: Clay

When he woke, the sun was rising and Karín was already dressed and gone. Ch0n was disappointed. He wanted to try this new experience again. He dressed and went outside. He was greeted by the remains of a human which had been partially eaten by an animal. He looked at the wolf. Then he walked to the main gate. In the distance, three men were walking alone with bundles on their backs. The sound of wailing came from close by. He looked for the source of it and found Karín with a woman whose eye was swollen and bleeding.

"This is Jaren, the wife of the elder, Arok who came to visit us last night. She tells me he beat her last night because she refused to go with him. She told him he was a lazy provider and that decent work would be the making of him but if he left, she would not go with him to wander aimlessly. They have no son. Their son, Pek, was the one who challenged your right to be king. She will have to be provided for."

"Your husband, unlike your son was a coward and died a coward's death," said Ch0n. "But that doesn't mean you have to suffer needlessly. Go to the woman Froncy. She will be needing cooks, healers, foragers and teachers. If you can be one of those things you will earn your daily ration along with the rest. If not, go to Eloi. Her work is harder but the rewards are the same. Nobody will go wanting once we have the system functioning here. "

He continued.

"Karín, if you have finished here, I would have you attend to me in my chambers."

"Yes, My Lord. I have finished. I will pass by the other wives' houses on the way to your dwelling. I will take no more time than is necessary."

"Look!" he said to her as soon as she came under the flap. "Look. This is the second time this morning. It has a life of its own. What happens if it does this in a public place?"

"My Lord, what will happen is that every woman in the village will look at me with eyes of green. Then they will avert their eyes because it is not polite to look openly at such things, even if they are of a kingly size. Now. I have a suggestion that I think you should adopt. It is this. When we are alone, we should never waste one of these things. You have missed far too many years for you to ever make up but you need to learn how to use that and to control it. You are suffering from that which affects boys when they first get their hair below. They are forever sprouting a stiff dewen. It cannot be helped in their case but it is not a good look for a King. So let us make it go down in the best way possible. If haste is necessary, this is the best way to relieve the pressure."

She reached back and flipped the skirt of her tunic so it revealed her buttocks. She bent over a stool and opened herself.

"Sheath it here, ChOn, while it is still stiff enough otherwise this will go on all day. Aah yes! That's the way. OK. Now clean yourself up and let's get back to the preparations for our departure."

"Sometimes it's good to be king", thought ChOn as he dropped his tunic and sauntered out of the flap.

They left after the mid-day meal. A platoon of soldiers had accompanied the sixty would-be Lancers and the four council members earlier in the day. Ch0n waved to the villagers as he and Karín trotted away. He was behind Karín again and the tlaque was unhappy to have to maintain the extra length in his stride. They trotted to the familiar water hole and checked it before watering the beasts. Then they made for the cave where they had camped a few times before in their transits. This time, they coupled again before sleep. Ch0n wished he had tried it earlier and Karín wished he were better at it but she knew that would come about.

They arrived late the next day. Jez was waiting for them at the gates. The Lancer barracks were finished and each lancer had her tlaque installed and groomed ready for inspection when Karín arrived. Her own tlaque was waiting in the stall for her, all brushed and shiny. She smiled at Jez by way of thanks. She inspected the stitched up bag and decided it had fully healed after the six extra days that had passed but Ch0n had been expecting that. As soon as she made to saddle it, he appeared as if by magic.

"Four more days. You don't want to ruin everything by being impatient. Just wait those four days. You have enough on your hands planning the arrival of the sixty. We will need to fetch more tlaque. This is happening faster than I had planned. Tomorrow we will select another thirty young males for gelding. Now we know the correct way to do it, it will be faster. We can do each one before the others are awake. The Lancers can help. That way each tlaque will have someone to look after it for a few days.

She put the tlaque back in the stall. She knew he was right. She had been foolish and impatient. The animal was the finest in the herd and she had been going to risk it. She chided herself by reminding herself she had shown more patience with

ChOn although she also admitted to herself it was because the prize was much greater.

ChOn had the villagers assembled as early as he thought was reasonable. He told them about the urn and asked if anybody knew where it had come from. An old woman from the very back of the group called out to him.

"King! My man made that urn and gave it to my father as a gift the day I left home to live with him. He made several of them. It was a skill he never passed on but I know he used to make them and then put them in a pit and light a fire around them. He said it cooked them but I don't believe it. I could never eat one."

"Old woman, where was the place you lived when he was making these things?"

"How should I remember, King? I was a young woman in love and I was more worried about how much dewen I would be fed than where he found the red mud."

The crowd roared and ChOn smiled. Three days ago he would have had absolutely no idea what she was talking about.

"She was from my village," called out the voice of Sonja. *"I have seen the red mud. Our village used to move there from time to time when we needed extra grass for the river floods there and the flats are rich pickings. I can show you where it is. It is closer than the Buq'ue village but not in the same direction. More towards the middle of the sun's path. Maybe a long day's forced walk from here."*

"In that case, take a squad of soldiers with you and leave this afternoon. Jez, take your leave now and organize it. Sonja leave easy sign for me to follow tomorrow with Karín. When we get there I will survey the place and see if we can set up a brick making quarry. Bricks are flattish stones made by hand that can be stacked upon each other to a great height if they are held together by the same mud we used to bind the stones together for the walls. With these bricks we can make cooking vessels big enough to roast a whole tlaque should we desire."

"While I have you all here, in three days we will have sixty more women arriving from the Buq'ue fort. Also four of their council and a platoon of soldiers. We need to make room for them. The women will stay in the stables with the Lancers until we build more stables. The council members will stay where Sonja can find space and the soldiers will live under the shelter that is the start of the single quarters. Eventually, a platoon of soldiers will leave here and the Buq'ue soldiers will stay for a while. Likewise the Cavalry troop. The resident troop will be called the King's Troop and it will be rotated between the Arw'an troop and the Buq'ue troop. When they are needed, they will be combined under the command of Karín. She will remain their commander but each troop will have its own troop commander. It is a good way to train leaders."

Boro took up the rest of Ch0n's day with inspections of the various walls and fortifications. The perimeter wall had grown another layer of stones and was now more than two men high. The castle walls were growing rapidly.

"We will soon need more stones, Lord. I am worried about the tlaque, though. We will need to keep them under control when the explosives are detonated or they will perhaps break down the corral and disappear."

"I think that if we have the Lancers mounted with the rest, they will be able to control their own mounts and stop the others from panicking. When the next group of women arrives they will be able to help. Meanwhile, get to work on the barracks walls. The men will need shelter from the wind as well as the sun. Tell Doni I haven't forgotten him. I will speak with him tomorrow."

Gavan Connell

"He has good news for you, Lord. I will not pre-empt it."

"Then I should meet him right now. Nothing like good news to finish off the day."

He went to look for Doni and found him as usual with the goats. He saw Ch0n approaching and ran to greet him.

"Lord Ch0n. I have good news. The dropping has begun and we have lots of twins. Your plan to separate the mothers with twins will come to fruition because there are so many of them. I almost feel sorry watching those with only one, knowing they are destined for the cooking fire. I have been allowing the villagers to come and see. Many of them were angry at having their stock taken in with the rest of the herd but they are all as excited as I am about the way things are turning out!"

"That I seriously doubt", laughed Ch0n, patting his beast master on the back. "This is a good omen for us. In a year we will have a herd of healthy fat young goats all running and jumping about ready for the fire and the next lot will all have been sired by our stud. How long before the females can have more offspring?"

"Usually we wait until winter before we allow the males in with the females but there is no rule to say we have to do that. Perhaps we could have half a little earlier or a third and then stagger the drop. That way we would always have young ready for the table and we would always have females in milk. We could never control that before because there were too many males but this is easy. Well easier. Just imagine. All those twins. I can't take my eyes off them."

"Well keep up the good work. Good management is important. Did you find out if there is a plant that is used for de-parasiting the villagers? I forgot to ask Kelda."

"She told me there is such a plant. Well it is the root of a plant that is very bitter to the taste and burns the tongue when it is chewed. Usually the women chew for the children and give them the mashed up root. She has been gathering it in big quantities for the last few days. She knows not why but she told me if you had asked for it, you must have your reasons."

"Mash the roots up in a hollow stone with a little water and force the goats to eat as much as a woman would eat. The tlaque will have the same as eight women. It will get rid of the parasites in their gut. They should be taken to one place the next day and made to drop their manure there. All that is to be gathered together and thrown onto the fire for the eggs will pass through and if they contaminate the grass, they will start another cycle. We will do it again in three moons and then after that, every nine moons. Talk to Kelda about the mashing. Kelda's women will need to do the work. Wait until you have enough to do the whole herd at once. The tlaque will be more difficult. Do the stables first. Then the geldings that will be sharing the stables and then the rest if you can manage it in one go. Otherwise do the females and then the young males yet to be gelded. This is becoming a big operation, Doni. Do you need help?"

"Help with the herd is easy to find because once, all the men were herders. When I need more men I just ask Boro or Jez if they can spare me some. So far they always have been able to."

"Good. Now I will retire for it has been a long day riding before we arrived."

"And a long night of riding ahead, My Lord if I'm not mistaken," thought Doni. *"You've softened somehow in the past few days. You smile and laugh more readily. It can only mean one thing. You have tamed the red-head. Or she, you. It is a good match."*

ChOn spent all the next day talking to the Lancers about tactics. He had a flair for it, having been schooled in minor tactics, but the role of Cavalry and how they had been used at their peak by the British in India and Russia and how the magnificent Sikh Lancers of the Raj had looked on parade impressed him the most and that was the era he went to. He used a sheet of glass over a white skin as a board. The entire village came out to see the glass when he produced it for it was the most beautiful thing they had ever seen. Then he took one of his precious markers and showed pincers, forms, charges and flank attacks against an advancing enemy on foot. At the end of each drawing, he had them form up on foot in two files and practise the manoeuvre that would get them into a line-abreast formation. Then he would do it at the run while a platoon of soldiers walked at normal pace. Karín hated all the training. She had planned to just go out and slaughter the enemy in her own manner but after a few hours she saw the logic of disciplined movements and ease of control, coupled with manoeuvrability and frontal or flanking weapons exposure. Or speed. Each formation had its reason for being and she quickly came around to ChOn's classes. By the end of the day she and the others were ready for a break. ChOn proposed they go to the stables and have a competition to see who could saddle their tlaque and have it standing on the line first, ready for action but Karín had had enough training for one day.

"It is women's day at the baths!" she cried. *"I say we all go and cool off. What say you My Lord?"*

ChOn looked at the sun and nodded his assent and fifty one females ran to the bath. ChOn went to the stables and walked along the line of beasts standing patiently in their stalls. Every one was brushed clean and shiny. Every saddle was hanging on a rail at the rear of the stall beside the ladder that led up to the bunk of its rider. Every lance was resting on two pegs across the side of the stall so it could be used by lifting it and rushing forward.　Every water container held water.　The woman had been right.　It was a good move to have women Lancers.　They were cleaner and more methodical and gentler probably with the beasts than men would be.　To test this thought he went to the stalls where the tlaque which were to be used by the stockmen were housed.　But he was wrong.　The same meticulous care had been provided to them as to their military versions.　He suspected the hand of Karín in the mix but then thought it possible that Doni might be overseeing the stockmen's mounts.

He continued to wander around the perimeter until he came to the entrance to the baths.　Because he was a full head taller than the tallest of the other men, he could see over the wall. His gaze was met with the sight of most of the fifty naked women all lazing about in the warm water.　He had not meant to stare but now he had seen, he looked longer than he might have.　One of the women saw him but said nothing.　She smiled at him and turned a little to face him, her knees apart displaying her trimmed ibuw.　He looked away and moved along the wall before glancing back.　The same woman was watching him unashamed.　Then she was lost from view as he walked towards his quarters.　He suddenly became aware of his erection and pondered the reason for it.

"I can understand it if I see Karín naked because she has conditioned me to it but I don't even know that other woman; only by name.　Reny.　She looked at me in a way that told me she would have me do the íjon with her and that alone was enough to stir my loins.　And what if I wanted to do it with her? Was it not allowed?　She is pretty.　I will ask Karín."

Jez was in the stables attending to the tlaques.　He had been a good squire for many months now and had learned to handle the tlaque, as well as Ch0n's array of weapons and communications equipment.

"Jez. The time has come for you to be promoted to 'Knight'. You have served me well but it is time for you to leave my service and become a Knight in your own right. What does that mean? It means you would still be garrison commander but it means you would have your own dwelling with your own tlaque and your own squire to teach. Usually the time a boy was a squire lasted many years until the king promoted him but you have achieved so much in such a short time that I wish to promote you earlier than the norm. As you know, I have five of every one of the weapons I carry, thanks to my dead comrades. I believe you are ready to bear one of them, either the kinetic pistol or the pulse gun. Which would you prefer?"

"My Lord, I am honoured and would accept this honour only if it means I can continue to serve you as a Knight. I am sure you will tell me my role in the castle when the time comes. Would I keep my helm as well for I feel it is important that we communicate?"

"We have but six helms. One is mine, one Karín's, one yours, two for the Ops at this point and one spare. I have a radio that we can bring back here as the base station with the antenna in the turret of the castle. That will extend the range of the helms a lot. The other option is to use the base radio as a repeater tower near the full range of the helms to double the range towards the Buq'ue village. If we do that, we may be able to get communications from here to there. I am sorry, I was talking to myself as much as to you, then.   Yes, you may keep your helm. So what say you, Sir Jez of Arw'an Castle?"

"Is that to be my title? How will people call me in a hurry?"

"They will call you, 'Sir Jez', as will I. We will have a formal ceremony tomorrow. Now go and pick yourself a tlaque. You may pick any that have been gelded apart from the fifty allocated to the Lancers. There are many fine beasts among them. Hurry now for in a couple of days the new recruits will be here and you will get the leftovers to choose from."

"My Lord, I have been looking at one since they first arrived, hoping that one day you might allow me my own. It was not taken by the Lancers even though it was gelded that first day for it is a lot taller than the standard size the commander ordered they get. He is as big as your own. I have been visiting him every day and whispering to him that one day soon I would ask you for him. Now I will go for him and if I may, I will house him here until I have my own lodgings."

"Good. A Knight needs a heavy steed for he has much to carry. Tomorrow I leave to follow Sonja towards the clay beds. In the morning we will find a woollen blanket for your tlaque and make him a sprayform saddle and you will have time to find him some stiff hides for a skirt. Before I go I will have a ceremony recognizing your promotion. While I'm at it I had better come up with something for the four. They have achieved a lot. Everybody has. Maybe it's a day for another feast when we return from the clay beds."

Karín arrived with her clean tunic and they went to the central eating area. Most of the village had already eaten but there was still enough for the late comers, most of whom were members of the Household Cavalry. Ch0n sat with Karín and they ate hungrily because they had both had a busy day of it. Ch0n was not used to talking all day and teaching and while he enjoyed doing it, he preferred to just do his rounds and talk to the key people. He wished it were men's day at the baths because he felt dusty and hot. He thought that after dinner he might go down when there was nobody else anyway. Karín was happily chatting away to her neighbour and Ch0n was taking stock of his Lancers. His eye fell on the woman, Reny seated a few rows in front of him. She was not looking directly at him but every now and then she caught his eye before looking away. She was talking earnestly to one of her colleagues, her hands making the motions of a pincer movement or a flanking movement or something and Ch0n found himself thinking she might be a good troop leader. Of course that decision would fall to Karín but this woman was all excited about what had really been a long day. She was in the middle of a long outflanking movement when she rotated her hips. Ch0n had an involuntary view of her ibuw for the second time that day. The noise around him seemed to dim and he felt a rushing in his ears and his heart began to beat faster. He looked up to find Reny still talking to her companion, still waving her hands about but looking him full in the eyes, knowing he had been staring at her below the table. Then her own eyes dropped and Ch0n felt himself blushing. His tunic was standing up under the table. Nobody close to him could see it but Reny could. She looked up at Ch0n and smiled at him again. Then she made a show of looking down at his raised tunic and feigning surprise. Or fright. She stood up and left the proceedings but not before giving Ch0n a slanted look that was an invitation to follow.

"Don't even think about following her, My Lord. If you do, I will kill her before you reach her."

Karín stood up and left the dining area along the same path Reny had taken. A few seconds later, she emerged from the path all smiles and sat down beside Ch0n again.

"My Lord, I think there has been a slight misunderstanding on the part of Reny. She thought you were making eyes at her but I know that isn't true. I watched her sit so you could see up her tunic and I felt the cloth on the side of your tunic pulling against my leg where I was sitting on it. It was her doing, not yours. You know not the ways of our world nor I yours. I can tell you, though, that you have the right to take as many women as you please and I may protest not. I would not even be shamed before the village because it is normal for a king to take concubines and to be the favoured one among them is

considered an honour. But I am not like other women and if you ever couple with another woman, I will kill her. I just told Reny that and she accepts it with grace. I do not blame her for wanting to lie down with you. Every woman within view would go to your chambers right now if you were to wish it of them. And then I would have to kill the entire Household Cavalry for now I have had you, no other may do so and live. It is a simple rule, My Lord. I will continue to serve you and love you but your concubines will have a short and probably not very satisfying time with you for you have much to learn and I am not going to teach you so they can benefit. Now that the tent you raised has been lowered, it is safe for us to retire. I think I should accompany you to the baths first though because I know you were thinking of going there. Afterwards I will show you something that Reny hasn't even heard of."

Ch0n woke with the sun as usual. Today was another important day in his short time on the planet. He padded from the bed and looked out the door. It was another fine day in a string of fine days. In fact it had not rained since he had arrived. Or had it? He couldn't remember. Today he would make Jez a Knight. That was an important step for the Arw'an because it showed them that effort and service would be rewarded with honours. Jez would be able to wander the plains as a Knight errant should he choose to do so, to perform heroic deeds for his king or stay in the castle and be the Garrison Commander. Whatever decision or combination of decisions he took, Ch0n and he would both need new squires. That was also on his list of 'to do' things. During the ceremony of Knighthood, he would be promoting Doro to the rank of Royal Architect and Doni to Royal Beast Master. Sonja would be the Mayor and Kelda the town Chief Logistician and Administrator. Nothing would change about any of their posts but the official-sounding names would lend importance to their work. He looked back in to the chamber at the woman and almost returned to her but he resisted the thought and went to the stable where Jez had the three tlaques already fed and watered and the stables mucked out. On a bench next to the stall where Jez's tlaque patiently chewed its cud, were two cans of sprayform, a tub of goat fat and a woollen blanket. Ch0n instructed Jez to rub the blanket with fat so the sprayform wouldn't stick to it. They threw the fatty blanket over the beast's back, placed the horn in place and sprayed it directly from the can. The spray mixed with the air and spumed up into a layer of bubbled foam. In seconds it was hard and they sprayed another layer. A strap of webbing was laid across the foam to act as a cinch and a third application and a fourth applied. Another, shorter strap with loops was positioned across the seat to provide adjustable stirrup leathers. Then Ch0n placed a rolled up goatskin at the front and rear of the pad and sprayed another layer. The saddle took shape suddenly with the rolled up hide and the horn and pommel firmly in place. One final coat and they carved out depressions for Jez's backside. A light coat filled in the knife marks and they were finished. The only remaining task was to trim the edges of the saddle to give it a finished shape and look.

"Let it sit for a while and you will be able to take it off the beast and clean the fat from underneath."

They fitted stiff stirrup cups to the leathers and adjusted them. What had taken Ch0n five days to achieve with the first saddle had taken one with Karín's and only a few hours with Jez.

"I'm getting better at this. I want you to ride mine to the ceremony with your full battle rig, including the helm. Nobody has ever seen you in it. They will be impressed, trust me. When you have your own lodgings and stable you will probably have your pick of the women. I have it on good authority that Reny is willing. And she will probably be commander of the King's Troop unless Karín lets jealousy get in the way of her decision making. She would be a good match for you. But that is none of my business.

Now there is one other thing I would like you to have. They are few. I have one, Karín has one and you will have one. Three remain. Fetch me a katana and your pulse gun from the weapon store."

Jez returned in minutes with the two items. Ch0n attached the holster with its built-in power source to Jez's pistol belt.

"Put on your armour."

He took the katana and attached the scabbard to the ties on the back of the sprayform armour so the handle was over Jez's right shoulder.

"This will set you apart from all other swordsmen. The classes we have done with the bamboo swords were to both keep me in practice and to teach you and Karín the way of the katana. You have seen her use it to execute men with a single clean and smooth arc. As I have said to you before, it is not an ax. It is an instrument of death. When we have the clay ovens we will be able to make more like this but not as fine for we lack the technology. I would train a platoon of assassins that wear black wool robes and masks that carry a version of this sword and they will be yours to command but first we need the clay. Then the oven. Then the iron and the forge. But that day will come. This is your day. Thank you for your loyal service, Jez. Find me one such as you before tomorrow morning so I can start his training. Now saddle the beast for it will soon be time for the gathering."

Karín was waiting for him in his chambers. She nuzzled his face when he entered.

"My Lord, you are getting better at the íjuw and I missed you this morning. But now I have to shave you quickly before the gathering. Hurry to the baths for we have little time."

Gavan Connell

The castle residents were gathered in the square when ChOn made his entrance to applause. He was dressed simply in a tunic and kamarband and sandals with no head covering. In his hand he carried Shiew in her scabbard.

"I call the elder Boro to come forward." Boro had no idea he was going to be honoured and came forward looking nervously at the sword.

"Boro of the Arw'an, I recognise you in front of your people. In gratitude for your work in designing and building the fortifications to this point, I promote you to the position of Royal Architect of the castle of the Arw'an!"

A great cheer went up, even though nobody, including Boro, knew what an architect was. And to ChOn that was half the point; the mystery of the appointment.

"This honour I bestow on you as an individual but in recognition of all the hard moons of work your men and women have put in to get to where we are now. So to you all, when you look at the Royal Architect, you may say, 'I helped him to gain that position and I am proud of my work'!"

Another cheer went up and ChOn motioned for Boro to stand beside him.

"Doni of the Arw'an, come forward! Doni of the Arw'an, I recognise you in front of your people. In gratitude for your work in the management of the herds of the Arw'an, I promote you to the position of Royal Master of Livestock of the Castle of Arw'an!"

Another cheer.

"This honour I bestow on you as an individual but in recognition of all the hard moons of work your men and women have put in to get to where we are now. So to you all, when you look at the

Royal Master of Livestock, you may say, 'I helped him to gain that position and I am proud of my work'!"

Another loud cheer. A raucous cheer.

"Kelda of the Arw'an come forward. Kelda of the Arw'an, I recognise you in front of your people. In gratitude for your work in designing and implementing the cooking, teaching and nursing facilities within these castle walls, I promote you to the position of Royal Logistician."

Another cheer.

"This honour I bestow on you as an individual but in recognition of all the hard moons of work your men and women have put in to get to where we are now. So to you all, when you look at the Royal Logistician, you may say, 'I helped her to gain that position the first woman in the history of the tribe to gain such a position of honour and I am proud of my work'!"

Another louder cheer.

"Karín, formerly of the Buq'ue, step forward. Karín, now of the Arw'an, I recognise you in front of these, your people. In recognition for your work in planning and establishing the Household Cavalry, I appoint you Commander of the Household Cavalry with the rank of Brigadier General. I have seen your capacity to plan and train and starting from tomorrow, we will see the King's Troop, resident in the castle mounted and in full training for the first time."

Another smaller cheer, mostly emanating from a small knot of young women at the flank.

"Jez of the Arw'an come forward!"

A murmur ran through the crowd as a man dressed all in black with a gold face, astride a tlaque and carrying the full battle rig of a space commando approached the dais. He shifted the tlaque so it faced the King directly. A strapping teenage boy walked beside him and when Jez dismounted slowly and theatrically from the beast, he handed the reins to the boy. He approached Ch0n with dignity as if he had been rehearsing the entire scene. The crowd was hushed. Was this the boy, Jez, who only a few months ago had been sent to Ch0n as his manservant? It couldn't be. Jez took off his helm and a gasp ran through the crowd. The young man had had Sonja shave his head clean in the manner of the King. Karín motioned to him and he passed the helm to her.

"Jez of the Arw'an, I recognise you in front of your people. In front of your father who brought you to me. In front of your mother who raised you alongside your father to be the man you now are. In recognition for your service to me as Lord of this castle and King of the Buq'ue and Arw'an, I promote you to the position of Knight of the Arw'an. With this position goes a plot in the castle on which will be built a stable and a rock dwelling. You will answer to none but me. You are confirmed as Garrison Commander of the Castle of the Arw'an and will take your place beside Brigadier General Karín at the council."

"Kneel before me, Jez."

Ch0n made a show of unsheathing Shiew with a grand flourish so the humming could be heard throughout the square. Ch0n placed the blade flat on Jez's shoulder with the keen edge touching his neck. Jez could feel a faint vibration along with the weight of the sword.

"Jez, of the Arw'an! With this sword, I dub thee first Knight of the Arw'an! Henceforth you shall be known to all as Sir Jez! Arise Sir Jez!"

This was followed by thunderous applause from those assembled. They had no idea what a Knight was or what he would or could or couldn't do but each of them saw themselves in the village boy who had risen through hard work, training and loyal service to a position on ChOn's council.

Jez rose and looked at ChOn. He unsheathed his katana, knelt on both knees in front of him and offered the sword to ChOn.

"I promise on this sword that I will in the future be faithful to thee lord Chon, never to cause you harm and will observe my homage to you completely against all persons in good faith and without deceit."

ChOn took his hand and helped him to his feet. He clapped him on the back and the crowd erupted. Down in the square holding the tlaque, a strapping teenaged boy looked on, wide eyed.

His name was Alik. When ChOn returned to his quarters, Alik was there. The wolf was barring his access to the chambers but allowing the boy to scratch his ears.

"My Lord," he said in a small voice. *"Jez told me I am to be your squire."*

"And what is your name, boy?"

"Alik, My Lord. I have no experience at all but Jez chose me from all the lads in the village."

"Well, that's it, then. It's done. Well come boy. Take the wolf to the stables with you. Just click your fingers and he'll follow. It helps if you have a morsel for him. You can share the stables with Sir Jez until he moves out. He will show you the way I like things. I suppose he will have a squire of his own, too."

"He does, My Lord. Beny"

"Good. By goodness, we'll have Knights running around all over the place before you know it."

Gavan Connell

"Will I become a Knight one day like Jez?"

"If you do your duties well and learn what you need to know, yes. If you slacken off on the job or don't learn fast enough, probably not but it is up to you. We must show you and you must learn. That is the rule."

Karín ducked through the entry when the boy had left.

"I think I should have a squire as well, My Lord, Ch0n. A girl to serve me and to teach. What do you think?"

"I think she would not be a squire for we will not have female Knights in armour. Knights will be solitary for the most part and Cavalry operates in groups. Your assistant would be called an adjutant. Usually it is a person with experience as a soldier who can assist you but in your case you will have to find someone without experience. I suggest a more mature woman than a teenage girl because she will have to have some credibility with the Lancers."

"And where would she live and work? We will need to extend the stables here. Jez's loft will be occupied for a while and mine has my things. Your two squires should move in there. I can move in here if it pleases you."

"You have a stall in the Lancer stables. It is currently occupied by one of the spare mounts but the space above it is unoccupied. She can stay there. I will tell Boro to put the priority for internal construction onto Jez's building. It will be simple. A bamboo double stable and loft, which will take a few days to build and then the stone house next to it. Once the loft is built, Jez can move into it and the boy, Beny with him. Jez's loft will be available for Alik."

"My Lord, you made no mention of my arrangements. Am I to keep my things in the loft or would it please you to have me move in here to your Quarters?"

"If you are living here with me would you still be able to be my bodyguard? Would you be able to carry out your duties as the Commander of the Household Cavalry?"

"If you take me in I can guard your body closer than it needs. I can perform the duties of Commander of the Household Cavalry and together we can discover the joys of our bodies. But for me it is more than that. I wish to be your woman and not your personal bodyguard and assistant. Already I am more than that. And, My Lord, you are not so bad at the íjuw, I was just teasing you as you do to me. But these things between a man and a woman take time to learn and practise. I could easily move my things into your quarters and you would not prevent it but what I seek is for you to invite me. That way I know you want me and don't just allow me to occupy a space in your quarters. It makes a big difference to me."

"Then please move your things into my quarters. I would have you share my bed but more than that, to be part of my life. You already fill my thoughts more than you could know and even when the woman, Reny made eyes at me I thought of you and if to go with her would be to betray you."

"If that is so, Ch0n, then it is the start of the thing we call, 'ébon'. It is that feeling I told you about that binds a man and a woman far stronger than coupling. It is a bond that stems from the centre of one's being. It is the feeling I have held for you since first you looked at my face and I saw the recognition in your eyes. I knew you had seen me in your dreams and I knew there could be none other for me but you and none for you but me. That day starts today when I become the woman of your dwelling. Others will see me and know you are mine and I, yours. Reny and others like her will never display their ibuw again unless you invite it. I will still kill them afterwards but that is just matter of fact. Now I will quickly go and fetch my few things and instruct the two boys to move upstairs into my loft.

Then I will tell Alik to fetch Boro to you so you can tell him to build Jez's stables. Then we will eat and ride after Sonja."

She skipped to the entrance. Then she skipped back and nuzzled Ch0n. Then she skipped away again. Ch0n felt a pang of something inside him. He had no idea he was in love.

They rode out shortly after eating. Jez had selected a plot next to Ch0n's much larger one. It was flat and on the main access track. Boro approached him and asked him where he would like to start the building and if he might spit lock the stone building so they could abut the stables to the wall.

"We will start this before the sun dips too far, Sir Jez"

"I thank you, Boro, Royal Architect of the Castle of the Arw'an."

They both laughed.

"We have a true leader at last," said Boro. *"He knows how to make us follow willingly, down to the last man and woman."*

"Aye that he does. And one day we will reap the full benefits of it all. I know not when or how but there is a divine reason he was sent to us and in due course it will be revealed for good or bad."

"Is it true the woman Karín moved in to his dwelling? The squire Alik is telling people he and Beny are to share what was her loft and that she moved her things in with him. Perhaps we will soon see a mating that produces a prince."

"Yes it is true. And it's also true that I need to box the boy's ears for him and teach him the first lesson a squire must learn is that of discretion. If you go for the workers I will mark out the boundaries of my stone building."

Ch0n and Karín pushed the tlaque hard and they caught the group of walkers well before nightfall. Sonja was striding out in front, belying her middle age and they had made good ground. When Ch0n drew alongside her, she didn't slacken her pace.

"We are fairly close now, My Lord. If we push hard we can camp underneath the fruit trees that abound there. There are some wondrous animals to be seen at dusk, tlaque and sometimes giant oruk, their cousins. There are birds of every hue including some that never leave their homes and if they are taken away they can always find their way back. They are large fat birds we call a dáguia. They are good eating. There is also a predator which kills silently and unseen. It is the dagononum, which changes its colour so it becomes invisible. We used to leave goats tethered for it when we camped here. Had it not been resident, we may have set up a permanent camp here but it was just too dangerous. Now I will stop talking for I need my breath to walk. I would go faster but the soldiers are holding me up."

"Stop before we get there. Stop when you can show me the way and I will go ahead for with my helm I can see the dagononum. If the red clay is as I hope it is, we will set up a quarry there and that will mean we need a permanent settlement with defences."

He turned away and spoke to Karín.

"I may need to kill the dagononum so we are safe and so the tlaque are safe. I would look upon the other beast, this oruk. If it is a cousin of the tlaque, it can be domesticated. The dáguia interest me for I have seen on the minitron when I was searching for means of communications that for many years a bird like this was used to bear messages from one place to another. This place excites me and I have yet to see it."

"I have seen the oruk. The king once took me to a place where water abounded and the grass was always green. It was a beautiful place for me to first experience the joy of…. Never mind why we went there but we saw a herd of the oruk by the

water. We moved among them for they are quite docile like the tlaque but much bigger. A male might be about the same height as a male tlaque but wider in the chest and lower at the rump. They do not have the antlers of the tlaque but curved horns that spiral around and outwards. The horns are a thing of beauty and I would have had one but even the king couldn't obtain one as a gift to remember our first... Well as a gift, anyway. His soldiers tried to kill a male but their spears were useless against its hide and it swept several aside with its horns and crushed another with its forehead before the king called them off. Even as they ran it killed another. It came at a heavy price, the lives of six men for the brief pleasure of a King, although it was not so brief now I think of it. Oh! I am sorry my agen. I became caught up in my memories. I should not have strayed so far."

"What does, 'agen' mean?"

"It is the word a woman uses when she is talking about the man with whom she lives, with whom she couples exclusively and for whom she feels the thing called 'ébon'. So you are my 'agen'."

"That would be 'husband' in my tongue."

"I find 'agen' easier to say but I am pleased you have a word for it. The word a man would use for the woman with whom he shares ébon and who would kill any other woman with whom he lies, is called, 'aget' or also 'agen'."

"In my tongue a woman who did that would be called a 'murderer'. But the correct word for 'aget' would be 'wife'."

"'Wyf'. I like that word. I will be your 'wyf' when you decide to tell me you feel the ébon. It is settled then. Why do we not use the skin of the dagononum when we have it? The last one you shot we left alone. It is like steel when it dries. I have never seen one but the king told me his father had formed the skin from the back of the beast around his breast and tied it to him

until it dried. He said the smell was fearsome but eventually when it was removed and scraped, it formed a breastplate like those we wear. He said a spear was unable to penetrate it even thrown from close range by the strongest man in the village. If we kill this thing, we should skin it and save the skin for such a purpose."

"We will do that but instead of tying it around my chest we will tie it around a tree the same size as my chest. Or your chest. Or the chest of the tlaque. What have we here?"

Sonja was waving to them. He pulled up to where she was standing.

"Yonder is the overhanging cliff with the caves that hold the red mud. Underneath it runs a river that has cut the cliff with its slow current. Upstream from the river the water is as clean as the.... glass you showed us but downstream the water runs pink for some distance and then where it passes through the reed beds, it runs clear again."

"Wait here. When you see the sun flashing from the base of the cliff, come to us."

They pushed the tlaque at a fast trot down the hill. The sun was still high enough to see clearly down the valley. As they approached the cliff, they saw a small herd of tlaque and some other small herbivores ChOn had not seen before. They were like the goats but with long silky hair instead of the rough woolly coats of their domesticated cousins. The fruit trees Sonja described were full of birds, some with scythed beaks. These walked instead of hopping and squawked raucously. ChOn caught a glimpse of one of the apes he had found dead on his first expedition. The walls of the cliff were full of holes and large birds were nesting there in their hundreds. Their droppings fell into the water and were cleaned away by fish in the slow current or trapped further downstream where their nutrients had created a luxurious pad of greenness over which the slightly pink water flowed. Smaller, colourful birds with pointed beaks were fishing on the wing and every now and then one would catch a small silver wriggling thing and disappear. It was like an oasis. It was an oasis. They both adopted the heat and thermal mode and searched for the dragon. Karín spotted it first. She pointed to it.

"Seen."

It was lying absolutely motionless, full length near a path that led upwards into one of the caves. It was watching them. It was the same pink as the wet clay on which it was lying.

"When it moves, it will change colour but the wet clay stuck to its skin will still be pink so we will be able to see it without the helms. I will go down and see if it attacks or runs. If it attacks, I will kill it. You can skin it if you like but Sonja may be better skilled. You are better at other things." He called the wolf and threw a sling over its neck. He handed the running end to Karín.

He dismounted and walked towards the dragon, which was still more than a hundred feet away. Ch0n didn't approach it directly. He wanted the creature to think it was invisible and to walk at it would give it reason for alarm and Ch0n would lose the advantage he needed, which was to get close before the creature moved. He had the pulse set on one hundred percent, just in case. There was no point in trying to kill something and failing to do so for the sake of a few volts. He was now only sixty feet away and was looking at the creature out of the corner of his eye. Its head was following him slowly. Without the thermal assist, Ch0n would never have noticed the slight adjustments if the dragon's head. At thirty feet, Ch0n stopped. He turned and faced the dragon. It stood slowly to its full height of twelve feet and suddenly charged. Ch0n sent the pulse straight at its chest and it fell dead on to the slippery clay. It slid straight at ChOn who jumped and rolled to one side just in time to avoid being struck full on by the open jaws of the huge reptile. He heard Karín scream as he jumped and then he heard her laugh. He stood up and looked at himself. His uniform was pink from head to toe, covered in the slippery clay. The chameleon was twenty feet past him where it had finally come to a stop against a rock. Its skin was already changing to the pale orange ChOn had come to know, mottled by the pink of the clay mud stuck to it.

Karín rode over to where he was standing and dropped from the tlaque, which was nervously snuffling the air.

"I will tether the tlaque and then attend to you, agen. I wish I had some way to record this."

ChOn reached into his thigh pocket and took out the tablet. He booted it and took images of the overhang, the beasts, the birds, the woman, the dead dragon and then he handed it to her.

"Just wait until the image you seek is showing and press the red circle."

She recorded his pink wet uniform and then asked him how she could take an image of them together. He set the tablet to 'timer' and propped it against the dead beast.

"Stand there." He adjusted the screen and pressed the button. He walked to the woman and put his arm around her shoulder as though she were one of his soldier buddies. She put her arm around his waist and smiled to herself. They saw the faux lens open and close. ChOn retrieved the tablet and showed her the image. She liked it.

"Is there a way to make a hard image of this?"

"No. Not here. We will have to get someone to paint it for us. We should signal the others to come down."

"No. Not yet. You are in no state to receive them. Take off your clothes and I will wash them for you."

He stood in his undergarment while she washed the clay out of his uniform. When he looked at her, he felt the same pang in his core that he had felt in the morning. She was everything he could want. She was a friend and now a lover. She was brave and loyal and smart. She was a freak among her people as was he. She was devoted to him. She looked up at him from the flat rock where she was working.

"What?"

"You will wet your clothes. Take them off or you will get cold."

"If I take them off will you capture me on the tablet?"

"If it pleases you."

"I would like you to have an image of me naked for those times when we are apart. To remind you of what you are missing."

"OK. That would be nice."

Karín stripped off her clothes and spread them neatly on the stone. She posed for Ch0n, who took several images and then a short moving image of her as she knelt down to finish her work. He dropped the tablet next to his clean pants and looked around at the rise where the others were waiting. He could see no sign of them. Karín finished rinsing his shirt and put it next to his pants. When she looked up she held out her hands to Ch0n, who was in a state of obvious excitement.

"This will have to be quick, My Lord agen. But you can make up for it later on."

A little later, they went into a sunny spot and Ch0n took a small signal mirror from a slide in the side of his helm. Karín felt hers and found one the same.

"This reflects the sun. It is called a mirror. Or in this case, a signal mirror. It has a tiny hole in the middle. The easiest way to send a signal to someone who is waiting is to stand in the sun like this, hold your thumbnail next to where the person is waiting and shine the sun on your nail and wiggle it around to make sure it hits their eyes. Now. Take this. Face the sun. It is low so this will be easier. Now hold your arm out like that. Good. Is your thumbnail over their position? Then look through the hole and shine the light on your thumbnail. No. Keep your thumb still and aimed at their position. That's better. We should see them coming soon."

Karín looked at the face of the mirror and saw herself in the small rectangle. Looking back at her was the woman in the images Ch0n had just taken of them. Her hair was now a couple of inches long and the red flames danced about her scalp in the breeze. She liked what she saw but she missed her hair.

"Ch0n, am I pleasing to your eyes? I have heard it said that I am raw boned and ungainly. A giant. A freak. Nobody has ever wanted me before other than the king and that was just for coupling. He was good at it but his manhood was in keeping with his small stature. Nobody has ever told me if I am pleasing to the eye. Malek, now, men just want her at first sight. She is considered a raging beauty and Reny, who coveted you, is also thought to be pretty."

Ch0n felt the pang in his chest for the third time that day. She was brave, intelligent, savage and loyal all at once and yet insecure.

"In my dreams a saw a woman of beauty. The image of her filled my waking hours all the next day. I knew she was to become something special in my life or she wouldn't have been in my dream. When a man has never even seen a woman and then dreams of one, would he not dream of the one he thought would be the most beautiful that existed? I dreamed of the most beautiful woman I could conjure forth in my imagination and then in the Buq'ue camp, I saw her reveal herself from under a black turban, the same woman from my dream. I know nothing about beauty or ugliness in reality but to me you are the most beautiful thing I have ever seen."

"Then I am beautiful because you say I am." She looked at herself again in the mirror and slipped it into its slide.

The group of walkers hove into shouting distance. They could hear Sonja calling to the soldiers to stop slowing her down. Finally they arrived and she just threw her bundle to one side, stripped off her tunic and kept walking into the river. The soldiers needed no invitation and before long they were all splashing about in various states of nudity. Ch0n and Karín kept their distance. Ch0n was studying the birds. He was much taken with the large bright orange ones with blue heads that walked along the branches and held the fruit in one claw while they ate. Their beaks were sickle shaped and their tongues were rounded at the end. From head to tail they were almost three feet long. They set up a constant cawing and chatting noise and seemed to be imitating the whistling noises of the smaller birds and one even made a sound like hooves drumming. He took images of them and the others before turning to study the birds roosting in the holes in the overhang.

They were more than a foot long, maybe as much as fifteen inches from what he could see. They had powerful wings that could carry them up to the curved ceiling of the overhang and fold in time for them to land on the edge of the holes they had excavated. They were smooth feathered and the same dull orange colour as many others of the species on the planet. About half of them had a darker collar and ChOn assumed the two sexes were colour-differentiated. He also thought the orange-ness of the inhabitants was due to the orange sun and the need for camouflage in the orange light. He was wondering how he might catch one of the birds when he noticed one of them fly to the ground where there was a flurry of movement and a fledgling came out of a shallow hole and the parent bird fed it by allowing the baby to put its beak inside the adult's and take food from its gut. He untied the wolf and let it run on the end of the lead. He let it cast wider circles out to where the baby bird had been hiding and at once the wolf found it. ChOn picked it up and studied it. It had a straight beak and strong long legs. The body was big breasted and the wings could be pulled right back until they touched without the fledgling struggling or calling out. He let the creature go and let the wolf search for more. It turned out there were dozens of them hiding in plain sight. ChOn decided to take them all back to the castle. He looked around for a suitable material and saw the reed beds. He called out to Karín.

"Are the Buq'ue women or the Arw'an women skilled in weaving?"

"If you're asking me, I am skilled in the use of weapons and hand to hand combat and I am also skilled in the ways of íjon but weaving is not something I know much about."

"Sonja!" Sonja seemed to be in the act of coupling with a soldier in the river but ChOn couldn't be sure.

"Sonja!"

She looked up.

"Do you know how to weave?"

295

"Of course, My Lord. It is a skill all women who are not Commanders of the Household Cavalry would be familiar with."

"Good. I want you to weave me a cage that will hold twenty of these birds," he called, holding one out to her.

"Right now, My Lord?"

"Have it completed before I leave tomorrow morning after we breakfast. And I need you to skin the dagononum."

"I'd like to finish skinning this boy, My Lord", she thought to herself, *"but the mood has passed. For now"*.

She climbed out of the water and went to the reed beds where Karín helped her cut an armful of the longest reeds.

"It only has to house them for the time it takes the tlaque to return to the castle in the morning." He changed from channel 11 to channel 1.

"Sir Jez, can you hear me?"

"Yes My Lord."

"Good. I want you to tell Doni I have a special task for him. Maybe two but certainly one. I need him to build a bamboo shelter as long as two men with a sloping roof and with a solid back, solid sides and a slatted front with the slats only so far apart that a man's hand will fit through to the heel of the hand. The floor should be of earth. The roof should be as high as a man and the floor as deep as a man could reach. It is to temporarily house birds that will grow to as long as a man's forearm. I need it by tomorrow afternoon. It is urgent. Are you with me so far?"

"Yes, My Lord."

"Tell him to look for someone in the village who keeps pet birds in cages. I know there are some. Appoint that person official keeper of the castle birds. Now here is the strange part. I need that person to make up a mixture of porridge and water just before we get back and to find a bamboo tube that his small finger will enter. When I get there I will show him the rest. I also need to know if the season for the tlaque to drop their young is near us. There were some obviously pregnant females in the group we captured."

"I will ask him, My Lord. Is the clay bed what you expected?"

"It is everything I had hoped for and more. It is a perfect place for a permanent outpost with a brickworks. Had I found it first I might have lived there alone forever and never found the Arw'an."

"I will sent the boy, Alik, for Doni and have him come to me. That way you can answer any questions he may have."

Sonja was sitting on the flat stone with Karín. They were weaving the cage together. Karín looked up at his step.

"This isn't so hard if you have someone to show you how. Now I know how easy it is for the women to sit around and gossip all day while they do this."

"I need to teach the OP commanders to read. Or I need to teach them to make signs. The birds instinctively go home. If they think their home is the Castle, they will go to the castle. If they think their home is the Buq'ue fort, they will go to the Buq'ue fort. The outposts, the OP. All we have to do is make them think their home is where we want them to go. I am going to take twenty of the birds to the castle and from there I am going to have them sent to the OP. They are so young they will think their homes are at the OP or the castle. We can move them back and forth and when we let them go, they will fly swiftly to their home base and we will have tiny messages on their legs to read. It is just a matter of making the paper, which is not hard, the pencils, which is not hard, and teaching people to make the marks that everybody will understand, which will not be easy."

"My Lord, you have so many things happening in your head at once. One day you will forget something important or you will have exhausted your brain capacity."

Sonja was fascinated with the idea.

"These birds breed rapidly. That is why they feed their young on the ground. As soon as they can flop safely to the ground, they are pushed out of the nest and another egg is laid. We could breed these birds for meat as well as for messengers."

"Each house could have a pair. Have you eaten the eggs?"

"My Lord. They have chicks in them. They have bones and fluff. Why would we possibly want to eat them?"

"Because, Sonja, eggs can be eaten.   In our survival training it says eggs are a good source of protein and they are readily available wherever there are birds. You just have to boil them in their shells and eat them. But enough of that. Before it gets dark I want to show you the clay deposits. They wandered to the cliffs where the soil was wet and pink. ChOn scooped a handful out of the ooze and squished it between his fingers. If this is mixed with human hair, wool or dry grass, it can be cooked to make rocks. You just form them in the shape you want and cook them. It's as simple as that. After that you stack them one on top of the other and mix the same mortar of crushed stones and water and they stick together. I have the directions on the minitron. We can make huge ovens of these and cook whole goats. Half a tlaque. A hundred rabbits. Rabbits! They can be domesticated so every house has rabbits to eat. Or we could start a rabbit farm. This is getting better all the time. And we could make bread. And water vessels and urns like the one at the Buq'ue fort."

"Yes, Sir Jez. I can hear you. Doni wants to know if there will be an area set aside in future to house the adult birds? Tell him, yes but for now we have to see how this works. Just the small one but if he wants to allocate an area for them, that's fine. And what about the tlaque breeding females? Are they almost ready to drop? I have a wonderful plan to raise oruks. Yes, oruks! But it will need tlaques in milk to work. OK. Listen. I will meet Doni as soon as I get back. The priority will be to feed these birds and then we will talk about oruks. Goodbye."

Chon ran the wet, red clay through his fingers again.

"I have read that it is good for the complexion if rubbed on the face," he laughed. The two women scattered. He made a mound of the wet clay and walked into the cave behind the overhang. It was musty and damp. In a corner was a pile of eggs, each as big as his head. Chameleon eggs. He was tempted to take them with him but decided it was too dangerous to have a reptile around humans. He picked up each one and threw it out the mouth of the cave and watched them smash on the rocks. There was no dragon in any of them. This puzzled him and he resolved to look up the answer when he had the chance. He was just about to leave when his eyes caught the flash of something in the fading light. He went over and dug it out with his survival knife. It looked like a dirty piece of pink glass as big as his fist. It was a diamond. On earth it was worth a king's ransom. Here it was worth nothing. He put it in his pocket and went back to the others. He had a grinding tool in his quarters. He would try and shape the stone to show off its beauty and then he would give it to the woman. He was excited about the diamond and the prospect there may be more but he was more excited about having a clay quarry.

Gavan Connell

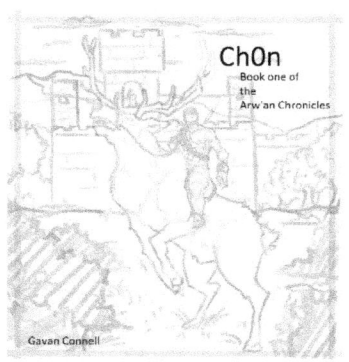

Mock-up Illustrations by Miguel Lopez Bernal

Mexico 2015

Chapter Twenty: A Menagerie of War

Approaching last light a herd of tlaque meandered in. Ch0n had to tether his beast and fight off the dominant male with the pulse, which worked well enough. The silken goats came in their scores to drink and eat the reeds and the green tufts of bushes that grew along the riverside. In the trees the birds gathered and chattered and screeched and finally grew silent and just as the last birds were settling, came the oruk. There were only sixty of them in the entire herd. They were led by an old bull that bore the scars of many battles fought and won. His horns were massive, spreading five feet across, each one six inches in diameter at the base and curling around back across the beast's forehead, over and then under his ears, finishing the great spiral outwards and upwards beyond his eyes. There were other bulls in the herd, none as big as he and the remainder of the herd was made up of pregnant females and yearling calves. Some of the cows were so big they looked as though they would burst open and Ch0n knew he had to act straight away or lose a year. He called to Jez.

"Tell Doni I need ten tlaque females with travois here by morning. It's a big ask but you should be able to lead them. Bring ten tie-downs as well and wool rugs. The oruk herd is here and I want to make sure that when they drop their calves, I am on hand to steal them. Back at the castle I will need all the goats in milk to be standing by for when the oruks arrive. If the tlaque females start to drop, so much the better. I will send you a homing signal for you to march to using the receiver on the helm. Stay as close to a straight line as you can. I will follow the herd if it leaves here and you can follow me in turn. This will be a test for your tlaque and for you. Luckily you have been practising on mine or you would be sore and sorry by morning. Have the females strung together behind you and a man in every second travois. Push your beast just as fast as the travois can travel. It is faster than a walk but slower than a run. Leave as soon as you can get the lot together."

"As you wish, My Lord."

"Karín, we may have to leave at a moment's notice. I want to be present when the oruk start to calve. I am going to steal ten calves, five males and five females. Tell Sonja that as soon as it is light, she should start back to the castle. Leave the bird cage here. I will catch the birds and we will take the cage back to the castle on the back of the tlaque. You and I will have to take turns running beside. Now I will probably have to kill the old bull. That is a sad thing but there are young bulls to take the herd forward and he would probably be killed by one of them soon anyway. If you would like the horns you will have to cut them off with your ax. Now. I have to go and calm the tlaque for he is bellowing another challenge to the wild male. He ran over to where the tlaque was both tethered and hobbled. The wild male was at the edge of the firelight. Ch0n loosed a pulse at the beast that knocked him to his knees. When he stood, Ch0n knocked him down again. Finally he staggered back onto the darkness. By his side the wolf began to sniff the breeze. He started to run into the darkness and Ch0n called him back. He put the lead on the animal and let him take him to where an oruk female was dropping her calf. She was upwind of them and so didn't start at the presence of the wolf. The wet bundle fell to the ground and the cow started to lick it clean. It bellowed once when the membrane had been licked from it and then staggered to its feet, falling several times before it was able to walk. The cow was still eating the afterbirth when the calf found her teat and started to suckle. Its tail wagged furiously as it sucked the precious colostrum from her. She stood still for it until she saw ChOn in the shadows and she lowered her head. Chon had been trying to guess her weight and settled on one and a half times a tlaque male. The pulse was set to fifty four and it knocked her out. ChOn took the calf in his arms and carried it back to the camp where he lay it down next to the wolf. The wolf licked it all over, which calmed the calf down and then it slept, its belly full of colostrum and a warm furry wolf to warm its back. ChOn looked down at its belly.

"A male. This will be my mount if we can steal no other." Off in the bushes they could hear the cow calling her newborn. After a while, she stopped. The calf was oblivious. It had already forgotten her scent and could smell only that of the humans and the wolf. The night was a long one with the calf trying to find milk and the tlaque periodically challenging a male who was now too traumatized to accept. During the night, ChOn found a female tlaque with a calf that was partly weaned and so he stunned the mother and carried the oruk calf to her udder. It nuzzled about until it finally got its head low enough to latch on to a teat and drank until its belly was distended. The tlaque woke up some minutes later a little groggy but none the wiser.

ChOn was contacted before first light. Jez was approaching the camp. As the sun rose he spotted the fire and rode towards it. He had the ten tlaque females. ChOn immediately strapped the calf to a travois and told one of the soldiers to take it back to Doni, leading the tlaque. He had travelled for eight hours to get there and now he would travel eight hours back. They covered the calf with a blanket to keep it from the sun.

Chon looked at the soldier.

"I know you, Marik. This is a great service you are performing for me. I will not forget it. That stands for all of you. Go now.

It must not dehydrate.   Neither must you. Drink your fill before you go.

We must look through the herd to see if there are others. This one was found by the wolf. Sir Jez. Use your thermal image enhancer and we will start right away. If you see one, shoot the mother with the pulse on fifty four and carry the calf back to here. Let me check the numbers. Good. We will tie them down and send them back in pairs, one led and one tied to the lead just as they came. Now let's go. You, Pary. With me. Step lively, boy."

Within five minutes they had two more and then ten minutes later, another two. When the cows came to, they were bellowing for their calves but that was twenty minutes too late. By then they were already trussed and on the way back to the castle. The herd was still quiet, thanks to the soundless pulses. After the first hour they found no more newborns. Then the old bull stood up and started to amble off. The herd stood as one. ChOn didn't want to be chasing oruk all over the plains so he made a calculated decision to shoot the bull. If it stayed put, the others would do the same. He called Jez to him.

"Quickly. Adjust your pistol to one hundred. Let me check. Good. Now move to the right front of the bull. I am going to the other side. On the count of three, shoot him. I will do the same. Two pulses should be enough but prepare to fire another one straight away if he looks like getting up. Now walk quickly but don't panic them."

They reached their positions as the herd was just starting to string out. ChOn counted with his fingers and they both fired. The bull went straight to his knees and rolled over. His chest was still and his eyes were bulging out of his head from the pressure. Blood came from his nose. The lead cows looked at him and stopped. They started to chew cud and finally sat down again. ChOn walked to the great bull and unsheathed

Shiew. With a mighty sweep he took the head clean off at the base of the horns. Bone and brains spilled over but none of the other beasts even gave him a second look. They were as docile as domesticated animals. That would change of course when they were herded and hunted but for the moment the pulses gave the humans the advantage of silence.

During the course of the morning they gathered the remaining five calves. They had to wait for seven to be born to get the right mix of males and females but once they had had their colostrum, they were quickly bundled away. Jez went with the last of them. Sonja and the soldiers had been on the trail since first light and that left Ch0n and Karín. Ch0n hefted the bull's massive horns. No other male on the planet could have lifted them in all probability. He carried them to the overhang. "I will put this on an ants' nest to be cleaned out. Next time we come here it will be bleached and ready for you. It is not a memento of your first tryst with a king as you had hoped but as a memento of the time I first called you, 'wife'. Now is it women's day or men's day in the baths?"

They set off with twenty of the chicks in a cage. Ch0n had no idea if they were male or female, he just supposed he would have about half of each. He put Karín in the saddle and tied the cage to the beast's rump. It would be a rough ride for them but they were packed fairly tightly. They were covered from the sun by a blanket but the sides were left open for ventilation. Ch0n marked the location on the inbuilt magnetic field positioning system, took hold of the stirrup leather next to Karín's war ax and they set off at the trot. Karín did not spare him. She put the beast into its long stride. She guessed Ch0n could run for miles at a time being half carried like this. After an hour he called for a halt and she stepped down.

"Give me a few minutes and I will be ready for another hour."

"We may not have a few minutes every hour, agen. The chicks are too important. Mount up. You will get your few minutes while I run. Don't spare me for to do that would be to insult me."

ChOn urged the beast forward and after a short while they passed Sonja and the soldiers. They waved a greeting and kept moving. In the distance they could see Jez leading a travois. They loped towards him until the woman called for a stop. They changed places three more times before they topped the rise and the castle came into view. Between them and the gate was the first of the oruk calves on the travois, with the cabot, Marik jogging doggedly ahead of the tlaque. They passed him just before the gate. ChOn was on foot and badly winded. Karín called to Marik,

'Well run, Marik. Go to Doni with the calf and then go to bed and do not rise from there except to eat. Tomorrow we will toast your endurance before the village. Doni! Doni! We are here with the birds and Marik is here with the oruk calf!"

"And I am here with the cage and the stockmen are over in the goat pen with the milking goats. Marik. Over there man. Goodness, look what you have brought us. Finny. Help Marik to the pens with the calf."

"Alik! Alik! Come here boy and see to the tlaque. He needs a scrub and a feed. Give him only one skin of water and wait until I call you again before you give him another. Get Beny. Tell him to rouse the Lancers from their stables and see to the female tlaques as they come in. Tell them about the water rations. If they have too much to start with, they will get bloated. Go now boy. Time is important. Marik. I told you to go to bed."

"Beg your pardon Brigadier General but I have just run for sixteen hours to get this creature a drink of milk and with your permission I'll see it done."

Doni was taking the birds from the cage one by one. Ch0n took the first and filled the bamboo tube he had requested with porridge. He stuck it over the chick's beak and persevered until it started to eat. From then on it was simply a matter of keeping the tube full, which they did using a goat's intestine to squeeze the stuff down to where the chick could access it. The castle bird man was right in his element. He had done this before on a smaller scale with his whistlers. Once Ch0n had shown him what he wanted he took the apparatus from him.

"Look 'ere now, milord Ch0n, if I'm going to be the castle bird 'andler you better let me get on with me work. If you want to do if for me, I might as well be at 'ome."

The oruk calf was stiff from being tied down and bounced all over the plains but it stood unsteadily by the bench where the goat was standing and it fastened on to a teat. It drained three goats before it stopped, squirted a yellowish brown stream of poop and wandered into a corner and dropped down. Ch0n arrived in time to see the last bit.

"Good sign, that. Doni? The yellow poop I mean."

"Yes, My Lord. If it is white and scoury it is hard to save them. We will know in short order how it handles the goat milk instead of the tlaques'".

"He's less than a day old and he's already had oruk, tlaque and goat milk. He won't know whether to bleat, or moo."

"My Lord, we have water for you, the lady Karín and Marik."

"Thank you, Alik. I would like you to see to the tlaque for the rest of the day. Stay with him and give him a lot of small drinks until nightfall and then let him drink his fill. Make sure he is dry and the saddle and other tack is hung in its place."

"Yes My Lord."

"Sir Jez will be here some time during the night. Before midnight. All I have told you about the care of the tlaque will apply to Sir Jez's. Tell the squire Beny all I have told you. He will not sleep tonight unless you help him. I am going to sleep now." He pointed to the sky. "Please wake me when the moon gets to there. Look also to the wolf. He can drink his fill for they have a different stomach to the tlaque. Go to the kitchens when you have settled the tlaque and find him meat and a leg bone. Do you understand all that?"

"Yes, My Lord."

"Good lad. We'll make a Knight out of you yet."

He stumbled off to bed and pulled off his boots. He did not hear or feel Karín slip in beside him.

He woke up hours later to Alik's calling him.

"Lord! Lord ChOn! The moon has risen to where you told me. Are you awake?"

ChOn looked at the sleeping form beside him and called softly to the boy. He pulled on a tunic and a kamarband and sandals and went straight to the pens with a flashlight. On the way he passed the cage and shone the beam down to the floor. The chicks were huddled together in one corner. He hurried to where Doni was still fussing about waiting for the next travois. He looked at ChOn and told him the first calf had accepted the goat's milk without scouring and so they should be able to keep feeding them on this until the tlaques came on line. Then they would twin an oruk with several tlaque calves so there was plenty of milk for all. ChOn counted seven of the calves already fed and penned. That left just one other soldier with two and then Jez with the last one. He recalled that the last five had been caught a little further apart than the first five but the others should still be getting close. Alik was standing off to one side of him.

"Alik, please fetch my helm from the equipment room." The boy ran off and returned quickly.

"Thank you Alik. Sir Jez, can you hear me?"

"I hear you, Lord. I have but one travois and am mounted so I have caught up with Farik and his two calves. We will be coming in together. I am atop the rise overlooking the gates."

While they were waiting, the sound of a newborn tlaque drifted in on the breeze. Ch0n and Doni ran to the corral. The doe was still licking the membrane off the calf and it was pushing upwards on unsteady legs. They watched until it found the mother's teat before Ch0n heard Jez's voice in the speaker. *"Well done Farik. We will go straight to the pens and you can go to bed."* In the background he heard Farik's curt reply. *"I'll sleep when I know my run was not for nothing if you don't mind."*

"So much for the gruff soldiers," thought Ch0n. They had all wanted to ensure their charges had arrived safely before seeing to their own needs.

He went to the pens to see the arrival of Jez and Farik. Jez looked relatively fresh compared to Farik, who was exhausted almost to the point of collapse. Willing hands unpacked three wriggling bundles and Farik shed tears of relief. Jez sipped from the saddle and was about to call for Beny when the two squires appeared at his side. Beny took the reins of the tlaque and Alik offered him food and drink. Jez smiled at the boys and motioned to Alik to give the food to Farik. The old Buq'ue soldier took it thankfully after nodding to Jez. They stood

Gavan Connell

together, Knight and soldier as their common goal was achieved before their eyes. The three calves drained the obligatory nine goats before trotting off to the corner of the pen where their brothers and cousins were sleeping, all huddled together. ChOn looked around the group. They were herders, soldiers, the two squires, the bird handler who was going to miss nothing of the excitement, at least one random villager, Doni, of course, Jez and ChOn himself. They were all staring at the ten bundles of fur and ears.

Doni walked over to where ChOn and Jez were standing.

"So now we have the oruk, what do you plan to do with them My Lord?"

"I am going to ride one into battle, as will Sir Jez. The oruks are not as agile as the tlaque but they are certainly imposing and will strike fear into any who oppose their charge. A Knight mounted on an oruk could just charge down a line from the flank and overrun an entire column. With the soldiers being shoulder to shoulder and their spears to the front, they wouldn't be able to turn their attention to us and even if they did, if the timing is right, it would be just as the Infantry are about to close with them so they would have spears to the front or Knights from the flank. Meanwhile, the Cavalry is picking off their rear and supply lines. Any enemy that doesn't have a similar show of mobility or tactics to defend against it will be massacred."

"And I have not even had a chance to get used to my tlaque yet," sighed Jez.

"The tlaque will be your daily mount and the one you will use to ride to and from the outposts. The oruk is the beast you will train daily upon and practise the art of warfare upon. It will know you and you will know it. When the day comes that we need to mobilize our defences and on those holidays where we will parade the military through the streets, we will ride the oruk."

"That accounts for two males, My Lord. What of the others?"

"Two more males will be gelded. That will make four. Two will be for war and two will be used to pull ploughs to till the earth and to pull anything else we may need to move. Stones, for example or trees.

"One male will be kept whole for breeding. The females will be used for breeding with the breeding bull. I am going back to the herd of oruk as soon as practical. I will have the Brigadier General accompany me with the entire King's Troop and we will drive some of the mature females out of the herd and bring them back. They are used to being in a mixed herd so if we push them along in the middle of thirty tlaque they will come easily. It will have to be soon, however, because once they have calved, the bulls will be looking for them to fill them for next season. I am going to try and cross them with my tlaque to see if I can breed a heavy mount for the cavalry. In ten days we will leave.

Today at mid day I would have the village assembled. I have some recognitions to perform. Meanwhile, I am going back to bed. I need to inform the Brigadier General of my plans."

The village gathered at mid-day as it had several days before. The line up on the platform included all those previously recognised.

"Sonja of the Arw'an come forward!"

"Sonja of the Arw'an, I recognise you in front of your people. In gratitude for your work in town planning and dispute resolution within these castle walls, I promote you to the position of Royal Mayor."

The crowd loved Sonja for she was truly one of them. They roared their approval. Even Silas was cheering, the gap in his teeth on display, as was Sonja's for she was grinning with delight.

"This honour I bestow on you as an individual but in recognition of all the hard moons of work your men and women have put in to get to where we are now. So to you all, when you look at the Royal Mayor, you may say, 'I helped her to gain that position the first woman in the history of the tribe to gain such a position of honour and I am proud of my work'!"

Another roar.

"Step forward the five who went to the clay beds with Sir Jez to bring back the oruk calves that will be used in the defence of the castle and the Arw'an and Buq'ue unified peoples!"

Five soldiers stepped forward in uniform.

Alik appeared next to ChOn. He was holding a cushion on which were six polished aluminium stars attached to olive green strips of material. ChOn had spent his little spare time during the previous weeks cutting them with his cutting wheel and he had asked a young artist from the village to draw two crossed swords with the engraving tool. They were beautifully finished.

"Marik, Kolin, Jafri, Pary and Farik; Soldiers of the Arw'an and Buq'ue united tribes, I recognise you in front of your people. Let it be known that these men have achieved a feat of physical endurance no man should have to perform unless his life depended on it. They did it because Sir Jez asked them to do it for me and for you all. While you were abed, they ran eight hours pulling two tlaque females to a place where I was waiting with ten oruk calves. Those calves will become war machines in the defence of our tribe and beasts of burden in time of peace. The calves were loaded on to the travois behind the tlaque and these five men ran eight hours pulling the precious cargo back to the castle. In a few days, Doni will allow you all to see them for they are things of beauty. To these five soldiers I award the Aluminium Star of Service. They will wear these things, called medals, on their street uniforms at all times. Look upon them when they pass and say to your neighbour, *'I know him. He bears the star of service'*. To you five I thank you."

He motioned the five to approach him and then one by one he velcroed the medals to their woollen tunics. Then he stepped back and saluted them in military fashion. The crowd cheered wildly.

"Sir Jez of the Castle of the Arw'an, step forward!" Jez moved from ChOn's side to a position in front of him.

"Sir Jez, for your part in the planning and execution of the foray to collect the oruk calves, I award you the Aluminium Star of Service." He velcroed the medal on to Jez's tunic- to roars from the crowd.

The next week at the castle was frenetic for Doni. ChOn was always at his side watching the progress of the oruk calves. The tlaque does had finally calved and the oruk were orphaned out to various among them. It turned out, the tlaque were not adverse to any of the calves, tlaque or oruk alike, using them as milk reservoirs. The first time they had tried to orphan an oruk they tethered the tlaque and leg-roped her to the rail but she didn't flinch when the calf searched for the teat and helped himself. And so it had been for all of them. The tlaque and oruk calves lived, played and fed all in one giant crèche where the next doe might have milk if the current one were empty. And then nature took over. The tlaque females started to produce more milk as the demand increased. By the end of the week, there were forty three calves in the pen with fat bellies. Ten of them were noticeably different in appearance but equally well nourished. People were coming with their children to look at the newborn goats, tlaque, and the oruk.

Meanwhile, in the bird pen, the handler was taking his job very seriously and the cage was quite large so he could sit in it while he fed the chicks. They were quite ugly by the end of the first week with feathers and tufts of fluff sprouting from various parts of their bodies. They had learned quickly, though, and when the handler entered the cage there was a cacophony of begging noises and flapping of newly feathered wings as they hopped crawled and flapped their way on to his lap and jostled for the best position. The man was the happiest he had ever been, despite the mess. His lowly position in the village had not given him latitude to indulge freely in his hobby and now the Lord Ch0n had provided him with the birds, the feed and the prestige of working for the Royal Livestock Manager. Under his loving care, not one of the birds was lost. He knew instinctively how to design the new cage and he had fussed over its construction. It had to face the sun but have a shaded area for the nesting cubicles. The birds should be allowed to fly free after they had developed all their feathers but they had had to move as soon as possible to the big cage or they would want to return to the small one. The perch at the entrance to the cage had to be on the very lip of a step with vertical bars so the birds could enter the cage after they returned from a flight by jumping down with their wings closed but could not leave because their wings would be open as they flew upwards. It was a version of a trap he had made as a child. Ch0n was impressed and happy.

"How long before they can fly, Mori?"

"How should I know, King? I am new at this just as you are. One day I will come in and they will all be perched up there on the sticks. Then we will know they can fly a little. When that 'appens I will let your boy know."

The rest of Ch0n's time was taken up with the Household Cavalry. One day after they arrived back from the overhang, the recruits from the Buq'ue fort had arrived with the council members and a platoon of soldiers. Jez was fully engaged in housing the men. Karín's new adjutant, a thorough woman called Carmodi, was fully engaged in housing the women and their tlaque. The councillors were billeted with their counterparts. Sonja was fully occupied supervising the shaving of heads and the boiling of clothes. Kelda was fully engaged in the administration of the village logistics and catering for almost a hundred extra personnel. Boro had to design and build more stables and at Sonja's direction had commenced the construction of a second set of baths adjoining the first. He was still working on the castle walls, both the perimeter and the main castle, Jez's quarters and he had to plan the next blast. They were heady times in the Castle. Years later they would still be talking about that one week when their community came together truly for the first time.

They had been practising daily now for almost a week, the King's Troop. Karín had warned them about their thigh muscles when they first formed the troop and they had been doing stretching exercises for days beforehand. Just so, the first day she restricted them to two one hour sessions mounted. It was as much for the tlaque as for their riders, she explained. By the end of the seventh day, she had them riding all day in pairs for safety. Some had fallen quite badly but apart from some bruising and a cut head or two, they were intact. Between Karín and Ch0n they had them controlling the tlaque quite expertly by the end of that seventh day. They knew they were in for a long, hard ride on the tenth day so they had the incentive to work hard.

The new recruits had an advantage over the King's Troop. They had their tlaques when they were formed so from the time they had made their saddles and tack, they were able to ride. They were only a few days behind the King's Troop in that regard.

On the eighth day, Ch0n had the King's Troop form up in their riding pairs in column. At their head was Karín. They looked splendid in their black wool pyjami trousers tucked into their calf-length moccasin boots, and their red-dyed wool shirts that Karín had chosen and had made. On their heads they wore the black turban of the style Karín had worn when he had first seen her, with just their eyes showing. They had had these new uniforms for five days now and wore them everywhere, drawing looks of admiration and not a few lewd comments wherever they went. They always went in pairs. Sisters they were called and sisters they were.

The Second Troop looked on. They wore the same rig but their shirts were of indigo.

"Look around you and you will see the King's Troop as they will ride from now on! This is called, Column of Twos. You have seen it on the wall in the training room. Now! Two troop, do the same behind the King's Troop. Yes! Over there, you! Here to me. Good. All the way back. With your sister. Good. Now hold that."

He rode to the head of the column and off to one side. He took the tablet from his thigh pocket and captured an image.

"Look around you. This is the Household Cavalry of the Arw'an and Buq'ue united tribes. It is the first time you have been assembled together. It is the first time Brigadier General Karín has sat at the head of the column that is her command. Look around and say to yourself, 'I am part of history.' I can tell you that never anywhere has a mounted force of women been assembled. Two troop, you may return to your riding practice until I call you to the training room. King's Troop, I leave you with the Brigadier General to practice riding in column. Tomorrow we will practice changing formations."

ChOn rode through the castle to the Lancer lines. He had to get ready for a lesson in tactics and formations. He had never been so busy and he was thriving on it.

Chapter Twenty One: The Overhang

They left for the overhang ten days after the oruk expedition. This time they aimed to drive some of the females back to the castle as well as capture more birds and ChOn was curious about the almost-white silken haired goats as well. At the last minute he had decided to incorporate the expedition with some military training so they left with the entire Household Cavalry and a baggage train of ten tlaque females towing travois laden with supplies for more than a seventy-strong force. For the first time ever, these were being led by some of Kelda's catering people mounted on tlaque. Karín rode at the head of the entire column as they left the castle. People lined the path up to and outside the gates and children ran alongside. She stood in the stirrups and turned around. Behind her stretched the two troops, resplendent in their uniforms and impressive in their formations. Each lancer carried a bamboo lance resting in a depression in the top of her right-side stirrup cup. Each lance was exactly eight feet long, tipped with a metal point and bearing a small woollen ribbon, red or indigo, to depict her troop. Karín had no such lance. She was dressed as was ChOn in full battle order, her katana over her right shoulder and her battle ax hanging from the saddle horn. On her head in place of the turban, she wore her helm with the gold visor in place. Her sling was around her neck as usual. Her only concessions to the Cavalry were two signal flags, one red and one indigo on short sticks tucked into loops on her saddle.

ChOn was riding off to one side of the column. He wanted Karín to feel the thrill of leading her command out of the castle.

"Meet me on eleven."

ChOn reached up and pressed the button until the number was shown on the heads-up.

"Thank you for letting me do this. For trusting my instincts above your own. Look at what we have done. Even if I die tomorrow I will know that you have given me the priceless gift of true equality."

"They look good but the true test of their mettle is yet to come. I will show you what I mean before the day is done. But, yes. You were right about them. As your King I give you thanks. As your agen I will thank you later."

"Look at this force, Ch0n. You are the only grown man among us. If you engage in íjon with their Commander will they not feel aggrieved? Alik is probably too young for them but he may yet prove himself man enough."

"You are right. I will try and do them all before I get to you. That way they cannot complain."

He heard her laugh into the mike.

"If you succeed it will be both the single biggest íjon ever undertaken by one man followed by the biggest massacre ever perpetrated by a lone woman."

"That would be a waste of good Lancers. Better to let them complain."

They reached the overhang in the mid afternoon. They checked for dragons and found none so they took the column down to the river.

"Get the cooking pots set up while we do some short training exercises!" shouted Ch0n to Kelda's team leader.

He took Karín out on to the plain and towards a small, linear copse of trees. They positioned themselves so the line of trees was abreast across their front.

"I want you to imagine that line of trees is a line of soldiers about to attack the spot we are standing on. They can move at walking pace and then they will jog. In a battle, I would have the King's Troop waiting over there in the depression. I want you to attack that line of trees in line abreast when I give the order over the radio. OK? Now take them over there and wait for my command. Tell Two Troop to come to me so they can watch and learn."

It took several minutes for Karín to have the troop ready. She described the ground in front of the depression and told the Lancers what to do. She wanted them to leave the depression in column, form two lines facing the copse and charge down the line of it. They all listened eagerly and nodded that they understood.

Up on the knoll overlooking the copse, Ch0n was telling Two Troop the pitfalls of a cavalry charge.

"There are two difficult things to do. One is to maintain the line so you all hit the enemy at the same time. The other thing is that the flank riders always want to get in the action so they attack the target instead of attacking past it in formation. It almost always results in bunching up in the middle, riders passing one in front of another and the whole thing looking decidedly unprofessional. I want you to watch as both of those things go wrong. Remember it is their first go at this so don't be critical. And one other thing. The commander usually gets caught up in the emotion of it all and ends up first to the battle by a long way."

"OK Commander, attack the left flank now!"

It was an impressive sight. The King's Troop filed out of the depression and did a nice manoeuvre on the move to put themselves in formation for the charge. Karín had the red flag held out at arm's length and flat. The Lancers held the line and then she had them walking, trotting and finally charging at the enemy.

It took about five seconds for things to start unfolding badly. Firstly, Karín was racing away with the katana held high outstripping the others by yards. The rest of the troop broke and ran at the enemy in a ragged line. Then the flanks started to push inwards towards the narrow enemy position and in the bunching, momentum was lost and the charge faltered. Only Karín made it at the gallop and she rode triumphantly through hacking saplings left and right, only to look back and find she was alone. The others arrived in dribs and drabs.

Some of those watching laughed. Ch0n was one of them. But it was not a laugh of sarcasm. It was genuinely funny what he had just seen. He put the tablet back in his pocket and waved for the mighty King's Troop to gather on him. They managed to find their sisters and arrived in a gaggle almost like a column with Karín bringing up the rear.

"Don't be hard on them, Commander," he told her as she trotted up the slope. "This was a training exercise and it went as expected. And more importantly, don't be hard on yourself. Now come and listen to what I have to say."

He gathered them all around in a semi-circle. It took up a large area, sixty mounted troopers. He removed his helm so he could shout.

"That went quite well except for a few little issues!"

This was greeted with peals of laughter from all concerned except Karín, who failed to see the funny side of it.

"The reason we do our riding in formation on the plains and not under pressure is so that we know how to do it in the heat of battle."

He went on to explain all the things that needed to be practised at the walk. Then at the trot. How it was important that the flanking troopers were rotated for reasons of dressing and direct contact with the enemy.

"Finally, I would like to congratulate your commander on single-handedly killing most of the enemy saplings and earning the king's bravery award for attacking the position alone."

A great cheer went up mixed with good natured comments about wanting to kill more than her share and so on. This time Karín smiled. He was right. He was always right with these things.

She stood in her stirrups.

"Lancers' day at the baths!"

They trotted down to the river under the overhang and took the tlaques to their roped off area by the stream. They hobbled them and raced to the water. Ch0n and Karín stayed where they were.

"We have a lot to learn, don't we?"

"We have time to learn it. We will learn the most important things first. That was the most important lesson today. By the way, you need to choose two troop leaders. You have no place leading a charge. On a parade you will ride at their head but in battle you will be needed where the decisions are being made. At the front of a charge you can command nothing and you may die in the first assault. You're no good to the cavalry dead. Or to me. When we get back I will show you how to plan an attack and to practise one. The Cavalry will always be used as a weapon of speed and manoeuvre. You will be called to turn a battle at the critical moment so practice is essential. By the way, I'm glad I'm not a tree sapling. You murdered dozens of them."

They rode to the overhang and Alik took ChOn's and Karín's tlaques. They went to the water's edge where sixty naked women were splashing around with abandon.

"This will be a test for you, my agen. If you become aroused, don't show it off. If you do, these girls will never think an Arw'an man is normal. I am happy for you to look at these women because I know I am more beautiful to you than any of them. You have told me. And if it arouses your passions to be among them? Well only we will benefit."

ChOn stripped naked and walked into the cool water. Heads turned to watch him and some of those watching spoke to their sisters behind their hands. A voice shouted,

"Karín, even my tlaque is not as well-endowed as your mount!"

There was general laughter.

"And no doubt you have sampled your mount, Shuzi!" countered another.

ChOn lowered himself from view and tried not to look at the acres of bare bodies frolicking only yards from him. Karín followed him and the sixty pairs of eyes followed her as they had followed ChOn for she was indeed magnificent to behold. Her skin shone pale orange/yellow in the evening sun. Her belly was as hard as a man's and the rows of muscles could be counted individually. Her legs were long and strong, joined at the top by firm buttocks. Her breasts were small and round and moved in unison as she walked. Her face was towards ChOn and she was smiling. Wisps of her short red hair lifted in the breeze. And then she was gone, just another head bobbing next to ChOn's.

"That was some entrance, wife. They couldn't tear their eyes away from you. Neither could I."

"Now they know what you have. Now they know what I have."

"The food will soon be ready. And the herds will soon be here. Don't forget your oruk horns. They will take up a whole travois on the way back. Time to get to work."

He left the water and dressed in full view of the women. He made no attempt to hide himself and they made no secret of the fact they were looking at him. This time there were no lewd jokes. The overwhelming feeling among the women was envy. Only Malek and her lancer-sister commented in low whispers.

"She is beautiful in her way but you are more so, Malek and you are tall enough. Wouldn't you like to sample that thing when it is angry?"

"I would love to but it isn't worth my head and that is the price she has put on it."

"Reny told me he was within a heartbeat of following her to the baths to make íjon with her."

"Aye but she forgets the part where Karín followed her and touched her on the neck with the sword she carries. Forget Ch0n's dewen. It is for her alone. Besides, you are too small for him. There are plenty of men to go around. I have set my eye for Jez. I hear he has been practising with the woman Sonja. Come. We are the last two."

"I will have him and my tiny form will be what makes him want me for every man desires that which is different from what he knows."

They ate well and doused the fires so as not to frighten the herd animals away. As the sun dropped, the birds set up their racket and the herds started to arrive to drink. Ch0n ignored the tlaque and watched the silken goats. The flock numbered more than a hundred and Ch0n could identify several males with wide spread horns. The females had smaller almost vertical horns and were a lot smaller than the males. He walked among them and they had no fear of him, just like the other herd animals. He wondered if they could be driven and decided to take the entire herd back to the castle if he could manage it. If not, he would stun a male and twenty females and lead them back tied to the saddles of the Lancers.

The oruk arrived last and went straight to the water. The goats and tlaque made way for them. There were at least thirty new calves at the feet of their mothers. The bulls were all scarred and some were bleeding from wounds that would eventually kill them. The passing of the old bull had created a power vacuum and they had fought themselves to a standstill until only one was able to continue. He was surrounded now by the mature cows and the other bulls were wandering the perimeter of the herd hoping to quickly mount a female while the dominant bull was distracted. Ch0n's tlaque was causing Alik all sorts of bother, despite being tethered and hobbled. He kept trumpeting his challenge but the herd bull had had enough of the pulse to avoid him.

"Wife, can we spare some of the sweet root for the tlaque? He is desperate for a fight."

Karín went to a large bag she had had brought along. In it were balls of the sticky root she had used to subdue her tlaque the first time she rode him. They were going to try and ride into the oruk herd and feed it to ten of the females with young at foot so they could be driven away from the main herd without panicking. In any regard they were going to push them away using sheer weight of numbers of tlaque. Ch0n had even considered trying to herd the new dominant bull away with some of his females or all of them and then cut out those they wanted at the last moment near the castle.

Ch0n went to the tlaque and fed him the sticky ball. In a few moments he was quiet and dopey. It was almost dark now. He saw a flurry of wings in the branches and one of the orange and blue birds disappeared into a hole in the trunk of a tree, high up.

"Alik. Do you think you could climb up there to that hole tomorrow early? I think there is a nest in it and I do so want one of those beautiful birds."

"Of course I could, My Lord. There are so many branches leading up to it, it is almost like a ladder."

"Just one. I want just one baby or egg. Leave the rest. It is a gift fit for the keeper of the birds and for him alone."

"As you wish My Lord."

They spent the early part of the night huddled in several groups listening to Ch0n tell of the future he had for the Overhang. The squire, Alik, was with them. The wolf was sitting at the boy's side, his eyes never leaving Ch0n.

"We are going to set up an outpost here with a square-based brick tower that can be defended. The red clay will be mined from over that side of the river and taken to a place downstream where an oven will be fired using wood from the branches of the trees. We will not touch the trees here for they are too beautiful and provide food and shelter for too many creatures. Where there is less water and the trees are tall and spindly is where we will make the pottery factory. The bricks we will mould and leave in the sun to dry. I was going to cook them but the damage to the forests would be too severe. They will cure almost as well in the sun. It will take longer, that's all. We will build carts with wheels that can carry the bricks anywhere we need them. The carts will be drawn by oruk. This will be an important centre for us. It will need to be a small village but organized properly. It will never have to move because the dagononum has been killed. Its hide is in the trees tied there to dry in the shape of a man's chest. It will eventually be cut for body armour or shields as will the hides of any others we have to kill."

Gradually the night wore on and people slept where they had been sitting. Karín snuggled into ChOn. The boy snuggled up to the wolf, which had moved next to ChOn. The Lancers snuggled up to each other. The sound of girls whispering was the only noise other than the rustling of the leaves.

ChOn woke up while it was still dark. He went to where the tlaque were tethered. Being all geldings they were not affected by the scent of the females and the dominant male had no interest in them. ChOn's beast was chewing cud with his short hobbles tucked in underneath him. ChOn surveyed the scene using the thermal imaging application combined with the light amplification mode and saw the oruk herd was still with them.

The sun was still well hidden. The 'eastern' sky wasn't even showing the first hint of silver but to him it was like broad daylight. He wandered back to the sleeping area with the visor active. He had to step past most of the Lancers to get back to Karín. Through his visor, they all appeared naked. He saw that some of them were now awake and were trying to pick out who was moving about in the gloom. He recognised Malek's lancer-sister as one of them. She stood up and appeared to look straight at him. He knew she could not see him, even if she had guessed it was him moving about. He stopped to watch her. She had to know he was watching her because she smiled at him. He turned towards the sleeping Karín and made the last few yards to her side. He looked back at Malek's lancer-sister again before he turned off the array. The last thing he saw was the girl motioning for him to follow her to the trees from where he had just come.

No. She couldn't see him. She couldn't.

ChOn lay on his rug and pondered the last minutes. It was almost pitch-black under the overhang. He tried to look through the darkness unaided but he could see nothing at all. Just blackness, even with his sensitive eyes. It was eerie. He put the helm on his head and selected the thermal and light amplification combination again. The overhang lit up like daylight. He could see the birds asleep in their tunnels in the roof and by turning his head he could see Karín. On his other side was the wolf, its eyes glowing hugely green, watching him. Two yards away one of the women was moving restlessly. She opened her eyes and ChOn saw the green pricks of light that were behind her pupils. He sat up quietly. Five yards to his left, Malek and her sister were located. He looked in that direction. He could see quite clearly the near-naked body of Malek. Her sister was still standing, seemingly able to look around the sleeping space. She stretched slowly and turned her face in ChOn's direction and appeared to look him in the eye through the visor. Her eyes were large and green like the wolf's. Then she smiled at him again and walked confidently out of the sleeping area in the direction of the tlaque line.

ChOn had to know. It was imperative that he know. Tactically and strategically she could be a weapon of immense importance. He stood up and motioned for the wolf to stay. He looked down at Karín, who didn't stir. He picked his way through the seemingly naked women and walked to where the tlaque was tethered. He could not see the woman. Then she stepped out from behind a tree and walked confidently to him with her tunic over her shoulder.

"I knew you would follow me. Quickly now."

She put her hand under his tunic and took hold of him. He stepped back from her.

"I have to know. Can you see in the dark? Put your tunic back on and stand away from me because if Karín comes, she will kill you and I need you alive if you can see in the dark. I watched you watching me. You watched me watching you. I saw the size of your pupils. It's true isn't it?"

"If I tell you the truth will you make íjon with me?"

"No. And if you do not tell me the truth I will have no reason to be here with you and Karín will kill you. Give me a reason. And dress yourself. If she comes and finds me thus excited she will kill you anyway. Just do it and come to your senses, girl, or you will not see the sunrise."

"Promise me an exchange if I tell you or you will never know for certain."

"An exchange? Am I prepared to exchange something for your secret? All right, I accept. What is your name?"

"Buyo. I will need time before I can tell you what I want in return."

"Buyo?"

"Yes. When I was a small girl I realized I was different from others. I do not know why but I have always been able to see in total darkness. I have never told anybody, not even my parents because I know how much my gift is worth as a secret and how little it is worth if people know."

"How far can you see?"

"Distance has no bearing on it. I can see. I can see as far at night as I can during the day. The black part of my eye is normal during the day but expands like an owl's in the dark. I have used my ability for different things but mostly I just play silly games. Like just now with you except that this game is serious. I wanted you to follow me. I wanted you in me. Now you know my secret. Actually, my two secrets."

"That is a wonderful secret and certainly worthy of an exchange but I would know your price before the end of the day."

"I shall tell you without fail but I have to think it through first."

"I will tell Karín your secret. Just the one about your eyes or she will probably kill you even though we have not made íjon. I will make you a spy if you will accept but it will be dangerous and you may have to use your body to keep your disguise and to gain information we need. You would need to be willing. The other secret, your desire to lie with me, had best remain between us."

"It would be a personal thing between us. The exchange, that is. Nothing too hard to give."

"Go back to bed, Buyo."

"Lord, Ch0n. Thank you for not mocking me for my silliness. I will be a good spy and as willing with my mind and body as you need. I will tell you the exchange you have promised me before the day is out."

Ch0n walked quickly back to his bed space and lay beside Karín again. He watched Buyo return to her space in the darkness. She smiled at him across the blackness and lay down next to Malek. Ch0n shook Karín.

"Not again, agen, surely." She pushed her backside into him.

"No, it isn't that. I watched the girl Buyo leave the sleeping area and go outside. She walked around the sleeping women as though it were daylight. I followed her with the helm and asked her if she could see in the dark. At first she was coy about it but then she told me. She has eyes like an owl, she says. Do you realize what that means? I told her I would have her as a spy and she has agreed. You will probably need to find a replacement for her in the troop unless she can juggle two different posts but she may have to spend long periods away and that would affect her sister, Malek's ability to perform."

"And you woke me up for that? It could have waited until morning. I preferred the last time you woke me. Now go to sleep and we will talk about it tomorrow."

ChOn sat up again and watched Buyo, whose eyes were open, staring at him. He really did like the idea of trying íjon with her but he did not want to betray Karín. What had she said?

"You have the right to lie with any woman you choose and I may not complain but I will kill them afterwards. You have the right."

"So it is normal for Arw'an and Buq'ue men to make íjon with other women," ChOn thought. "Karín's objection is on personal grounds and not moral ones? If there are no moral ones then I do have the right and if I have the right, I should protect any woman I made íjon with by hiding her identity. That sounds strange logic. I will have to think about it. But, my! She is a pocket sized beauty.

He stared at the girl and she stared right back at his visor with her huge green, unblinking eyes.

He must have slept because he woke up with a sore neck and his helm still in place. The sun was just starting to show above the dark orange horizon. Alik and the wolf were gone. Half the Lancers were dressed and tending their tlaque. Karín was stirring and Kelda's assistant had the porridge on the boil. ChOn went to his tlaque and saw a group of the women watching Alik climb the tree to the hollow in the trunk. He reached in and fumbled about for a few seconds and then produced a pale-orange egg. He put it in his kamarband and easily returned to the ground.

"One egg as you instructed, Lord. The nest had but two. This will have to be kept warm as though the female were sitting on it. It needs to be safe from spilling and getting bumped."

Ch0n had already thought of how he was going to solve that problem. He called to one of the Two Troop Lancers.

"You, girl. What is your name?"

"Kora, My Lord."

"Well Kora, I see that of all the women here you have the best place in which to keep this egg warm. Please place it down the front of your tunic and keep it safe in the cleft between your.... down there."

There was a shriek of laughter from all present. Alik blushed and Kora cupped her ample breasts.

"It will be safe and warm in here, My Lord, have no fear. And no hand but yours will retrieve it."

More laughter followed, even from Karín, who had arrived late on the scene.

"Everyone to breakfast for the oruk may move without warning. We will leave as soon as we can pack up. Commander, please have the King's Troop go to the far side of the oruk herd with me. I would like Two Troop under yourself, to herd the white silky goats. If they will not be herded, stun one male and twenty females and drag them back on ropes when they awake. Put the pulse to twenty. Show me. Twenty. Good. Step lively and eat fast. When I mount up, I want the King's Troop ready."

They rounded the back of the oruk herd before the bull stirred. By riding the tlaque right up to the faces of the oruk cows, they were able to make them stand and then they crowded them together in a bunch with the tlaque around them and among them and they all started to move towards the trail to the castle.

The cows went quietly enough with their calves following and ChOn thought he was home free when the bull stood up and started to walk in the other direction. The cows paid him no heed because they could not see him moving and he was downwind of them but the bull could smell some of his cows leaving the herd and he bawled for them to come back. By crowding the cows, the Lancers kept them moving. ChOn checked the bull and drew the pulse. He set it to one hundred and did a self-check on it. He peeled off the back of the group and rode towards the bull.

Karín's troop had had to stun and rope the goats because they kept splitting up into small groups and scattering. She was on the ground supervising the roping of the creatures and when the rest of the girls re-mounted, she was still tying her oruk-horn trophy to the travois. The oruk bull started to trot angrily towards his wayward cows and he spied Karín on the ground off to one side of them. ChOn saw the bull change direction and start the charge and in a split second saw he could not fire the pulse because Karín was in the danger area. He slid from the tlaque and ran at Karín, shouting at the bull as he ran, and drawing Shiew at the same time.

"Hey bull over here! Hey bull heyheyhey over here!"

The bull checked his run at Karín and swerved towards ChOn but then turned back for Karín. She was standing stock still in a crouch.

"Hey bull over here! Hey bull heyheyhey over here! OVER HERE!"

Karín looked long at ChOn and smiled. She waited until the bull was ten feet away and jumped to the side opposite ChOn, who arrived almost at the same time as the bull. He slashed at the bull's forelegs with Shiew and felt a wave of panic because he did not feel any resistance against the blade. He was sure he had missed but the creature fell flat on its face and its rump went over its head in an untidy somersault. It was screaming in pain and rage and trying to stand up on legs that were not there. Ch0n raced to it and slashed it and slashed it and slashed it through the head and then again through the neck and the mane. He was screaming with anger and relief at the same time. When Karín called him to stop, he was splattered with gore and his breath was ragged from the exertion and the adrenalin rush. Some of the Lancers were cheering. Others were dumbstruck. A few wept with relief.

"What kept you so long my hero?"

"I thought you were going to wrestle it. I was placing bets on you with Alik. He thought the bull would win," grinned Ch0n. "I thought I was going to lose you."

"Not so easily My Lord. Come on we have to get this lot back to the castle."

And so the legend of Ch0n the bull slayer was born. Seventy witnesses all had a different version of how he had slain the creature with nothing but a sword but all had one thing in common.

"He did it for her." They would say later. *"She just stood there smiling at him while he ran in and killed it for love of her. An oruk bull. With nothing but a naked blade. One bull against another."*

Doni was almost frantic when they arrived. Even with Makin the Buq'ue Beastmaster helping, he was rattled.

"My Lord, we will need more corrals. Oh how beautiful are those silken goats! How are we going to house these oruk? Aren't they magnificent and they have calves at foot! There will be more milk. We will run out of grass. Oh! Look at that

beauty! I suppose we will manage them if we re-arrange a few things."

"Kora!" called Ch0n. "Kora, I need you."

"If she's not available, I certainly am, My Lord," cooed a voice from Two Troop to laughter all round.

"Here I am, My Lord", panted Kora."

Ch0n was feeling a bit pleased with himself. He looked at Karín and raised one eyebrow as he did when asking a question. She read his mind and nodded. Ch0n went to Kora and without a word, pulled open the collar of her tunic and put his hand between the girl's ample breasts.

The Lancers went wild with delight and Kora put her hands behind her head to raucous laughter. Ch0n made much show of looking for the egg and when he finally held it aloft, a huge cheer erupted. Karín was helpless with laughter and Kora was playing the crowd for all she was worth.

Alik appeared with the keeper of the birds.

"Mori, Alik has a gift for you. He climbed a tree and fetched it himself from a hollow trunk." He motioned for Alik to accept what was in his cupped hand. "Tell him what it is, boy."

"It's the egg of a giant orange bird with a blue head."

"The kwidada?" He looked at Ch0n and the boy. *"The kwidada is a bird of legend. Me grandfather's grandfather once saw one perched on a man's shoulder and it spoke to the man in the man's own voice. I 'ave never seen one. This is a gift fit for a King. Thank ye, boy. Now I must rush away and warm it for we know not 'ow many days ago it was laid, nor 'ow many days it will be before it 'atches."*

"Brigadier General Karín and troopers of the Household Cavalry! Gather round so I don't have to shout so much! In the past two days we have had an adventure such as some of you have never had before. Savour what you have experienced. Think about what it meant to you as a person, as a woman and as a trooper for I will tell you this. The bond that a soldier feels for his fellow soldier is a bond like no other. It is a bond that will stick firmer than the ébon between an agen and an aget. It is a thing that will make a soldier get up in the middle of the night and leave her lover and go to die in the company of her sisters in the defence of all. That bond is formed by shared adventures, the silly games and jokes, the sharing of a secret, the hardships and the shared fear and the shared triumph. No training school can teach you how to form a bond. I share a small bond with you all because we have done this thing together and shared the teamwork we needed to employ to keep the herd together when the bull would have re-taken his cows. All that will out in battle. You can not share this with your families, tho' you try. They will not understand what you are trying to share. That is why the life of a soldier is a lonely one and yet one filled with colleagues. Look at your sister. Look at her! You will come to know her better than her mother knows her. Look at the trooper on the other side of you. You will come to depend on that trooper more than you ever depended on your family. Now look at your Commander. She will be life and death to you for when the bond is formed, you will gladly give your life rather than see your sisters or your cousins the Infantry found wanting. That I offer you and that I promise you. You will find that everything will be a little easier tomorrow because two days together in the field are worth twenty in the lines. I thank you for your work gladly given these past two days. Now. Go to your stables and check the beasts for parasites on their skin and blisters under their saddles. Rub them well and whisper sweet things in their ears for they have borne you without complaint for two whole days. In the morning, Two Troop, we will be back in the training room.

King's Troop will be under the charge of the Brigadier General practising changing-formations-on-the-move and in the afternoon we will attack another copse of trees and this time I hope we don't lose the battle."

It was a long speech but ChOn was happy with the troops and happy with their work. They would never be the same after those two days and as time passed they would change more and more as they became more disciplined and more practised.

"It is women's day at the baths," said Karín. *"If you like I will go and see if there is anybody there and if not I'll let you know on eleven."*

"I imagine the entire Household Cavalry will be there as soon as they have quartered their tlaque."

"They have seen you naked now and you, them. Nobody will care if you go down. It is only the civilians I am thinking about." She strode off along the wall to the baths. ChOn started towards his quarters but a voice stopped him.

"Oh! it's you, Buyo. You'll be late for the baths."

"I have to tell you the price of my secret, My Lord. Remember? You promised me an exchange."

"Of course I remember. Now what value have you put on it?"

"I have been thinking all day of my value to you as a spy. You told me it may be dangerous and that I accept. You told me I may have to use my body and that I also accept for it is just a body like any other body and I would not be doing anything I have not done before. There may be a time when my actions save many lives, is that not so?"

"One or more."

"So here is my price, my exchange. I wish to be taken out of the Household Cavalry and placed on your personal staff for training and tasking. But if I am so placed, it will be obvious to all that something is afoot. So I wish it to appear that I am on Karín's personal staff; not like Carmodi her adjutant but as her personal assistant. As Alik is yours. To serve her in her quarters as Alik serves you. Has she not told you she would have a squire?"

"Yes, she has."

"Then I want it to be me. I can live in the stables next to the squire, Alik. When Sir Jez's quarters are finished, he and Beny will move out, Alik gets his own loft and I get mine. Karín has her tlaque in the stable next to yours and Karín has her squire. But it is a front for your spy. Nobody will suspect I am in your service. It will be a secret service with Karín providing the camouflage. Reny should be appointed Troop Commander so Malek can sister up with Flora. Reny brings in two of the reserves in training and the King's Troop is complete again."

"This morning you said it would be a personal thing between us. So far you have mentioned only logical military reasons, all of which make sense but none of which involves a price for your telling me your secret."

"But they are all connected, My Lord. I get to be on your personal secret service. I get direct access to you on matters of secret missions and you get to train me personally in all aspects of spying, including the use of weapons and poison, disguise and subterfuge and so on. That is my exchange. I get to be near you and when Karín is otherwise indisposed, I will shave you and bathe you. That is the personal thing between us. Nothing more."

"I can see that is all well thought out. You are bright as well as... well, pretty. Karín will agree to it all because it suits her

337

Gavan Connell

needs. I will lay down the boundaries of your secret service training and tell her where she may not interfere. As to your getting to shave and bathe me in Karín's absence, I think Sonja will have something to say about that."

"I can be very persuasive, My Lord as you will discover to your delight. Now I can go to the baths. Will you be there?"

"If Karín tells me there are no civilians there."

"Then please don't tell her of your plans for me just yet. I would hate to be classified as a civilian and miss out on seeing you take your bath."

Ch0n wandered to his quarters via the bird cage. He shone his flashlight to where the birds were huddled in the corner. Was it his imagination or were they more feathered up than they were two days ago? He was still looking at them when his helm crackled into life. It was under his arm and he had to put it on to activate the mike.

"There are a few Lancers here but no others. Come quickly while there is still room."

Later they were sitting in their quarters discussing the trip away when Ch0n suddenly said,

"I forgot to collect more dáguia chicks in my haste to herd the other animals. Someone will have to go back and get them. Maybe in another ten days we can take the King's Troop back there, collect some and take them straight to the Buq'ue fort. I don't want to be too long away from there without checking up on it."

"Good idea, agen. I also want to return to that den of traitors and see how Izaki is managing. But I have a request. I have asked you before and you were not in agreement but this whole commander business is more than I can manage with my other

duties to you and the new troop. I feel I need a squire as well as an adjutant."

"I was going to raise that very thing with you tonight. I have been thinking hard about the value of the girl, Buyo and her gift of night-vision. She is far too valuable an asset to have as a lancer. I need a way to bring her under my personal control and to do so without a pretext would start people wondering so here is what I propose…."

"Would she agree to that plan?"

"She stayed behind at the pens and we discussed it then and again briefly at the baths before Malek came too close for us to speak privately. She is excited at the prospect of what she calls her 'secret service' to the Arw'an and it was she who came up with the pretext of doubling up as your squire. It is a perfect disguise, right under everybody's noses. As the shaman, Pik said, you don't have to be invisible to disappear in plain sight. All this will come about when Jez is ready to move out. I will check Boro's progress tomorrow but the stables should be ready by now or if not, in a day or so. That will free up one loft for the girl and your tlaque will have her own stall as well. Alik can concentrate more on his training while Buyo attends to your needs and undertakes her training with me. One thing, though. If I need her, I get her and Alik can help you out until she is available again. Her training may take her away from here for days at a time. I will give you as much notice as I can but it is a necessary condition."

"No wonder you forgot the dáguia. You have too much on your mind and too many plans running around in your head. You need to slow down and consolidate what you have started. Boro is exhausted. Kelda is extended beyond what she should be able to produce. And Doni gets a new herd of beasts every time you go through the gate. If you don't slow down you will kill us all."

Gavan Connell

"You're right of course. I will plan no new projects until some of the current ones are functioning properly."

"Speaking of functioning properly, I have decided to take your advice and appoint two Troop Leaders so I can concentrate less on detail and more on learning how to command. Who do you think might be suitable?"

"Well, the night Reny showed me her ibuw, I watched her talking to her sister about the lessons we had been learning that day. I have watched her since as I am sure you have albeit for different reasons and I think she would be good."

"I had thought of her or maybe the girl Jesup. She has been very quick to learn but I think Reny has been quick to learn and also quick to teach for she has been actively helping the others where they were lacking. She is more of a leader, I think."

"And Two Troop? I barely know them because I have not had much chance to spend time with them. The girl who was helping you tie the goats is one I noticed more than most."

"The fact she had the perkiest ikimwamwas in the baths tonight may have sparked your memory might it not?"

"Perhaps a little."

"I chose her to help me this morning because she has always been first to help in the lines and the first to finish everything. She is strong and loyal. I have known her since she was born, as I have known all the Buq'ue Lancers. She is a favourite of mine. You were right about her. Apart from her 'wamwas, she has other qualities."

Ch0n laughed.

"Then it's settled? Reny and Wamwas? Malek gets Reny's sister and two of the trainees as replacements. What of Buyo's mount?"

Karín laughed with him.

"'Wamwas' is called Eloik. She is the daughter of Eloi. Thus the 'ik' on the end. As for Buyo's mount, will she need one as a spy? I think it would be hard to be invisible on a tlaque. Does she need one as my squire? Neither Jez nor Alik has had one. I think she could do without it. Perhaps it could be used by those who need one from time to time. If you are at the Buq'ue fort and you send for something, a dispatch rider could be.... well, dispatched. She will not be happy about it because like all of us she has grown fond of her beast but I don't think she needs it. Certainly not on a full time basis."

"It could be kept in the King's Troop stables and used by them as well if one of their own goes down for some reason. I think that's a good way to keep it in work. The reserve Lancers are performing the work of grooms so its care will not be a burden on anybody."

"So when do these changes take place? I would think tomorrow. Will you announce the promotions? I think it should be me."

"Most definitely you."

"Now we have discussed business all evening, there is the not so small matter of your actions this morning at the Overhang. I recall my previous bull killing all those men who were trying to take its horns and you go and jump in front of one in peril of your own life. Already they are calling you 'The Bull'. 'One bull killed the other,' they are saying. You frightened me. You saved me but you frightened me. I am supposed to be your bodyguard, not the other way around. What would we do without you? Where would our dreams disappear to? I am forever grateful to you and I know you would have done the same for any of us but we need you too much to lose you. I

Gavan Connell

need you too much to lose you. Not now I have finally found you."

"Remember my dream? Remember I told you I was in the battlements with you? That has to come to pass before either you or I die or why would I have dreamed it? I am not going to say we are immortal or anything silly like that but I believe in my dream. It was too real and you were in it and I had never seen you before. I can imagine dreaming a dream now with you or Jez or Boro or Malek in it because I know you all but I dreamed of you *before* I knew you. It has to be an omen of some sort. By the way, why did you smile at me before you leapt away and why did you jump to that side?"

"I smiled because if I had have died, I wanted it to be the last thing I ever did and the last vision you would ever have of me. I jumped to the other side to give you room to swing Shiew. Both actions were thought out. I was just waiting for you to turn up. So, My Lord and agen. I owe you my life. Not that it makes a difference for it was yours before this morning but now it is truly yours. As your wyf I should thank you for it and teach you how to make íjon like the bull you reputedly are. You are getting better but a bull you are not. Don't look sad. These things take time to learn. It's like leading a Cavalry Charge. Sometimes you get there too soon."

Chapter Twenty Two: The King of the Buq'ue

It took one day to finish Jez's stables and one more for Jez and Beny to move out. Then Buyo moved in. Karín had her two new Troop Commanders and Ch0n had his live-in spy. He tried hard not to start any new projects and apart from suggesting a factory to spin wool with what the minitron had decided was mohair, he was successful. He had instead spent a lot of time in the classroom with Two Troop under Eloik's command. Like the King's Troop they were quick learners and Eloik soon had them doing formations like veterans. Reny was having similar success with the King's Troop.

Ch0n decided it was time to practise a walkthrough charge against a live 'enemy'. He used Two Troop dismounted as the enemy. He had them form two skirmish lines and stand facing Ch0n and Karín. When Ch0n told Karín to deploy the Lancers, she raised the red flag and pointed it to the position, raising it and lowering it twice, in quick succession. The King's Troop walked from their position of cover towards the enemy and walked from column to line abreast with Reny falling back into the middle of the front rank. They walked all the way to the 'enemy' skirmishers and walked past them in two straight lines with no bunching. They continued past the position and Reny raised her hand and made circles in the air. The Lancers turned about, regrouped and went back through the enemy with what had been the second rank now leading. They continued through the position and once again Reny gave the about turn signal and an open handed chopping signal. The Lancers walked their mounts down among the enemy and milled around stabbing with their lances.

"Very good. Now have them do it at the trot. Exactly the same thing. Exactly the same but faster. This will test them."

Karín waved the flag and pointed it at the place they had been waiting. The Assembly Area, ChOn had called it. They found their formation and stood waiting for Karín to signal a new attempt. This time, when she signalled with the flag, she used her other fist to indicate that they were to trot. Two exaggerated pumps, for trot. The troop topped the rise and trotted down to where Reny signalled the change of formation. This was the Forming-up Point and where the troop had to quickly adopt their assault formation. Reny gave one exaggerated fist pump and they walked. Two and they trotted. They kept their line pretty well as Reny dropped back into the front rank. The flankers kept their eyes fixed on a point where they were to sweep through or past the enemy as well as making sure they held their line. They managed quite well apart from some bunching in the middle the first time they turned about.

"I am going to walk down to the enemy position while they set up for a practice at full speed. I will give you the signal. I want to talk to the troopers below about the noise and the shock value of a cavalry charge from the flank or rear." He gave the reins to Karín and he and the wolf trotted down the slope to the small mound where Two Troop was waiting.

"OK. Imagine you are attacking up to where Karín is standing. You are under fire from archers and slings and are struggling to make way." He waved to Karín. "Your colleagues are screaming out orders, falling down wounded, crying for their mothers and goodness knows what else. You are concentrating on making sure your shield is in the way of the next volley of arrows and stones and you hear this."

He had timed it perfectly. While he was talking to them and shouting at them, the King's Troop had left the Assembly Area and formed up. As if on cue they charged and the assembled Lancers looked in astonishment. They had not even seen the movement out of the Assembly area and all of a sudden the thunder was upon them. Some started to move out of their position.

"STAND STILL!" roared Ch0n as the King's Troop swept over them in a reasonable formation and then turned back and swept them again and finally rode among them. Reny was wide eyed and kept shouting at them and signalling for them to reform on the far side and they followed her command and reformed in two orderly ranks on the crest of the position from whence they had charged. The Two Troop Lancers were covered in dust and tlaque spittle. One had been knocked down and was nursing a sore shoulder and a cut cheek. All had learned something.

"I want you to imagine spears, arrows, stones, lances and perhaps swords added to the noise and weight of thirty tlaque. Imagine that while you are recovering and they are regrouping, fifty Infantry spearmen hit you from the front. Now imagine this. Imagine a line of Knights on oruk bulls leading the tlaque, smashing through the position first and keeping on going out of spear and arrow range. Imagine it. You saw the power in that bull at the Overhang."

"But you killed that bull with one stroke of your sword, My Lord."

"If you say so, Eloik but it was a sword like none other. My oruk will have frontal armour made from the back of a dagononum and our enemies will have short swords. At least for the first battle and that is when we want to annihilate them."

Karín rode on to the position leading Ch0n's tlaque. She addressed the King's Troop.

"That was quite good for a first try. Now we know the basics we can practise one of these every day. In three days, Two Troop

345

will do the same with the King's Troop on the mound. Now, go back to the lines and clean up. You can be first to use the new women-only baths. Sonja and Eloi announced this morning that they are ready. I am sorry My Lord but you will not be able to bathe with your Household Cavalry again."

"Aaah, Brigadier General Karín! That pains me but if I want to do it I will call for another expedition to the Overhang where it is always Lancer Day. Who would return for another adventure?"

They all cheered, including Karín.

"Soon we will return there but on light rations. We will collect some of the tlaque and dáguias and take them to the Buq'ue fort under full guard. We will march into that fort and people will line the streets to see us. Soon. In about ten days we will go."

The time passed quickly for the entire castle was busy. Three days before the Household Cavalry returned to the Overhang, the elders from the Buq'ue fort left with a platoon of Arw'an soldiers, their heads full of ideas and three tlaque females towing travois. Their calves trotted beside them and the does were full again, thanks to Ch0n's male. Doni had built more pens for the mohair goats, some of which had dropped kids and as with the other herd, the females with twins were being separated.

The oruk calves were several weeks old now and were filling out much faster than their tlaque cousins. All but one of the males, the strongest, had been gelded along with the tlaque males. The dáguias were in full feather and lived perched high in the bigger cage and ate porridge and loose grain. Mori had told Ch0n he was going to release the strongest of them on the other side of the castle and see if it had the homing instinct they all hoped for. The kwidada egg had still not hatched but Mori had shown Ch0n how to put the egg in a bamboo tube and shine a narrow beam of light through the shell to reveal its contents. They had done it twice now together and Mori confirmed to Ch0n that there was a chick inside. Mori had the egg wrapped in wool in the sun but he checked the temperature every few minutes to make sure it was not overheating. Twice a day he sprinkled water on the wool to increase the humidity.

"Me small birds pluck their chest feathers and sweat on the eggs; so eggs must need moisture as well as 'eat."

Boro had Jez's quarters ready to be roofed. They consisted of a square stone box of three small rooms with a door on one side, a passage running to the back and three open windows. The stables abutted the blank wall and there was also a space for a small garden at the back, where Beny was already digging-in the manure.

The castle walls were creeping ever higher and the roof of the first floor, which doubled as the floor of the second storey, was in position. The perimeter walls and main gate were finished. It had required another explosion to fracture enough rocks to continue and now Boro had enough to build the castle walls another ten feet high as well as finish the barracks for single men.

Sonja ruled the streets with an iron hand and would not allow any building extensions without good reason. She had built the new baths because the population of the castle was always increasing and the system of men's and women's days was just too cumbersome.

Kelda's administration and Logistics team had diversified. Some in the town had declared their desire to become barbers and tailors. Others specialized in cooking and yet others in looking after young children while their parents were working. Kelda had discussed ways these people could be rewarded for their work other than by being part of the communal kitchen at meal time.

"I will have to put something of value into the community so it can be traded for. One shave for one 'thing', and one day looking after your children for two 'things'. It is called money but swapping goods or services can also be used and that is called 'barter.' If I shave your beard, you will have to look after my child for the time it took me to do it. Something like that. I will think on it. Whatever we use has to have some value. It has to be restricted so it is worth something. I have an idea but it will need some working on."

Buyo was ensconced in Ch0n's stable and was ostensibly and actually Karín's squire. Ch0n had had little time to spend training her as a spy but he was not concerned. That would happen soon enough. For her part, she was happy to be close to Ch0n.

Alik was a fast learner and Ch0n had only to train him up to be a sparring partner with the sword. That was taking time but his other duties with the tlaque and Ch0n's weapons stores and uniforms he was managing with minimal supervision. Meanwhile, he, Karín, Beny and Jez practised daily with the wooden katanas.

In the knowledge that all in the castle was under control, Ch0n confirmed with the Household Cavalry that they would be leaving for the Overhang and the Buq'ue fort in three days. He told Karín the schedule he planned to keep and she passed on the information the Troop Leaders needed to know. Kelda was tasked to provide hard rations for the trip and Ch0n planned to kill what meat they needed as they travelled. He told Doni he would need three more tlaque with Travois. The dáguias were now flying about their aviary and the one Mori had released in the castle grounds had flown several circuits of the walls and then dropped down to the coop. It took it quite a while to work out how to get back in but soon it was happily perched with its cousins and Mori was racing to tell Ch0n of his successful flight. On the back of it, Ch0n ordered cages for twenty more of the chicks at the Overhang. Makin, the animal master on his way to the Buq'ue fort had the bamboo on a travois to make the first holding cage as soon as he arrived.

The night before departure, Chon called a meeting of the council and gave them their priorities for the next ten days and told them he would be in contact by radio relay through the OP if his plans were going to change. He was more than satisfied his people could run things in his absence with Jez staying behind to maintain control of any flare ups. Jez could also communicate privately with ChOn as far as the Overhang and most of the way to the Buq'ue fort so ChOn would still be able to exercise control from afar.

The castle was abuzz the next morning because the entire Household Cavalry was to be forming up in full rig and leaving through the main gate after breakfast. Most of the population was lining the streets to watch them as they passed in all their splendour, their red and indigo shirts standing out in the bright sunshine, their turbans hiding all but their eyes. Each of them rode with her lance resting on the top of the stirrup cup, the troop ribbon fluttering in the breeze. Karín rode at their head, her katana handle over her shoulder, moving in time to the tlaque's gait. Her ax swung from the horn. The two troop leaders were at the heads of their columns, each identical to her Lancers apart from the pennants that fluttered from their lances, which set them apart. ChOn left at the rear of the Lancers but ahead of the three tlaque females and their travois. Alik was astride one of them with ChOn's and Karín's essentials dragging behind. Buyo was astride another with the cages on top of some supplies and one of Kelda's quartermasters astride the last with the rest of the supplies. ChOn stood in the stirrups and made an image of the convoy in front of him and one of the three pack animals. Buyo smiled sweetly at the camera and Alik waved. Kelda's quartermaster just held on.

Gavan Connell

They set up as they had done the previous time with the tlaques hobbled and the sleeping area by the river. They arrived well before last light and ChOn decided to explore the area at the back of the formation. He had to cross the river and go around the end of the hill before he could climb and explore the land that stretched away green and flat almost to the horizon, broken by rocky outcrops of a white shiny stone that caught the sun in places. He could see dots on the plain that turned into tlaque, goats and oruk under magnification. He rode to the nearest of the rocky outcrops and dismounted. He picked up a piece of the rock and put it in his analyser and it came up 'gold-bearing quartz'. He took an image of the rock and the screen with the analysis result. He walked carefully over the rocky ground until he saw what he was looking for. It was no bigger than a dáguia egg but orange and shiny when he rubbed it. Just for proof he analysed it in the machine and it confirmed his decision. '24kt gold'. He found several more nuggets in just a few minutes and decided to send the Lancers here before they left the following day. He took images of the nuggets and returned to the Overhang where the Lancers were bathing. He was tired and dusty from the ride so he stripped down and plunged in with no ceremony. He waded to where Buyo was rubbing soap onto Karín's back.

"Tomorrow, would you please send the Lancers to the back of the overhang? I have found something there that will be of use to us all and I need lots of hands to collect it. I will show it to you when we get out of the river. In my world it is called 'gold' and it is very valuable as jewellery and for parts of some machines. It is a shiny orange stone and there are many of them scattered around the broken escarpment behind the overhang."

"I know this stone. It is common in the Buq'ue land and also one that is shiny but not orange. They are both too soft to do anything with so we never bothered to collect them. If you can use them we can collect bags of each colour. I will talk to the

Troop Commanders now. We will be busy in the morning collecting the chicks, rounding up the tlaque and collecting the stones."

"The other stone is probably the one called 'silver'. It is not of as much value as the gold where I am from. Of the three tasks, the stones are the least important. I can collect them any time. I would prefer to do it now while we are here because I don't want to make these trips any more than I need to but the animals and birds are far more important. There are many things to do in the Castle and the Buq'ue fort and whilst we all enjoy the freedom that comes with these trips, they do take a lot of time. Had it not been for the urgency of trapping the chicks, I would not have suggested this trip."

"My Lord," cut in Buyo, *"will the dáguias form part of the spy communications? They are quite big and I could hardly carry one with me and pretend it was a pet. I will need a better way to communicate back to you than that."*

"Spy stuff," said Karín. *"OK, time for me to leave the discussion. Buyo, I will need you after your bath to set up our sleeping space while I am with the Troop Leaders. Alik should have it all unloaded and in place, it will just be for you to lay it out and make sure the ground is dry under the skins."*

Yes, Karín. I shouldn't be long here, should I My Lord?"

"No. But you are right about the communications aspect of your work. I will have to come up with something that you can use when you need it. Let me think about it. It will have to involve a radio somehow and that can only mean a helm but you can't exactly go around wearing a helm."

Buyo started to rub soap on Ch0n's back with a woollen pad.

"You had best see to Karín's bedding. This is a dangerous game you like to play."

351

"I like to play it because we both know you like me to play it. I am patient. I know it is just a matter of time before you have me. I know that because I can see the doubt in your eyes."

"You know I will not. And yet you are right I do desire you."

"I know that and I accept it. Now I will go. Now I know for sure."

She arranged the bedding so she was sleeping beside Karín. Alik had a place on Chon's side and the wolf would fit in there somewhere. After the plans for the following day had been announced and Ch0n had told them stories about his former life, they retired. Alik gave the tlaque some of the sweet root as soon as the herd started arriving and before long they were almost all asleep.

Ch0n lay awake, restless, listening to the night sounds. He had his helm on standby so he turned on the thermal imaging and light amplification modes. The Overhang roof lit up as it had done the previous time. By tilting his head he could see the wolf, which went from being asleep to awake as soon as he moved. Alik was asleep with his mouth open and beyond him were rows of green glowing women, their warm bodies showing naked on the visor thanks to the thermal imaging. He turned his head and watched Karín sleeping with her tongue lolling out the side of her mouth. He lifted his head to see past her and looked into the enormous green pupils of Buyo. The girl smiled at him and rolled over.

Ch0n was deep in thought. During the night when he went to check the tlaque he expected her to follow him but she didn't, even though she watched him return to his bed space with that knowing smile on her lips the whole time.

Ch0n estimated they had collected ten pounds or more of the nuggets. And that was Two Troop alone. The King's Troop caught the twenty chicks and selected a dozen female tlaque with male calves at foot and by mid-morning they were cutting a line directly towards the Buq'ue fort, thanks to ChOn's tablet magnetic-field positioning system. ChOn called Jez to advise him they were on the move. He was also in contact with the OP. He conducted radio checks all day until he found the limit of communications by helm from the castle. He still had the OP in range and they had the castle. It wasn't until the second day that he lost communications with the OP and that was when they were almost at the rise overlooking the main gates where the Infantry was waiting. The councillors had already entered the city some hours before and had paved the way for a grand welcome and to organize a bird handler at short notice. It was only a matter of knowing the time of arrival. ChOn told Karín to send messengers ahead and she selected sisters from Two Troop, the Buq'ue troop. They cantered ahead two abreast, their little ribbons fluttering. And their hearts.

The Household Cavalry rode into the gates while the Buq'ue villagers were still rushing to get a view. The lancer-sisters were waiting for their troop at the gate and formed up at the rear like seasoned veterans as their troop passed. Izaki had the guard fallen out to welcome their king. ChOn rode at the head of the column and he went past the crowd direct to the main square where he stopped, facing the throne and he let Karín give the orders for the Household Cavalry to form up behind him in troop abreast. Alik ran from the supply section and took the reins as ChOn dismounted. ChOn climbed the several steps and stood before the throne. The people were cheering him, albeit not with a lot of enthusiasm.

"My fellow Buq'ue tribesmen. I bring you my Household Cavalry to show you what we have been doing these past moons. Just as you have been busy making changes directed by your most able Garrison Commander, your council members have been busy learning the way of the future for us all. I am very pleased to enter these gates and not find someone trying to separate my head and for that I thank Commander Izaki and all of you.

I have several proclamations. The first is that I have taken as my aget, my wife, the woman you knew as Karín, the former charge and bodyguard of the recent king."

At this there were a few sniggers from the crowd and one man yelled out,

"Well he had no further need of her in his bed, did he?"

That brought some sporadic laughter from the crowd but fetched a scowl from both Ch0n and Karín.

"If you would care to come forward and repeat that comment to me man to man I will kill you for it with my own hands. If you are the coward I think you are, hide among those who know who you are and pray they do not betray you. And if the old king were here he would have killed you for it as well. And Karín yet may."

"You see before you what we call my Household Cavalry. Brigadier General Karín commands it. As you can see, it is made up of two troops, one from the Arw'an and one from the Buq'ue. Their mission is to serve us all in times of peace and war. In peace they will patrol from village to village protecting our grass and our people. They will provide entertainment for us merely by their presence. Any of you may watch them training and any girl among you may join them in time if you are good enough. I am going to leave here the Arw'an troop to help your army train and defend the outposts. They will stay for six moons and then they will return to Arw'an Castle and Two Troop will come here. For the time being we will have only the two troops. The troop at Arw'an Castle will be known as the King's Troop. As you can see, they look well here on parade and I can assure you that they are just as pleasing to my eyes when they are training in the field." He took the tablet out of his pocket and took an image of the troops on parade.

"The next thing I will do is commend to you your councillors. Makin the master of the beasts, of which there are twelve female tlaque and their calves, twenty dáguia chicks and your goats but soon there will be oruks and goats of a different race. Makin will be setting the herders apart to manage the animal program. He has been working side by side with the Royal Master of Livestock at Arw'an Castle and will do well. Heed him. He speaks with my voice. The animals will be on display when Makin is ready with the pens and cages.

Cyris will be the town planner and builder. He will be selecting a team of builders to do any construction and destruction in the fort. All of it will be under my direction. Some of it will be by request from other councillors or the Garrison Commander but he also speaks with my voice. He has been working side by side with the Royal Architect.

Eloi, whose daughter you see before you as Troop Commander of Two Troop with the indigo shirts, will be the town Mayor. That means she is responsible for the planning and layout of the town and for any alterations to it. Also she will be making rules which will determine how the town works and the Garrison Commander will enforce those rules. She has been working side by side with the Royal Mayor of Arw'an castle. She is the first woman to hold that position here and she speaks with my voice.

Finally, the woman Froncy will be responsible for all the administrative work in the fort. She will work with Eloi to make sure the fort is fed, bathed, the children are taught and the sick are attended to. This is a most important position and she will be called the Head of Logistics. She speaks with my voice.

In my absence, the king's council will be presided over by the Garrison Commander, Izaki of the Buq'ue.

I mentioned dáguias. The dáguias are large birds with an instinct to return to the place they were borne. This makes them suitable to carry messages from one village to village. The twenty I have brought with me today are already under the care of a bird keeper. He is being shown how to feed them and house them. In two moons they will all be taken from here to the different Buq'ue outposts, which the cavalry will visit shortly. The heads of those outposts will be able to send messages back to the bird keeper, who will pass them to the Garrison Commander. This is critical to the defences of the tribes and means that some of you will need to learn to write and read a few words and symbols.

Now go back to your work or your dwellings and resume what you were doing before we arrived. I will tour the fort and see how you have fared in my absence."

The crowd was about to disperse when Karín stepped forward and pumped her fist in the air.

"ALL HAIL KING CH0N!"

"ALL HAIL KING CH0N!" they responded more enthusiastically than when Ch0n had first appeared.

"It's amazing what not cutting people's head off can achieve," she said.

Ch0n spent the rest of the day touring the works Izaki had implemented. The wall had been raised on both sides of the main gate. The moat had been partially dug and the two sets of baths completed. The latrine had been re-sited and dug. The pens for the tlaque had been built and Ch0n's quarters had had a stable built for two tlaque. A space had been cleared and the stables for the Lancers were nearing completion.

"They will be finished within days, my King. I have had every available man working on the construction of the various works and I misjudged the time it would take to finish thirty two stables and lofts. As you can see the walls are completed and the bamboo and mud for the roofs is over there."

"Talk to brigadier General Karín and ask if her Lancers might help with the labour. Thirty extra hands will make a lot of difference."

Izaki grinned at him.

"I had hoped you would say that. With them working alongside the builders and soldiers we will finish this two days from now instead of three or four. But are there not double that number?"

"You have done well, Izaki. Now the four have returned you will be under less pressure from outside the garrison and will be able to appreciate the tasks the others are doing. Yes, there are double thirty Lancers. But the next priority is for us to pull the outposts back in."

"My King, I would have sent soldiers with the message but they were needed here on the works and I didn't want to send them individually. It is not for one man to walk for days towards the frontiers of the Matáng lands."

"You decided well. It is the perfect task for the Lancers. They can ride from village to village while their cousins are building their own stables. It is fitting that the Buq'ue troop be the one to go and pass the message. It will be better received. They can leave tomorrow if their commander is willing. And she will be. You had no more problems with treasonous villagers, then?"

"We had a few complaints about the summary justice meted out by Karín but nothing more. I am not going to say that everybody is perfectly happy as you so unfortunately overheard today but we have no real issues as far as we know. By the

way, I have learned the identity of that person and he will disappear before morning."

"No. Have him dragged before Karín. It was she and the former king who were wronged and it will be she who has the last word. I have no doubt it will be a just punishment."

"As you wish my King."

"Have you seen the dáguia chicks?"

"No but they interest me. I do have my concerns about knowing how to decipher the messages, though."

"They will be as easy as I can make them. Smile for friendly. Scowl for enemy. Arrows for past and future. Suns for days, moons for nights. Big for big, small for small. Square for here. Crosses for there. So that this," he wrote on the ground, "would mean what?"

"Small friendly future there three days….Small friendly group your location three days."

"Good. Now write large enemy force arriving here in six days." ChOn watched as Izaki drew the symbols. "Good work. There will be more but not so many that you will be confused. The most important are enemy and time. The rest we can work out. Let's look at the messengers, then."

They found the cage already assembled and the bird keeper squashed up inside feeding his charges. He was so similar to Mori at the castle that ChOn had to look twice to make sure it wasn't him. He was cooing to the chicks as he fed them, oblivious to all around him. The routine was the same as it had been for Mori. He had to force the bird's beak into the tube and squeeze the intestine attached to it to make the porridge come out. Once the chick felt the food in is beak, instinct took over and it would feed greedily. He was almost finished with the entire flock.

"His name is Puntik."

"You are doing well, Puntik," said ChOn. The man just nodded his thanks and didn't look up. He put the bird he was feeding with the others he had finished and took up another.

"I had better go and talk to Karín about her Lancers," said ChOn. "I am well pleased with your work here." Izaki bowed his head in acknowledgement and watched ChOn walk away. He stood watching Puntik until he had finished another chick and then went to his own quarters.

"No!" said Karín when ChOn had pointed out that one of them would have to go with the Lancers and the other would have to stay. *"It is my job to protect you. How can I do that if you are out there or I am? There must be another way."*

"The helms are too valuable to give to just anybody and I certainly don't want one to fall into the hands of a Matáng patrol or something similar. I need the outposts to pull back to radio range in case we are fighting there and need someone from here to help in some way. The dáguias aren't good for two way traffic so it has to be you or me. I will be fine with a troop of Arw'an Lancers here or with Buq'ue ones if I go. There is no other way."

"I know. Then it will be me."

"Yes. Now go and brief Eloik. They need as much warning as possible. How long will it take?"

"There are five outposts. The first is three days ride from here. Maybe less. How close do you want them?"

"Three days' forced walk. One day's ride. It depends on the radios. OK. Three days to the first. You will have to mark out the place for him to withdraw to. You had better take Izaki to make the tactical decisions like where the new sites will be. Alik! Alik! Fetch me Izaki. No. Don't. He has no mount and if he took mine he can't even ride. It's up to you. Look for places that can be defended. Think of how the castle is positioned with obstacles protecting it. OK. Three days to the first. Then how long?"

"Two to the second, one to the third, three to the fourth and one to the last and then another two to here."

"Twelve days. We could save time if we sent a patrol to the fifth or the first. Make it the fifth. If they leave tomorrow as well, the fifth outpost could be moving in about five days instead of ten. OK you go to the first four and come back. Reny can arrange the other one. Now you can go and brief Eloik. You will need five days hard rations and you can forage for the other six. Forage as a first option so you have rations to spare. I will have Alik and Buyo get your things ready."

Karín went to find Eloik and Ch0n went to his stables. Alik and Buyo were still cleaning up their kit from the previous two days' ride. He told them to concentrate on Karín's tlaque and prepare several spare uniforms for her ride, to get five days' worth of porridge and dried meat from the kitchens. He went to his private pack and took out a second tablet.

It was late when Karín returned to the chambers. Ch0n was already in bed with the tablet, logging his activities as was his custom. She jumped into the terracotta urn and washed herself in the cool water before throwing on a clean tunic and plopping down beside him.

"This is a spare tablet. I have five more stored away in my fort near where I crashed. I had this in case I lost or broke the other one but the time has come for you to have one. I am going to programme it to you first so nobody else but you and I can use it."

He booted it and a blank grey screen shimmered into view and stayed.

"Put your hand on it and keep it there until I tell you to take it away..... Ok. Take it away now." He pressed a green button that appeared in the corner of the screen and the same grey screen appeared again. He put his own hand on the screen and then after a short time, removed it.

A menu flashed onto the screen with dozens of icons. He pointed to one in the shape of a circle filled in with green and blue and with lines coming from the two ends.

"This is a positioning system. Once I activate it, it will map the area where you go. It will leave a line on that map so you can follow it next time. Every time you take an image, that image will be stored in the memory but will also be stored in the positioning system so that if you take a picture of this room, which I suggest you do, it will register this as the place the picture was taken and you can always find your way back here. OK. Take one. Put the lens facing us and we can both be in it. Good. Now see here you can label the picture if you could write. Mmmm. Bit of a disadvantage, never mind, you'll know when you touch the picture and it comes up."

He downloaded the existing map from his own tablet to Karín's and went on to explain the various properties of the tablet but concentrated on the image, video and voice recording functions.

"It will map where you go automatically so you can forget about the map unless you get lost and have to go back to the last point. Take photos of every hill, water source, strange animal, every village of course and the place where they have to go. You can't take too many and they will all provide waypoints on the map. Now. If you look like you are going to get captured, you must not let the weapons be found. Bury them or destroy them. Here is a weapon of great destruction. It is called a fragmentation grenade. It blows up like when a fire explodes and sparks go everywhere. The case will splinter into thousands of needles that will kill or wound a person within the distance from us to the urn. If you do not want to get captured, you can use it to kill yourself and blow up some of your enemies and the weapons. I leave that up to you. Before you do that, remember my dream. You can throw this and it will explode where you throw it but don't hold it too long or it will explode in your hand. This is how you arm it"

He explained the process of arming and disarming the grenade and made her practise it twice before he was happy.

"Now, come here and make me explode." He turned off the lamp and plunged the room into darkness. Moments later Buyo patted the wolf as she lifted the corner of the entry flap. She walked several paces into the gloom and stood transfixed as she watched ChOn kneel above Karín and then join her. She watched for several minutes before she smiled and left them.

ChOn rose with the sun and went outside. This was a habit he could not break. He was so used to checking his perimeter and starting his daily routine that he just did it. These days he didn't check his perimeter but he did check his surroundings. He went to the stables to make sure Karín's things were ready. Her kit was laid out waiting for her to put it on. The tack was hanging on the rail all cleaned and oiled. He looked up at the lofts as he turned to leave. Buyo was rising from her bed. She had not seen him. She pulled her sleeping tunic over her head and turned to pick up her day tunic. Then in her peripheral vision she saw ChOn watching her from below. Instead of covering herself, she turned to face him. ChOn was embarrassed at having been seen and left quickly. He didn't see Buyo grinning as he turned away.

Two Troop looked resplendent on the square as they waited for Karín to arrive. She was making some last minute checks to the saddle and her armour in the stable before she mounted. She was obviously deep in thought or troubled about something, Ch0n could see.

"Are you feeling alright?"

"Yes, I am now but I have been thinking very carefully most of the night about what I am going to say next for it is not easy for me and goes against my personal feelings. I will be gone for eleven or twelve days, perhaps more if things do not go as smoothly as we have anticipated. That is a long time for you now you have finally discovered how to make íjon. You have a strong need. Stronger than any I have ever known and I think it is because you are still discovering the joy of it. If your needs are so strong that you can not wait for my return, then you have the right as a Buq'ue male, and more so as the king, to take a lover. I know I vowed to kill any who lay with you but I see things more clearly now than then. I ask that you be discreet. There is no shame in it for me but I would have it a secret just the same. Even from me."

"I don't think that situation will arise but thank you. Now mount up. Your Lancers are waiting. I will miss you at my side. Go well wife."

"Stay well, My Lord."

He walked behind her as she trotted to the square and received a salute from Eloik. She took her place at the front of the ranks and watched Ch0n as he mounted the steps.

"My King! Two Troop of the Household Cavalry is standing by for your order to depart for the outposts!"

"Go well Commander. The people of the Buq'ue and Arw'an bid you a safe and successful mission!"

Karín turned and rode to the flank of the Lancers. Eloik gave the order and moved to a position behind Karín. The troop changed from two ranks to two columns as they moved off. It was a sight to behold. They marched down the road to where the guard commander had stood the guard to attention while they passed.

ChOn went straight to the bird aviary. The construction of the large coop was about to be commenced under the watchful eye of Makin. Piles of bamboo were being brought from the store of building supplies Cyris had had stockpiled in his absence.

"It will be finished by mid-afternoon, My Lord," he proclaimed. "Old Puntik will be in his element. It will be almost the same as the one at the Castle. I am going to put the landing platform half outside so they can walk inside before they jump. I think they will find it easier to find the entrance."

ChOn went to the smaller cage and found Puntik at his work.

"How goes it, Puntik?"

"Aye, they are better at it this morning, king. Some of them were a bit hungry after not having a full crop last night but we've managed to fill all the ones we've started so far. The fact they all made it through the night after being in the hot sun for almost two days surprises me."

"Well we did wait until after they'd been fed before we left so they hadn't been the whole two days without food but yes. They must be hardy birds. Keep up the good work."

His helm crackled into life.

"Are you there, ChOn?"

"I am. Meet me on eleven. Is everything going all right?"

"Yes. I just wanted to check the communications. What are you doing?"

"I am up with the dáguia chicks. From here I am going to visit the tlaque pens and then inspect the baths, the latrine and the moat. It won't be as much fun without you to accompany me, especially to the latrine but I will try not to get bored."

"This is the first time we have been apart since the day we met. I swore on that day I would never leave your side. And here I am leaving you for twelve suns. I miss being on the front of the tlaque with you behind. Those were days filled with exploring of the land and innocence between us. When we get back to the castle can we go away for a few days with just the one tlaque?"

"We will ride one and lead one or maybe two. I want to take you to where I crashed and show you the ship I came in. I will have Reny follow us a day behind leading as many tlaque females as are available. I have a lot of stores back there that will need to be transported to the Castle. And I forgot to tell you, if you see any of the orange or shiny stones along the way, bring back what you can carry. I have a plan for them. Now concentrate on your navigation and recording the landscape on the tablet. We will talk later."

"I feel the ébon for you, Ch0n. The centre of me is heavy without you and flies when I am with you. I should have told you that before I left. It was on my tongue but it didn't seem to fit with the other thing I said about using someone for your needs. But I am telling you now in case something happens and I don't have the chance later."

"If that it is what the ébon is, then I feel it for you, too. Perhaps one day we will have offspring when we are ready. When the work has been done to the point we can relax."

"Yes. I would like your child. Now my mind is settled I can leave you alone."

365

"I am not far away. Change back to frequency one."

By the end of the day, ChOn had examined every nook and cranny of the fort. He had been accompanied by the four at different stages and had told them what he wanted. The moat was a priority. The fort could not be defended from all sides at once so they had to force the enemy to attack from the side that was best defended. The moat also served to stop enemy engineer sappers from digging a tunnel under the wall and attacking from within. The latrine was located at the bottom end of the fort close to the water so the waste would be carried away from both the fort and the moat but would render the water unfit to drink for some distance downstream.   He eyed the men's bath and remembered he had his own in his quarters so he trudged back there and called for it to be filled. That task fell to Buyo as Karín's 'squire' and she soon had the bath ready and a jug of scalding water on hand to top it up.

"Will you be wanting me to shave you, My Lord?"

ChOn ran his hand over his face and head.

"Yes I would, thank you."

Buyo told Alik that ChOn was taking his bath and was not to be disturbed. She skipped away to where Karín kept the blades for shaving ChOn's face and head. When she returned, ChOn was sitting on a leather chaise waiting for her. She took the woollen cloth, wet it from the hot jug and put it over his head and face. She shaved his head first; using the blade ChOn had first given to Sonja for the purpose and which Karín had recovered. It was a simple matter to pull it over his smooth scalp once it had been lathered with the precious soap. She sat on a stool behind the chaise, re-heated the cloth and pulled ChOn's head back so he was reclining with his head in her lap. She managed to cut him once on the point of the chin, otherwise she was deft with the thin blade. When she was done she put the hot cloth back in position with a few drops of spice and massaged his face. Ch0n lay in her lap breathing in the fragrance and enjoying the feel of her fingers on his face and head.

"If you don't get into the water it will be cold, My Lord."

Ch0n pulled the tunic over his head and stepped into the warm water. Buyo added the hot water from the jug and without asking, took up a position behind Ch0n and started to wash him. He leaned forward so she could reach his back with the soapy cloth and then when she had finished, he lay back, reclining against the back of the tub. Buyo moved to the side of the tub and started to wash his chest.

"It must be pleasant to be King and have someone tend to you in your ablutions, My Lord."

"Usually I bathe myself. Sometimes a change is nice. Your way of shaving me was very relaxing. I almost went to sleep under your fingers."

"I will shave you every day while Karín is away since you like it so much. And bathe you as well if it pleases you. You need to slow down and relax more. Your duties are many and you punish yourself by working so hard. Nobody can understand why or how you are able to sustain your levels of intensity. If I can help you relax, I will do so. If you liked my head massage you would like my body massage. Here. Finish washing. You can reach the rest of yourself. I will prepare the bed for you and fetch my things."

Karín stopped the troop in a copse of trees as it was approaching dark. She had already checked it for dagononums and found none. There was a spring feeding the trees and she could see for miles in every direction if she climbed a little. She told Eloik to post sentries all night and to wake her if anything unusual was happening. Then she radioed Jez to see if he was in range but he wasn't. She called Ch0n instead. He had just finished his bath. She gave him a full run down on her day's advance and he asked questions about the terrain, water, food sources and shelter. Karín had diligently made images of every water course and rocky outcrop, the one cave she saw and a few groves of fruit trees. She had not seen any gold or silver. The troops were all in good spirits. Ch0n then asked her to describe how Eloik had set up the bivouac and Karín explained that the tlaque were tethered in lines next to the water with the Lancers on the perimeter.

"Did you have them rub down their mounts and then put the saddles back on for the night?"

"No. They have tended to them but the saddles are being used as pillows as at the Overhang."

"At the Overhang we are well inside our own territory, we have the wolf to warn us if anybody is approaching and I am there with you. Where you are now you are in unknown territory. You may be stumbled upon by a Matáng war patrol and you would have no chance against them fighting at ground level. Your best defence and your best weapon is speed. If you have to fight, best to run, regroup and then sweep them from two directions in a pincer. Let the front section be the anvil and the rest can sweep through from the flank like you practised. I should have told you all that before you left."

"There wasn't much time, Ch0n. You were busy with many things as well as making your farewells. You have to stop taking control of everything and let others do it for you. You have surrounded yourself with the best of the Buq'ue and Arw'an. Let us take responsibility. Be passive. Relax. We will do our best to please you. Now I will go and talk to Eloik about the saddles. We will make it a normal part of the change from day to night routine after the sentries change. Keep your helm handy. OK?"

"OK."

Ch0n had just spoken to Karín and was already making his entries in the tablet's log when Buyo returned some time later. She was carrying a skin bag that held something heavy. She put it down and went to Ch0n's bed and pulled the woollen rug up to the pillow.

My mother was a healer. She taught me the skills of body massage with hot stones. It is very relaxing but it is also quite painful if I find a muscle that is too tense. The final result though is that you will be completely relaxed and will sleep like a baby. There is just one rule. You must not fight against me, but be like a woollen doll with no bones. Now come here.

Ch0n did as he was told and walked to the edge of his bed. She took the hem of his tunic and lifted it almost over his head but she was so tiny that she could not reach and he had to help her. She hooked her thumbs into the band of his undergarments and pulled them to the floor. He stepped out of them and stood waiting. Buyo's heart skipped a beat.

Face down first My Lord. Let me take control. Be passive. Relax. I will do my best to please you.

The stones were so hot she had to put a thin blanket over him to stop them from burning his skin and she used them to knead from his shoulders to his toes. It was mostly pleasant for him but also painful at times.

Roll over.

Ch0n rolled over, conscious of his nakedness but Buyo simply covered him with the blanket and continued with the hot stones. Then she paused.

"My Lord, there remains just one thing to complete the massage. To truly relieve the tension from a man's body, he

369

has to release the tension from within and that requires him to have a discharge. It does not mean making íjon because that is an active release as distinct from a passive one." She took a small wool cloth from the bag of rocks and placed it over Ch0n's eyes. Then she finished her work slowly and expertly.

"Now My Lord, sleep. You will be more relaxed than you have ever been." She covered him with the blanket. Ch0n donned the helm and was asleep before she had finished cleaning up.

Buyo took her stones to the loft and stowed them. Her body was burning. She took her night tunic and went back to Ch0n's chambers. Once there she slipped quietly out of her day clothes and stepped into the still lukewarm tub. It was pitch black in the room but to her it was as clear as day, just a bit green. After a long soak, she stepped out, dried herself and pulled the night tunic over her head. She walked to Ch0n's bed and watched him sleep. She was going to lie down with him but he was sleeping so deeply she didn't want to disturb him.

"Not tonight, King of the Buq'ue but perhaps tomorrow," she whispered. *"Tonight you will not know me but please forgive me; you have made in my body a fire that has to be quenched. Tonight I will wake Alik and see if he is yet a man."* She looked at him again through the blackness.

Ch0n watched through the visor. He had woken as soon as the wolf growled at someone approaching his chambers. He had stopped growling when he realized it was Buyo but by then Ch0n was on full alert. It had been easy to feign sleep with the helm on and the visor down. Buyo was one of half a dozen who knew he slept with it on when he was waiting for a possible call for help. He also had the minitron plugged in to his ears. But Ch0n knew she could see him if she looked so he lay stock still watching her undress, bathe herself, don her tunic and finally walk to his bed. His heart started to beat wildly when it seemed she was going to lie with him. But instead she looked at him and spoke to him quietly but audibly. She turned away and he knew he didn't want her to lie with Alik.

"Buyo."

He saw her start.

"My Lord? You are awake but feigning sleep? You have been watching me?"

"Since you entered."

"And does the King of the Buq'ue usually spy on his subjects?"

"Sometimes a spy has to be spied upon so he or she knows it is not possible to relax without being caught out. This has been a lesson for you."

"And you heard my whispered words?"

"Yes."

"And what of them?"

"I am confused by my feelings after hearing you say you were going to lie with Alik. I do not wish you to make íjon with him."

"The king of the Buq'ue has but to wish something and it is my command.   If you do not wish it, you command me not to do it. I am but the assistant of your woman, her servant and yours. Does the King command me to lie with him instead? Will the King of the Buq'ue douse the fire in my belly that he has lit but commanded me not to quench with another?"

"I wish it."

"Then you command it my King and I obey but please remove the helm. I want to look at your face while we do it. It is important to me to watch you in the dark."

Gavan Connell

"You will have me at a disadvantage, Buyo."

"Yes, I will, my King but you will benefit from it."

She pulled the tunic over her head and stepped to the bed. The king of the Buq'ue looked at her one last time before he took off the helm and everything went black.

Chapter Twenty Three: The Washing of the Lances

Karín woke to the sound of her troops stirring for the day. A fire was revived and the women washed and cleaned up after eating. They led their mounts to the water and stowed their kit before Eloik gave the order to mount. Eloik rode to the front of the two ranks and stood in the stirrups.

"We are riding towards the Matáng territory." She shouted. *"It is unlikely we will see any of them but be aware. Each of you keep a look out to your side of the column and if you see anything, don't shout about it, pass the word forward to me. If we do come across a Matáng patrol, we will use the first five pairs to feint from the front and hold the enemy's attention while the remainder will circle around to the left or right and we will do to them what we do every day in practice. Except for one thing. The dummies will be real men. Do not look at them as real men but as dummies and if you have to stick one, remember to let your lance loose in the wrist thong so it can go behind you for a recovery. That is why we practise. To get it right when we come to the real thing. Remember the words of Our Lord, Ch0n, the King. No man on foot can withstand the force of a cavalry charge. Brigadier General Karín, where will you ride?"*

"I will ride with the ten and assist where I can."

"Very good. First five pairs, raise your lances. OK. You will be the anvil and hold their attention. The rest will ride with me. Pay attention now."

She rode to the head of her Troop and they moved into column of twos behind her. Karín trotted alongside her.

"Good work, Eloik. We chose well when we chose you. Remember also what the king said about being calm and not charging ahead of the rest when the time comes."

She told Ch0n to change to channel eleven and spoke. He answered instantly.

"Good morning agen, we are on the move. We chose wisely with Eloik. She just gave a nice set of orders to put the troop on alert."

"Good morning, wife. I want you to look around from now for a suitable place for the village to move to. I don't want them any further than a day's mounted patrol. If we need to get there quickly we can put the beasts to the forced trot and get there in half a day or a bit more. Are there any hills near where you are?"

"Not near and not on the line of march but off to one side of us is a rocky hill with some trees in the gully near it. Will I look at it? It will not take us too far from our path and if it is suitable it would have been worth it."

"Yes. Hills may have caves. Rocks mean fortifications and trees mean water. It may be possible to build a fortified village with caves at the back as an inner fortress. Go to it and if it is suitable, tell me. There is a cable in your helm near the speaker. If you look closely you will see a patch that can be pulled half away. It reveals the cable. Pull the free end out carefully and put it in the hole at the bottom of the monocular where the little plug is located. If you do that and select channel eight, that's the one with one circle on top of the other, you will be able to send me images of what you are looking at. It may not work at this range but we can try it out. I should have told you sooner but I had forgotten about it, probably because I haven't had any reason to use it. Do that now and see if it works."

Karín removed the helm, pulled the monocular from its cradle and positioned if in front of the visor. Then she searched for the cable, located it and inserted the gold plug into the small hole on the monocular. She selected channel eight and Ch0n's voice was immediately in her ear.

"Now listen. It's a bit snowy but I can see well enough. You can't speak because the transmission of the image has captured your microphone. Silly but that's the reality. What you have to do is disconnect the cable and tell me to meet you on eleven if you have to speak. If you don't have to, just transmit and listen to my orders. I can tell you when to change. OK? Nod your head or shake it."

Karín nodded.

"Now look at the hill you told me about. No. Not like that. You have to move your head slowly or I can't see. That's better now zoom in. Make the image bigger. That's good. No. You'll have to go and look. If you like it, leave a trail for the villagers to follow when they relocate. You should be out of radio range soon after mid day. The camera will fail soon enough too. Try to transmit through the monocular from the rise. Or is the place you stayed at last night suitable for a village? Meet me on eleven."

"No. It is flat and nothing more than a copse of trees where a spring of water comes to the surface. The water is moving in the middle but does not get any deeper. The edges just disappear into the sand."

"It would have been good if there were more shelter. Permanent water is a gift that should not be wasted if possible. OK, I trust your judgement on this."

"We are still close. I will switch to eight and show you."

375

Gavan Connell

ChOn surveyed the scene on his visor. She was right. It was not suitable.

"OK. I've seen enough. Meet me on eleven."

"I will talk to you from the hill and see if the monocular works from there. I missed you last night. We have not been apart for so long it seems strange."

"Yes. It felt very different without you here. Now keep a look out for Matáng and talk to me when you get there."

"OK."

ChOn wondered what to do with his morning. He had spent the entire day previous doing his rounds but there weren't the things to do here in the Buq'ue fort that he had at Arw'an Castle. Over there he had several different construction sites, several herds to look at, the birds, the training of the Household Cavalry, and he could always go for a ride to his old fort for a couple of days if he wanted to. Here, things were well established. The moat and the latrines were the only construction apart from a birdcage that would be finished by now anyway. He couldn't really leave his quarters and do anything that involved removing his helm for at least another hour. Perhaps it was time to teach Alik some sword techniques or Buyo some ways to disguise herself.

He thought back to the night before and the nymph who had wrung every drop of pleasure from him. She barely came up to his chest she was so tiny but had had no physical issues 'quenching her fire' as she had put it. Or his. If anything, she had made it burn more fiercely for she had demanded much more of him than Karín. *"I have to make the most of the short time I have with you before she returns to claim that which is hers".* She had returned to her loft before the dawn so Alik would not find her. Now it was time for her to return.

He went to the stable and told Alike to send her. He had barely returned to his quarters when she hurried in.

"Yes My Lord? How can I serve you further?"

"It is time for you to start your training as a spy. There are things you will need to know. One of them is the manner to disguise yourself. I thought it would be a good place to start."

"If you say so My Lord. From whom will I be hiding?"

"You will be hiding from everybody if you are spying. You must be able to hide even from people in your own village. From people who know you. The whole aim of being a spy is to be invisible in public but not always in private. Your disguise must have a purpose.   For example, the shaman of Boro's village was able to return to that village and walk among the villagers who knew him well.   He was invisible in plain view of everybody. How did he do it? How would you try and do it?"

"I would try and dress as those I am trying to be are dressed?"

"And?"

"I would try and act like they are acting, speak like they are speaking and look the way they look?"

"Would that work if I were to send you to Arw'an Castle and tell you to spy on Sir Jez?"

"No. He would just call me by name and ask me what I was doing."

"So in that situation you would have to look different from everybody instead of the same?"

"Yes but if I were different would I not appear out of place and attract attention?'

"That isn't always a bad thing. Be invisible in plain view. I will tell you about the shaman, Pik. According to Karín, he told the king he could make himself invisible and he had a soldier to say he had walked through Boro's village in plain view and nobody had seen him. So the king believed them. Now how does one make oneself invisible in plain sight? For me it would be impossible by day because of my size but I could do it at night with the helm and dark clothes. I would be invisible to those who can not see."

"But not to me."

"Aaaaah! Now you see why you are so important. Your skills mean you need to work at night when people are skulking around in the shadows of darkness. But you also have to have a reason to be there in the first place. You see, clothes and speech and mannerisms are not everything. Pik became a beggar. He WAS a beggar. He was dressed like one, he walked like one, he talked like one and he went to the places a beggar might go. He probably only ate what people threw at him. Because he was a beggar, nobody looked at him. You see, nobody really wants to look at a beggar because they are repulsed by them. When one passes close to you, what do you do?"

"I look away in case he asks me for something!"

"Exactly. So when you are thinking about what you will disguise yourself as, you need to think of all those things. Now. When you want to be noticed, what do you do so men will notice you?"

"I put colour on my face and lips and put these out. Or I might jiggle them just a little more than usual. Or I might follow them in the darkness and try to grab their dewen. But I usually only do that with kings."

"And when you do that, do they see your face? If they are with their agens, do they look at you?"

"They pretend not to look but they do and then they only look at my wamwas."

"Now your face. What are the features of your face? "

The speaker in the helm beside him crackled into life. He put it on and indicated for Buyo to stay silent.

"We are at the place. I think it is suitable. The trees are growing beside a small stream that runs from a spring nearby. There are three big caves and many of the rocks are small enough to handle. With an OP on the hill the village could be called back inside a wall to defend it with slings and bows. We need more bows. How do we make them? Yours are made of materials we can't get here and the trees are brittle. Would the bamboo work?"

"Maybe it would. I have thought of it but never tried it. I think it is too weak. There must be some way. Change to channel eight and try the camera."

The image from the camera was too hazy to make out any detail.

"Meet me on eleven. It doesn't work."

"OK. I need you to mark the spot. Perhaps your blue ribbon on a stick. It has to be something obviously yours. Take images of the place and also movies. I will have a look when you get back. Get back on track to the village and have them follow your tracks backwards to the new place. Tell them this is non-negotiable if they want to count on our protection from the Matáng. Tell them to move within one sun of your leaving and to take only what they can carry. Burn the rest. Leave nothing a Matáng patrol might use to sustain itself for the return to its base. Fill in the wells or kill a goat and leave it in the water. That will be effective for months. They will have to stop and turn back for they will only have supplies for the distance they are expecting to travel. This is a great defensive weapon, the buying of time. Next time they come it will be to put their own outpost in place so they can raid further in to Buq'ue lands or they will come in force because they will need more supplies. You have done well. Now get moving because you have lost almost half a day."

"We will water the beasts here in the stream and get moving straight after. I will call you periodically to test the range of the helm. We need to know the limits of communications do we not?"

"Well done. You are thinking more and more like a Brigadier General all the time. Yes. And take an image of each place you call from. Do it from places you think you would prefer to fight from. No cover for enemy Infantry and space for your Lancers. And if you do engage a patrol, leave no survivors. I do not want the Matáng to know we have mounted troops or they will do the same before they come and we will lose the advantages of shock and speed."

"Thank you My Lord. I will try again when we are back on line."

"I will be waiting... Now, your face, Buyo. What are the features of your face?"

"My chin, mouth, teeth, nose, eyes, hair."

"Think. What else?"

"My ears?"

"Your skin and your cheeks. And your eyebrows. They are all prominent but you take them for granted. The eyebrows you pluck daily can be left to grow naturally and they will change your entire face. You can make your face rounder by putting woollen rolls inside your cheeks and your skin, which is so clean and yellow now, can be made dirty or darker with clever use of charcoal dust. The other things you mentioned are also important and can be made to look different with shading or false warts or sores or in the case of your hair, growing or cutting or dying it or even hiding it. Now. You are not well known in this village. There are those who know you as Karín's assistant but you are still a relative stranger to them. I am going to give you a little exercise. I want you to make yourself invisible in the village for the entire morning of tomorrow. If you succeed you will have proved a good student. If you fail, you will have to make up a story to the person who identifies you that does not involve your training as a spy and it will have to be convincing enough that they believe you. You have the rest of the day to plan what you will do and to gather the things you will need. "

"As you wish, My Lord. This should be fun. I will run along now to plan my disguise but I will be back in time to shave you."

"You shaved me yesterday."

"And I will be here in time to shave you today, My Lord. And tomorrow. And every day. I told you that. Every day until Karín comes back and I am relegated to my loft and the embraces of Alik for it is unfair for you to wish me not to engage in íjon with him while Karín is reaping the benefits of the time I have spent teaching you my tricks."

"Leave me now with your talk of Alik. Get ready for your test. I will see you here for my shave and not before."

Buyo left him with a black look on his face but she was grinning. She had touched a raw nerve. She would play it for all she could get from it and Alik might not be a bad option after all. He was young and strong and very close at hand and she had seen him in the darkness. He was not Ch0n but he was no stripling either. She went to the loft and lay on her paillasse. What was she going to do? What was she going to be?

Gavan Connell

The helm came to life again as Ch0n was walking to the bird cages.

"Can you still hear me, Ch0n?"

"Yes. The signal is still fairly strong. Make an image and call me again later."

"I'm bored riding all day with nobody to teach me the alphabet."

"Practise the song but you can't afford to get bored. You are the commander of those Lancers. Talk to Eloik. You should be thinking, *'what if I saw a patrol over there right now... What would I do?'* Bored is not an option. Bored means you lose precious time and maybe get people into a situation you wouldn't have had you been concentrating. This is not a ride to the Overhang with me behind you. Do you think I was switched off all that time? No. I was constantly looking out for places, water, resources, wolves and dagonunum. If I were there asleep on the back of the tlaque would you be bored? Of course not. You would be looking after my back. Well there is more responsibility with the entire Buq'ue Troop. What you can do to relieve the boredom for them is have them half relaxing and half looking to the front, flanks and rear. One sister at a time. You and Eloik. Then you can spend half the time being alert and half singing your alphabet song but ready to lead if you have to do it."

"You're right of course and I have been watching out but that doesn't mean I can't be bored at the same time. I'll talk to Eloik about the things you mentioned and I'll talk to you again soon. I think I had better do it more regularly now the signal has dropped in intensity."

"OK."

Puntik was feeding the chicks in the big cage. He was more relaxed with the extra space but the chicks still huddled together in a corner for shelter and warmth. They were more advanced, Ch0n noticed than the first ones and some of them already had feathers sticking out of their backs and necks. Ch0n did not disturb the man on his way to the tlaque pens. The beasts were quietly chewing cud with Makin watching.

"Do you have any of that sweet root that Karín used on the males?"

"Yes, My Lord. She gave me some of it when we first received them. Do you think it is time to start them on the travois?"

"They are placid creatures as you have seen. I think they will take the travois without the root but have it on hand just in case they get excited. I want to go exploring for a day or two to look for different types of trees as well as the bamboo. As soon as we have one that is happy to walk around with the travois I will leave. These must be full again because my male has shown no interest in them. "

"I noted at the Arw'an Castle that when the females mounted each other the male would become excited and join them. The female goats do it too. It must be their way of telling the male they are ready to be joined. If these start it I will advise you straight away so we can join your male to them. Now I will make a travois and see if that one over there will take it. She is the most docile and can be touched without it upsetting her. Will you leave the calf behind? If you do she may fret. The calves are used to trotting along with their mothers so I would take him. The distance you travel in two days will not worry him."

"Then I will take him. Let me know when she is ready and I will leave the next morning."

He went back to the stable where Alik was busily brushing down the tlaque with a wet piece of skin. The beast was standing with its eyes closed chewing cud.

"He likes that, Alik. Have you been riding him at all?"

"No. I fell down the ladder and hurt my hip. I tried to ride him yesterday but I couldn't open my legs wide enough to sit astride him for the pain. There is nothing broken but I will probably be grounded for a few days. Buyo took him briefly yesterday. She said she likes to keep her thighs stretched in case she has to ride for any length of time. While Brigadier General Karín is away, Buyo says she has to ride yours or she will stiffen up."

"I am going away for a couple of days. I was going to suggest you go with me but if your hip is sore you won't be able to. I will go alone. It will be strange to go alone after all this time. I have only done it once since I made contact with the village of Boro. I will give you a night's notice. As soon as Makin tells me he has a tlaque that will pull a travois I will let you know. I am thinking it will be the day after tomorrow. I was going to take you for some sword classes today but you are not ready for them yet, either. If you need help with the tlaque from Buyo, just ask her."

"Buyo has gone, Lord. She told me to tell you she had to go back to Arw'an Castle with the caravan of traders that left just a while ago. She said you had given her leave to go when the right moment arrived and she heard of the caravan and rushed away with them."

"So soon? I didn't think she would be leaving so soon. Well never mind. We can manage without her to help us. Go to Froncy and get someone to put a poultice on that hip. And take the rest of the day to rest in bed. You should have told me when you hurt yourself. There are no extra points for being silly. But thank you for your dedication."

Ch0n went to his quarters to escape the midday sun. He was no sooner in his tent than his helm crackled into life again. This time the reception was weak but he could understand what Karín was saying.

"We have come to a small hillock with a few white stones of the type where you found the orange gold. I will do a quick search before we move on."

"The signal is weak where you are and if you are on a small hill this will be the limit of our communications. Mark it with something like a pile of the stones while the Lancers are searching for gold and silver and call me before you leave. Don't forget to take images. We will not patrol further out than this place because we need to maintain communications with our patrols and OP. Now look around. Is there a place close or have you just passed which would be suitable for an OP? It needs a place with shade and water for the people and the birds."

"Not too close but we passed through a place that would be suitable. I took images because it was quite pretty with a few trees and a small spring at the bottom of the hill. I can see it from here in the distance."

"Even better. If they see an enemy patrol we will be in range of radio and less than a day's forced trot away. The birds should be in their cages within the hour from there flying fast and straight."

"What is an hour?"

"It is the time it takes for..... Never mind I will show you when you get back. It is a measurement of time. I have six machines that measure it. In fact, I have twelve because the tablets have it. Let me see. Take out your tablet. Tell me when you have it booted...."

"I have it booted."

Gavan Connell

"On the opening screen look for a circle with pointy sticks on it. One long and one short. Tell me when you find it and have opened it."

"I have it."

"You will see there a lot of circles with dots between them. The first two circles are days or suns. The second two are hours. The third two are minutes, the next two are seconds and the next two are parts of seconds. Below you will see a circle and a cross. OK?"

"OK."

"Touch the display. The hours, the minutes, seconds and parts of seconds will flash."

"OK."

"If you press the circle the seconds and parts of seconds will start counting quickly and the minutes will follow. If you look at it you will see the same numbers I have shown you. Press the circle now."

"Oh! I have done it. The last ones are going so fast I can not see them. The others are slower but the middle ones are not functioning. Did I do something wrong?"

"No. Every set of two goes slower than the ones to their right. Watch for a little longer and you will see the number one come up. Here it comes....."

"Oh yes! This is a wonderful thing. So that is one minute? "

"Yes. There are sixty of those in an hour. So now when you look at it and the next pair says 'one', you will know how long an hour is."

"I love this thing! It will teach me the numbers."

"It will help. When you get back I will program the days. The clock will not program itself to the length of a day but the hours, minutes and seconds are always the same. Now you were going to take some images and get moving again. I want you to stop well before dark and make sure the sentries are well programmed. No fires tonight. You are a lot closer to the Matáng. Be careful and call me from a similar place between the second village and their new position. I am going on a patrol of my own in two days to look for trees suitable to make bows. Go well."

"Stay well, Ch0n. I love this tablet."

Ch0n took off his helm and lay down. Waves of tiredness rushed at him. He had not slept a lot the night before, nor the one before that when Karín was saying her goodbyes. He dozed off and dreamed a dream. In it he saw the red headed woman in full armour in the company of the Household Cavalry charging down a band of soldiers and scattering them. She was wielding the katana with merciless precision and the Lancers were stabbing and thrusting and knocking men to the ground with their tlaque. Then there was a great cheer and the woman looked into his eyes and smiled.

He woke with a start, reached for the helm and called Karín. Three times he tried but he received no response. She was out of range. He contemplated mounting the tlaque and following her but that would mean there was no communication link between them to the fort. In the end he forced himself to see reason. It was a dream. She was with thirty fairly-well trained Lancers and if she couldn't win a skirmish against men on foot, the entire exercise was already wasted.

He was bored. She had said she was bored but at least she was out there. He needed something to do. Alik was injured. Buyo had disappeared. He had already been to the cages and the pens and the afternoon before he had toured the entire camp's facilities. He decided to go to the gatehouse and see how the sentries were doing. By the time he arrived, they had been informed of his coming and they were all turned out, spic and span. He smiled to himself and turned to the guard commander.

"If your sentries are as efficient at warning you of intruders from outside as they are about telling you of my whereabouts, Cabot, we are in good hands. Carry on."

"Aye My Lord", grinned the Cabot, *"we are indeed."*

He continued to the baths. He rubbed his chin and looked at the line of men waiting to be shaved. It seemed longer than usual but he wasn't accustomed to waiting to be shaved. He hailed Eloi and asked Froncy If she could arrange for his urn to be filled and whether or not Alik had been to see her. Alik had and while she was telling ChOn about Alik's hip, she dispatched several girls with hot water to ChOn's quarters. He dawdled back and arrived just as the last of them, a fat girl in her teens was scurrying in with her jug full.

"My mistress wants to know if you would like someone to shave you, My Lord, seeing as your servant girl left this morning."

"Yes. Have her send someone up. I feel the need for relaxation and a shave would be just the thing." The girl left and ChOn stripped off his tunic and sat on the chaise with a woollen towel around his waist. Froncy herself came up.

"I couldn't let any of those scatterbrained girls loose on you with anything sharp. They'd be too busy swooning to wield it safely."

ChOn pointed to the soap and the razor.

"Be careful with the blade. It is a lot sharper than your flints."

"I brought a flint, My Lord. I think you will find it works perfectly well."

She shaved him expertly. It had been a thing of surprise to ChOn that the Arw'an and Buq'ue men had a custom of going shaved. Their hair was usually worn long but they had no facial hair.

"It is because of the food, My Lord," Karín had told him. *"They don't like the thought of food getting stuck in their facial hair and smelling. The Matáng wear beards and they stink of rotten meat all the time but they are used to it."*

He slept early and woke with the sun as usual. He went outside to look around and then did his exercises and katas alone. He had become accustomed to this ritual ever since he arrived and he enjoyed the self-paced routines that he made himself perform harder and more intensely as he went along. When Karín was with him they did them together and she had shown him she was every bit as intense as he was after he showed her the forms. Alik was a different story. He preferred the weapons and he was quite adept at the sword katas and enjoyed the combat and one on one drills ChOn made him practise. It was a relief from the seemingly endless cleaning of stables, tack, uniforms and weapons that made up his day. He didn't realize it at the time but it was ChOn's way of teaching him self-discipline.

Malek came to him after ChOn had been to the central eating area for breakfast. Froncy was fussing about over the rations and the kitchen staff. ChOn picked out a few he recognized, including the fat teenage girl who had helped fill his bath the night before.

"The tlaque is ready to lead, My Lord. She just stood and let me fit her with the travois and then I had one of the herders lead her around for a while with it weighted down. The calf just ran beside her."

"OK. I will leave tomorrow morning at this time. If you have her ready to leave I will have Alik get my tlaque ready and Froncy can provide me with two days' rations. "

He passed by the bird cage where Puntik was at his work as usual. He was cast in the same mould as Mori, gruff on the outside but tender and patient with the birds. They were clambering at his legs now after just a few days. He continued his rounds, stopping to look at the herders making travois so they could train the rest of the tlaque. They were looking forward to not having to carry everything from place to place and competition was fierce to be among the few who would be handling them. The neutered calves were to be used as mounts and to lead the females with the travois. That would not be until they had grown strong enough but Izaki had his eye firmly fixed on one he hoped would be allocated to him as the Garrison Commander.

Some distance away, Karín and Two Troop were within sight of the first Buq'ue village. As they approached it, she thought it looked deserted but remembered the reaction Boro had described when his villagers first saw ChOn. It would be logical for them to hide from thirty strangely dressed people mounted on beasts they may never have seen. But as she drew closer, an uneasy feeling gripped her. She put the monocular on to zoom and looked at the village. Some of the shelters had been knocked down and there was a body in the middle of the central square. She called Eloik forward and told her she would ride into the village with the first five pairs and for Eloik to move to a flank and adopt a line abreast formation ready to charge the village.

"This is real, Eloik. It is not a practice. Look for the flag signals as we have practised them and tell the girls to look sharp and remember not to bunch up or ruin the formation."

The first five came to her.

"Form line abreast with me in the centre. Do not get in front of me. We will walk to the village and wait at the edge and see what happens. Under no circumstances are you to charge. If anything happens I will open up with the pistols and I will call the others through from the flank. This is not a practice. OK?"

She looked each of them in the eye and they each nodded.

"Now. Lancerrrs……….. ready!"

Ten lances went from the vertical to the horizontal in unison. Karín drew the kinetic pistol and checked it. She put her thumb on the screen and it read her print and booted. A green light showed. She removed her thumb and the light went out. She raised her free hand and waved them forward.

"Walk!"

They walked to the edge of the village and halted just on the edge of spear range.

"Buq'ue people, I am Karín of the Buq'ue and bear orders from your king. Come out. You are safe!"

A man's head showed through a flap and he looked at Karín and those with her. She took off her helm. Her red hair was short but easily identifiable.

"I see you, Karín. Well come but late. The Matáng left us not long ago taking with them all the goats they could round up and all the young women and some children. They killed the elder, Gronik, and took the food stores. They went that way but they will be slowed down by the goats and captives. If you can help us we would be forever in your debt."

"You will be forever in the king's debt. Round up what is left of the goats and all you can carry for a two day walk. Burn everything else and fill in the spring. If that can't be done, kill the weakest of the goats and put it in the water to rot. You will *be moving to a mount I have selected for you. Follow our tracks back until you find it. It has three caves and a ribbon the colour of the shirts of these soldiers. The other villagers will follow when we free them."*

She waved her flag for the rest of the troop to join her and briefed Eloik.

"We will follow them at the trot and come up behind them. The ten will go around to the rear, which will be their front, to block their retreat and you will go to the left or right, whichever you decide is the best to form up. This time we know blood will be shed. Separating the villagers from the Matáng will be the first aim. Leave that bit to me. When I rush in, I will stop short and the Matáng should come out to meet me. The villagers will be told to lie on the ground. They should be tied together in a small group and easy to avoid. Anybody standing is to be killed. Try not to trample anybody. The goats will probably scatter but they are expendable. The women are not. Watch my flags carefully and remember to kill with the first thrust and let the thong go loose. Anybody who falls from her mount is to run for it. Do not try and fight on the ground. OK, column of twos at the trot."

They set off at a forced trot and saw the enemy group after just a short ride. A shout came up from the Matáng and a group of four or five ran towards them. This was something Karín had not anticipated so she signalled for the ten to join her and they changed formation on the run and charged line abreast at the Matáng.

Karín signalled for them to take the Matáng and she shifted her own line to the left. They hit the Matáng at the gallop and didn't even slow down. They fell as one stuck through the bodies, their spears still in their hands. Karín wheeled around to the left and outflanked the main group, wheeling to the right again before halting just outside spear range. As expected, the

Matáng, some dozen or more rushed forward in a line of skirmish and crouched, ready for an attack.

"Buq'ue villagers, lie down on the ground!" shouted Karín. When they complied, Karín raised her flag and dropped it. The Matáng heard the charge coming from their right and were in the process of changing their formation when Karín let go a burst from the kinetic pistol that took three down. It served to distract them and then it was too late. Two Troop of the Household Cavalry scythed through them and kept going. Six were still standing but they started to run, a situation made for mounted troops. The troop turned and the rear rank became the front. Eloik led them slightly off centre so she could claim the outside Matáng soldier for herself. And then it was over. A spontaneous ululating broke out among the Lancers as Eloik ordered the regroup where the villagers were lying and Karín went on foot with the katana and accounted for twelve heads in one group and five in the other.

"Take their swords and spears and anything else of value. Do not harm the bodies but bring them all to one pile so the birds and wolves don't have far to search and to serve as a warning to those who would follow. The Matáng commanders will not know how they were bettered, only that they were speared through the body. We maintain the advantage of surprise." She took an image of the corpses when they were gathered and stripped and then the victorious Lancers rounded up the goats and the women drove them back to the site of their village where the others were still packing up. A great hubbub broke out as families were united and stories were told until Karín had them organized and moving.

Karín was ecstatic. She wanted to tell Ch0n. She wanted to shout it out to anybody who could hear. Instead she told Eloik to assemble the troop.

"Lancers of the Household Cavalry of King Ch0n of the Buq'ue and Arw'an! Today we have struck the first blow against those who have raided us for years and stolen our people, our best land and beasts for their own use. I have dreamed of this day my whole life and now the Lord Ch0n has given us the means. This is no small victory against a Matáng patrol. This is the beginning of the end of them. They will send a bigger patrol to look for this one and they will find it over there. They will be filled with rage but by then our tracks will have been washed away by time and they will not know where to look. They will have no supplies for their return and they will lose much face and maybe some of their men. They will know we have slapped them and they will come for us in force but again not knowing where to look. The Household Cavalry will strike their flanks and tail until we defeat them out on the plains and then they will have to invade with their Armies. That day will see the end of the subjugation of our tribes under the banner of Ch0n. Savour this moment, this small but significant victory, for it is the first blow struck in our quest for freedom."

The villagers left the site a burning ruin with half a dozen dead goats fouling the only water supply.

Chapter Twenty Four: King of the Castle

ChOn was wondering about the patrol and his dream and he was also wondering what had happened to Buyo. She had disappeared out the gate and not been seen since. He was not happy with her failure to meet the challenge he had set her. He had lied to Alik to protect Buyo's position and she had let him down. He went to lunch determined to find out about the Household Cavalry patrol but more perplexed about Buyo. As usual the eating area was packed at meal times and the kitchen staff were working hard and fast. The herders came and went quickly and the sentries took their rations back to eat at the gate house. ChOn liked to eat by himself or with one of the council members but today he sat with Eloi and her crew before going back to inform Froncy that he would be needing rations for two days and then he went to the stable to tell Alik what he would be taking on his exploration trip.

He had to help Alik and the afternoon passed quickly. He did his rounds quickly before retiring early. When he arrived, his bath was full. He looked around for Froncy but saw instead the fat teen he had seen various times during the day. He wondered why he had never noticed her before but put it down to not having been around long in the fort. She was putting a jug of hot water next to the chaise.

"Is Froncy coming to shave me?"

"I don't know My Lord," she answered in a small, frightened voice. *"I will ask her to come if you like but I was hoping I could learn to shave you when my lady is away and her beautiful assistant Buyo is not available."*

Gavan Connell

"Have you ever shaved a man before girl?"

"Shaved? I have bedded the King himself, My Lord," replied the girl in Buyo's voice.

Ch0n laughed and slapped his thigh.

"My stars! What a fine plump teenager you make, Buyo. Now show me your disguise as you remove it and tell me how you came to think of it."

Buyo took off her bonnet and revealed her fair hair. She took two wads of wool from her upper gums and her face lost its fat look. She took off her tunic to reveal a blanket wrapped tightly around her breasts and stomach to flatten the former and enlarge the latter. She unwound it and her plump breasts plopped free. The sandals were old and worn. She threw the tunic back on and started to chatter excitedly.

"I came up with the idea of being a girl because I am so small. It was obvious, really and being a girl nobody took the slightest notice of the fact I had never worked in the kitchens before. They all thought I was just starting out. My grimy face is rubbed charcoal and my hunched shoulders are a form of submission. The voice was easy. I hardly ever uttered a word. But I really wanted to fool you and to do that I had to play the part well before you were expecting it. You were looking for me today, I could see you but you looked at me without seeing me because you saw me yesterday. And now that girl is a part of the village. I can be her whenever I like and nobody will think it strange she comes and goes because she is so unimportant that they don't even see her. Froncy does but only while I am working with her. Outside those times she just looks straight through me. Oh! How exciting that I was even able to fool you at close quarters like just now and you know me better than anybody. Did I pass? Did I?"

"Yes, you did and easily. Your planning was first rate and the idea to go into the role early was a masterstroke because I was looking for you and I didn't see you because I saw you last night. You are right."

"Froncy says you are going away for two days riding. Can I go with you? Alik has hurt his hip and can't even sit astride but I am ready and would love to go. I could steal out of the gates under cover of darkness and you could collect me later."

"No. I have the right to take you. Alik is injured and everybody knows it. They know you are on our household staff so it would be natural for you to take Alik's place. Will you be ready in time, we leave after breakfast tomorrow."

"I am already packed. Where do you think I have been sleeping? I returned here and slept last night. I was going to surprise you but that would not have achieved my aim of fooling you. And I was here at the time to shave you, just that I didn't do it. Now I have to return during the night tonight. I will say I changed my mind about going and came back early. Now, I will shave you and bathe you and then I will jump into the urn and wash the charcoal out of my skin and make myself squeaky clean. And then you will give me my prize. What is it?"

Ch0n reached into his pocket and brought out the diamond Pik had given him. Then he reached into the other pocket and brought out a matte black clasp knife with a five inch blade. He opened the knife and put the two items next to each other on the chaise.

"Pick one."

Buyo's eyes went to the glittering jewel. It was worth nothing but it was indeed a thing of exquisite beauty for its own sake. The light from the window played on it and sent prisms around the room and into her black eyes.

She picked up the knife and tested the edge then tried to close it. ChOn showed her how. She hefted it in her right palm and opened it again. The wicked tanto point was as dull in the light as the diamond was brilliant.

"This is the choice of a spy who can see in the darkness. The blade will not reflect light and so no-one will know I have it until it is too late."

"You chose well. In my world, the stone would have bought a king's ransom but here it is just a pretty bauble. Do not allow that blade to fall into enemy hands because it will raise many questions they will want to know the answers to. Now if you were to shave me with it, it would work because it is sharp enough but if you fetch the razor, it will be more suitable. After you bathe yourself you should return to the loft so Alik knows you are there. Tell him you have been with me and that you are to accompany me on my patrol. Tell him to lend you a helm for the trip. It will mean we do not have to shout at each other and you will have the benefit of the zoom lens. The other functions you don't really need. I will tell you the letters of my tongue to pass the time. You will need some basic writing skills to send me messages. Writing is the scratchings you have seen me making and reading on the minitron."

ChOn called a meeting of the council for that night and left all with their instructions. Alik was to maintain communications with ChOn via the last of the helms and to pass any messages to Izaki for action if needs be.

They gathered in the stables the next morning. ChOn was as usual in his full battle armour. Buyo was dressed suitably for riding in her cavalry trousers and moccasin boots and a short tunic. She carried the blade in a pocket she had sewn in the inside thigh of her trousers where she could get it but it would not be found by accident, only by a deliberate search. Malek had brought the female tlaque early for Alik to load the travois.

Buyo placed her personal belongings next to ChOn's. The wolf was trotting around the little group in excited anticipation of an adventure. ChOn mounted the huge beast and pulled Buyo up behind him. They set off down the track to where the guard was waiting in line to farewell their king and passed through. ChOn pulled the tlaque around away from the morning sun and followed the river upstream leading the female with the calf trotting beside her.

"Where are we going, My Lord?"

"This is a direction we call 'East' towards the rising sun. If we follow the river we will see many different trees and animals maybe. I am looking for a tree that I can use to make bows. It has to be strong and light and flexible so that when it is bent against the force of a thread, it will shoot the arrow instead of breaking. I also will be looking for things I have not seen before and to see if I might have a use for them."

"Near my old village was a pool of black water so thick a man would take half a day to sink into it. But if he moved to escape, he would sink faster. We learned this when a herder tried to rescue a goat that was sinking and we could not save him. It smelt strong to the nostrils and in the mid-day sun it became so hot you could not touch it and it ran more readily."

"I would like to see that. I will look for information on such things on the minitron."

They rode at a slow walk for almost half a day before ChOn veered towards a copse of trees with long pointy leaves. He slid from the tlaque and went to where the copse had mostly saplings. He took an image of it to mark the location and then used his axe to cut a sapling twice as tall as himself and used his survival knife to trim the top. It was as thick as his arm at the base and had no branches for the first three metres of its height. It was so hard the axe chipped away at it for some time before Ch0n finally managed to fell it.

"This looks promising. If we split this down the middle and carve it and dry it in a light bow shape we may have something." He looked at the taller trees but they bore no fruit and so had no birds or animals living in their tops. He noted that there was no surface water nearby and decided they must have a deep taproot and be slow growers to be so hard. He wondered how his mind could arrive so readily at such a conclusion and then he dismissed the thought. They mounted again with the sample stashed on the travois and followed the river to a spectacular place where grass grew to the water's edge and the far bank was cut into the sandstone. The water was still and clear. Ch0n took an image before dismounting and letting the two beasts drink. The calf also took the opportunity to suckle. Ch0n looked around for signs of a dagononum but saw none. There were hoof prints close to the water but that was to be expected with so many herd animals on the plains. The trees that grew there were similar to the ones at the Overhang with fruit in the leafy branches and birds flitting to and fro. He saw some of the dáguias near the edge upstream.

"Wait here. I am going to see if there are dáguias nesting upstream."

He and the wolf walked along the river's edge and around the bend where a second pool revealed itself but this one had a cave at one end and there were the dáguia nests in the wall and the roof. He lowered the visor and checked again for signs of any dagononum but once again there were none. He took an image of the site and watched the wolf sniffing at the long grass at the edge of the trees. He came out with a dáguia chick, which he lay down and devoured in short order. Ch0n's own stomach rumbled and he started back for where he had left Buyo. When he rounded the bend he stopped and watched her. She was swimming naked in the clear water. He took the tablet, zoomed in and made a moving image of her. He went to where her clothing was neatly piled and was soon at her side.

"This place is beautiful. More so than the Overhang. This will be our place. Even though we will have to share it with the others, I will always look at it as our special place. When I am away on a mission and I ever have to run, this is where I will come. It is close to the fort but not so close as to give anybody a chance to cut me off. And you will be able to come here for me quickly."

"I am happy for you to do that but why is it our special place and not just a place where we stopped for a swim?"

They set off after she had showed him why. He had marvelled at the warmth inside of her body when the rest of her was cool to the touch and she had fallen spent on his chest. As they rode she leaned against him and did her best to distract him with her hands.

They saw nothing that was really different from their known flora and fauna and Ch0n wheeled the tlaque around away from the river well before sunset.

"We will find a place to stay out here somewhere safe. Then in the morning we will ride back and arrive in time to get these beasts cleaned up and ready before nightfall. We need a cave for the tlaque. I used to sleep under rocks when there was just me and the wolf but now it is more difficult to find suitable places without having the Household Cavalry to provide sentries. As soon as we see a cave we will stop there."

They rode until it was almost dark before they saw a cave in the distance. They both scanned for signs of dagononum and saw none. When they finally arrived they discovered it was barely big enough to take the three beasts so they themselves were forced to sleep at the entrance with the wolf. Ch0n set his electronic surveillance devices out and they settled down under the same blanket to pass an uncomfortable night.

"When does it rain here? I have been here for many moons and haven't seen it rain but there are rivers and springs all over the landscape."

"The rains come all at once. They are not far away now, maybe one moon before the wet starts and it rains every after mid day for two moons and that's it until next time. When the leaves on the trees start to fall we know it is time to move some things to higher ground for the river rises half the height of a man and stays there for the wet season. Sonja and Eloi have been careful to put the baths high enough so they can be used during the wet. And Boro wouldn't let anybody build the wall too close to the edge because it would wash away. You are fortunate to have such people looking after your interests while you are away."

"Does the land flood or can it still be crossed?"

"It can still be crossed. It is strange how the water just disappears into the ground as though the underneath is a big hollow space. We think that is why there is so much water here. The rivers run from the hollow spaces in the hills."

"So the wild herds are never in danger?"

"No. We have to manage our own herds, though and make sure there is enough high ground for them to move to while the lowlands are wet in the evenings but when the sun comes up they can go back down until it rains again. It is a busy time for the herders."

"Why do you not have a man?"

"I have had men, My Lord. I have not met one whom I would have for a mate until now and he is taken. I am content to be

his second woman when his first woman is away. I trust that he and she will provide for me in every way a woman needs. And if something is lacking I can always use Alik but what he has in his tunic would be a poor substitute for that which I have come to know."

"Well when Karín returns you will have to make do with Alik because she has made it clear she will kill any woman who lies with me while she is not absent."

"She will have much need to be absent with her Lancers, My Lord. We both know that. And I can be very persuasive. There are times in the moon's cycle when she is not available and she will come to allow me to be with you during those times. When she is with child it is forbidden for a woman to lie with a man to protect the unborn offspring so she will encourage you to be with me then. Why all of this? Because she can control whom you are with if she allows you a second woman. If you have no second woman you will lie with anybody who shows you their willingness. Then she would have to kill them. It is easier this way and it has always been so. She knows you are with me now even though she is far away. In her heart she wishes it were not so but her mind tells her you will not wait for eleven or twelve nights without a discharge. She knows I will look after you and will be discreet. We have spoken of it many times in an indirect way. There is no shame for a woman if her man takes a second woman and there is no shame for a woman to be the second wyf as you call her. On the contrary. For two women to be happy with one man is a great honour for the man and therefore indirectly to his women. Karín does not admit it yet but that is where this is going. She knows it and I know it because I am already fulfilling the role. And now you know it and you have slipped easily into the role of a King with two women."

"She told me she would understand if I were to make íjon with another in her absence. You are right in that regard but she wants it kept discreet. A secret even from her. Had she not said that to me I would not have lain with you."

Buyo laughed softly.

"My Lord, you are such a loyal man but you would have stood no chance against me. Having Karín's permission only delayed what was always going to be. Now if we are not going to sleep, I think we need to make better use of the time we have."

They cut further north and found a small herd of the white silky goats. ChOn tried to round them up but with one tlaque he was unable to do so. He took their image and decided the Lancers could come out later and herd them back to the fort. Or drag them like the previous herd. They found several other types of trees and took saplings back but overall, ChOn was disappointed in his two days away, apart from Buyo's attentions. They arrived back at the fort and ChOn took the saplings to Alik and showed him how he wanted them split with a short sword and a wooden hammer. He had had some weak signals from Karín and wanted to go and wait until she were in range again.

Two days after the skirmish with the Matáng, the first of the villages had been relocated at their new site and Karín was finally able to tell Chon the story of the Household Cavalry's first charge. He congratulated her heartily and told her about his dream. She told him about hers: a dream she had had of making the Household Cavalry a force to be reckoned with. And now they were.

"And what have you been doing in my absence, My Lord?"

"I have been doing king things and have just this after mid day returned from a two day exploration patrol."

"Did you go alone?"

"No. I took Buyo. I was going to take Alik but he has been injured for seven days and can't sit on a tlaque."

"Oh… And did you discover anything new?"

"I found a place where the dáguias are nesting betwixt the fort and castle. I have found four new types of hardwood trees that Alik and Buyo are going to split and carve for me. I am hoping that at least one of them will make good bows. Buyo told me of a place near her old village where there is a pond of black water that the minitron says may be a tar pit. It is not something I can explain but it is a sticky, thick, black naturally occurring substance good for sealing against water leaks and it burns. There must be a use for it. I am thinking that if it burns it could be used as a weapon but more that it could seal the roofs of the dwellings better than mud. I also want to see if we can use it to stick the points and fletches on the arrows. I think I will ride over there in two days to see it. I am also impatient to return to the castle. This fort is too well established and there isn't much for me to do. When you return I will send the Lancers out to round up a herd of the silken goats I found and we will return with Buyo and Alik. Izaki is doing an excellent job here. I am not needed except to be the king. So you need to keep moving. And keep your eyes open. I doubt there would be more patrols but you cannot afford to be complacent. Reny has ridden out to move the fifth village but she lacks the communications data that you can provide. I told her to go to a place where they could have walked in three and a half days. That should be close enough. I will talk to you during the move of the third village."

"I have missed your presence, Ch0n. I feel the ébon strongly for you. I do not like being away from you."

"As I feel it for you, Karín. So get moving and we will be united as quickly as possible."

Gavan Connell

"OK. I will call you from the next possible site."

It was eight more days before Karín arrived. In the intervening time, ChOn and Buyo made a three day trip to her old village site, which was now a grassy area with no sign anybody had ever lived there, apart from a few piles of stones where fires had once burned. ChOn took back a sample of the black substance to play with. The analyser confirmed it was tar and ChOn burned some out of curiosity.

Karín had barely had time to get settled on her return to the Buq'ue fort. But she had been warned in advance of ChOn's plans and the Lancers had ridden through the gate to the square to a thunderous reception. Each of the Lancers had received a wreath of leaves around her head with the promise of further recognition. They had gone to their stables with Eloik having been told the general whereabouts of the dáguia nests and the herd of goats, and Makin was already building the new pens. Buyo was fussing about Karín like a mother hen and Alik was treating her like some sort of war-goddess.

After Karín had bathed and soaked and rested, ChOn took her on the rounds of her village to see the changes wrought in such a short time. The moat was almost dug. The baths were finished. The stock pens were in various stages of completion and the dáguia chicks were a mess of feathers and fluff but were still only able to clamber onto Puntik's lap to be fed. They did their rounds together while Buyo and Alik started the process of cleaning and washing all her kit. When night fell, Karín took ChOn by the hand and led him to their quarters. There in the darkness she reacquainted herself with his body and Chon felt the difference in the coupling between Karín and Buyo. His feelings for Karín were strong and his feelings for Buyo were more physical than emotional. Standing unobserved in the darkness, her big eyes taking in all, Buyo sensed it in him and felt a pang of disappointment but not jealousy. She was the second woman, the king's only concubine and that was a position of great prestige once she was recognised by him and his wyf. And she smiled when Karín made comment that ChOn's capacity had improved in her absence and that she imagined Buyo had played some part in it. That in itself was virtual acceptance of her role by Karín.

The following morning ChOn called the council together. He gave them all instructions on the direction he wanted their departments to take. He told Izaki that he would have the Lancers in support of the fort but that they would remain essentially an independent command of Eloik and through her to Karín. Karín had given Eloik a training and patrolling schedule for the next moon cycle by which time there would be an interchange of dáguia and communications between the two areas would be a little better.

The big issue was that Izaki could neither read nor write and so ChOn told him to select two of his trusted people to go to the castle on foot to where ChOn would set up a school for messengers. They were to leave as soon as possible so that when the interchange of dáguia took place they would have basic reading and writing skills using the symbols but also some letters.

As usual the final meeting was long and left many questions unanswered. ChOn was happy for the five to make decisions inside their own areas but for Izaki to have the final word if there was an issue touching two or more areas. Finally it was complete and ChOn returned to his quarters with Karín where they changed into their full battle rig for the journey and mounted up.

The Entire Household Cavalry was lined up along the route to the gate and One Troop followed them from the fort to the knoll in the distance, Karín rode along the columns and farewelled each of the One Troop girls in turn before turning her back on them and riding alongside ChOn towards Arw'an castle. Two

Gavan Connell

Troop, the King's Troop for the next six full moons, fell in behind.

They stopped at the usual cave on the way. ChOn established communications with Jez at the castle and told him they would be returning the next afternoon. Jez had no important news to tell him, which relieved ChOn. That night ChOn slept with the helm on so Jez could reach him if necessary. Buyo slept as usual beside Karín and Alik beside ChOn. The wolf disappeared into the night but came back shortly afterwards and took up his place at the mouth of the cave making crunching noises for a while until he too fell silent.

They topped the rise overlooking the castle and ChOn looked across at Karín. The view had changed considerably in the twenty days they had been away. The outer wall which had been finished before they left was the same but the castle had risen from the hill and was now an imposing structure. ChOn could see from the rise that it was as high as four or five men and more in places. There were workers scurrying about like ants on the walls with stones and bags of mortar. They trotted down to the gate where Jez met them with the guard.

"Well come, My Lord. My Brigadier General Karín, Eloik and members of the King's Troop."

"Well met, Sir Jez. I see from yonder rise that the castle walls have risen by much in the time we have been away."

"I will let Boro tell you of his achievements at the council meeting tonight, My Lord. Meanwhile I suggest you relax and unpack. Beny will assist Alik and Buyo."

"Relax? I have been relaxing for days. I want to tour the castle. Boro can tell me of his deeds at the meeting but in the meantime I want to do my rounds. Let the King's Troop retire to their barracks and clean up. The Brigadier General Karín can do likewise if she chooses. Alik and Buyo will start on the tlaque and the kit but I am going to walk. Alik! Take the beast to the stables. The material for the bows can stay with you. Keep them well greased. Now. Sir Jez. Show me around."

Beny took Jez's tlaque and Alik and Buyo took the others. Karín spoke briefly to Eloik and then accompanied Ch0n on his rounds. They walked the perimeter at first, stopping by the new baths and then continuing past the cooking area to the bird cages. This was where Ch0n had wanted to rush but he knew they would still be there when he arrived so he allowed Jez to take him via the perimeter. Mori was at the cage as usual but outside it. When Ch0n arrived, he opened a hatch in the side wall and the birds flew out one by one until there was a flock of twenty circling above their heads, wheeling and rising almost as one. It was a spectacular sight and one the villagers obviously enjoyed for things seemed to grind to a halt everywhere Ch0n could see while people watched the flock.

"Hola Mori," grinned Ch0n. "They look wonderful. How long do you leave them out for?"

"Well come, King. They will tire of flyin' around soon enough and land on the roof of the cage. If I were to let them they would probably stay out for most of the day but I prefer to let them out three times so they get their exercise and come back to be fed. Look! They are circling lower now after just a short flight." He closed the flap and started to bang on a bamboo tube. It made a hollow ringing noise and the birds dropped to the landing platform, walked a few steps to the bars and jumped into the cage. They fought over the grains and seeds Mori was scattering on the floor.

"In one moon I want to take them to the Buq'ue fort where they will stay. Each day I will have them release one to see how long they need to be kept in one place until they call that place their home and return to it. Will that be enough time?"

"We will 'ave to take 'em out each day a little further so they get flyin' practice, milord. Perhaps tomorrow to the rise in front o' the main gate and each day afterwards a little further and in a different direction. I 'ave asked Doni to make up a travois with a cage built on to it so they can be easily transported and released. It has been finished for some days now and is behind the main cage if ye would like to see it."

They went around behind the cage and there was the travois in question. The cage was robust and had a square hole on the top where the birds could be dropped in but they couldn't fly out and the front of the cage was hinged to allow it to open fully. Inside were perches for the twenty and more birds. A frame to hold a water bowl was built in.

"You have done well, Mori. Tomorrow we will take this and the birds to the rise."

"Milord, I have somethin' else to show ye." He went to the small cage and reached towards a hollow bamboo tube. A scraping noise issued forth as soon as he opened the door and when he put his hand into the tube he withdrew it with a half feathered, half bald chick. It was making a rasping sound and Mori responded by putting a small bamboo tube into its beak and taking his finger off the top to allow the contents to flow. The ugly chick made gurgling, choking noises as it swallowed the porridge. This process was repeated several times until the creature lost interest. Mori wiped its beak and stood the chick on his finger, which it grasped with strong-looking talons.

"This is the kwidada chick your boy gave me before ye left. It 'atched out fourteen days ago and ain't stopped eatin' since. It is a male and as ye can see it has imprinted on me. In another moon it will be fully feathered but before that I will carry it on me shoulder for all to marvel at. It likes the nest still but it will leave naturally when it is ready and then I will carry it."

Ch0n looked at the ugly thing. It was hard to believe that it would turn into one of the majestic birds he had seen at the overhang. He studied the crescent shaped beak and the talons, which were not like the dáguias'. It had opposing toes that gripped with much more dexterity and he recalled the adult birds standing on one leg and holding their food to their beaks with the other foot.

"It will be a wondrous thing to have in the castle, Mori. As are you with your patience towards these birds. Your importance to the future security of the tribes can not be understated. There is one like you at the Buq'ue fort. He has the same dedication to his work."

"Did your boy give 'im a kwidada too?"

"No. There is but one for the royal bird keeper. We will find something else for Puntik. It will be something he too can show his villagers."

"P'raps ye can find the nest of an owl. They are cruel birds that 'unt live animals like mice and lizards by night. Their eyes can see equally by day or night and they fly without makin' a sound. I have seen them in the forest nearby. If ye were to find an egg, this Puntik would be well pleased. I would ha' been 'ad ye given me one tho' this kwidada is much more of a prize."

They left Mori to his charges and continued to the pens. Ch0n wanted to see his oruk calves. In twenty days they had grown quite large. Ch0n found himself thinking that his neutered male would support his weight within weeks and that as soon as it was able to, he would start riding it daily to get it used to the situation as it grew to full size. The bull calf was being handled daily to make him docile as a grown beast but whether or not this worked would be resolved later. In the meantime, the ten oruk females were seemingly pregnant with half tlaque offspring to produce a heavier mount for ChOn and for mounted Infantry in the future.

The other oruk calves were all neutered and grazing with their mothers or surrogates in the fields outside the perimeter but when Doni beat the bamboo bell and whistled them in they ambled to him like large dogs, went to their pens and dined on fresh-cut forage.

The mohair goats had dropped mostly twins and the occasional triplet. The ones with just the one kid were tagged for slaughter. The breeding buck was prone to charging the herders and they made a game out of avoiding his horns, which were the length of a man's arm from point to point.

The domestic woolly goats were separated into breeding females and 'the rest' with the males being kept with the breeding females. The females were the biggest of the females and all had borne twins or triplets. The three biggest males were now the only ones with access to them. All the other adult males had been slaughtered or were awaiting slaughter and now only neutered kids and females ran with their mothers. In another four moons the first of the selective breeding kids would be appearing.

The hides of the slaughtered goats were being cured by Kelda's crew. They soaked the skins in a tea of water and the leaves of a local scrubby bush. After a few days of soaking, the skins were pegged on bamboo frames and then stacked for use as floor coverings and even sewn together to make the walls of the shelters. That part of the castle was in the furthest downwind corner of the castle for it had a fearsome smell about it. ChOn resolved to establish a plant downwind and downstream from the perimeter wall.

The final point of call was the inner castle with the keep. The wall of the keep was as high as four men and joined the side wall of the main building at the two front corners. The effect was that the main castle was a structure fifty paces square with a walled front keep the full width of the castle and twenty five paces deep. The keep walls were castellated and a ledge was under construction at the top of the existing wall. The final wall would be chest high to the ledge and troops fighting from the ledge would be well protected from below by the castellations. There was one set of wooden gates set behind a drawbridge so that the doors couldn't be rushed. Above the gates was the gatehouse with a hole for stabbing and pouring boiling water and sewage on any attacking force below. Essentially it was a smaller version of the main gatehouse. An area had been set aside in the keep for a troop of Lancers to rush the doors if they were breached. Towers were already under construction at the two corners of the inner wall and these would be manned by bowmen and soldiers with the kinetic pistols firing along the walls and the approaches to the gates.

The main building was already as high as five men standing. Essentially it was a square box with slits for windows every few yards. The ragged walls were reaching higher still until they would stop at a height of ten men. The ground floor was now complete and was divided into a kitchen with its own well, a dining room and several other large rooms which in all could house the entire population of the castle if the outer perimeter were to be breached. The doors were wide and secured by a wooden bar that crossed the two doors and lifted into brackets on the wall. Any enemy had to breach the outer wall and then the inner keep wall before they could get into the main castle.

The second floor had wooden floors made from tree trunks floated from upstream and then split with wedges and smoothed with iron adzes. These made up the ceiling of the ground floor. On the second floor was the accommodation for Ch0n and Karín and their future household staff. Separate accommodation was set aside for the members of the council

413

during an attack. The squires would stay in the stables, which abutted the main castle and were enclosed within the keep.

The ceiling of the second floor would also form the fighting deck on the roof from where Ch0n could direct the battle and bring fire to bear on the enemy with bows, slings and the rail gun. Also on the roof Ch0n had planned a water tank to provide water pressure to the floors below; to the toilets, which were flushed into bamboo drains below the surface to the river. The final construction was to be a bamboo tower on which he would place the antenna for the landing module's radio.

He walked around the ground floor and marvelled at this creation, which Boro was bringing to fruition. He mounted the internal steps to the second floor and there he was greeted by the reason the walls were going up so much faster than before. Boro had invented a system of bamboo scaffolding that was growing with the walls and making the carrying of stones and mortar a lot easier, quicker and safer. Boro himself was directing the process.

"Well come, My Lord. I had planned to bring you here after the council meeting but I see you are eager to observe the progress."

"This is just a marvel of construction you have here. With just a few drawings you have made all this and the scaffolding is a wonderful invention."

"I wish I could claim it as my own but one of the builders came up with it. He told me he was sick and tired of climbing the walls with one stone at a time and he thought that if we built a system of interconnected ladders and platforms we could just pass the stones and paste from the floor to the next level and to the next while the fastest of the stone layers could concentrate on placing and pasting the stones into position. We could work faster but we have to do one layer at a time and make sure it is

dried before we go up. The internal walls are all tied in with the outside walls so they won't fall down the first time someone lobs a stone into them. Also the sizes of the rooms are determined by the length of the trunks we can manage. The top of the castle will be narrower by five paces in width and length than the base so the walls are leaning inwards and supporting each other with their own weight. I thought of that when I was stacking the bamboo into piles that wouldn't fall over. I think it will look more pleasing to the eye as well."

"You are a marvel. All this time you were the head man of a semi nomadic village and yet you had the capacity to build this from a picture on the minitron, a few drawings and an idea. Had I not chanced upon your village you would never have fulfilled your potential and we still don't know where your limits are. I am amazed. In my language the men who lay the stones and mortar are called 'stone masons'. It is a noble trade and one which has died out over the centuries as building methods and materials changed. Your men will be called the Royal Stonemasons."

Boro's face lit up.

"It is a fine name for them who have worked so hard. The Royal Stonemasons."

Chon turned to Karín who had been silent throughout.

"This is where we will live. On this floor with a view across the village to the plains on one side and up and down the river on the other. This is where our offspring will grow up, playing in the battlements. And downstairs will be the place where we invite those who have served their people well to dine with us from time to time.

"Is this the place of your dream, My Lord?"

415

"I think it must be so that means at some point in the future we will be attacked by the Matáng or even another army which is trying to bring down the Buq'ue and Arw'an tribe. We know from the dream that the castle is finished so that battle is in the future. In the meantime we can assume that within the full moon they will be looking for their lost patrol and after that we may need to relocate the entire Household Cavalry to the Buq'ue fort and patrol the western lands. They will come in ever-bigger forces if we continue to massacre their patrols and massacre them we will because we have to maintain the element of surprise we hold as long as possible. But when the castle is finished, we will move from our current quarters to here and one of the councillors may have our existing dwelling. Now that I have seen all I needed to see I can relax until the council meeting tonight. First, a shave and a bath and food. Suddenly I am hungry."

Karín pestered ChOn for the opportunity to go riding alone with him and so he planned a trip for the two of them to his landing site. They were to take just his tlaque and the King's Troop would follow them a day later with a convoy of tlaque females and travois. They decided to take a dáguia with them to see how it would manage finding its way back from so far away, about the same distance as the Buq'ue fort. They were ready to leave the day after they arrived back from the Buq'ue fort but to get the King's Troop away for several days took far more preparation. Finally, six days after their triumphant return, they set off towards the East with the wolf following. Karín rode up front and ChOn spent the first morning reciting the alphabet and joining in the song. He spelt out a lot of basic words for her and as she had spent a lot of time at the messenger training sessions, she could visualize the letters as he spoke them. Then he quizzed her about them and was surprised at her ability to remember. All day he pointed out the waypoints he had used on his various patrols before he finally set out to find intelligent life. There were the fruit groves, the bamboo stands and the place where he had killed the dagononum. Over there in the distance he had found the wolf cub and had first seen the tlaque herd and the ape carcass and had killed another dagononum. Finally they came to the place they were to spend the night. It was by water and in amongst tall trees. They swam and coupled and then Ch0n set up his perimeter and they slept. When the sun rose they swam and coupled again and set off for Ch0n's fortified cave.

The wolf ran ahead excitedly and even the tlaque seemed to want to surge ahead as they rounded the slopes of the rocky outcrop that had been their home for months. When they arrived, Ch0n let the dáguia fly free and watched it circle around the hill a few times before making a beeline back in the direction they had just come. He then took Karín to see the remains of the landing module still covered with brush and then he climbed the tree and recovered the radio and antenna. He unearthed all his bins full of supplies and laid them out for her to see and she was enthralled, picking up each thing in turn and having its use explained to her. She loved the synthetic blankets for their fine weave and green colour and she loved the crossbows and the slingshots. Ch0n immediately gave her a slingshot and a pound of the dense balls which she put in her pouch with the stones. The slingshot she put in the thigh pocket of her uniform. But she couldn't take her eyes off the crossbow.

"I can see that this is a mechanical bow and that the manner of it makes it more accurate than the one you shoot from the tlaque. Of all the things I have seen, this is the thing I most covet."

"More than the katana?"

"Hah! You would have me make a choice between them? This is a weapon for more than fifty paces I think and the katana is for two. There is no comparison in their roles but if you were to

tell me I could have but one, I would take this and use my ax instead of the katana."

"Look at the design of the crossbow for that is its name. Why do you think I take the horse bow to battle instead of this even though this is more accurate?"

"Show me how it works and I will answer your question."

ChOn took the bow and strung it. He put the end of the bow on the ground and pulled back the cocking lever so the string was captured in the trigger. He inserted a bolt and fired it at a nearby tree. The bolt sped away and hit the target with a satisfying 'thunk'.

"It can be fired just once from the back of a tlaque because of the need to hold it down on the ground to prepare it."

"Correct. This weapon will be fired from the towers at either end of the walls because it needs to be armed where the user is protected from the battle."

"What a pity. It is such a beautiful thing."

"Your kinetic pistol and pulse gun are much more effective even if they do not appeal to your sense of style."

"I will become proficient with the sling you gave me. That also is a thing of beauty and will serve me well when I do not want to announce my presence. What purpose served these on a flying vessel?"

She was holding one of the mirrors that were usually housed in the hull of the module, only to be deployed so the spotter could see under and around the hull. Each mirror was roughly one foot by eight inches and Karín was looking at herself. ChOn explained their purpose.

"If the vessel will never fly again, this will serve no further purpose. I will have this to help me with my hair. I like this mirror. It is much more suitable to a woman's needs than the small one in the helm for signalling. Might I have all four others to give as gifts?"

"I was thinking of using them as signal mirrors but you may have three. I will break the other one into smaller pieces." The way she grinned at him told him she had been after two.

"Thank you My Lord. Now what else is there? What is this beautiful material?"

"It is silk. The dome is used to slow things that are falling. The material is an ancient one called 'silk' made for thousands of years by worms who weave a shelter for themselves before they turn into flying creatures."

"Hah again! You would have me believe that?" I am not so dairinaiya as to believe that. This would make a beautiful garment, would it not?"

"Such as neither of us has ever seen."

"I could dress the entire Household Cavalry in silk with these five domes."

"If you were to do that, you would be one among many. If you have just one, the garments will be unique. I will give you one of these five 'chutes. The rest I would keep. I may yet find a use for them." Her expression told him she had wanted at least two.

She looked at every article with wide eyes. All the synthetic materials she wanted and Ch0n gave her some of everything. The lightweight double-bladed axe he had left at the cave soon found its way into her arsenal. The handle was long enough for two-handed use but the head was light enough for it to be wielded with one. ChOn wanted the axe to cut timber but she had pounced on it as soon as she saw it, her eyes shining with delight. So he had succumbed to her pleas.

They ate grilled rabbit by the entrance. ChOn suddenly realized he missed the simplicity of his life at the beginning of his time on the planet but knew there was no turning back. This place was rudimentary at best. The water supply was adequate and there was game to be had but if he were looking for a place of sanctuary now, he knew he could easily find an exotic place like the Overhang or the twin pools he had discovered with Buyo recently.

That night they slept close together on the platform made for one. Karín was eager to thank ChOn for the many exotic gifts he had bestowed on her and he accepted her thanks with equal enthusiasm. The tlaque was in its pen with the other and the wolf lay at the place where his cage had once stood. Outside, the sensors recorded the movement of a few small animals going about their business but no more.

The following day they saw the King's Troop approaching from a distance. ChOn and Karín had spent a fruitful morning stacking everything in piles that a travois could manage. Karín had her own pile of treasure and ChOn made sure the weapons were not all on the same travois. After a long afternoon of inspecting everything, the Lancers finally packed all the items and tethered the tlaque ready for an early start the following morning. They were disappointed not to find a swimming hole and that the cave was barely big enough to accommodate them all but they saw out the night without incident and the following morning the train headed back to the castle at travois pace.

Progress on the castle went quickly for the next month and the second storey and roof were completed except for the sealing of the roof. ChOn sent one of the men from Buyo's old village with a train of travois and they returned with enough of the tar to mix with sand and to seal the gaps in the gently sloping roof. They then mixed water and the limestone dust and 'painted' the roof white. A drain and spout enabled the water to run off so the actual roof need never have water sitting on it.

Mori had the dáguia out every day flying and returning to their aviary. The return of the bird from ChOn's cave was cause for a celebration and proof that the proposed plan of communicating by dáguia would work within the limitations of literacy. ChOn cut small lengths of flexible cable conduit and attached them to the birds' legs with cable ties. They soon got used to having the small tubes permanently attached and stopped pecking at them. Making paper had not presented any problems and the thin scrolls were made to length. A wax cork made up the set. Teaching the messengers was proving to be more difficult than ChOn had hoped and confirmed that he would have to keep everything as simple as possible. The idea of symbols seemed to be the best option for all and so it was adopted over text.

One day Boro came to ChOn and told him the castle was finished and that all it needed was to be furnished and occupied. Doni and Kelda had been curing and joining hides for moons in anticipation of this day and so when ChOn and Karín moved out of their quarters and into their rooms on the second floor of the castle, they had wall to wall rugs of goatskin underfoot. The rest of the furnishings were quite spartan and consisted of their bed, a few cushions to sit around on and some rudimentary drawers for their clothing. All their uniforms and kit stayed with Alik and Buyo in the stables. Their apartments seemed bare and cold and Karín decided she would put some colour into the place and hung woollen blankets dyed the colours of the Household Cavalry along the walls on the first and second floors. She ordered long wooden tables and benches for the dining room on the ground floor and then announced to ChOn that she wanted Buyo to move into the room next door so as to look after them better as a squire and household assistant. Buyo was ecstatic at this development and thought Karín was going to announce to the villagers that she was appointed to the position of Royal Courtesan but that didn't happen. Just the same she knew now that Karín expected her to fulfil that role in her absence.

Ch0n had Boro build the tower of bamboo four men high on the castle roof. It was strong enough that a man could climb to the top to install the long antenna that reached even higher into the sky. The radio was installed on the second floor with a cable to the antenna. The frequency stayed on band one. Ch0n had considered changing it to another frequency because he knew that any ship passing by the planet would be monitoring frequency band one and would be able to gain a lot of intel from listening for even a short while. He left it because they would be scanning the full range of frequencies looking for some sign of intelligent life and it was only a matter of seconds until they found an alternate frequency anyway. The important thing was to see how much extra range they had managed to gain from the more powerful radio, the extra height and the extra antenna, designed to transmit and receive transmissions through hundreds of miles of space.

They had an open day so the villagers could see what their castle looked like with Ch0n and Karín ensconced in it. They were amazed at what it looked like inside and it was the talk of the entire town. Jez had developed a plan for defending the inner keep and the castle itself which he and Ch0n refined and then implemented. The makeup of the defensive force was determined, and bowmen, spearmen and the crew of the rail gun were all briefed and shown their positions as the days passed. Ch0n ran a standard up the pole on the bamboo tower. It was made from a silk parachute with glue holding the edges in place. It was red and indigo in colour to match the cavalry troops and Ch0n had spent weeks drawing a coat of arms on it. It was crossed katanas with a stylized soldier in the vee made by the swords. The people below cheered wildly when he unfurled it over their castle. Over his castle. He waved to them from the ramparts with Karín by his side.

"This is not the dream but it is very similar. This is the realization of a different dream. One I have had to unite the two tribes of the Buq'ue and the Arw'an under the one banner. That banner flying above us. Now I feel like I am getting somewhere. Finally I feel like a king."

"You are a king indeed, My Lord and not just because you have built this castle. You are a king by your deeds and the way you treat us all. You are King Ch0n. King of the Buq'ue and now King of Arw'an Castle."

Gavan Connell

Chapter Twenty Five: The Matáng

The king of the Matáng was demanding answers.

"Why hasn't that patrol returned? They were to bring me another of the Buq'ue women for my harem. I am tired of those I have. I need new blood to maintain my enthusiasm. And we need more goats. Our herd can't keep up with the growing population. We have to keep building and expanding our pastures or we will stagnate. Fetch me the soothsayers. What do they have to say?"

The soothsayers threw their magic bones and other knick-knacks in order to see what had happened to the lost patrol. They consulted among each other before the leader spoke.

"My Lord King, we see that they have been defeated in a battle and all have been killed. Their bodies are piled up and are rotting as we speak. The manner of their deaths is closed to us but that they are dead there can be no doubt. All the signs point to it."

"So the herders have finally grown a spine then? Perhaps they lay in ambush, for no Buq'ue soldier alive can match it with a Matáng foot soldier. Send out a force double the size. The king of the Buq'ue will soon see that to defy me and to deny me is cause for his concern. Critang. Take a patrol of thirty men. No. Fifty. March with all speed to the village where the others were sent. Bring me every woman of age and every child. Kill every male over the age of twelve. Leave their heads on sticks for the King of the Buq'ue to see. I will not be denied and I will not allow that tribe of goat herders to better one of my fighting patrols. Go now. Now, I said! Go NOW!"

Critang left for the barracks. He had been waiting for such an order and his commanders were on high levels of readiness. He called to two of his platoon commanders and told them to be ready to leave for a nine day patrol by mid-afternoon. He went to his quarters and took out his own battle dress. It consisted of a leather helm, a thigh-length tunic and hide sandals. His upper body was protected by the Matáng breastplate of goat hide dried in the shape of his body. His only weapon was a short sword which he wore in a leather scabbard hanging from his kamarband. From his bedspace he took a rolled up blanket and a water bladder made from the stomach of a goat and covered with skin to protect it from damage. Another skin bag he filled with the dry porridge mix from the central cooking area. By mid-afternoon he was watching the two platoons forming up in marching order. The king came out of his rooms and gave a rousing speech about Matáng superiority and then disappeared into the shade. Critang raised his hand and signalled the troops forward.

They force-marched all that afternoon and bivouacked near a spring. The following morning Critang was adamant that they drink their fill and fill their water skins for the day's long march. It was known that at normal pace, the march would take five days but they aimed to do it in four. The return march always took a lot longer because of the goats and slaves and this time they would have the additional burden of many children.

The second night they had another bivouac near water and once again the following morning they drank deeply and filled their skins. It was the last water on the route they were taking so what they took would have to last until they could refill at the Buq'ue village in two days' time. The men were trained in the conservation of water and marched with a stone under their tongues to keep the saliva running in their mouths. By the end of the fourth day when they were within sight of the rise overlooking the village, though, they had little or no reserves to call on, most drank the last of their water when they saw that they had arrived.

They topped the rise and marched confidently over. They had never been challenged by the Buq'ue before and even though they suspected their former colleagues had been ambushed, Critang felt sure that a sixty-man patrol would not be opposed. He looked down on the place where the village had been. There was no sign of anything other than a black hole in the plains with green shoots of grass protruding from the ashes of what had been the village. He checked his landmarks to make sure he was in the correct place before signalling the patrol forward. The men quickened their pace as they approached the spring but the leading platoon commander halted them with a gesture. In and around the spring were the rotting carcasses of the goats left to poison the water. Critang looked around him in the vain hope he would see either another spring close by or a Buq'ue patrol he could massacre. Anything to satisfy his anger and frustration. He told the two platoon commanders to get the carcasses out of the rank water, to search the scrub nearby for anything of use and to send out patrols in every direction looking for clean water. Within minutes one of them called him to where the bodies of the former patrol lay with the seventeen heads neatly lined up nearby. Critang looked at the head of his brother who had commanded the patrol. It was barely recognisable but the bushy beard plaited at the corners was a clear sign. He looked at every body and what he saw shocked him. They patrol had not been ambushed but massacred in a skirmish. Every corpse except three had spear wounds through the chest and out the back as though they had been driven in with great force. The other three had no such wounds but their bodies were torn and the flesh as far as he could tell for there remained little of it, was almost shredded from their arms. He went back to the heads and found three with the flesh similarly torn.

427

"These three have been killed by a wild beast. Possibly a dagononum and then brought here and their heads taken. I can see no other explanation for it."

The platoon commander picked a small dull sphere from the eye socket of one head.

"What is this thing? It is heavy for its size. Perhaps the Buq'ue have found a way to cast these little balls and to fire them from a sling at close range to blind an enemy and then cut off his head while he is unable to see."

Critang took the pellet and examined it.

"That is plausible but where did they find the material to make it and how? Perhaps it is naturally occurring like round river stones that we use in our own slings. One thing is for certain, being so small they would only function at very close range. Maybe just outside sword range and then as you say the enemy steps in the extra step and takes the head. It is a tactic we will need to plan for when we confront them. Perhaps a woven facemask attached to the helm would be a good idea." He put the pellet into a fold in his kamarband and took a last look at the bodies. The other puzzling thing was the force at which the spears had entered the chests. Usually the hide armour was enough to lessen the force and sometimes even save the wearer but never had he seen a spear pass through the body of a soldier wearing armour and he had no idea how it might have happened unless the men were taken prisoner and the spears rammed through their bodies by more than one person.

"They have found a way to defeat us when we patrol in small numbers. We will have to attack in force if we are to prevail, and prevail we will for this is an insult to us and a threat to our domination of the region. I will inform the king of all I have seen and he and the soothsayers will know the next step." He turned to the platoon commander. *"But now we have a more serious*

problem. There is no water for a two-day march and no food at all for the return journey. This was a planned act of sabotage. They knew we would come and they knew we would need water and food because we have always done it the same way. We were too predictable. They have a new commander I am sure of it and he is no fool. And now we will suffer for it. I fear many of us will not make it back to the stream. We will march only at night when it is cooler. Inform the men that they have to make do with what water they have if any. There is no compulsory sharing of water for each man started out with what he could carry and some used it all and some didn't but they have to make do with stones for two nights' walk and one day's rest plus today. This will test the mettle of us all."

Darkness fell and they set off back along their own tracks. The moon was bright enough for them to find their way. By morning they were all thirsty and even those who had water at the start of the night were loath to use it because they knew they had another day and night before they could fill their bellies and skins. They walked until they came to a thin copse of trees where they slept in the feeble shade. By mid day none of them had water and most had not drunk anything for three days and two nights. Men with parched throats were unable to raise saliva even with the stone under their tongues and they stopped sweating despite the heat. The sun beat down and they started to overheat despite being told to remove all their clothing. Here and there a man vomited bile because he had no fluid in his stomach and then one of them started to shake involuntarily where he lay. His skin was dry and red from the sun and when he stopped his tremors he stayed unconscious. By the time night started to fall, more than half of them were too weak to stand and three were dead. Critang tried to reconcile what was happening. He knew it was heat and dehydration causing the symptoms and that there was nothing he could do about it. He made the necessary decision to allow those fit enough to walk to leave the others behind. There was no question if them returning with water inside a whole day even if they made good time overnight, filled their bellies and all the skins they could carry and came back at a run. It was simple. Get to water or perish out on the Buq'ue plains. As soon as he felt that the temperature had dropped sufficiently he called them to stand and form column of twos. Of the original sixty, only thirty seven were able to take their places and many of them were barely standing. He ordered them to march and they set off on what would be an all-night trek for a strong few, while the weak and the stragglers would be left to die where they fell. And fall they did. After the first five miles, only twenty four remained; after the next five, only sixteen. When they reached the half way mark fourteen of the sixty still shuffled along in some form of order but things took a turn for the worse soon afterwards. Men started to stagger away from their little group and the others had no saliva to wet their lips to even call out. Some returned to the ranks and others just fell and stayed where they had fallen. Critang and the two platoon commanders were three of only seven who saw the sun rise. When they reached the little stream, the five remaining threw themselves bodily into it and sucked the precious clear water through parched lips down into their bellies. One was so weak he drowned face down in two feet of water and his comrades didn't even notice until it was too late. Critang told them to rest for the day and that they would leave again just before dusk and arrive at the next water in the early morning. He slept most of the day and when he did wake, it was to drink more water and sleep again. Late afternoon came and he decided to wait a little longer before leaving. He slept again and when he woke the moon was high. He called his few remaining charges to form up and leave but he was greeted with pleas for more time to rest. He himself felt so weak he doubted he would make it back to the village so he allowed them all to sleep again. When the sun rose they staggered from the oasis into the plains following the tracks they had made just seven days before when they were full of confidence and marched along singing their battle songs.

Critang led the sorry group on and on until he decided they should pause at the final spring. He turned to give the order to halt but there was nobody following him. His brain started to tell him he was almost home but he was too hungry to listen. He ate the sweet grass at the edge of the spring and washed it down with yet more water. He knew he would not make it back if he slept so he decided to walk on. He saw the tracks they had made on the outward march and followed them all through the night until he saw the lights from the gatehouse ahead. He started to run towards them and he fell agonizingly short and tried to rise but he couldn't. He shouted to the sentry who couldn't hear him. He managed to crawl a few more yards towards the gate and that was where he was found when the sun rose and the sentries changed their routine. He was delirious by the time they carried him to the king's chambers. He told them of the massacre at the site of the village. He told them of the strange ball he had found. He told them of the poisoned water and the trek back that had cost them sixty lives. He told the king that the only way to defeat the Buq'ue was to send the entire army with a supply train of slaves as porters until they found the Buq'ue village and were able to resupply. He told the king that the Buq'ue must have a new commander who was a strategic thinker and that they would need to change the way they operated or they would surely suffer for it. And then a major blood vessel exploded inside his head.

The king of the Matáng looked at his senior commander and oldest son. One side of his face had collapsed. One side of his body suddenly gave way and he fell to the floor. His eyes tried to move from side to side. He clutched at his head with his one good hand but the pain would not be controlled by such a feeble manoeuvre. He whimpered for a short while and then his body shut down completely. The death toll from the patrol had now reached sixty one. The king had lost two sons to the Buq'ue in less than one moon. He screamed for the soothsayers.

431

Gavan Connell

The Matáng could congregate and fully equip an army of more than two thousand men on reasonable notice. Three with time. The king was not inclined to allow them time so when the invading force left for the Buq'ue lands a week later, it was only five hundred strong with a supply train of half a hundred porters carrying water and porridge and driving goats. It was a fine looking force of men divided into five companies of ninety four under the command of the king's third and last son and his advisers. Each company was further divided into three platoons of thirty with a commander and three aides. They marched well and in straight lines beneath their standards of various colours and they soon outstripped the baggage train. The first night they camped by the same spring that Critang's patrol had done and on the second night they camped at the same stream. Two days later they arrived at the former site of the village and decided to try the water. The spring had replenished itself many times since the removal of the goat carcasses so they were able to use the water, unlike Critang's force. The problem was that now they had no idea where to look for the Buq'ue village. The commander decided to set up a permanent camp at the water and let the goats run free. He then sent two of the five companies out on four day patrols looking for signs of Buq'ue life.

Chapter Twenty Six: A Plan comes to Fruition

Ch0n and Karín were back in the Buq'ue fort when things started to fall into place. The radio antenna on the castle roof gave a signal well past the OP and so the OP were moved closer to the Bu'que fort where they could provide better warning to the Arw'an Castle than before. Ch0n and Jez had roamed the pains for days at a time finding the extent of the radio signals and now had a good idea where they could guarantee reception. The dáguia had been interchanged between the fort and the castle as well as out to the Buq'ue OP forward of the outposts. Each of the outposts now had a few birds homed to their villages so an OP could release one bird to the outpost and another to the fort. The OP themselves were under strict orders never to engage with the Matáng but to melt away as soon as it looked like their positions were going to be compromised. The bird cages were to be dismantled and the sticks hidden. The water holes were to be left alone so as to allow the OP to be occupied as soon as possible after the Matáng had passed. The villages themselves were to be vacated. The inhabitants were to carry what they could to a predetermined hiding place and then they were to walk towards the fort until they were met by friendly troops. Once again there was to be no actual contact with the Matáng patrol unless they were taken by surprise. Ch0n's plan was to keep the Matáng Patrols wandering on the plains without ever finding anything of substance and so they would have to return or perish. He had no idea that his strategy had already cost the Matáng sixty of their finest and had caused the angry Matáng king to advance to contact much earlier than he should have done.

And so it happened that one afternoon just before they were due to return to Arw'an Castle a dáguia arrived from the western OP. It caused a scramble at the cage as Puntik hurried to retrieve the precious rolled up paper and rush it to Izaki as were his orders. Izaki swore under his breath and ran to where Ch0n and Karín were getting their kit in order.

"My Lord, the Matáng have been seen at OP4. The bird arrived just now."

He handed the scroll to Ch0n who looked at the symbols for 'enemy',' big', 'coming', 'one day'. A large enemy force was approaching the OP but was still one day away. Large? Large was more than a lancer troop. So more than fifty. Probably a hundred. Three platoons and a headquarters.

He looked at Karín. "Fall out the Lancers and send them straight to the western outpost to meet the villagers and escort them to safety. Short rations. Move now." She rushed to tell Eloik.

"Puntik, send this to Mori." He scribbled a few symbols and words on two scrolls and gave them to the bird master. "Your best two birds, man. This is not a practice. Go now.

"Izaki. I have just sent for the King's Troop to come here. They should arrive tomorrow night if they push it hard. Karín and I will ride with them after they rest. We will go to the site of OP4 and see what we can see without being seen. It would be nice to have birds homed to their location but it will be a logistic nightmare to maintain them. At least we have the advantage of one way warning. Now if they are a hundred strong we will not be able to attack them with one troop of Lancers. With two troops we might manage it but we need to split the force if we can. If not, we will pick at the flanks and rear without actually engaging in a full battle. This is just the beginning of it by the way. We will kill their hundred. I think we probably killed thirty by poisoning the water and they have come in force. If we kill the hundred, they will have to mount a full invasion of the Buq'ue lands and we will lead them to ground of our choosing. But right now we need cavalry. Your soldiers will have their glory, don't worry but not just yet. We need to exploit our mobility while nobody knows we have it. The next step will be mounted Infantry carried behind male riders on the biggest of the beasts. The soldiers will dismount and fight the ground battle while those mounted sit back and pound the enemy with arrows and manoeuvre to pick up their brothers at the critical moment before the cavalry sweep. It will be a joy to behold and even better to be a part of. For the moment, though, we will hit the supply train and hope the company commander splits off a platoon to defend the tail. If they do, we can sweep the remaining two by engaging them and holding them while the second troop comes in from the baggage train to roll up the flank. Alik! I need to be ready right now boy. Let's go. Full battle order and have Buyo set out Karín's. Move boy. We are off to war!"

"The beauty of having an autonomous cavalry force in barracks is that they can be kept on short notice to move," Ch0n had once told Karín. "If your soldiers are quartered with their mounts, they can just fall out of bed and into the saddle. See to it that yours can do that. One day you will see why."

Karín went straight to Eloik's stall and quickly told her the situation. Eloik roused the Lancers and then listened to the end of Karín's instructions. By the time she had finished, the troop was ready to mount up.

"We will follow in a few minutes as soon as I get back and get dressed. Buyo will have my kit ready. Remember do not engage with the Matáng until we assess the situation or unless they are already attacking the villagers. If they are just going to keep wandering, the Lord Ch0n will explain the tactics we are going to use to harass their tail and flanks. Ride well now and keep the villagers safe."

The indigo shirts rode off into the murkiness along the now worn trail and Karín ran to Ch0n's stables. He was waiting beside his mount fully dressed. He said nothing while Alik and Buyo dressed and armed her. Ch0n gave her a once-over kit-check himself before they mounted.

Reny was getting her orders at the same time Ch0n and Karín rode through the main gate and trotted after Two Troop. The dáguia had taken exactly one hour and ten minutes at an average speed across the ground of just over fifty miles an hour. Mori had run to Jez with the message and Jez had run to Reny. Reny had them riding through the gates an hour later. She didn't notice the dáguia casting a wide circle overhead before making a beeline towards the west.

While their birds had stirred up a hive of activity in the two main centres, the members of OP4 were watching the Matáng patrol as it approached. There seemed little doubt they would pass right over the OP so they released the rest of the birds and dismantled the cage. By the time they brushed over the flattened grass and checked the space for rubbish, Eloik was already heading for the village and Reny was rousing the King's Troop.

The villagers at the western outpost started to pack up. They could move in just a few hours and the Matáng patrol was more than a day's march away. The cave where they were going to hide their belongings was hard to see from low down on the rise and even harder with the stones strewn over the entrance. They shouldered their belongings and walked to the cave, hid everything including the cave's entrance, brushed away all the signs from the rocky ground and then started towards the Buq'ue fort.

The Matáng company commander ordered his lead platoons to check the high ground on both sides of the line of march. He was feeling as though he was achieving nothing with the grid he was searching. They had found nothing and in another day they would have to return to the main position and rotate with another company. The going was slow and hot and he had other things he would like to be doing. A shout from the scout followed by signals for him to go forward snapped him out of his reverie. It took him half an hour to reach the high ground that was on the right side of their centre line. The platoon commander explained to him that the forward scout had found the grass flattened as though something had been sitting on it for a long time. They searched the entire knoll and found nothing apart from a pile of bamboo sticks all the same length, some of which smelled of manure.

"Scout, what do you make of this?"

"I think two men have been here for some time. Perhaps as long as a moon cycle. This grass is flattened in the place that allows someone lying here to see down the plain towards the direction from which we have come and yet not be seen from the lower ground. These sticks are probably the remains of a cage that housed rabbits or birds for cooking. The manure seems more of birds than rabbits so I am going to guess they had a diet of mostly birds that supplemented their porridge. It is something we should consider for our own forage. The dáguia bird is big and slow when it is fledging and we could catch them and take them on a long march. The only problem is it would take a hundred birds just to feed one platoon. This worked because they were only two. Perhaps even one. I am guessing they have long left and are probably running back to their main position to let them know we have arrived."

The company commander laughed.

"And you get all that from some flat grass and a few sticks under a bush. Amazing work. Well we have lost the element of surprise but we know we are heading in the right direction. Well

done. Move out, now. Find their tracks. We need to keep moving if we want to find that village or what's left of it."

The two observers had indeed run from their hide. But they had not run to the village. They had no need to warn the village because the dáguia had already done that. Instead, they ran towards the place where the Lancers would be riding to intercept the villagers. It was part of ChOn's plan. Lead the Matáng away from the village but let the Lancers chop them up in the open ground off to one side. The villagers themselves were going to a third position where the Lancers would meet up with them unless they cut across the Matáng first. It all depended on the speed of deployment of the Lancers and the ability of the Matáng to read the signs on the OP.

ChOn and Karín had long caught up with the troop when the observers ran across their path at the designated rendezvous point. They told ChOn, Karín and Eloik that there were twice as many soldiers as there were Lancers and that they had stayed watching until they had seen the scout point in their direction and start the advance again. They were only a couple of hours away.

"Wait here for the villagers and tell their head man to walk back towards the fort until he comes to the spring. Tell them to wait there. You stay here and keep an eye out for our return or for the Matáng if we miss them or they get the better of us, which is most unlikely."

He looked at Karín and Eloik.

"It will be dark soon. They will set up camp. We should ride hard for a short time to get closer and then walk quietly until we see their fires. At that point Karín and I will go with two sisters until we can dismount and go in on foot. The sisters will stay with the mounts and wait for our return. We will cause a bit of havoc in their camp and see how their morale is in the morning.

If they are any good, they will be camped in three platoon positions, all self-defending but mutually supporting."

The troop trotted west for half an hour and then slowed to a walk until they saw the light from several fires. Ch0n and Karín peeled off with two Lancers and they rode quietly towards the camp until they reached the last of the cover. Ch0n stopped and they all dismounted.

"Look at that big rock up there," he told the two Lancers. When you see this again," he flashed a laser onto the rock and it showed as a green point of light, "mount up and get ready for us to arrive at a run. I am hoping that we will be able to walk in and out but if the commander is good, he will have assessed this bush as a likely enemy approach and he may have a plan to counter attack it. If you see this flashing off and on and off and on, mount up and take the tlaque away from here and back to the troop. We will run in that direction and if you send out a small patrol for us in the morning we will meet it. Do you understand?"

"Yes, My Lord."

"Good. The most important thing of all is that they do not know we have the tlaque under our command. Better both Karín and I die than that."

They melted into the darkness with their helms on full night operations mode. The two Lancers waited uneasily in the darkness for any signs that the others had reached the Matáng camp safely. They kept their eyes on the rock and their ears listening for tell-tale signals.

Ch0n saw the sentry from fifty feet. He was leaning against a tree playing with the point of his spear. He took out the pulse gun and set it to forty. Enough to stun a tlaque, enough to kill a sentry. The pulse reached out into the darkness and hit the man full in the chest and he went down instantly. They waited a few moments in case the sentries were in pairs and then sneaked easily to the edge of the camp. Most of the men were asleep with their blankets under their heads. Some were sitting around the fire. There were too many of them awake for a rush so Ch0n signalled Karín to go backwards into the darkness. He followed her and took two fragmentation grenades and a smoke grenade from his utility belt. He whispered into the mike for her to turn her back and close her eyes and when she heard the noise, to run back to the tlaque as fast as she could but on no account to turn around or she would be blinded temporarily by the light from the flashes and the flames.

"Do you understand?"

"Yes."

"Do NOT look back. Say it"

"Do not look back."

"OK start walking I am going to throw two explosives that will make a lot of noise and one that will make a lot of smoke. That one I will have to throw so the smoke covers the camp. Move now. Here we go on three. One.....Two....... Three."

He readied all three grenades. He lobbed the first fragmentation grenade and the momentum armed it and fired it three seconds later, then the white phosphorous and then the second frag. When the first one went off, he told Karín to start running.

Ten seconds later he shone the green light on the rock and they slipped into the copse. Behind them, men were screaming and shouting and forming up. Dense white smoke and flames covered the Matáng position and the riders were screened from view as they leaped into the saddle and raced into the black.

Eloik heard the explosions. So did the observers and so did the villagers. They all knew only one person had the wherewithal to make them happen so they knew Ch0n had struck the first blow.

The Matáng company was a shambles. The fragmentation grenades had killed two men and injured seven more. One of those had his face half missing and the rest had minor shrapnel cuts to various parts of their bodies. The white phosphorous had started fires in tents and had burned dozens of men as well as starting a grass fire in the middle of the position and it was spreading quickly. By the time they extinguished it they had lost a lot of their equipment and they were terrified beyond words. Their commander was trying to come to grips with the noise and injuries and how they could possibly have come about. He had no doubt they were Buq'ue tricks but the scale of the shock was beyond his comprehension.

When the sun rose, Ch0n had the Lancers hidden close to the Matáng position in dead ground. He, Karín and Eloik were lying under a bush watching what was happening less than two hundred yards away. The Matáng were walking around their position searching for something. Clues.

"They won't find anything really of any use. The fragments are tiny and only useful out to the height of two men. They'd do better to look at the wounded and see what they can recover. When they set off, we will start attacking their rear supply people. They won't last long with no food or water so far from home. Karín, you take half the troop and Eloik the other half. I will attack the rear and you two can do lightning raids on the flanks. Now then. They are going to see we are mounted on tlaque so it is important that nobody from this group survives. Nobody. And there is no reason why any of us should be a casualty. We have weapons that can defeat everything they have. No charging in. There are too many for a charge. They will stop and form squares and do all sorts of things. When they do, Brigadier General Karín and I will use the kinetic pistols and the pulse guns. Only when they run will you run them down. Not before. And watch your flanks."

The Matáng commander was trying to decide whether to push ahead for the Buq'ue village or to go back to the main group and report failure and defeat. In his mind, though, he knew he had to go ahead so he gave orders to that effect. His soldiers were skittish from the outset and it took them a long time before they were stretched out in proper patrolling formation.

It was the scream that brought them up short. A piercing, woman's scream. They looked around and saw a lone creature with a golden face astride a tlaque. It was dressed from head to foot in black. It was just sitting on the beast doing nothing. Then it turned slowly and rode away behind a crest. A few seconds later it appeared again on the opposite flank. The same creature all in black. And suddenly there were two of them. The platoon commander of the closest platoon barked out an order and the platoon formed a reluctant Roman square. The figure rode to just beyond spear-range, raised his hand and pointed something dull and black towards them. There was a rattling noise and the front rank of the square crumpled and fell. The second row was splattered with blood and bone and bits of flesh. The creature raised its arm again and there was another rattling sound and the second row went the way of the first. Then the third. Ch0n had just wiped out almost a third of the Matáng force in less than a minute. The creature on the other flank lifted its arm and pointed a similar device at the platoon commander who dissolved in a pink spray.

They rode at a walk around to the next platoon. The horror of what they had just seen struck terror into the hearts of every soldier present but they stood firm. Ch0n was impressed with their discipline and noted it for future battles. He called to the porters.

"All you who are not soldiers and who wish to return to the Buq'ue tribe go over there. If you wish to remain with your Matáng masters, you will die beside them. Go or stay now!"

The slaves rushed to where Ch0n was pointing.

"Those soldiers among you who would join the army of the Buq'ue and Arw'an put your spears on the ground and walk over with the slaves. You will be treated fairly but you will have to serve me. I give you this one chance to save yourselves. Where is your commander?"

"I am their commander and I command them to stand fast and fight." Ch0n pointed the kinetic pistol at the company commander. A small red dot appeared on the end of his nose. Then his face disappeared. Another officer, the second platoon commander stepped forward to take his place but he said nothing.

"That is the fate of those who would fight. I have no desire to kill all of you but I have the means and I will do it. I cannot let any who would be our enemy return and tell your king what they have seen. As soldiers you know that. I too am a soldier and I have no desire for needless bloodshed. I offer you the honourable life of a soldier or the honourable death of one."

The third and final platoon commander stepped forward.

"Before we can serve you we need to know what manner of thing you are with your gold face and no features. You who command the beasts of the earth." He pointed at the tlaques and the wolf who was sitting next to Ch0n. *"You who possesses weapons the likes of which we have never seen. How do we know you will not take us back to the Buq'ue and enslave us?"*

"I have no need for slaves. The Buq'ue and the Arw'an work as one and they have power among themselves. Their soldiers

443

are invincible because they have tactics you do not have. We have the manner to invade the lands of the Matáng and slaughter you all or enslave you but why would we do that?" He activated the mike and told Karín to signal for the troop to come over the hill at a walk.

"We know you are one company of many. Our observers have told us what is happening. If your other companies continue towards us, threatening us, there will be a massacre the likes of which these lands have never seen. It is in their hands what happens tomorrow just as it is in yours now. As to what I am, I am like you all." He removed the helm to reveal his bald features.

"There. Now you see me. Now see them." He pointed to the rear of their position and a murmur broke out among the soldiers for now they were truly frightened. Thirty Lancers in two ranks were lined up not fifty yards away, their lances up.

Karín decided to impress them further. Off to one side and out of their view, for they were all fixed on the Lancers, she signalled with her flag and their lances came to the horizontal as one. She signalled for them to walk and they walked in formation ten yards and she signalled them to stop.

Ch0n replaced the helm.

"Well done, Brigadier General Karín. You made your point beautifully. But no closer because they may yet need to fight and we need the advantage of distance." She nodded in reply.

"What say you, commanders of the two remaining platoons? Fight or fealty?" He waited five seconds and shot the closer of the two platoon commanders. "Too slow! I need commanders who can make quick decisions! You now! Fight or fealty?"

"Dark soldier, you have killed my brothers. I will not join you but I would ask that you give me the chance for vengeance. I will then let these speak for themselves."

"No, ChOn!" It was Karín.

"So be it." ChOn dismounted and called the platoon commander to come forward. He holstered the pistols and stood with arms akimbo until the Matáng officer was ten feet away.

"This will be a waste of your life, boy. And you have honour. I need men like you. I do not need dead officers who could otherwise be in my service commanding their own people. Your brothers were soldiers. I knew them not. They died as they would have chosen, in the field of battle. You may still do that, die in the field of battle but it doesn't have to be here and now. Let it be in a battle worthy of fighting in a place worthy of defending. To die here on a dry plain in foreign lands is not how someone like you should die. Kneel now and swear me your oath and I will spare you and all who follow you. If you die they will come to me anyway or they will all die and their blood will be on your hands. You know that. What is your name, boy?"

"I am Alangadale and I will die here so my father will not call me a coward and they will decide for themselves."

"So be it, Alangadale. I am ChOn, a galactic soldier from the planet Earth, marooned in your world. It has been an honour to know one such as you, even though it has been for such a short time." He reached over his right shoulder and unsheathed Shiew. She sang a single note as she brushed past the metal ring on the scabbard. He took up the horse stance, left foot forward and his body at forty five degrees to Alangadale. The naked blade pointed at the sky over ChOn's right shoulder. The boy's short sword looked like a toy by comparison, for a toy it was. He took one step towards ChOn who stood stock still. He took another step and saw ChOn's left shoulder twitch as the fibres in his body exploded into action. Alangadale's practised reaction to the twitch was to withdraw a step but before he moved, ChOn stood up and bowed to him. Nobody knew exactly why or what had happened except ChOn; certainly not Alangadale for he was dead. His body stood balanced and erect before it finally fell forward and the head separated from his shoulders.

"If any man among you has the courage and honour of that boy, I would have him in my service. He died for you all. Now it is your duty to live for him." He nodded to Karín and she signalled to the Household Cavalry. Their lances came down as one and the Lancers made their mounts shift as if they were eager to charge. The Matáng soldiers had lost their four officers and watched thirty of their comrades die. They were looking around uneasily waiting to see if someone would be the first. Nobody was. Instead a roar started somewhere in their group and they charged spontaneously at ChOn, who was still dismounted. He drew both pistols and fired at the charging mass. He winnowed them down and Karín joined in from her flank, signalling the Lancers to charge. They hit the Matáng at full throttle and opened up a space for ChOn to withdraw into. He was mounted within seconds and cutting and slashing at the edges of the melee. Then the Matáng broke and ran and ChOn reined in his tlaque. The Lancers ran them down and rode through them until not a man was alive. The bloodlust was on them and Karín had difficulty attracting Eloik's attention to call them to reform. When they did, there was a tlaque standing alone near the formation.

"Find her!" shouted Eloik and they searched amongst the gore for their fallen sister. She was easy to find from her indigo shirt. She had lost a leg below the knee where she had been slashed with a sword and she had obviously fallen from the tlaque and

been killed on the ground. Her wounds were horrible to see but there was nothing to be done about it.

"Bury her with the boy in the shade. They deserve to be together in peace. Afterwards we will ride to the villagers and take them home. The King's Troop will be here by nightfall or by morning at the latest and then if the Matáng come to us, we will see if they still have the stomach for battle. Pile up the dead for the carrion eaters. This hill will be known henceforth as The Hill of Tears for the senseless loss of lives that took place on it."

He was quiet as he lay beside Karín after dark. It was a side of him she had not seen. A more sensitive side.

"Do not grieve for the boy. He did what he thought he had to do. And you did what you had to do."

"I would happily have killed the rest of them to have him survive. He knew he was going to die and he knew it would achieve nothing for him except the respect of his troops and his enemies alike. That is true bravery and honour and we may not see its like again."

"I know that but you should not torture yourself for his decision. Would you rather he had bettered you and that he were alive this night and you buried in the copse yonder? I think not. Now go to sleep because tomorrow morning you will have to decide if we are going to look for the Matáng companies or let them wander through our lands unimpeded."

He did sleep and he did not dream because he knew she was right and it cleansed his conscience to know it.

The morning broke cool and cloudy.

"The rains will be upon us within two or three days, ChOn. It is not good weather to be waging war, even from the back of a tlaque."

"But we have to know where the Matáng companies are before we can send the villagers back. We are already here and soon the others will arrive. We can send the villagers with the observers while we fan out and look for the Matáng. Everybody within sight of the next pair. You in the middle with me. Rain or no rain we have to engage the Matáng or make sure they have left the area. My guess is that they are further north because they are well trained and would not be searching the same area as this patrol. That is where we will look first and if we find them we will tear into them like wolves. This time we can use the King's Troop to stand off with the new bows and slaughter them until they are weak enough for Two Troop."

"Always something new to learn, ChOn. With you there is no standing still."

"No and when we have mounted Infantry we will have battlefield mobility with Infantry muscle. Cavalry can win you a battle but without Infantry the victorious side has no way to hold the ground. Also, sometimes you need Infantry to block the enemy and engage them before the cavalry can sweep through. Archers and Infantry first, Cavalry next and Infantry last. But that's for another day."

The King's Troop arrived mid-morning. They were tired from the forced march so ChOn told them to rest the beasts and water them ready for an afternoon march. Of course they were keen to hear of the two victories Two Troop had won and so while the beasts rested, the Lancers didn't until ChOn ordered them apart.

The villagers were unpacking their village from the caves when the Household Cavalry arrived in force. It was an impressive sight and everybody stopped to watch them passing through. Ch0n had decided they would patrol a day's ride north-west and see if they cut the tracks of a Matáng company. They did so early the following morning and the signal mirrors and flags called the outriders in. Ch0n gave Karín her orders and she passed them on. They trotted down the line of march and within the hour they had the Matáng rear platoon in sight. The King's Troop didn't even break stride and hit the platoon from the rear while the platoon commander was trying to form them up in a defensive square. The two lines of fifteen Lancers took out the entire platoon in the first charge. By then the company headquarters had sent out runners to the leading platoons to consolidate but Ch0n and Karín rode through the headquarters group with swords slashing. The two platoons were isolated with two troops of Lancers between them. Ch0n surveyed the ground and decided the right front platoon was in the more vulnerable position because the ground gave them nothing. The other platoon had a shallow wadi protecting them which the tlaque could not negotiate at a run. He nodded to Karín and she put Two Troop in position while the King's Troop drew their new longbows from their saddle boots. They were six feet long and needed all the power most of the women possessed to fully draw. But they had carefully matched the bows to individual women and the first flight of arrows rose and fell among the Matáng platoon seconds after the order was signalled. The long arrows were weighted with tar at the front of the shaft and they fell heavily into the heads and shoulders of their prey. Some who had looked up had arrows in their eyes and faces. The second flight followed and then the third and the fourth. Most of the soldiers were wounded or dead by this time although less than a minute had passed. And when they heard the thunder of hooves as Two Troop started to sweep down the gentle slope, they broke and ran.

Karín was delighted with the progress of the fight but Ch0n, the soldier, wanted an end to it and when the Cavalry had reformed he rode quietly to the remaining platoon and called for their commander. A young man stepped forward and stood defiantly in front of his men.

"Do you know Alangadale, boy?"

"I do but I do not know you or what you are."

"Alangadale is dead along with everybody else in the company of which he was a member. They went the way of these you see strewn around but it did not have to be that way. I offered him what I offer you. Surrender to us, swear fealty to me and I will take you back to the Arw'an village and place you in the Arw'an army with full honours. Refuse me and I will kill you and then all your men. Alangadale chose death. You may choose life."

"I swore fealty to the king of the Matáng. How can I then break my oath and swear to you? How could you trust a man who would break his oath just to save himself?"

"I would trust the word of a man who swore to save the lives of his men, even though his own life be forfeit."

"Then kill me and take my men if they wish to follow you. It is their choice, not mine."

A soldier stepped from the ranks. He was a middle aged man and wore the posture of one used to being in a position of authority.

"Show your face and we will talk. We see not your eyes. Ah! So you are a man after all, not a God. Well, I will speak for the men. Our commander has offered his life to save us but if he dies you will have to kill us all. If he lives and swears to follow you, we will follow him. There will be no other way!"

Ch0n looked at the platoon commander.

"What is your name, boy?"

"I am Mikares of the Matáng. And you?"

"I am King Ch0n of the Buq'ue and Arw'an. Now you have it in your power to save or kill your men. But decide quickly for we have a long way to go before we reach the Buq'ue fort."

"Then, King Ch0n, I swear fealty to you. I will serve you as you desire and my men will serve you alongside me unto death."

"So be it for death will be the price if you break your oath just as it will be if the King of the Matáng were to hear of your making it. Now. How many more companies are there and where are they located?"

"There are three. They are located at the site of the Buq'ue outpost where we lost our first patrol one moon cycle or more ago. They are waiting for us there. And of course for the other company."

"Good. You have passed your first test of loyalty. Had you lied I would have killed you all. Now. It is a four day walk to the Buq'ue fort. We have rations aplenty and water to make the journey. You will be escorted back by Two Troop. When you arrive at the fort you will report to the garrison commander, Izaki. You will all shave your beards and hair and boil your clothes. That way there will be no infestations of body lice in the fort."

"But Lord, our God requires us to have beards. We will not shave them."

Ch0n unsheathed Shiew.

"I can arrange for you to meet your God or I can have you shave your beard, boy. I care not for your God but I respect your right to believe and now I respect your right to change your mind. If you insist on having a beard when in my kingdom we insist on no nests for lice, we have a fundamental area of disagreement. If I have to shave you, I will do it with this."

"Well, since you put it that way, we can but hope that our God, whom we call, Aduwen, will see it in his heart to forgive us this small thing."

"Sheath your swords and form up in double file. You will walk and the Lancers will follow. Eloik! They are not to break ranks or draw weapons at any stage until you reach the Buq'ue fort. Have the village send word that you are on the way with thirty new soldiers for Izaki. He is to meet you outside the gate with Froncy's team to shave them. Mikares, I have your word that you will serve me. Eloik serves me as you do but she speaks to you with my voice. Izaki will speak to you with my voice. To obey me and my laws is to want for nothing. To disobey my people is to disobey me and I have already told you that to break your oath will cost you your life. Do you understand me, Mikares?"

"I do My Lord. We all do."

"Good. Eloik? Start back as soon as they are formed up and ready to march. Stay a spear throw behind them. If they break ranks or try anything at all to slow you down or defy my order, kill them all except the platoon commander. Him you may wound if you have to but at the end of the day I want to try him myself if he plays me false. Do you understand, Eloik?"

"Oh yes, My Lord. I do understand."

"Brigadier General Karín!"

"I am here My Lord."

"Make sure your Lancers are provisioned. We are going to visit the Battalion Commander. Recover as many arrows as you can. They will be needed again unless I am mistaken. I want to leave before dark. Rest while you can. It will be a long night and tomorrow when the sun rises over the Matáng camp there will be another battle."

They reached the final Matáng position before the sun rose. ChOn had them rest again in the dead ground while he went ahead on foot. Karín had orders to advance to where the bows could inflict damage on the nearest positions and to provide ChOn himself with support if he needed to withdraw under covering fire. Karín was unhappy for him to go in alone but she knew that communications was the key to the plan and she had to wait with the Lancers. She watched ChOn find and kill the sentries and then he disappeared from view into the camp. He reappeared at a run just as the first of the tents caught fire. He stopped outside spear throwing range and placed a red shirt on the ground.   Then he withdrew another twenty yards and waited. Out of the confusion came Matáng soldiers but they stopped when they saw the strange apparition fifty yards from their perimeter. The sun was rising behind him and they had to shield their eyes to see just his silhouette.

"Matáng soldiers. Send for your commander!" he roared and soon enough a man walked from the camp and separated himself. He walked slowly towards ChOn, stopped at the red cloth and picked up something off it. Karín watched him inspect the small black thing closely.

"I am offering you the chance to surrender your force to me. They will be treated fairly and will have the chance to enter my service. You have the power to save them or kill them. Which will it be?"

"I know not what you are but I assume you speak for the Buq'ue herders. You are but one and we are three hundred. And two hundred more returning here. They should be here within hours."

"Alangadale and all the men in that company are dead already. Mikares has surrendered to me. They are never coming back. I am here to kill you all or have you as allies. It matters not to me which option you choose."

"You have killed a hundred of my men?"

"One hundred and sixty. Thirty survive and are as we speak marching to the Buq'ue fort to enter the Buq'ue army. I give you the same chance."

"I am a battalion commander of the Matáng. I will never surrender my men."

"So be it. Soldiers of the Matáng Army! Your commander has condemned you to death. For that he will die first."

Ch0n raised his hand and pressed a button on the remote control. The Matáng commander felt the dull black object vibrate. He looked down at it in surprise just as it detonated in his hand and blew the top half of his body to pieces.

"Karín, bring them into range."

The Matáng soldiers were still recovering from the shock of the explosion when the Lancers topped the rise with the sun almost behind them. Ch0n walked back to where Karín was holding his tlaque. He mounted it slowly and nodded to her. She moved them forward at a walk and halted. At the signal they freed the longbows and nocked their arrows.

Ch0n walked his tlaque closer to the Matáng. Their formerly well-ordered position was now just a tightly-packed gaggle of frightened, angry and curious soldiers standing watching events. Ch0n manoeuvred the tlaque so it was able to run parallel to their front and not have to turn first. It enabled him to get a few yards closer. He had the kinetic pistol in one hand and the pulse in the other. Both were booted and armed.

"Where are the company commanders and platoon commanders?"

A group of men appeared, pushing their way through the crowd.

"Look at your men. They are in no position to fight. It would take time to form them into squares and by then my Lancers will have killed them to a man. I am offering you what I offered the others who came to kill us. Serve the Buq'ue and live. There is nothing to be gained by dying here."

One of the platoon commanders drew his sword. Ch0n aimed the pistol and when the red dot was on the boy's right eye, he fired a single shot. A growl erupted from the Matáng soldiers.

"We have the means to do this. You are wasting time here." He shot another commander, waited a few seconds without a reaction from the other two and so he called to Karín to loose arrows and he shot the others.

The Matáng troops were outraged and surged forward towards him but thirty arrows fell into their midst before they had advanced more than a few feet. Ch0n and Karín let loose with the four pistols as they trotted along the front rank. The second volley of arrows cut dozens more down and while Ch0n and Karín were retiring, the third rain decimated what remained of the lead companies and many of those behind. Someone broke ranks and ran. First a trickle of his comrades followed and then a torrent. Karín gave the signal and the bows were sheathed and the lances lowered. They charged through and through the panicked Matáng like a solid wall and then returned as they had practised, sparing none. They reformed where they had started out.

"Find all the civilian followers and round them up."

"Yes My Lord."

Ch0n wandered through the mass of bodies, killing the wounded. It was a task he hated but there was no other option. They would die quickly by his sword or slowly and painfully of their wounds and thirst over several days.

"Take everything of value but do not defile the corpses."

He went to the group of civilians. There were forty seven of them, mostly women, all Buq'ue slaves as he discovered.

"Men and women, you have the chance to return to your Buq'ue people willingly or not. I am sorry for those among you who have children in the Matáng camp but I can allow nobody to witness this day's events and report it to the Matáng king. Let him come himself and find out as these have done. We are pressed for time so you will leave everything here except what you are wearing. The rest will be burned. You will ride behind the Lancers to the Buq'ue fort. Tomorrow you will not be able to walk but it will pass."

They burned all the clothing and left the dead where they lay, minus their swords and trinkets. The carrion eaters would be busy for weeks and months. They set off for the fort just as the first fat drops of the wet season fell to ground with cone-shaped puffs of dust rising where they landed. The Lancers were full of the battle and their success. Ch0n felt sick in the pit of his soldier's stomach at the slaughter. He knew at that moment from what he had seen of the Matáng soldiers and leaders there would be war to follow. It would take many months for the Matáng king to raise his army and caterpillar it to the Buq'ue and Arw'an strongholds but he would do it.

And Ch0n would be ready and waiting.

Chapter Twenty Seven: The Calm Before

They arrived triumphant at the Buq'ue Fort. Ch0n had a stirring presentation of the medals Alik had been storing for weeks. Karín and the Lancers of Two Troop received the Military Cross of Courage. The observers received the Star of Service. The family of the dead girl received her sword and lance and her medal. Puntik received the egg from the nest of a white owl that Buyo had been searching for since she first saw the mother bird near the village.

The Matáng platoon was received by the Arw'an guard. They were not happy to have been shaved and washed and their Matáng clothes burned. They were fitted out with the Buq'ue wool pyjami uniform and tunic and started training immediately under the watchful eyes of Izaki. He was not a fan of foreign troops in the Army but had to admit that he himself had started out as one.

Ch0n spent little more than a few days in the Buq'ue fort before sending the Matáng platoon and the King's Troop back to Arw'an Castle. In the next two days he gave orders for the establishment of a platoon of mounted Infantry. Until there were sufficient tlaque, they would learn to ride behind the Lancers but eventually each would be paired with another soldier and would then take turns in being the rider or the ground soldier. The first priority was to spend time astride the beasts so as to accustom their legs to riding.

The dáguia program had proven itself and was to be expanded so that every village had a small cage of birds and a writer and reader of messages.

The goat breeding program was to be implemented and the silky goats combed and their fibre spun and woven into garments.

The construction and maintenance program was ongoing and Ch0n would review it on his next visit.

The OP were to be re-established and maintained. The success of the previous battles had been as a direct result of early warning by the observers and the efficiency of the dáguia message system. They were to be given priority in terms of logistic support and manpower turnover. The dáguia were to be released every two weeks and rotated with the observers to ensure they homed to their correct bases.

There was little time for relaxing and Ch0n was looking forward to their return to the castle. He never felt completely relaxed or at home in the Buq'ue fort. Karín had grown up there, however and knew everybody in the village and now that she was the king's official aget, she was more accepted than before when she had been just a freak and the previous king's bodyguard and occasional bed partner. She enjoyed her elevated status and Ch0n noted that at times she was not backward in subtly settling old scores. In the darkness she was warm and insistent and Ch0n looked forward to their nightly sessions, unaware that Buyo was almost always watching from the darkest corner of the chamber.

They left for the castle as soon as Ch0n had everything in place. He had planned to arrive at the same time as the King's Troop and have a medal presentation on arrival. He radioed ahead to Jez as usual and the entire force marched through the gates while the guard presented arms. The Matáng soldiers were in awe of what they were seeing and knew that their domination of the Buq'ue and Arw'an was forever over. The crowd cheered wildly when the accounts of the battle were told. They had no idea that the new soldiers were Matáng recruits and Ch0n had made it known that they were not to be presented as such at least until the celebrations were over. The King's Troop were presented with their Military Crosses of Courage and Ch0n was delighted when Karín called the crowd to silence and presented Ch0n with one. The cheering went on until Ch0n hushed them with his hand.

"This was but a skirmish that we won and one which will result in the Matáng invading our lands with the aim of conquering us all. We have perhaps eight to ten moon cycles to get ourselves ready. The stock breeding will take time. The oruk calves will not be ready for six moons. What seems like a long time now will pass quickly. Make sure every effort is made so that when we need to defend this place, we have the manner to do it. We will need to store grain and seeds and cut hay for a siege. If the Matáng Army can hold us here in the fort we will need to eat everything and make sure the water is clean and the sanitation levels are maintained at their highest or the walls will mean nothing. We will get sick and die from within while the Matáng wait outside. Know this and know that I will be driving us all towards a victory from which the Matáng will never recover. Ever."

Ch0n needed to sleep but he needed to do his rounds more. He was driven by a personal desire to know everything that was happening, even if he had the leadership qualities to delegate. He called a council meeting for that evening in the main dining area. Kelda's team was to cater for a working dinner. Mori was invited to attend as a special guest as well as several of Boro's head masons and key members of all the teams. But after the medal presentation, Ch0n took Karín around the village to see how things were progressing. The Matáng soldiers were in the male baths singing and splashing about. Ch0n could hear them wondering aloud why they had never had such luxuries in their own village. A trickle of Lancers was arriving at the female baths. Ch0n and Karín made their way past the latrines to the bird cages and stopped to talk to Mori and congratulate him on the success of the dáguia program, of which he was the single biggest influence and true architect. ChOn marvelled at the size of the parrot sitting on Mori's shoulder. It was now almost full-sized and certainly fully plumed. It talked incessantly and cooed like a dáguia in Mori's ear and occasionally punctuated its words with Kelda's voice shrieking out 'hurry up you idle wench!' Or to bleat like a goat. ChOn was fascinated by this.

"This bird is a true wonder. The minitron calls it a parrot, of which there are hundreds of varieties, the largest of which are the cockatoos of Australasia and the macaws of the Americas. This is more like the macaws I have seen images of. You have done well with him as you have with the dáguia."

When they arrived at the corrals, ChOn wanted to see the oruk calves first. He wanted to know how soon he could ride one. Those which had arrived with their mothers seemed further advanced than those on tlaque milk. They were a little taller at the shoulder on average and the males were wider in the chest but ChOn was not concerned because the one he had selected as his personal mount was easy to handle and an inch or two in an adult oruk steer wasn't going to amount to a big issue. Doni had put a hole in each side of the oruks' noses and through them had put two precious spring clips to which to attach the reins. The future work-beasts had a single hole in the septum with a karabiner attached. They could all be led around easily. ChOn sized up his oruk and decided that in two weeks he would try and mount it. The creature was already almost as tall as his tlaque and was only four months old.

"Have the female oruk come into season again?"

"No, My Lord they are carrying young. It seems your tlaque has successfully mated with them. If they bear healthy young, your plan for heavy mounts will have come to pass."

"It will be too late if the Matáng invade when I think they will. They will have to be a long term thing. We will have to put a breeding tlaque bull with the Oruk herd next season before the oruk bulls mate with them. That way we will have a wild herd of heavy tlaque or light oruk to harvest. These ones were just an experiment. It will be almost two years before they can be ridden into battle. But these two oruk will be ready if we train them properly. They will have to be exposed to noise and crowding and the smell of blood as early as possible. I will ride mine in two weeks and Jez will ride his. Start putting progressively heavier weights on their backs so they are accustomed to carrying something. I will send Alik and Beny up every day to lead them around and turn them. Their noses must be desensitized before we can ride them. I see this one has started to sprout horns. Their development is faster than I imagined it would be."

"They grow spikes so the mother knows when to wean them. Like goats. The mothers will not feed them if they are being pricked in the belly all the time so they stop the calves from feeding. It is the Gods' way of allowing the mothers to rest for the pregnancy that follows."

The second night back in the castle, Karín bathed and shaved Ch0n and told him she had called for Buyo to fill his needs for the next few days.

"I know you coupled with her while I was away on the patrol because you were not the same when I returned. She has not said or done anything indiscreet since I returned so I trust her with you while I am bleeding. Buyo has also been patient. Alik is not one she would lie with as he is your squire. Jez has Malek as a bed partner so the only man Buyo would lie with was forbidden to her. I think you should take her as your concubine now. It will give her status to be recognized as such and it will give me status for allowing it."

She signalled to the door and Buyo entered. She was wearing a silk tunic cut from a parachute. Karín had made herself several of them and had allowed Buyo to do the same. Buyo went to ChOn and took him by the hand. When ChOn looked around, Karín had gone.

A month passed. ChOn was driving everybody to their limits in an attempt to get the castle ready for a siege. The stables inside the keep were piled high with tightly packed hay and wood was stacked along the walls of the lower floors of the castle where it could not catch fire from an enemy torch. The well was kept clean despite its daily use. The sanitation was altered when it was found that it could be blocked by an enemy sapper digging down to it from outside the keep. It could now be diverted to splash down on enemy forces trying to scale the wall near the river. The dáguia were all released two days after a patrol set off with replacements from both ends. The oruk and tlaque calves were growing. The goats were providing meat, wool and now a fine long hair that was easy to spin and weave and was much lighter than wool. The mounted Infantry project was well under way. Karín had expanded the King's Troop to sixty-six so that two full platoons could be carried behind the Lancers. It did slow the Lancers down somewhat because they had to find new girls and train them as well as train more tlaques. ChOn and Karín had adjusted the tactics of both the Household Cavalry and the Infantry so that when the Lancers needed speed, they would drop the soldiers who would march as before until they were picked up again. When they encountered an enemy patrol of force, the Infantry would be dropped and the two bodies would resume their normal roles.

It was as a result of watching the integration of the mounted Infantry that ChOn noticed the former Matáng Platoon Commander, Mikares, spending a lot of his spare time with one of the lancer girls. He had no issue with it in principle but it came on the back of Mori telling him that Mikares had been asking a lot of questions about how Mori had raised the birds and trained them to home and the distance they could fly and so on. Once again, there was plenty of interest through the whole camp in the birds but when Doni told ChOn that Mikares was starting to spend time at the corrals, the alarm bells started to ring in ChOn's head. He decided that Mikares needed to be watched closely for a while and told Buyo her first real mission was about to unfold in the castle.

"I want you to watch the Matáng officer, Mikares. He is very curious about the dáguia and the tlaque. So are a lot of the villagers so it may be my imagination that he is over-interested. He is also seeing a lot of one of the new Lancers from the King's Troop. Karín knows which one. Once again that's OK with me but I am now thinking, what happens if he takes information on all we have accomplished here and he manages to get back to the Matáng with it? They will delay their attack, which is fine but they will spend that time training dáguia and tlaque and what if they train a whole herd of oruk instead of a herd of tlaque? We will have lost the element of surprise we need to defeat a larger force. Mikares also knows that we are strong here but that the Buq'ue fort is less so. We want them to attack us here, not there. So. Watch him. Listen to him. See if he is drawing anything. I want to know what he says to his girlfriend in bed. In short, I want to know everything. You are relieved of your duties here until you have something to tell me, even if that something is that he is not up to anything. But if he is, I need to know before he leaves or perhaps as he is leaving so he is caught in the act. I am sorry, girl because in a day or two you and I have an appointment do we not?"

"I will try and find a way to do it all, My Lord but if I miss our regular time together I will make it up to you somehow. Now if you will forgive me, I have to make myself invisible."

Karín was all for just killing Mikares there and then but ChOn was determined that justice needed to be served first. He knew he was risking something in not killing him but the best Mikares could hope for was a few hours' lead and Ch0n would make sure that wasn't enough. He summoned Jez.

"Sir Jez. I have a Knightly errand for you. I want you to be prepared to hunt down a traitor should we discover that the person we are watching is indeed one. It is my intention to let him leave the castle by whatever means he chooses and then for you to bring him back. Alive. For trial. If there is more than one traitor, then we will send the King's Troop after them but it will fall to you to bring me the leader."

"And who is this possible traitor, My Lord? Why do you not just kill him now?"

"Because Jez and Karín, this is the new era of fairness for all. Besides if we kill him now and he is one of many, how will we find the rest?"

"I am sure there is a way, My Lord. There are many ways to ask such a question of his associates."

"Just be ready, Jez. It will happen if it is going to happen in the next few days or so. If it doesn't we will force the issue so he thinks he is running out of time. You may leave now. Thank you for coming."

"So Buyo is going to find him out?"

"Yes, Karín. Or prove his innocence. I am happy for either outcome. I would prefer him to be innocent but if he is guilty I would prefer it to be with all his former troops. If he is alone, how will we ever be able to trust his men? It worries me that we may have to kill them all for his actions."

"Buyo will find out or if she doesn't, I will question him on your behalf. I am sure he will be only too willing to tell me his secrets if I ask him pleasantly enough."

"I'll keep that offer in mind, my sweet one. Now. Buyo will be busy for the next few days so it is up to you to make up for what I will be missing because you will both be absent."

Buyo was indeed invisible. Ch0n looked for the teenage girl in the kitchens and didn't see her. He looked for her everywhere but he did not see her. He looked for Mikares at various times of the day and when he saw him, Ch0n tried to see anybody nearby who was Buyo in disguise. On the morning of the fourth day, Buyo walked into his office and plumped on to a stool.

"He is a traitor. He is gaining information on the dáguia, the tlaque, the dimensions of the castle, the flow of the river, the distance from the wall to various copses of trees, the location of all the wells and the kitchens. He is sleeping with the girl Marelik. By the way, she is inexperienced in the ways of the íjon but she is a willing enough partner. He is a bit rough for my liking but she seems to like it. She certainly makes noises as though she likes it."

"That's it after three whole days? That she is a willing and noisy partner with which to make íjon?"

"I just thought it might please My Lord to know that she is willing if inexperienced, My Lord. Just in case you should tire of me and my tricks."

"I will tire of you as a spy in a minute. Now what more is there to know?"

"What is a minute, My Lord?"

"A minute is the time it takes a woman to drown if she were to be held under the water in my bath for not answering my questions."

"Then I had better finish my report, had I not? Well last night, I was standing near the foot of their bed watching them as usual

when he suddenly told Marelik that he wanted to make her his aget. She was overcome with joy and promised to be a good aget to him even if it meant she had to leave the Household Cavalry. Personally I think she is too immature to be anybody's aget but that is my opinion and has nothing to do with the report. He told her he wanted to take her back to the Matáng village where she would become his aget and a princess of the Matáng and their future queen because he is the only remaining son of the king. She did hesitate but after he pleasured her he asked her again and she agreed. They will leave under cover of darkness tonight on her tlaque. He will leave on foot and she will tell the guard she is on a secret mission to the Buq'ue fort and they will meet at the rise overlooking the main gate. From there they will go around the OP towards the Overhang and then towards what you call the West."

"Well done, Buyo. You have proved what I suspected. All that remains now is for us to trap the two traitors on the road and bring them back. But I have a question for you now. How did you disguise yourself? I have been looking for you all this time and did not once see you."

"Well My Lord, I just asked myself where the biggest chance of finding the truth lay and it certainly wasn't in following Mikares all over the camp trying to look like I had a reason for being everywhere he went. You already discovered he was seeking information. No. I knew he would have to include Marelik. The Matáng territories are too far to walk alone with the Lancers in pursuit. It had to involve a tlaque and making space in the chase by going in a different direction. He could not steal a tlaque because he could never get out of the gate with one so it had to be his reason for starting up a relationship with the girl. She is young and silly and he is her first lover. As soon as she felt his dewen inside her she mistook it for ébon and she was vulnerable. Had she been one of the more sexually active girls, and there are many of them in case the king of the Buq'ue is

interested, she would have just bedded him. He is a smart operator, this Mikares and he told the girl he has been planning this since he first set eyes upon her beauty. I think he has been planning it since he first surrendered to you. Personally, I don't think she is pretty but that is just my opinion and has nothing to do with the report, either. I feel sorry for her. He has used her innocence and naivety to commit treason."

"But you have not told me how you disguised yourself."

"Aah, My Lord. I didn't tell you I was going to disguise myself. I said I was going to make myself invisible. I went to Carmodi's stable and told her I was doing some work for Karín. I have been there all this time in plain sight, watching the training and visiting all the Lancers in turn asking them if they are happy and reminding them of your great power and influence in the region. That is how I came to talk to Marelik. She was one of the last because she is one of the newest. But she told me of her affair with Mikares quite openly and from there I knew when and where she would meet him and with my gift of night vision I was able to creep into her loft under cover of the noises from the cot and watch and learn."

"Ask Jez to come to me if you would. And go to Karín. She will have need of you after so many days. Well done on your work. You have proved your worth yet again. I am sorry that I can not give you a medal for this or any form of public recognition because of the nature of the work you do."

"That which I sought, you have given me, My Lord. The whole castle knows I am your official concubine. All else is of lesser importance to me." She bowed to him and turned away.

"It is confirmed for tonight, Jez. He will leave on foot some time today and go to the rise overlooking the gates. The girl, Marelik will leave after dark on the pretext that she has a secret mission from Karín in the Buq'ue fort. She will ride to the rise and pick him up. They will head north towards the Overhang to avoid the OPs. Then they will turn west and ride for the Matáng lands. I am guessing he will kill her as soon as he is mounted on the tlaque or he will abandon her somewhere on the way. Either way, she will be unable to tell us his plan. I want you to ride out now. Find a place beyond the rise where you can ambush them. I don't care about the girl but he must come back alive. I suggest the pulse gun on charge seventeen will knock him off the tlaque. You will need some rope to tie his hands. Drag him back if you have to. If she wants to come, she may ride but lead her tlaque and bind her hands to the saddle horn. Remember she feels the ébon strongly for him so she will try and save him. Accept nothing she offers. Nothing. You can collect your reward from Malek when you return. And from me. Use channel five so we can talk privately. Karín will be listening with me. Go as soon as you have your things. I will tell the guard commander to let Marelik through tonight because he would surely stop her on such a flimsy reason for leaving. Do you understand your mission?"

"Yes, My Lord. The Matáng comes back alive and the girl if possible. You will tell the guard commander to allow the girl passage."

Many miles away the commander of a small Matáng fighting-reconnaissance patrol, Mastel, surveyed the former Buq'ue village. He looked at the way the bodies were concentrated and the strange wounds in their heads, shoulders and even faces. He picked up an arrow and looked closely at the way it was made and the weight of it. The groove in the back end was of particular interest to him and the fletches. He threw it as far as he could and it straightened and arched gracefully to land point first almost sixty feet away. He walked to where a body or at least half a body lay decomposing and partially cleaned by carrion birds and wolves. It was obvious that the body had not been chopped apart. The damage to the ribs and spine was not clean and the hide armour was ragged at the edge and not a clean cut. In the eye sockets of some of the dead he found small, dense spheres, all the same size.

"I think from what we see here that there is no chance any of our soldiers survived this massacre. It is the manner of their deaths that worries me, though. They are bunched as if they were all running in one direction, towards something near this half of a body. Most of the fatal wounds have hit them from the side as if they did not know the enemy was there. The ones at the front of the rush have these in their faces, which means they were launched from the front. And finally we have that other group spread from here to the other flank with spear wounds in their backs because they were running from an enemy which was running faster than they were. How do you account for all this strange pattern of fighting that made our men dispense with the tried tactic of all round defence and the fortified square?"

His deputy shook his head.

"These small spears weigh nothing. To cause damage they must have been travelling a lot faster than a man can throw them. These grooves in the end tell us they were fitted to a sling of some sort. We will need to take this back and experiment with it to find out how to propel it. The small balls are made of something I had never seen until Critang brought one like these to the king. They are obviously launched at great speed from close up. A sling would do it but from perhaps two arms' distance and no more. They are too small to travel great distances. But what puzzles me most is what they are made from."

"I suspect there is magic involved. These small spears I can see that they might be propelled by some device but the small black stones must be the work of magic. If they were launched from two metres away, the enemy would be overrun in two

469

more steps by the second rank of soldiers. Something is very wrong here."

The deputy spoke again.

"How many men would it have taken to kill three hundred in such a small space with no evidence of losses to the other side? And to have killed two hundred more out there somewhere. They must number in the thousands by now for them to have had the numbers here as well as the numbers stalking the other companies."

"Not if they are using magic," insisted the commander. *"I will report this to the king. We need to return as fast as possible and report this development. The Buq'ue have a powerful magician commanding their army. There can be no other explanation for it in my mind. They have soldiers who can be transported from one place to the other using magic and then they launch small spears from on high to give them speed and they use magic to launch the magic stones. Unless you can come up with something more plausible, that must be the enemy we have to combat."*

"If you say so, commander but if I were to go into their midst as a spy I would have the answers. Meanwhile you could take back the little spear and the ball and try to find out how they work. I am already more than a day's walk inside their lands. I should be able to find their village and spy on their ways for a short while. I could probably be back in the Matáng village within a moon, perhaps two. It makes sense to send me."

"Then do it, Palik. But shave first as they go without beards. And if you get caught there will be nothing but death for you. And not a pretty one."

Jez rode quietly out of the castle and turned towards the area where the tlaque were grazing. He rode at a walk through the herd and stopped for a while to talk to one of Doni's men. He made a great show of pointing back towards the castle and waving his arms around towards the river and every direction other than towards the rise to the north. The herder was completely bemused at Jez telling him he was doing a wonderful job with the beasts and that one day Doni would have the herds grazing on the other side of the river and the castle walls were looking good in the sunlight were they not? He waved back to Jez when Jez bade him farewell and rode along the bank of the river and was lost to view by the copse of recently trans-planted bamboo stalks. Doni had discovered when he built some of the corral posts with green poles in the wet soil that the trunk of a bamboo tree would shoot roots and shoots and grow at an enormous speed without losing any apparent quality or durability. He had also discovered that by bending and tying the saplings as they grew, he could grow curved trunks, which would be perfect for water transportation around the castle.

From inside the castle, Mikares watched Jez pass through the gates and ride away. He watched him talking to the herder and pass along the river and out of sight. During his month at the castle he had got used to watching everybody and everything working and Jez was the one he had never come to grips with. He was the garrison commander but had no other formal duties as far as Mikares could tell. He rode everywhere and always alone and in battle order. There was never a pattern and never a challenge. He might as well have been Ch0n himself. The fact that today he had ridden west along the river created no suspicion in Mikares' mind because yesterday he had ridden out the gate and turned east and had not returned until after dark. The day before he had just ridden around the camp and out into the ground in front of the castle to check the sentries were alert. He looked at the sun and saw that soon the guard would be changing. During the change they would not challenge an officer who was leaving the castle dressed as though he were on official business. It would be a simple

Gavan Connell

matter, if they did, to say he was going to the rise to check the appearance of the defences for Jez and to make sure that the road to the front gate was free of obstacles in case the Household Cavalry had to deploy along it later in the evening. When he did finally pass through later in the afternoon, he was not even glanced at. Not even by ChOn, who was inspecting the new guard as they took over their watch. When he looked back, ChOn was tugging at the armour of one of the soldiers and berating him for having it on crookedly. A few minutes later he was home free and hiding in a small copse of trees he had reconnoitred days before. If he looked under one of the low scrubby bushes, he could see the gate from his hide. Now all he had to do was wait for the lonely and somewhat gullible Marelik to arrive with his transport and rations.

Karín went to the lancer barracks late in the afternoon to talk to Eloik about something and to take the opportunity to walk into every stall and check the tlaque and the tack. It was something she did every few days. It also gave Marelik the opportunity to tell Karín in private anything that may have been on her mind but she greeted Karín formally and showed her around just as she did every other day. Karín was barely able to contain her anger but left smiling and even told the girl her tlaque was in fine condition, that she was fitting in well to the troop and that one day she would be a veteran and some other girl would be here in the end stall.

"If you have something to tell me, girl, now is the time. I am giving you every opportunity," she thought to herself.

"Thank you Brigadier General Karín. I will not let you down," said the girl.

Some hours later, the same girl rode quietly out of her stall towards the gate. The tlaque's cloven hooves made almost no sound on the sandy forecourt of the stables where the Lancers did most of their training in formation. When she reached the gate, the guard commander halted her and asked why she needed to leave the castle after dark. She told him she was on a special mission for Brigadier General Karín and he signalled for the gate to be opened. She walked through looking a lot calmer than she felt and even waved to the gatekeepers as they closed the gates after her. She wanted to gallop up the rise to Mikares but he had specifically told her she must not break out of a walk or even look around. It took her only a few minutes before the ground started to slope in front of her and she pricked her ears waiting for the sound of Mikares. When it came, it was off to the flank and she turned towards it. In the gloom of the trees she could barely make out the blob that was calling to her. She dismounted and ran to him.

"I can't believe we are here, Mikares. Now mount up quickly. We need to speed away all night before someone realizes I am missing. If we dawdle we are lost. The Lancers will not be able to follow a single track by morning and that will slow them but if they fan out and we are not well away they will find us."

"Put me in front. I wish to learn how to guide the beast and you will be able to rest during the night so that you are fresh when we need you tomorrow."

He mounted somewhat awkwardly and settled himself in the saddle. His inner thighs felt a little stiff, he thought, but obviously that would pass quickly. He pulled Marelik up behind him and she wrapped her arms around him with joy and pressed her face against his back.

"The ébon is strong between us, is it not, my agen?"

"It is, woman. Now how do I make this thing move forward?"

"Just dig your heels into its sides and it will know. To stop it, pull back on both ropes but not too hard or it will fight you. To make it go left or right, pull gently on that side and its head will turn. After that it is just practice."

They moved at a walk down the far side of the rise and when the moonlight showed the way before them, Mikares urged the beast to go faster. It broke into a trot and Mikares was just starting to think he was in control and maybe didn't need the girl any longer, when the beast shied suddenly to one side and they were both thrown. It wandered off a few paces and stopped, looking at the dark shape that had spooked it and was now standing over the traitors.

Mikares recovered first and recognized Jez.

"Sir Jez. Thank goodness you are here. I have discovered that this woman is a traitor and I had lured her into my trap. I was just about to turn back for the castle and reveal her to you when the tlaque threw us from its back. Arrest her for treason."

"I will indeed arrest her, Mikares, for you are right. She is a traitor to her people, her profession as a soldier and to her king. You, on the other hand are a loyal soldier are you not?"

"I am, Sir Jez. You know it."

"Loyal to the king of the Matáng, even though you swore an oath to Ch0n. You have betrayed your oath even though you have not betrayed your people for you were never one of us. You have always been a Matáng and were just waiting your chance."

Mikares rose to one knee and Jez swung the katana and hit him on the side of the head with the flat of the blade. Mikares went down again, dazed and Jez casually put a cable tie around his thumbs and tied a rope to the nylon bindings that were as strong as metal. He tied the other end to the saddle horn of Marelik's tlaque, kicked Marelik into action and led the beast to where his own was tethered. He tied the reins to his own saddle horn and turned to the girl.

"You have heard what he had to say. He says you are a traitor and he was about to turn you in. This is the man to whom you gave your heart and body. He used you like a silly little girl for his own ends and you played into his hands. I have orders to take him back alive but I have no such orders for you. I have to take you back but it is all the same to me if I have to kill you here and take back your body. You have the choice. Mount your tlaque and I will tie you as I tied him or I will kill you and throw your body over the saddle."

"Sir Jez. You have it all wrong. I am not a traitor. I was just going to go to his village and be his woman. I knew they would try and follow us but what is wrong with a woman following her agen to his village? It happens all the time. I was doing no wrong."

"And the tlaque? Is that yours to give to the Matáng so they will know we have cavalry? And is it right that he has seen all our weapons and our tactics and our castle and measured the walls and studied the breeding of the dáguia and the other beasts? He would have revealed all to his king as soon as he arrived and you would have slowed him down. I have no doubt he only needed you to get him from here to where he could kill you and then ride on alone faster. Now mount up or die. I have to return."

He reached up to his helm.

"Are you there, My Lord? ……….. Yes, I have them both. I am returning now I will be at the gate soon."

"Sir Jez. What will happen to him?"

"He will be tried before the king and executed"

"And to me?"

"Probably the same."

475

"But that isn't fair. I didn't set out to commit treason. I am just being a foolish woman. Surely you understand that."

"I understand you left the camp with a traitor bearing secrets that would damage the Arw'an and Buq'ue in the hands of the Matáng."

"Sir Jez. If you put in a good word for me I will do anything for you. I will be your mistress. Let me show you how willing I am to please you. I will kneel before you. All I ask is that you do not speak badly of me." She knelt at his feet and started to fumble with his uniform.

"You think my honour and position was so easily gained as to lose it in an instant because you would do that? I can get that any day from a woman who is true to ChOn and Karín. Now do you wish to return alive or dead?"

"Alive. The lord ChOn will hear me."

"Then mount your beast and put your hands on the horn."

He tied her hands to the horn and set off for the gates. They were met half way by Karín.

"Well met, Sir Jez. Take Mikares and leave me with the girl."

Jez shrugged and slipped the reins off the tlaque. When it went past him he took the rope and steered Mikares down the road leaving Karín and Marelik alone.

"You have betrayed my trust, you silly girl. I came to you this afternoon hoping you would tell me what you were up to. We have known for some time. Now you will have to die because you placed at risk the entire people of the Arw'an and Buq'ue and for what? A dewen to fill your ibuw once in a while. Now I want to know one thing more and I will ask it only once. Is Mikares alone in this or are his troops also involved?"

"There is a cabot who was to remain behind and wait until the attack began. At that time he was to try and start a fire inside the main castle where the hay and wood is stored. That would have forced everybody into the open. The others are all happy to stay here. He thought them weak but he had no choice but to accept them or give away his own intentions."

"When we pass through the gate you will point out the cabot to me and I will put in a good word for you to the lord Ch0n."

"As you wish it Brigadier General Karín."

Ch0n was waiting for Jez when they arrived at the gatehouse. Mikares was sullen but not cowed. He knew his fate and as a soldier had always suspected he would die by the sword. His mission was not completely lost. His trusted cabot was still here under cover and if all went well, he would be able to assist the Matáng Army when the time came. Ch0n looked him in the eye.

"Before the sun sets tomorrow, you will pray for death to hasten unto you."

Mikares jerked his head up. Now he was shaken. He had expected a trial of sorts and as a member of the Matáng high caste, to be executed by the sword. Now he was not so sure. He had seen Ch0n close up for more than a month and knew him to be a hard man and fair. But this was an angry side of him he had not seen. Jez led him to the guard house where he was stripped naked and tied to a beam in the roof.

Karín entered the gates with Marelik.

"She has revealed to me that the traitor was not alone. One of his cabots is also plotting to assist the Matáng Army when it arrives. The others according to this one are loyal to you. I will beg for mercy on her behalf when her sentence is passed. Now, Marelik. Take me to the other traitor."

Mikares' mood dropped even further when his cabot was strung up next to him.

"Your slut has told all. I warned you she was not to be trusted."

"She will gain nothing. Her life is forfeit along with ours."

The entire village was present for the trial. The sorry story was heard leaving out the part where Buyo had stood at the foot of the bed and listened to the pillow talk. The girl was called to speak in her own defence and she pleaded for mercy on the grounds she was a silly woman who had never intended to be a traitor but was just following her heart. Ch0n found her guilty of treason in that she had stolen a tlaque and was intent on taking it and Mikares to the Matáng king where the military secrets of the Arw'an and Buq'ue would become known to the enemy. He sentenced her to death. Karín stood before him and pleaded for mercy on the grounds she had revealed the identity of the second traitor. Ch0n nodded his head.

"On the basis that Brigadier General Karín has pleaded for mercy on behalf of the accused, Marelik, I sentence her to death by beheading instead of death by torture!

Cabot Garik what have you to say in your own defence?"

"I have no defence, My Lord. I am a simple soldier loyal to the army of the king of the Matáng. One of his officers offered me the chance to serve him as I had sworn when I first entered his service. As a result of that I find myself here."

"Such honesty becomes a soldier but you also swore to me and for breaking that oath and plotting to assist an invading army conquer this castle and its people, I find you guilty of treason. You are sentenced to death. Your own soldiers whose lives you risked will perform the execution at the end of this session. Sir Jez, please make the necessary arrangements.

And now to you, Mikares. You claim to be the last remaining son of the king of the Matáng but I have heard none of the Matáng confirm it. It matters not anyway. What have you to say in your own defence?"

"I am an officer in the service of my father the King of the Matáng. I was offered the opportunity to live or die at your hand. I saw the chance to live and to save my men. When I saw what you have at your disposal I knew the Matáng could not take it with their current technology and strategy. They are the people of my blood. I decided to escape and take the knowledge of what I had seen here back to the King and accept whatever reward he chose to bestow upon me."

"You swore an oath to me in the field when I might have killed you. You owed me your very life and that wasn't enough for you. You had to play me false. Along the way you coerced another of your men to join you and you seduced the mind and body of a maid of the Arw'an with lies of wealth. You convinced her do something she would otherwise never have done. Your actions have cost both of them their lives. I find you guilty of an act of premeditated treason and sentence you to death. Your death will be at the hands of Marelik and her mother. You will receive no food or water from this point. They may kill you in whatever manner they choose. As soon as you die, Marelik will die by the sword. The longer you live, the more time she will have at her mother's side. As they remove the life from your body, I hope you have time to reflect on your actions. I would have given you a soldier's death in the field as I gave Alangadale but you chose the snake's path and so you will die the death of a betrayer. Sir Jez! Take him away to the place where his sentence will be carried out. Assign two soldiers to guard him so he doesn't try to escape or kill himself."

Mikares was on his knees now.

"Lord. I beg you to sentence me to a soldiers' death. This punishment does not fit the crime."

"Tell that to the mother of the girl you seduced and whose life is forfeit because of your deceit."

"Now, former soldiers of the Matáng. Your officer and one of your cabots have risked your lives this day and in days gone by with their plotting. I was going to kill you all to make sure that I had rid myself of any traitors among you but my sweet Brigadier General Karín has convinced me to trust you. Now in order for me to do that I ask you to line up between Alik and Beny and throw your spears at your cabot, who is under that bag and tied to the stake. Throw well. We want him to die a quick death for he was not the ringleader and seems to be a good man."

Jez formed up the troops and called for another of the cabots to order the execution. The whole thing was over in seconds.

"I take no joy in these killings," he told Karín when they were alone. "She especially pains me and if there were a way I would spare her but treason must be a crime punishable by death. To spare her would make me appear weak."

Jez appeared at the entrance to their suite.

"My Lord, the Matáng is dead. Marelik killed him with a dagger. She says she has no wish to see him suffer and that his crime has been punished by his death. His betrayal of her was a lesser crime than that of his treason and he did not deserve to suffer for days because of her silliness. She calls on you to carry out her sentence so all may see that justice was done."

Ch0n looked at Karín.

"Is that the action of a woman who has betrayed her king? Is that what a coward would do? Has she not shown that mercy is a virtue? How can I kill her with a clear conscience?"

"You don't have to kill anybody, My Lord," answered Karín. *"I will kill her. She betrayed me as well as you and I have no such qualms."*

"Jez. Tell Marelik she is free to go. Tell her she will live out her days as the slave of her mother. When her mother dies, she is to kill herself so they can be buried together. She is to be shunned by the rest of the village. None may speak to her or look at her except for her mother. None may give her food, water, help or shelter apart from her mother. She may not take a man or bear a child under pain of death to both parties. She is not to speak to anybody except her mother. She may take her own life at any time to pay her debt to the villagers. If she performs some deed of valour that deserves a review of this sentence, I will review it. Tell her and tell the villagers. She will be a living reminder to those who see her that treason is a crime not to be suffered."

"My Lord. This is a punishment far worse than death," said Karín. *"Remember she gave us the cabot."*

"Ask her mother which is the better outcome. There will be no more discussion. She is lucky to be alive and she will cherish her life, hard tho' it will be. Jez! Go now and pass the word."

"Now. Karín. Come with me. I have something to show you. It is very important."

"As you wish, My Lord."

Ch0n took Karín to a room on the ground floor of the castle. He showed Karín a rock with a series of grooves as thick as the rail gun ammunition cut deep into it with the grinder. They were identical in every way to the naked eye.

"I have been making these. They are for moulding gold and silver. When we have the grooves full we will know that each bar weighs the same. That means they will be of equal worth.

We will call them a peso. It means 'weight' in one of the earth languages and also it is used as the name for money in most countries. So we can use silver and gold to make them. Silver can be ten pesos and gold can be one peso. Gold is worth less here because there is more gold than silver it seems. We measure them out and when they are cold we can use them to change for things. That way if you wanted to sell your silk dress, for example, you could decide because it is so rare, that it might cost twenty pesos. The gold and silver stones we can change here for their weight but they will be worth more as money."

"How do you melt the gold and silver?"

"With the special lenses I brought from the ship that Kelda sometimes uses to cook. They concentrate the light from the sun. We place the gold on top of the grooves and melt it so it runs down into them. Later we will build brick fire pits. Then we open the moulds and the cold metal falls out. We cut it into identical sized pieces and we have created money."

"Money?"

"It's a difficult concept to explain but I'll try."

Palik had been wandering for seven days. He had been walking in the early morning and the late evening, avoiding the heat of the day. He had driven himself hard at the morning sun and maintained his direction the whole time. He was a good bushman and had no trouble finding the little food he needed, plus water and shelter as he walked. When he saw his first signs of civilization, he had already missed the Buq'ue fort and had arrived at the track that separated it from the castle. He was a shadow of the soldier who had left the site of the Matáng massacre but it was his choice. He had eaten little and had survived on a small amount of water each day. His face was gaunt and his clothes filthy and ripped from the bushes. When he saw the track he knew he was close to something. He had not found a single village in his seven days. He maintained his easterly bearing confidently now but on the lookout for anybody coming in the opposite direction. He was going to become a beggar in the first village he came to and just watch and listen. They would all be talking about the great victory.

He passed through a shallow valley and saw a lake with trees behind it. Up to the north was a small hill with a cave in the front of it. He made a mental note of it in case he needed a place to stay on the way back. He did not see the observer just below the crest opposite, nor was he to know that the same observer passed a radio message to the castle informing them that a wandering beggar was treading the path to the castle.

Ch0n was with the oruk when Jez came to him with the news. It was unusual for anybody to walk the path alone. Beggars usually stayed in the outposts or where they found success. For one to trek for four days from the fort to the castle would almost certainly be for a reason. Ch0n wasn't overly concerned but Jez indicated they would check him when he arrived. Ch0n continued to lead the oruk around the corral and to force it to dodge obstacles on the ground while it walked and trotted. It was Ch0n's new exercise routine, trotting with the beast behind. It was as docile as any of the tlaque and eagerly accepted the fruit treats Ch0n gave it every now and then. This afternoon he had called to it from the fence and it had come to him for a treat and Ch0n was feeling quite pleased with himself. It made a nice change from reviewing the Lancers training with the Infantry, although they were doing very well.

Two days later, Jez was called to the main gate by the guard commander. The beggar was approaching from the rise. Jez put the tlaque off to one side of the gate and waited to see what responses the beggar would give the guard.

Palik topped the rise and looked down the slope at the most amazing thing he had ever seen. The castle was an imposing sight thrusting towards the sky with the tower atop it and a cloth fluttering at a pole. The whole village was walled to the river and there was only one way to approach it. He had planned to just wander in to the first place he saw but that was out of the question here. He took note of the herds of tlaque being tended by the herders and the goats off to one side.

This is a place for the picking if I can work out how to conquer it. He had to rethink his strategies in light of the fact he would have to pass through the main gate. It was too late for him to change his guise of beggar but he was going to need a reason for being here and he was going to have to think of it in a hurry.

The guard commander watched the beggar approach. When he arrived at the gate, the gatekeeper opened it and ushered him into the space between the two sets of gates. Ch0n was inside listening to proceedings.

"What brings you here vagabond?"

"I seek a change of fortune. Times are hard in the outposts. The Matáng raided a village I was about to enter not ten suns ago and I was one of those who escaped. I have seen the site of a great massacre where the Matáng were laid down like so much grass before the wind. I got lost in the rainstorms and stumbled on a track to follow two days or more ago. I have been living on water and grass with some fruit when I could find it. But I am used to going without food. People are not generous to those of us with no skills and no real interest in work."

"None may pass through here without going directly to the baths and being shaved and having their clothing boiled. In your case it will have to be burned. You will be taken there. Pass."

The gatekeeper opened the second gate and Palik followed his escort through. Palik was looking down the slope towards the activity by the river and didn't see Jez until the tlaque moved. He jumped back in surprise and almost ran. Standing over him was the huge tlaque with a black-clad being astride it. The being had no face but a gold light in its place. Over his shoulder was the handle of what was obviously a long-bladed sword and he had a curious array of hardware at his waist. Next to his left thigh was a long staff with a string attached and under his left thigh was a tube holding a score or more of the little spears, only the feathers showing. So this was the creature that had killed the three hundred. No point in lying because he would be found out. While he was taking stock, the thing raised the gold screen to reveal a face underneath.

"When did you see the massacre?"

"I did not see it, My Lord. I saw the results of it ten suns ago. A patrol of Matáng soldiers, some twenty or thirty in all raided the Buq'ue village and I ran from them. They paid me no heed for they were after the women and goats as usual but I ran in the wrong direction. I came to a place where an old village used to be and there I saw hundreds of dead Matáng piled up in lines."

"Ten days ago you saw this?"

"Yes, My Lord. With my own eyes. There was one body split in half from the waist and no top half in view."

"You say they raided your village before that and you fled?"

"Not my village, My Lord. I was wandering on the plains and was about to enter the village. Even now I imagine the women and goats have arrived in the Matáng fortress. The king will have the best of the women in his harem and the rest will go as spoils to the patrol although there are many women there with no husbands because of the patrols that have been massacred in the last several moon cycles."

"Go and get cleaned up. Your information has earned you a set of clothes and a meal."

Jez rode quickly to the castle and called for Ch0n. He told him the beggar's story of the raid on the village and how he had escaped and seen the site of the massacre.

"If the Matáng had raided the outpost I would know of it by now. The OP would have reported movement of a Matáng patrol and the village would have sent word to the Buq'ue fort. Have a dáguia go to the fort asking them to report the situation in the outposts. This doesn't sound right. Keep an eye on the beggar. He sounds authentic because he knows about the massacre and even the body that was blown up. We know at least that he has seen the site of the previous village. Offer him a bed in the stables and assign a soldier to watch over him from a distance."

"He has an accent from the west countries, My Lord. But the Buq'ue outposts and the Matáng have a similar way of speaking. I will get that message off but I think I should also ride out and see what I can find out. I could take Two Troop with me beyond the Buq'ue fort."

"No. Ride direct to the western outpost and then to the western OP. If the Matáng have had a patrol in our territory so soon after we killed more than five hundred of their finest I will be surprised. It may be a different group of rogue soldiers or it may be a trap of some kind. When you get to the outpost, sent two dáguia to the Buq'ue fort with a green paper if all is right or with red if the beggar is not what he seems. If he trips himself up I will allow Karín to question him further. Get that dáguia off to Izaki and then leave. Ride swiftly. Look for signs of Matáng activity at the old village on the way back. If you need Two Troop ask Izaki to send them."

It was a month since Marelik had left the camp with Mikares. Ch0n wanted to tell Karín the news of the beggar but she was indisposed and Buyo was sharing his quarters. She was most interested in developments and offered her services as a spy again but Ch0n would have none of it.

"Not this time. It will be impossible for you to be invisible when he will be begging around the dining area and moving through the camp. He will be watched. In a day or two we will know if he is telling the truth or not because the dáguia will have had time to go backwards and forwards. Now. I have to go to my oruk for his training. When I get back I shall be needing a shave, bath and one of your special stone rubs. That will do to begin with."

"As you wish, My Lord."

Palik arrived at the baths with his escort. The soldier ordered him to throw his clothes onto a pile of coals near the entrance and to seat himself where a woman was waiting with a flint to shave her next customer. The woman called for him to seat himself and he obliged, praying to his God to forgive him for shaving his beard twice in rapid succession. In short order his face and head were clean and she was ushering him to the water. He threw his undergarments onto the fire as he passed through the entrance, shaved his pubic region as he had been instructed and then he was lost in the warm water of his first ever bath.

He was standing rubbing his bare chin when a group of rowdy soldiers pushed past him on the way out of the baths, heading towards the barracks. A couple of them looked hard at Palik before continuing.

"I tell you. It was Palik I saw. He was the platoon commander of one of the platoons in our company before he got sent to the company headquarters. I'm sure it was him. He's here to spy.

He has to be here for that. He certainly can't take the castle himself."

"I knew Palik, Cabot. It looked like him, to be sure but this one was far too thin and I am sure Palik was taller."

"No. It was him. What should we do? I have no desire to return to that hell hole where there are no baths and the prospect of being on the wrong end of ChOn's cavalry is the best we can hope for. I'd much rather the cavalry was on my own end."

"Perhaps we should tell Sir Jez. Cabot. You could go to his quarters and tell him. It would hold us all in good stead for our loyalty to be on display and you might even get a promotion. Besides, we would never be allowed to go back. Not even against our will. The ChOn will have no witnesses to his plans survive to tell the tale."

"All right. I'll do it as soon as I'm dressed and fed. He isn't in a hurry. He only arrived today."

Palik emerged from the baths and took a clean undergarment from the wall alongside the entrance. Not more than a few feet away, a group of young women were bathing but he could not see them. They were laughing and talking about mounted Infantry and how much they slowed them down, especially when the commander was so scared of falling which was most of the time, and that he had his hands wrapped tightly around Eloik's wamwas.

Mounted Infantry? What is that? Mounted on what? Those tlaque? Could it be possible? Palik's mind was racing. Every minute he had been in the village he had been confronted and challenged. Firstly it had been the enormous stone fortress and the ordered village inside the wall. Then once inside, the mounted black soldier and then the shaving and clean clothes and now the women laughing about their soldiers being mounted. And why and how would the commander need to hold a woman's wamwas to perform his role. He would waste no time finding out all he could and then he would just walk out of the gate as he had walked in and fourteen days later he would report to the garrison commander at the Matáng fort.

"Hey! You. No loitering near the women's baths. Who are you anyway?"

"I am Pa…Pasaro. I am just a beggar who has had the fortune to have had a shave and a new set of clothes and the black soldier has promised me a meal."

"You don't much look like a beggar standing there in your undergarment. That is the body of a fighting man or I've never seen one. You even have a scar on your left side where you were too slow to dodge. I am Marel. I shaved you. That is my job here at the castle."

"Once I was a soldier but when I was wounded they let me go. I was in one of the Buq'ue outposts when I was wounded in a training accident. My cabot told me I zigged when I should have zagged. Who is the girl?"

"She is Marelik. My daughter. She doesn't speak or hear. She has your clean clothes. Take them. You will have to go to Sonja to get your bed and to Kelda for your dinner."

Palik smiled at the girl. She was pretty in a sad sort of way. She wouldn't even look him in the eye. Perhaps he could have some fun with her while he was here. The shy ones were often the most fun in the end and one who was deaf and dumb would probably be grateful for some attention as well.

Buyo gave Ch0n the full treatment and then left him. She had heard enough of the new beggar and wanted to see him for herself and check the situation. She had been warned off the role of watching him but her curiosity made her determined to know at least something. She went to the central eating area and looked round for a stranger. She picked him out quickly. He was eating at a bench with Marel and her daughter. Marel was giving him the once over and Marelik was eating head down and looking at the ground as she ate. She may as well have been invisible. *She may as well have been invisible!* She strode confidently to the table and spoke to Marel.

"Is Marelik supposed to be eating in the company of people other than you, Marel? Is this what the lord ChOn had in mind when he said she was to be shunned?"

"She is with me. This man came and sat with us. He is new here."

"Then you are responsible for making sure the decree is heeded. You know the penalty for it. She is alive only to be your slave. She has no right to be socializing here while she eats. You place me in a hard position, Marel. If ChOn were to walk in now and see this he would surely rescind his commutation of sentence. What am I to do?"

Marel looked around for support but none was forthcoming, even from the stranger, who was obviously confused at the proceedings.

"Buyo. You are favoured by the lord ChOn. You do not need to make our life worse than it is. I will send her away if you decide to leave well enough alone this time."

"Then do it. But remember your role in this. And hers. Remember she is a Matáng sympathiser, alive only because she wouldn't let you starve and flay the traitor, Mikares."

She stormed off, leaving the three of them in the midst of a crowd of onlookers.

"What was that about?" asked Palik

"It is nothing that concerns you. Marelik. Go home. Take your bread with you. I will see you there shortly."

Marelik stood and walked away. She faded into the darkness beyond the glow of the central fire. Unseen by the diners, Buyo grabbed her by the arm and dragged her quickly to her dwelling and inside the door.

"Marelik. Listen to me and listen well. I have a job for you that may restore your position in the village. That man is a suspected Matáng spy in the guise of a beggar. His story is being checked even as I speak but it will take a couple of days to confirm it or not. You have a chance to talk to him. Note I have exposed you as a Matáng sympathiser so you can expect him to somehow try to get information out of you regarding Mikares. Tell him everything, including the part about how you were in love with him and how much you miss making íjuw with him. This one will want to lie down with you and he is not an ugly man. Your mother has eyes for him but that is dangerous for her. If you lie with him you can maybe find out if he is indeed a Matáng spy and if you reveal him to me I will make sure Ch0n reviews your station, even to the point of trying to get you re-instated in the Lancers. Will you do it? Hurry girl for I can not be seen here. Yes or no?"

"Yes! I will do anything to rid myself of this burden I bear. Anything. I would lie with a goat if I had to. Give me until this time tomorrow night. I will go to him where he is sleeping. He thinks I am a deaf mute anyway."

Palik could get no more information from Marel. She was making eyes at him and he was thinking he had not felt a women's body for weeks but he was more interested in the daughter. Had she known Mikares? What was a Matáng sympathiser? What was this punishment she was suffering and who was this Ch0n he was hearing about at every turn? Was he the black rider from the gate? Surely he was. He would have to be discreet in his enquiries and stick to the common living areas. To go snooping around during the day would be foolish. Perhaps when he had been here a few days and knew his way around he could move around a bit more at night.

High in a rocky crag, a pair of orange and brown hawks and their young were sleeping on full stomachs. The two hawks had earlier been hunting at the same time because neither had managed a single kill for the day. Two dáguia had flown low and fast underneath them. The hawks had gone in as a team and hit their prey hard and fast. They arrived at the nest together with the two birds and started to pull the feathers away from the birds' breasts and tear at the flesh for their fledglings to eat. They flicked the aluminium tubes over the side of the nest and took no notice of the two pieces of red paper fluttering slowly downwards......

Marel was a little put out when the handsome 'beggar' didn't respond to her looks. She decided he was too young for her and just a beggar anyway and left him alone at the bench. He had tried to get more information from her regarding Marelik's punishment and she had told him nothing. She arrived at her dwelling and the girl was already asleep. She looked sadly at the form under the blanket and put herself to bed.

Marelik was excited for the first time since the fateful night with Mikares. She waited until all was quiet around her dwelling and stole through the shadows to where Pasaro had said he was sleeping. He had been given a place in the stables as befitted the status of a beggar but it was clean and dry and dark. She didn't see him leaning against the entrance but he had been watching her approach in the moonlight. He had known she would come. He didn't know why or how but he had known. When she was almost at the door he stepped into view and she gasped. She went straight to him.

"You are a beggar and I am shunned. It is fitting that you should make eyes at me and that I should want you."

"I thought you couldn't speak or hear."

"My mother says that to hide her shame. I am not permitted to speak or be spoken to by anybody."

"Why not?"

She looked around and took him by the hand and led him inside. She pushed him down on to his bedding, lay close beside him and told him the story of Mikares and her relationship and the attempted escape. She embellished it a little to make it more as though she had suggested they escape together on the tlaque and that when they were caught she couldn't stand the thought of him suffering so she had killed him quickly thinking to be with him in death. Ch0n had prolonged her life and her suffering until her mother's eventual death but she would escape if she could and roam the plains rather than live the life of a slave in her own village. Palik listened.

"How did you get here, Pasaro?"

"I walked for ten days after I saw the Matáng massacre. I stumbled across the path to the castle and turned in this direction. The plains are bleak and I saw only one place of true beauty the whole time. There is a lake with fruit trees around it and on the slopes there is a small hill and a cave where a man or a woman might seek peace together or alone and enjoy the solitude if they had a mind to do so. It is almost two days from here. One day if you need to leave this place you could go there and become a recluse. I might just as easily have gone the other way when I came to the track. What lies in the other direction?"

"The Buq'ue fort where the lord Ch0n killed the king in single combat to claim the throne of the Buq'ue. He has since united the two tribes and done all you see around us."

"Are there other Matáng here?"

"Yes. There is a platoon that surrendered with Mikares. They have been absorbed into the Arw'an army and are quartered here in the castle."

"Are they loyal to this Ch0n?"

"Yes."

"Tell me about the Lancers as you call them. How do they fight?"

"Why do you need to know? It is not a thing a beggar would ask. Even a beggar with a scar such as yours. Not unless he were not really a beggar." She nestled in against him and her hand crept to the hem of his tunic and lifted it to his waist.

"As a former soldier I am always interested to see advances in tactics and strategies."

"I don't believe you. You are a friend of Mikares come to see what happened to him and to rescue me from my plight. You are a Matáng spy just as he was. But you are much bigger than he was down here. I miss making íjuw with him. He was so good at it he could make me cry out with pleasure. It is such a pity he was caught by Sir Jez. By now we would have been together in the court of the king Seth. Mikares was the only surviving son of Seth, he told me."

"Sith, not Seth," Palik corrected. *"And Mikares was no son of his. All the king's sons are dead on the Buq'ue plains near their Northern outposts. Now lift your tunic and straddle me before you make me finish. We will see if I can make you cry out."*

494

Palik knew he had to leave the castle as soon as possible. If there was a platoon of Matáng here and that platoon had been under the command of Mikares, there was a chance he would be recognized, although none had seen him without his beard. He spent the best part of the night coupled with Marelik before she told him she had to leave him.

"It is death for me to lie with a man and for him as well. I will come to you tomorrow night at the same time. Mikares was a boy compared to you. I have never had a lover who could make íjuw as well as you do."

Palik was well pleased with himself. He had been in the castle less than a day and he had already bedded a former lancer of the Household Cavalry and during another session under the blankets with her she would tell him everything he wanted to know about their numbers and how they worked. He would hardly have to trouble himself to look and see. He asked her to wait a while longer.

Ch0n sent Alik to Mori as soon as it was light. But he returned with no news or messages from the Buq'ue fort.

"They should have arrived by now. Check again before breakfast. I don't like this a bit."

Before and after breakfast there was still nothing. Ch0n called Jez but he had been riding hard since mid-afternoon the day prior and was out of range, even using the OP as relays. He wrote two more messages and took them to Mori.

"Something is wrong. Perhaps neither of yesterday's birds made it through. We have been losing them for more than a moon cycle now. I suspect there is a hawk pair nesting somewhere on the route. Send another two together. One of four should make it safely." Mori selected two birds, put the papers into their tubes and released them. They circled twice around the ramparts and then sped together like arrows to the west.

"Sir Jez told me you had earned a meal last night, beggar," said Kelda to Palik. *"He said nothing about this morning. If you want to eat in this castle you can either work for your food or eat what scraps come your way from the others. Please yourself but you get nothing from me either way. Or you can ask the Lord Ch0n. Here he comes."*

Palik turned and saw a giant of a man striding down the path from the main structure. He was wearing strange black pants with skin boots and an equally strange looking tight green garment on his upper body. Palik estimated that the man was at least a head taller than anybody else he had ever seen and was a head and a half taller than Palik himself. His arms were muscled and light-skinned, not at all like the rest of the Arw'an and Buq'ue and certainly not like the Matáng, who were darker still. He carried himself erect like a soldier and was greeting everybody as he passed them. Beside him padded a wolf. He arrived at Kelda's post and greeted her warmly.

"My Lord, this beggar wants breakfast but I have told him he has to earn it."

"Beggar? He has scrubbed up well for a beggar. He looks like a soldier to me. Are you a soldier, man?"

"I was once, My Lord."

"Then we will sit and talk about that time of your life. That way you can earn your meal. When were you a soldier? And where?"

"I grew up in one of the northern outposts not far from the Matáng lands. I had ambitions of becoming a soldier like my father had been. He made me into a soldier from the time I was old enough to walk in a straight line. March here. March there.

He even allowed me to carry a sword from an early age. Thus my bearing I suppose. I told the village headman I wanted to join the army and he allowed me to join a patrol we had in the village. I was with them for a short while until I was wounded one day sparring. My father was not happy with my performance as a swordsman and we had words. It ended up that I walked away from the village and have wandered since from outpost to outpost. I was so wandering recently when I saw a Matáng patrol raid one of the northern villages and so I ran. It rained and I lost my direction. A day after I ran, I came to a place I knew as having been the site of the village closest to the Matáng lands and the one that used to get raided the most. There I saw a sight I had never imagined. There were hundreds of dead Matáng soldiers all lying in lines as though they had marched to their deaths and just fallen and stayed where they fell. At their front was half a body that looked as though it had been bitten in half by a monster. I did not want to be there if the Matáng patrol arrived so I walked towards the sunrise for ten days until I crossed a track. I had the option of turning left or right. I found myself here yesterday. That is the story of my life as a soldier. The soldier who wasn't a soldier."

Ch0n was doing calculations in his head. Yes, it was possible a Matáng company had been further East than the ones they had found and killed. It was possible that they had raided a village and it was possible that this man had run and come across the massacre of the Matáng battalion. He had obviously seen it.

"How did the Matáng soldiers die?"

"I know not. Some had spear and sword wounds. Some had wounds to their heads and shoulders and faces. Some had their whole faces removed and of course there was the half a body."

"What work did you do in your village apart from playing at soldiers with your father?"

Gavan Connell

"I was just a herder of sorts like the rest of the men."

"Who was your village elder?"

"Am I on trial here for being a vagabond, My Lord?"

ChOn stood up. The wolf stood up. It growled and raised its hackles. ChOn stilled it with a wave of his hand and it sat down again, watching his every move. From his boot ChOn took a weapon of such beauty that Palik could not take his eyes off it. It was silver and shiny to look at. It was as long as his forearm, slender and coming to a point. Near ChOn's hand, two smaller blades flared, ran parallel to the main blade and then flared out again to points.

"You are not on trial but if you can not answer my question I will kill you anyway. We do not have vagabonds wandering for days at a time from places we do not know having escaped from skirmishes we know nothing about. Now, who was your village elder?"

"His name was Doranik, son of Doran and Anei. Husband of Malik and father of Damion and Anelik. He was a herder before he was an elder but he was also a shaman of sorts when the village needed rain."

ChOn was somewhat taken aback at the complexity of the answer and so he accepted it on face value.

"My Lord, I have never seen a knife so beautiful as that. If I am to die, I would happily die knowing that a thing of such beauty had caused my death. Might I look more closely at it?"

ChOn put the sai on the bench and took a step back out of reach. Palik noted the movement and approved of it. It was a soldier's movement, born of long hours of training. It was something he would have done. He took the sai and felt it. It was made of something he had never seen. It was lightweight,

498

not forged but looked as though it had poured itself into the beautiful lines and curves. It was balanced where the handle met the blades. It told him nothing about the massacre of the Matáng battalion and it told him everything. He took it by the point and lay it on the bench. As Ch0n stepped forward, he stepped back. The move was involuntary and he realized too late that he had done it. It had not gone un-noticed by Ch0n but neither said anything. Taking up the sai, Chon sheathed it into the boot.

"If you are the son of a herder, report to Doni up through there and you will earn your mid-day meal."

He clicked his fingers and the wolf rose and stood at his side. The discussion was ended.

Palik turned and walked away towards the stock yards. On the path he passed an old man with a red bird perched on his shoulder. He was talking to the bird and it was talking back to him. Palik was again astonished and started to give a little credence to the theory that magic was involved. That was further enhanced when the old man told him that the other birds were used to take messages to the Buq'ue fort.

"But how do they know where to go old man?"

"I'm not so old I couldn't better you, boy! Magic. They know by magic. 'ello parrot. Are you 'appy?

"'ello," said the parrot. "'ello Mori. 'ello! 'ello!"

Palik arrived at the yards to see Doni in full flight separating the silken goats from the others. He was using a chute with a gate at the end and was putting some on one side and some on the other. Behind him was a pen with several of the beasts the Matáng called oroks. They were being handled by the herders as though they were completely docile but every Matáng soldier had seen a raging orok bull kill several men before it was overcome. This was magic indeed and he felt as though it was indeed a major factor in the Buq'ue victory over the Matáng. How else could it be explained that they were lined up as though they had been watching a dancer or a play instead of being in battle formation? Could it be that the red bird had flown to their position and started telling them a story? And how was it that a man or woman could ride a wild beast and have it do his bidding? And the Ch0n had controlled the wolf with a single hand movement and click of his fingers. He waited until Doni was finished and told him that Ch0n had sent him to work. Doni put him to mucking out the stalls where the milking goats passed the night. It suited Palik. From the shadows he watched everything that happened in and around the yards. Before long, Ch0n arrived with the wolf and he stood at the fence and called softly in a strange tongue to one of the oroks. It looked in his direction and ambled slowly to where Ch0n waited. He rubbed its muzzle and its ear and then vaulted the fence and started to attach ropes to two strangely shaped shiny things on the beast's nose. Then he attached a curved structure to the beasts back by tying a strange looking strap under the beast's belly. Finally, he took the beast's mane in one hand and vaulted the height of his own head onto the beast, landing in the curved seat. The orok did nothing. Then as if by magic, it started to walk around the corral turning left and right. Ch0n looked small on its back but the creature was under his compete control. Palik's heart was thumping at this further show of magic but it paled into nothing when he saw in the distance a group of what seemed to be about fifty women riding tlaque in two lines. They stopped briefly and a group of soldiers raced from the low scrub to the side of each beast. As one the women raised their legs and the soldiers placed a foot where the women's had been and swung onto the tlaque behind the women. They the women replaced their feet in the cups and trotted away in perfect lines, their spears skyward.

"Mounted Infantry!" He realized. *"They use the women to take them to the battle and to return them to their base so they have speed over the field. Genius. No wonder they were able to outflank us."*

Palik had seen enough. He decided to leave the castle immediately and report back to the Matáng. He could not risk being caught out. He left the stables and walked quietly to where his meagre belongings were located. Then he simply walked to the gate, told the gatekeeper that Doni had sent him to the tlaque herd and virtually disappeared. It was at that exact moment that Buyo was talking to Marelik in ChOn's stables.

"He is definitely Matáng. I caught him out with the king's name. I knew the king's name was 'Sith' but I called him 'Seth'. And he said that Mikares was not one of the king's sons. How would he know that if he weren't a Matáng?

"Well done Marelik. I will tell ChOn. Go back to your mother now and wait for me to come to you."

Buyo found ChOn at the yards with his oruk. She told him of Marelik's task to uncover Palik and how things had unfolded. ChOn went to Doni but Doni told him Palik had disappeared. ChOn told Buyo to get his tlaque ready and ran to the guardhouse. The gatekeeper confirmed the beggar had left under instructions from Doni to go to the tlaque herd and ChOn knew he had a hunt on his hands. He ran back to his quarters calling for Karín but she was still bleeding and could not go on a long ride. He told Alik to get Eloik to him immediately but the Lancers were out with the Infantry. He almost sent for Buyo but her days as a lancer were past her and she hadn't been in the saddle for months. He thought of Alik but he wasn't ready either. He would have to go alone. No. Alik would have to go too. He called the boy to get two tlaques ready and himself in full battle gear less the katana and together they rode down to

Gavan Connell

the gates in search of Palik. ChOn was angry with himself for playing silly games with the beggar when all signs pointed to his being a spy. Waiting for confirmation from the Buq'ue was just one piece in an otherwise complete jigsaw.

When they arrived at the gates, Marelik was there dressed in her lancer uniform. ChOn didn't give her a second thought and told her to mount up behind Alik. He ordered one of the guards to give her a spear and they set off along the track, up the rise. ChOn wanted to get ahead of the beggar, who was on foot and lie in wait along the track, perhaps even at one of the OP and search the flat plains with the thermal imaging lens. He was sure that he would find the man because he had left with no provisions and no water. The nearest water was along the river and then the lake but that was a full two days' walk. Yes, it could be done in less by a disciplined soldier travelling at night. ChOn decided to follow the track in case he was being watched and then to cut back towards the river. He wished he had the Lancers to fan out and help with the search but he didn't. He had no doubt they would follow when Karín had the chance to speak to Eloik. He resolved also to make sure that Eloik had a helm when Karín was indisposed.

They pushed forward for some time and then cut to the river. They watered the animals and themselves and ate a little dry porridge that Alik always had ready in case of a sudden departure. The girl kept to herself at first but then plucked up her courage to approach ChOn.

"My Lord. I would speak with you."

"Then speak, girl. Buyo has told me of your part in this and had it not been for you we would not be looking until later today. What is it?"

"He told me of a place of great beauty near the trail where a man or woman might seek peace and solitude. It is a lake with

fruit trees and overlooking it is a hill with a cave where he said a person might shelter. It is the only place he mentioned in a flat plain."

"Aah. That is what happens when you are hiding. You do not see the things of beauty because you live in the low ground like a serpent. When you are exploring you see many places of beauty but I know the place. One can see it from the path and I have stayed there myself. You will like it. It is likely he will go there because of the water. He will use the river for water the first day and then cut across to the track to find the lake on the second day. We will meet him there. You did well, Marelik. I know from Buyo that it was not easy for you to get the information as you did. When this is over I will not forget."

They left the river and went north to cut the trail and when they found it, Ch0n signalled for them to go west again. After a few hours they came to the place. Ch0n checked for signs of the chameleon but saw none. They rounded the slope and set up a small camp on the reverse side. Ch0n went along the crest until he found a spot where he could see under a bush and they cleared the ground smooth and set up a system of watches starting with the night watch. The girl first, then Alik and finally Ch0n. He had set things up so he and Alik would be the most likely to see the beggar when he approached. Ch0n calculated that it would not be until the following day anyway. It was still mid-afternoon so Ch0n told Alik to take the girl to the lake for a swim and to pick fruit. He warned them of the chameleon and told Alik to use the helm at all times to keep watch as well as to be ready to speak to Ch0n.

"Take the pulse set on seventy. Here. Show it to me. Yes, that's good. Leave everything else here. Tether the tlaque. Don't hobble her. If you see the dragon, mount her and ride back here as fast as you can. If you need to shoot it, do it fast and then get out. It will knock the thing over but it won't kill it. I

503

will keep watch from here as well. Listen to the helm, Alik. Do you understand me?"

"Yes, My Lord."

"Good. This is your first big test. Don't fail yourself."

He watched them go and called the OPs. They answered in turn and he warned them to keep an eye out for a lone person on the trail. If they saw him, they were to advise him immediately. He called the castle and told Jez to find Karín and tell her where he was and to have the Lancers ride via the river to the OP first thing in the morning and fan out north to south and search the area. They were to try and capture the beggar if possible but on no account was he to escape. He was to be killed if there were no alternative.

He put the helm to thermal and scanned the surroundings. There was no indication of anything at all. He scanned the lake again and zoomed in. Alik and Marelik were approaching the shore. There was still no sign of the chameleon. He watched them dismount and heard Alik through the live mike.

"Well are you going to swim like that or are you going to take off your clothes?"

"Your mike is live. Alik. Unless you want me to hear every word you say, you should turn it off and just listen out."

He watched Alik reach up to the helm and even at that distance he could see the boy was smiling. The girl was already half naked, obviously ready for her first real social contact in more than a month and Alik was tearing at his uniform but he kept the helm in place. Ch0n watched them through the zoom until it looked as though things might get a bit private. He surveyed his surroundings again. He didn't normally get much time to just lie around and think but this was different. He had all afternoon. He went back in time on his tablet. He had been here more than eleven earth months. Measured in cycles of the moon, he had been here a little more than a local year. The rains had come and almost gone. Twelve moons had passed. Three hundred days of twenty earth hours each. He had not stopped to smell the flowers for more than half a dozen of those days in all that time. He realized he was tired. He needed to take a break but the Matáng would soon be upon them. There would be no break this side of a war with them and he had no idea if he would come out the other side of it. If the war resulted in a resolution favourable to the Arw'an, he would have to negotiate the peace with the Matáng. Was that why he was here? To wage war and unite the various tribes of the planet? It didn't even have a name. He would find that out as soon as he could speak to Karín again. He looked around again with the thermal imaging and the zoom but all was quiet. Alik and Marelik were still swimming. He checked to see if Alik were listening and as soon as he mentioned the boy's name he saw his head jerk up and he looked in Ch0n's direction. He waved and the boy waved back.

Ch0n's thoughts went to his two women and their roles in his life. Karín he was sure he loved. She was physically designed to be his woman. She was a warrior like him and together they made a formidable couple. She had given him no signs really that she would like to settle down and be the queen of the Buq'ue with a family. He hated being away from her even for a few days and they never had a cross word with each other. Then there was Buyo. Buyo of the tiny body that gave Ch0n so much physical pleasure. He loved Buyo as well in a way but there was not the depth of missing her when she was not with him. He found that he could be revelling in Buyo and wishing Karín were not away somewhere purifying herself or whatever it was she did for three or four days a month. Buyo adored him and wanted more than anything to bear him offspring. She would whisper in his ear during the íjuw that she wanted his seed to sprout in her. He was not sure why it didn't. Maybe they were not genetically compatible, the people of earth and the people of here. He wanted offspring though. He thought he was probably ready for Karín to bear him offspring but not Buyo. Why not? Why did he want offspring more with one than the other?

His thoughts turned from love to the impending war with the Matáng. He knew there would be one because there had to be one. There would be a war just because Ch0n had killed six hundred of their finest and so mocked them and taken away their source of slaves and livestock. How would he control it? He had barely five hundred men and women at arms against a force that could afford to lose a few hundred and then back up with a battalion at short notice, also massacred. Ch0n knew from the way the battalion had been deployed that it was a reconnaissance-cum fighting patrol sent to investigate previous losses but the next deployment would have to be on a huge scale with the entire force advancing to contact, consolidating with their logistic tail before moving on to the next point of conquest and consolidation. They would have to maintain an enormous logistic component to feed and water a force numbering more than perhaps two or three thousand men at a time. He had put most of his eggs onto the one basket with the castle but if they decided to go for the Buq'ue fort and never attack the castle, he would have to mount a lengthy mobile defence of the Buq'ue lands. Could he concede the Buq'ue fort in order to have the enemy close on the castle? Should he deploy the King's Troop as a screen to force the enemy to fight and deploy every inch of the way delaying their advance and depleting their supplies? This seemed the best option but he would have to ensure that they were not engaged so much that they were not available for the defence of the castle. One advantage of deploying them was that they could lead the Matáng away from the Buq'ue fort straight to the castle and therefore Izaki's force, once bypassed, could become a useful reserve force attacking from the rear. He looked around again.

Alik and Marelik were almost back at the hill. There was still no sign of the chameleon.

They tethered the tlaque fully kitted for the night and they slept hard with one on watch all night. ChOn had spoken at length to Karín about the deployment of the Lancers and she assured him they would be available from first light and would deploy. She would ride with them for purposes of communications. ChOn was a little annoyed at this because he wanted her to be able to delegate to Eloik but he decided to allow it and trust his link to Jez.

The early morning rays were starting to glow in the east when the thermal showed a faint green dot in the distance. ChOn watched it carefully until he knew that it was not a rabbit or a wolf but something much larger. As it drew closer it became obvious that it wasn't a dragon. ChOn turned the thermal imaging off and looked through the night image intensifier but it was too light in the pre-dawn glow and the screen went white. He turned the thermal back on so as not to lose the subject and he followed it to the edge of the lake where it got smaller and finally did disappear.

"Gone swimming have we? That's OK, you'll have to get out and heat up again and if it gets light before you do I'll just pick you up on the scope."

Palik picked the fruit and dropped it on the ground before he waded into the cool water. It was so soothing to his tired body he was tempted to stay in the lake all day but he wanted to get where he had a view over the valley and the cave entrance would provide that. He was hoping the girl would follow him. He put his head under the water, drank deeply and held his breath as long as he could. It was like a weight was being taken off his shoulders every second he was below the surface. He stayed submerged until he felt his lungs burning and then he exploded to the surface and waded to the edge, a new being.

His wet tunic kept him cool as he strode towards the mouth of the cave but soon his exertions warmed him and he felt its weight pulling at him.

It took a while but eventually a blob started to materialize as the wet Palik started to warm up again. He was walking straight at the hill where ChOn and the others were waiting. ChOn had wondered how to deal with the situation when it arose. He didn't want Alik to be involved too intimately in the killing because he was still quite young. He was happy for Marelik to do the job because she had earned the right to redeem herself if she wanted to. He was happy to do it himself because it was against him eventually that the information would have had the most impact. He watched the blob get hotter and hotter. He turned the thermal off and watched through the normal scope as the sun started to touch the hill. It was definitely Palik. He was striding up the slope purposefully with some fruit in his hand. He was planning a rest here probably until last light and then he would cut further west and onwards through to the Matáng land and safety.

Palik was watching the first rays of the sun touching the hill when something flashed down the left slope of the crest. He had no idea what it might be but he instinctively knew it might be a threat. His soldier's brain made him keep calm and continue his original route until he was out of sight of the bush from where the flash had come.

ChOn woke the others and put a finger to his lips. He pointed over the crest and signalled for them to crawl forward. Soon all three were watching Palik as he approached the forward slopes of the hill. In short order he would disappear from view and no doubt would seek refuge in the cave. ChOn stood up and dressed himself in his full battle order. Alik did the same. Marelik was already dressed in her old lancer pantaloons and shirt and had only to pick up the spear and she was ready.

"Marelik. Wait here with Alik. I am going to do this." He mounted the tlaque and rode quietly around the slope to the front of the hill. He had expected to see Palik climbing to the entrance of the cave but he was nowhere to be seen.

Palik ran fast to his right heading for the slopes of the hill where he could outflank anyone watching from above or circling around from his left. When he felt it was safe to stop, he crouched behind a rock and watched. A lone soldier dressed all in black with the sword sticking out from behind his right shoulder appeared around the crest and went straight towards the entrance to the cave. It could have been the one they called Jez. It could be Ch0n but Ch0n was at the castle so it had to be another. Perhaps the Arw'an army was full of these dark riders. He had no desire to fight one so well-armed so he sneaked further around the slope and started to run down the other side to where there was a small copse of trees in which to hide. The rider would have no way of knowing where he had gone. He would have to dismount and search the cave and that would give Palik more time than he needed to get hidden. He would escape yet and deliver his news of strange weapons and magic to king Sith. King Sith! The bitch had said King Seth! What else had she said? Mikares. He had told her Mikares was not the king's son. She knew! And she had told Ch0n. But this could not be Ch0n. He had run for most of the two nights and nobody would have missed him until dark. This must be an outpost with a dark rider to patrol it. The place was an obvious place for travellers to take water. But nobody would know. Not yet anyway.

Alik was holding the tlaque on the reverse slopes when he caught the movement.

"Marelik! Look!" he said just loudly enough for her to hear. "It's him. He must have seen us and he's running for those trees."

Marelik ran to the tlaque, spear in hand and vaulted into the saddle.

"Tell Ch0n. You have the helm. Tell him now that I am giving chase behind the hill and for him to come quickly." She urged the tlaque down the slope and after the fleeing form of Palik. She had covered most of the distance when he heard the hoof beats and he turned around to face her. She was tempted to charge him down and run him through but she halted the tlaque and then walked it around him so he was between her and the hill and she was between him and the trees. The movement took Palik a little by surprise because it was the movement of a soldier, trained to isolate her enemy.

"You came quickly, Marelik."

"I always come quickly. It's why I like the íjuw so much." She laughed at her own joke.

"Who is the dark rider on the other side? If you are here it must be the Ch0n. You Arw'an have it all over us poor Matáng when it comes to mobility."

"You have no idea what your people are up against. If you ask the lord Ch0n he may show you before you die."

"I shall. It would be interesting to see how the magic works. Aah. Here he comes now. How did you warn him so quickly?"

"If you ask him he may also show you that before you die."

"Do you kill all your lovers?"

"Two still live but that will soon be one."

Ch0n pulled the tlaque to a halt near Palik but not opposite Marelik. Palik noted it and moved a little to put himself between them but Ch0n moved again.

"My Lord, ChOn. Marelik says you may show me what my people are up against before you kill me. Would you?"

ChOn shrugged and took out the pulser. He booted it, set it to ten percent, armed it at Palik and pressed the enter button. An invisible cone swept across the grass and knocked the Matáng off his feet. He was dazed but not hurt. He stood up.

"So it is magic!"

"It's a kind of magic called 'science' that we do not have here just yet but one day I imagine it will arrive." He pulled the kinetic pistol from his belt.

"Hold out your hand like this. Look at it. You will see a small red mark on it. Now hold it as still as you can and look very hard at the red dot." He pressed the trigger and a single dense ball flew from the muzzle and went through Palik's hand where the dot had been. Palik shouted in surprise but not for the pain. Pain was something he could endure.

"Is that the small black ball they found in the eyes of the fallen?"

ChOn nodded.

"I can shoot a hundred of those in a heartbeat. If I shoot them at your face it takes the whole face away."

"And the little spears? How do they get their speed?"

ChOn took the horse bow from behind him and nocked an arrow.

"Hold out your other hand like you did before."

Palik knew what was coming. He held out his hand. He watched the bow arch and then he saw it flex and straighten. He dropped his hand and the arrow flew past with a faint whisper.

"Such a simple concept. We have a spear and we will soon work out the mechanics of how to launch it."

"It isn't that easy but good luck anyway. It will take at least three or four suns to make the bows even after you find the right wood and cut it on the cross and work out how long it should be and how to string it. Then you have to learn to shoot it. It isn't as easy as it looks."

"Is that all you have?"

"No. I have something that can blow you in half but I don't want to waste one on a demonstration that you wouldn't really appreciate. Marelik. Give Palik your spear."

Palik caught the spear and Ch0n dismounted. He took Shiew from her scabbard and they all heard the hum as she cleared the locket.

Ch0n spoke as if to himself.

'Alik, can you see me?"

He pointed up the hill and Palik followed his finger.

"Raise your two hands in the air and wave them."

Palik could not believe what he was seeing.

"This is a trick. You are sending him a signal."

"What would you have him do?"

"Stand on one leg"

"Alik, Palik would like you to stand on one leg."

"No! So this is how you knew where I was?"

"I can talk to the castle from here. In fact I need to do it now."
He changed frequencies.

"Karín, tell the Lancers not to deploy. We have the beggar. I
will be back tonight with Marelik. She will be moving back into
her loft tomorrow."

"As you wish My Lord."

"You have one wish yet to be granted. I will now grant it."

"And what is it? I have wished for nothing else."

Ch0n moved towards Palik and the Matáng adopted a
defensive stance with the spear in hand.

"So you are going to kill me like this? What if I prevail?"

"Aah, Palik, if you prevail, we have two witnesses here who will
tell all the Buq'ue and Arw'an that they have a new king by right
of single combat."

Palik advanced and thrust the spear, feinting to test Ch0n's
reflexes. Ch0n took up the horse stance and stood stock still.
Palik advanced and withdrew, thrust, feinted and even made to
throw the spear but Ch0n was like a statue. Suddenly Palik
went in for a stabbing stroke and Shiew sang her single note.
Palik was left holding three feet of wooden handle. Ch0n went
through a flowing kata that ended with the katana sheathed in
her scabbard. Palik bent down and picked up the four feet of
spear point. The two men circled each other and Ch0n reached
down with both hands to his boots. The twin sai flashed briefly
in the sun and Palik smiled for now he understood Ch0n's
previous comment. He looked at the blades, which Ch0n was
moving in a sort of dance in front of his body and then off to the
side as his posture and foot position changed. Ch0n allowed
Palik to get within stabbing distance with the spear and when
the move came he leaned backwards and thrust the sai at the

spear, deflecting it with the trident blades. When he righted himself he had done a half turn. The left sai was now in front of his face and he had shouldered Palik off balance. As the Matáng fell, ChOn kicked his feet out from under him and he fell heavily. The spear was still in his grip and he thrust it clumsily at ChOn's groin. The sai moved downwards and outwards and the spear was caught again. ChOn flicked the other sai overhand with his fingers and the point came to rest on Palik's eyelid. The spear was under ChOn's foot trapping the Matáng's hand with it.

"Recall now the words of death and love you spoke to the sai, just yesterday, Matáng! Your wish is granted."

ChOn eased the point of the sai through Palik's eye until the two outside points were resting against the Matáng's forehead and the main shaft was protruding five inches from the back of his skull. He held it in place until he felt the life drain out of the screaming Matáng and he withdrew the blade with a flourish, wiping Palik's blood on his own tunic even as the body fell to earth. Finally he took up the half-spear and handed it to Marelik.

"This short spear will be carried by you in a special boot we will make on your saddle cloth. You will bear it always to show the Lancers it was you who caused the officer Palik of the Matáng to die before he could reveal our secrets. Now go and get Alik. I will meet you on the other side of the hill. We are going to the Buq'ue fort."

He called Karín again and told her of his plan to visit Izaki. She told him she would meet him there. The trio arrived at the fort late that night. Karín had sent a message advising Izaki that they were arriving and they went straight to a council meeting to discuss progress. ChOn was pleased as usual and at a village meeting promoted Izaki to the rank of Brigadier General. He explained to the council that when Karín arrived they would hold a council of war where Ch0n would discuss and lay down the plan for an impending battle with the Matáng that would unite the third of the tribes for better or worse. He slept well in his bed after the long night on the plain the night before and once again he had his dream. This time he was directing the battle from the ramparts while Karín was firing the crossbow, her flaming hair streaming away from her face. Below, the Lancers were charging into the fray and he saw the girl Marelik wielding the short spear like a trophy.

The following morning he did his usual rounds. The program of training the mounted Infantry was as progressed at the Buq'ue fort as at the castle. For Ch0n it was the lynchpin of his strategy. He had to exploit his mobility to the fullest in the face of what would certainly be vastly superior numbers. He told Izaki that all males of age were to receive basic military training in the use of the bow and that production of both bows and arrows was to increase. The use of tar to fix the heads and fletches to the arrows sped up the process as well as aiding the efficiency of the arrows by adding weight and range. The bamboo shafts for all their perfect shape had been lacking that one characteristic to give them the extra punch. The tlaque females were now all equipped with travois and that alone would make it easier to engage in a mobile battle where the logistics had to match the fighting force's requirements.

He found he was missing Karín's planning ability and logic as well as her company and when she arrived late that night with Buyo and the King's Troop in tow with their Infantry mounted behind, he could barely wait to tell her of his plan so she could pick at the edges of it. She had the warrior spirit in a fight but she had the female eye for detail and they worked late into the night on his strategy before she finally took him by the hand and led him to bed. They had not been together for a week and she was as hungry for his body as he was for hers. Unseen and unheard in the darkness, Buyo watched their reunion with a mixture of happiness and envy.

It took Ch0n most of the next morning to lay out a model of the Buq'ue and Arw'an lands as he knew them. His tablet had covered most of the territory and he supplemented it with the downloaded maps from Karín's and the aerial photographs downloaded from the mother ship all those months ago. By the time the council, Karín, the lancer and Infantry commanders were present, it was just shy of the hour to eat.

"I want to explain this model to you all. It is what your lands look like from the sky. For the past twelve moons, my tablet and Brigadier General Karín's have been drawing them as we moved around. This is where we are now. This is Arw'an Castle. These are the OP, the outposts and the limits of our radio communications." He continued for a long time because the idea was hard for them to grasp but finally he was satisfied they understood the concept of scale and knew the distances on the model relative to the time it would take for them to traverse it on foot and on tlaque back.

"Now we will go and eat. When we return, I will ask more questions about the model and then I will outline the strategy for the defence of our lands against a Matáng invasion."

For simple herders and soldiers accustomed to walking and fighting on foot and in the case of the Arw'an, not really fighting at all, the plan seemed complicated. Ch0n made sure the various elements of his army had their own roles well known and their interaction with the other elements understood at a basic level. It was Ch0n's plan to make sure the commanders knew how to interact with each other and to make sure they could change from one phase of the defence to the next. He anticipated that any attack would take place not before four more moons by which time the Matáng would have had time to regroup following their losses, raise and mobilize their army and start their advance to contact. He explained that the bigger an army, the longer the logistic tail and to shorten it, they had to consolidate every couple of days, usually near water. That would result in the fighting troops having a large civilian group immediately behind them whenever they were stationary with an ever longer but less bulky supply line stretching back to their stronghold. The role of the Lancers during this early phase would be to attack the logistic tail and flank guards and not worry at all about the main body of troops. He explained that that would force the army commander to redeploy troops from the main body of the advance to protect the rear and to bring in his flank guards or increase their strength. That would slow down the advance and require more food and water so the logistic effort would increase until they were under stress just from their own levels of consumption. The tactic of fouling water supplies would also be a priority. It would mean that all water for consumption would be suspect and would have to be cleared of carcasses, allowed to renew itself and then boiled in the relatively small iron and copper containers. Everything in this phase was designed to slow down the advance, make it more dependent on logistic support and cut that support off. No actual fighting would be needed apart from harassing the rear and flanks. All this would be possible because of the mobility of the Lancers. After this battle, the element of surprise would be lost and both sides would have Lancers so it was essential that this be a decisive victory to bring the Matáng under the one ruler.

"During this phase, the outpost villages will have to leave their present sites. They may return when the Matáng Army has passed because they will never return in a state fit to threaten any of the villages again."

The second phase of the battle would be to draw the Matáng away from the Buq'ue fort to Arw'an Castle. This was a delicate phase and would require closer contact and the use of the mounted Infantry to engage the enemy's advance guard and flanks on one side to turn the advance off its axis unless that axis suited Ch0n.

"The Lancers will drop the Infantry, they will set up a position that will force the Matáng to deploy a force big enough to move them and just before actual contact is made, the Lancers will sweep the enemy flank on the way to collecting the Infantry. This is known as mobile defence and is a tactic designed to make the enemy deploy time and again against his will until he reaches our main defensive position, the ground of our choice. Of course if he doesn't deploy a force at any stage big enough to cope with our Infantry, the Lancers will sweep through and the Infantry will mop up. We win on both counts.

The need for this phase to succeed is born from the fact that the Buq'ue fort will be stripped of its defences and the population set up to move at short notice. We have to make sure the Matáng Commander realizes he can not divide his force. If he does discover this fort is lightly defended and tries to send a part of his force to capture it, we will change our strategy to all-out attack on that smaller force while he continues towards the castle with the rest of his army. We will have plenty of time to overtake him after this battle is won. Izaki, I will tell you what I need from you in the way of obstacles and diversions later.

The final phase of the battle will be the defence of Arw'an Castle. I have designed that fortress so that a complete victory over us can not be obtained without occupying the castle building itself. Inside the outer wall will be the villagers and the domestic animals we need for survival. The rest of the herds will be driven away so the enemy can not use them for meat. Everything they will need apart from water will be inside the walls with us. The standing army we have at the castle will defend the walls from within while the Lancers harass and attack from outside. The mounted Infantry will resume their role as before and join in the defence of the walls. We have available there all the weapons I have brought with me including one which has yet to be used. It is called a rail gun and is similar to the metal storm kinetic pistol you all know but it is designed to be used in a defensive role and has the capacity to inflict enormous casualties on an enemy within its killing zone. The archers on the walls will provide the additional defence and the Infantry within will provide a mobile reserve to counter any beaches of the wall and the remainder will wait for my order to storm out of the gates and engage with the enemy when they are depleted enough to guarantee us a victory. Once we reach this stage there is no turning back, it is all or nothing. Karín will direct the Lancers from the castle with flags. I will direct the overall battle the same way, except that I will have radio contact with Sir Jez in the rail gun turret."

He looked around at a combination of awestruck and incredulous faces.

"This will work. We have at least four moons to prepare it. In two months I will return and confirm the strategy. Meanwhile, we will set up the western OP with helms and with dáguia communications to the nearer villages. Until now I have wanted the OP to protect the castle but now we need them on the edge of the Matáng lands to give us early warning. They will withdraw as the Matáng army advances so we will know where the battle is as it unfolds. When they are back in their present locations with communications to the castle, there will still be plenty of time for us to bring in the people and disperse the herds."

Karín told the Household Cavalry that in two months they would be rotated to enable final training to be stabilized. She reminded them all that the clashes between the Buq'ue and the Arw'an were a thing of the past and how much better things were. She then told them that when they defeated the Matáng there would be a period of sustained peace. That was her dream and when it was fulfilled she and the rest could settle down and be women again as well as soldiers. And that their soldiers could settle down and become husbands again.

"That is what we will be fighting for. I thank the Gods for sending us ChOn with his new ways. He has made us all better for his coming. Now we enter the final stages of the war that has plagued us for generations. Plan well. Train well and follow orders well and we will prevail for the king and for our people."

They rode back to the castle and ChOn outlined his plan to the council there along with the King's Troop and the Infantry commanders who had already heard it once. The council immediately started preparations on the defensive structures ChOn wanted in place outside the walls. They took to having practice drills to get the villagers inside the keep, which would become necessary when the main wall were breached as expected. The herders went with the Lancers to where they were to take the herds during the battle. Each archer and soldier knew his place on the wall. Each of Kelda's team knew his or her role in maintaining the troops fed, watered and in arrows. They set up a rudimentary aid post inside the main castle to wash and treat wounds in a hygienic way. They even had a team of women to sew up any wounds that needed it, using needles and thread that had been boiled. As the weeks passed, things became routine and then it was time for ChOn to return to the Buq'ue fort and step up the proceedings. The villagers stood and lined the path to the main gate as the King's Troop left them on their rotation. There were more than a few long faces among the Lancers and also the men remaining.

Two Troop was ready to return to the Castle. Karín had told them that the six-month rotation would be reduced to two months until further notice to relieve the Buq'ue-based troop, which would be on almost constant patrol before long. The OP were collected along the way and taken to the Buq'ue fort ready for deployment further west. The spare helm was given to Izaki so he could maintain communications with the OP. The dáguia, which were also being rotated, would provide information back to the castle. Ch0n went through his detailed instructions with Izaki, who was now mounted and kitted out like Jez. Ch0n took away his rank of Brigadier General and dubbed him, Sir Izaki, Camp Commandant and Second Knight of the Buq'ue and Arw'an.

By the time Ch0n, Karín and the new King's Troop left the Buq'ue fort, the OP were in place, communications had been established, everybody had shown that they knew their roles and Ch0n was happy that he was far enough away from the battle to set up the final defence but close enough in time to launch the first phase and oversee it from the front. All they had to do was wait.

The war had begun.

Gavan Connell

Chapter Twenty Eight: The Storm

Sith was ready.

It had been months now since it had been confirmed that his prized battalion had been wiped out to a man on top of his earlier patrols. He had lost three sons and all for nothing. Their usual quota of breeding animals and slaves had not been replenished this season. The Buq'ue had bloodied their noses which was bad enough but there had been no information from any of their spies, who had either returned half starving from the Buq'ue lines having not even found the villages, or had not returned at all. His trusted Army Commander had led a special patrol out to discover the fate of his battalion only to return with a small spear, a few of the strange heavy balls and the news that his second in command was going to the Buq'ue and Arw'an lands to find out what was happening and why they had overnight become a military force to be reckoned with.

Mastel strode into the king's presence.

"All is ready, majesty. We have rebuilt the lost battalions. The camp followers have been assembling the stores and rations for weeks. The rains are long gone and we have sent our scouts forward. The army has assembled and awaits your orders."

"What of the new weapons? The arcos."

"There are more than a hundred functional, majesty. The spears lack the fine finish of the one we captured but they fly true. The arcos themselves need special care for if they are bent too far they break but we have established their limits and I am satisfied they will do their job. We can start the advance guard moving any time. All we are waiting for is your order."

Gavan Connell

"Mastel, this must not fail. We are going to leave this land with few defences in order to subjugate the Buq'ue. And the Arw'an. Two thousand five hundred men marching across the plains in my name must carry the day so I can claim the thrones of the Buq'ue and Arw'an forever. We must have a ready supply of slaves and meat or we will perish. Our numbers are too many for this poor terrain and were it not that it is ours by God's will, we would be able to leave it for better grazing. We have to conquer those tribes because if we do, we know that it is God's will that we have all the lands we need in which to thrive. Access to slaves will be easier. We will have herds of goats and talake for food. This is a holy war we are undertaking. God is on our side and he will defeat the magic. I will wave to the troops as they leave. Tomorrow I will join the march with the main body as befits a king."

Mastel bowed low to his king. He wasn't so sure that the God, Aduwen would protect them from the magic. He had not done it so far. He was more confident in numbers, discipline and in the new arcos. The Buq'ue and Arw'an could never muster an army of more than a thousand between them and now the Matáng had the weapons to reduce the advantage that had been obvious when they lost their battalion. He marched to the head of the column which had been waiting all morning and told the battalion commander to start the advance.

The war had begun.

The Matáng advance scouts were long gone but when the order came to move at last, the long shaking out process began. The lead soldier of the forward section of the forward platoon of the forward company of the forward battalion took a step forward on a march that would determine the future of three tribes and three cultures.

It took what seemed forever before the last soldier of the last section took his first step. By that time the first man was a mile ahead and the flanking units were still making their way out to their required distance. Behind all of the troops, the enormous camp following group shuffled forward with their sleds of water bladders, bags of porridge, cooking utensils, herds of live goats and assorted women and children who simply could not be left behind. When night fell that first evening, the tail of the advance was still in sight of the fort. Sith donned his war bonnet and armour and set off to join Mastel in the centre of the main body. When he topped the rise outside the fort, he could not see either the beginning or the end of the line of men and women.

Four days later, the advance party reached the site of the initial skirmish with the Cavalry. The individual companies and battalions set up camp and waited patiently for the tail to catch up. The men dined on hard rations and water and slept hard. They were used to it and none complained. Nobody would have listened anyway.

By the time the first of the units had set up its defensive position for the next day or more, the OP had reported to the Buq'ue fort that the Matáng army was on the move. Izaki sent two dáguia to the castle and then two more for good measure. He had a return message from Ch0n before nightfall that the Lancers and mounted Infantry from the castle would leave and ride all night. He should pre-position those from the fort late the next day where the two troops would eventually unite and ride to meet the Matáng. Both the castle and the fort buzzed all night with the news and the movement of Lancers, Infantrymen and logisticians making last minute preparations to the travois before heading off the next morning. They would move ahead of the Household Cavalry to begin with just to establish a firm logistic base. This was one advantage the Matáng could not counter, the ability of the logistics to almost maintain pace with the main body. There were no live animals to kill, the water was largely carried on the individual soldier and the mobile logistic forces had the ability to divert from the line of march to resupply or take forage of opportunity.

By the end of day five, the Matáng force was consolidated at the line of the former Buq'ue outpost, bivouacked on top of the bones of three hundred of their countrymen. The Household Cavalry was bivouacked half a day's hard ride or three days' march away on the Matáng axis of advance. Karín was at their head. ChOn had resisted the temptation to ride with her and had detoured instead to the Buq'ue fort to oversee the proceedings. From there he could get first-hand the radio transmission from the OP, which were now on the next line of hills to the front of the Matáng advance. Alik and Buyo were with him. Jez was back at the castle making sure all the things they had been rehearsing for months were ready to implement in the coming moon cycle.

Karín deployed her Lancers loosely for the last time. She called them all in around a cooking fire and told them again of their roles.

The King's Troop were to leave their Infantry in place, outflank the Matáng army on the southern side, keep riding until they passed the rear company of soldiers and were alongside the logistic tail. They would sweep just once through and once back, killing anyone that got in their way and ruining any stores that they encountered inside their axis of assault. They would then ride south until they were out of the line of sight and turn east again and return to the bivouac site. Meanwhile One Troop would outflank the army to the north and sweep just once through their flank guard and return via the north to the bivouac site. By then the entire Matáng army would be stationary, wondering what had happened and trying to deliver reports to their commanders.

Dawn broke and the two troops, each now sixty strong set off on their missions to the cheers of their Infantry saddle companions. One Troop struck first, riding down on the hapless company that formed the left flank guard. Before the three platoons had a chance to fully establish their defensive posture, the Lancers were through them in two ranks. They left the entire outside platoon dead or wounded in their wake. By the time the next closest platoon was deployed to repel an attack the riders were out of sight over a small rise. The company commander ran to the site of the attack and surveyed the damage. Men were shouting from the adjoining platoon about women riding talaques through their position. Wounded were screaming in agony. The news passed from lip to ear like a wave to the main body where Sith and Mastel heard it.

"Mastel. I want this confirmed. Women fighting from talaques? I don't believe it. Have a runner sent out to the flank. Pull the other flank in closer and close up the line of march. Halt in place until we know what is happening."

The runners sped away towards the right flank leaving Sith and his commander to ponder this development. Mastel was nothing if not a good soldier and he was weighing up all the possibilities.

"Sire. This is a disturbing development if it is true, and could explain the massacres we have suffered in the past several moons. If the Buq'ue have mobility they can outflank us almost at will. We are in grave danger as we are deployed. We need to bunch together to stop them picking off the edges. Get the arcos to the left flank ready for the next attack. They don't know we have arcos yet so we have the element of surprise. Bunch the Infantry and call forward the archers to the vanguard and the left flank. And our tail is vulnerable. We need to consolidate here and make them attack us in force while we draw the tail up to the main body."

Sith was listening.

"Very well. Do it. Send a runner to the arcos companies and have them come forward. Send another to the right flank and have them close up hard to the main body. Send another to the rear guard and have him bring up the tail as you suggested. Then the rear guard can redeploy behind the logistic tail to keep it moving and also to stop the Buq'ue from attacking our weak underbelly. From now on we advance in small waves with one battalion always on the ground in defensive posture."

"As you wish, Sire but there is one more option. We withdraw back to the fort and rethink this whole war."

"Withdraw? Are you mad? We lose maybe twenty or thirty men from a force of two and a half thousand and already you want to call it off? It has taken six moon cycles to put this together and we are not yet six days into it. We don't even know for certain what happened yet. I will hear no more talk of retreat. It is your job to counter what they can throw at us. Get the arcos up here and we will see how they like that!"

Reny took the King's Troop far to the south and then cut back north. They watched the flanking units of the Matáng from the dead ground and only put themselves into view when they came to the water carriers. It was a simple matter for them to sweep through thirty wide, turn about and return with the second rank now leading. The rear guard had time to turn and watch what was happening and then it was over as quickly as it had begun. They ran to assist their porters but they had lost almost forty of them and the water bladders were mostly slashed beyond use. The company commander sent a runner straight to Mastel with the news. It was received with disbelief and shock.

"Sire. I beg you to rethink this advance. They will cut us to ribbons. We have to withdraw and give ourselves time to get troops on line which can match them."

"We are half way there, Mastel. Do what you planned to do. Draw in the flanks and the tail and we will continue. We will prevail. We are on a mission from God to conquer new lands for our people. We will usurp their land and take their talaque. We will have our own mobile army. Now. When all is in place we will advance to the next line of hills and consolidate again. Keep the arcos to the front and to the left flank. Move man. We have to maintain some sort of momentum."

Reny and Eloik were back at the rendezvous telling Karín of their success. The Infantry soldiers were keen to know how many were in the Matáng army and how they were kitted out. Were they well disciplined? What weapons did they deploy? The Lancers answered as best they could but they had had little time to look at the force they were up against and had just charged straight through them. Karín passed the news back to Ch0n.

"They will be wary now. If their commander is worth his command they will draw all their forces together to make it harder to pick off the stragglers and the loose edges. Now listen carefully. You have lost the element of surprise so they will have to come up with something to counter your speed and manoeuvrability. They may have slings. They may have bows because Palik said they had found arrows and were trying to work out how they were launched. You will need to be strictly disciplined and maintain your distances. Next time, sit off their windward flank and shoot arrows at them and see how they respond. Do not allow them to close with you. Never are you to get involved in a battle. If you cannot isolate them, withdraw. Let them come to us. Remember that we have the ability to make them deploy whenever we like. If they are short of water they will need to send out scouts to find it. You know where the water is. Pick off the scouts and make them deploy a force to defend the water carriers. Every delay plays into our hands. Let them have tomorrow free. They will not know if you are coming or not. It is just as effective for us either way so take the easy path and rest the troops. They will get plenty of work soon enough. Good work to the two commanders and yourself. You followed my instructions exactly. That is all I can ask."

"Is Buyo with you?"

"No. I will send for her later."

"This is all very exciting for me. It makes me hunger for you. Thinking of you with her will not ease my need but inflame it."

"Do what you need to do. But stay in command. This is not a game. They are thinking of ways to defeat your Lancers and you must second-guess them. Now go and talk to your commanders about tomorrow. Make sure they are aware and wary. The entire game changed as soon as they were seen."

Ch0n went to brief Izaki and the council. Karín went to brief her commanders. Afterwards Ch0n took Buyo to his bed as he always did in Karín's absences and she as always made the most of her infrequent trysts with him.

Karín lay on her blanket and felt the heat in her that would not leave. From nearby came the sound of a woman in ecstasy. She imagined Ch0n lying down with Buyo and felt cheated. Not jealous but cheated. Chon deserved her this night. She was on fire for the íjon. She went quietly to where Eloik was lying.

"Sister. I need you. I know we have not lain together since we were young but tonight I am on fire because of the battle. Will you let me lie with you? Will you quench the fire for me?"

Eloik laughed quietly in the darkness.

"We are all feeling the need. The sisters are talking of nothing else. Some are lying with their Infantry brothers. Some are lying together and some are playing the game of slippery finger as was I but we are all in need of the sensation. I remember

well our nights together under my father's roof when we were discovering what our ibuws were for. Come here to me and show me what you have learned from the lord ChOn."

Marelik was alone on her blanket. She, too was feeling the need. She had lain with three man in her short time as a mature female. Two of those she had killed. The third was just a boy waiting in the Buq'ue fort for his master's orders.

Mastel passed the night moving from commander to commander making sure they had complied with his orders. The force was now much smaller in size but higher in density than before. The arcos were deployed with the vanguard and as left flank guard. The king was convinced they had things under control. By the end of the following day he was beginning to think he had overreacted because they had advanced without any form of contact. They bivouacked near water and planned the following day's march. Their scouts had not seen any sign of a Buq'ue village. They were advancing to contact in known enemy territory and with no idea what or when things might start to happen.

By mid-morning the eighth day, things changed for everybody. Karín dispatched the King's Troop to the left flank again to harass the flank guard and to make sure the column didn't veer right and head for the Buq'ue fort. She had to keep them straight or veering slightly left. The Lancers topped a rise and watched the enormous force stretched out before their eyes. They rode further north and cut back to the flank guard. They had to adjust their position several times to allow for a favourable wind and the success of that manoeuvre was seen when the volleys of arrows started to fly. The Lancers fired downwind into a mass of soldiers. The Matáng arcos fired into the wind at riders well spread out. The Matáng arrows fell well short into the breeze while the One Troop arrows fell heavily into the midst of the arcos killing or wounding several soldiers. The second volley was equally effective from the Lancers and felled several more of the enemy. They stayed out of range of the arcos, retiring only when they were threatened from their flank by more arcos running in from the vanguard. Reny wanted to sweep through the flank guard but she had been ordered only to harass them and not to engage. Just to confuse the enemy further, she decided to push south to the edge of the main body and make them deploy. Just by her movements she caused the closest company to reform into a defensive block.

On the south side, One Troop was harassing the right flank guard. They were more affected by the wind and had to get closer to cause casualties but they were able to create confusion and delays to the march. By mid-day they were back in the bivouac with the King's Troop planning the next move. Karín wanted a night raid but ChOn would not allow it.

"Your role at this point is to delay their march so they use up resources for little or no territorial gains. Any night work will be undertaken by you and me alone with the night-vision equipment. Our force is small and I don't want to risk taking casualties or having our bows captured."

Mastel called his battalion commanders to orders.

"We have to retake the initiative. But we also have to change our disposition. The arcos to the flanks did not work because the wind was in their faces so they need to be deployed where they can launch with the wind or at least across it. Secondly, we need shields to combat the shafts. So the heavy Infantry will take the van and we will advance with no flank guard but on a wider front. All outside platoons are to bear shields. The arcos are to be accompanied by heavy Infantry so that when they are being used, they have shields to assist with their protection. Tonight we will deploy arcos on the high sides of a cutting that the scouts have told me approaches this position from the rising sun. If the Buq'ue riders use that cutting again

tomorrow we will ambush them. Also tomorrow there will be a change of axis. We will march off the axis to the left for one thousand paces and then turn to the sunrise again and consolidate before continuing. We will leave fires burning here and march all night. We need to gain ground and force the enemy to engage us in a set-piece battle. That way we will have the advantage of the numbers. By moving only at night we will save energy and reduce their mobility. Let them come to us in the daylight when we are ready and then let them try and restrict us as we advance by night. Bring the camp followers forward and put them inside the defence when we stop. They can not be exposed during the day. The riders will not come again today. They need to revisit their tactics now they know we have arcos. Let us take advantage of the time we have. Go to your units and tell them of the new plan. When I give the signal we will stand up and march one thousand paces in that direction, bring in the camp followers and stop for the remainder of the day to rest up for the night march. Arcos remain here, keep the fires burning and when the sun has passed its mid-afternoon point, start your march towards the cutting with the scout. Wait until dark before you take up your positions in ambush. After that, stay until the sun reaches its high point and if they have not passed, join us on our new axis. The scouts will lead you. Go now all of you and be ready for my signal to move to the left of the axis."

"I picked you well, Mastel. You are indeed a strategist. We will win this war and when we do I will let it be known you were the one who planned the victory."

"Thank you Lord but a plan does not win a battle. It only sets the scene. We have not even seen a single Buq'ue village and we have already lost seventy men and women. I am only trying to gain ground so we can find something they will have to defend. Then the war of attrition will begin and we know the numbers lie with us."

The observers at the western OP watched the cloud of dust from their position atop the cutting. One zoomed in but could not make out any detail.

"They are on the move." He called to his companion. *"But it looks as though they are not coming to us. I think they are moving to the north."*

"Watch them for a while and then tell Ch0n and Karín. We will stay here until tomorrow and if we have to re-deploy further north to watch them we will do it then."

Some time later the dust cloud subsided and the watchers waited for renewed activity. When there was none, they made their report.

"They are changing their axis of advance. They hope we will lose them but they forget we have the tlaque and they have no idea we have the radios. They are waiting to see if we will harass them further today. I am guessing they think not. This short move surprises me. Their commander is a thinker. He wants to restrict our advantage. How can he do that? First he changes his axis, even by a small distance. Perhaps he thinks we will approach his force as it was deployed and blunder into the vanguard. If that happens we would be engaged in a skirmish we were not anticipating and perhaps we would suffer casualties. That is one advantage we would lose, not knowing where they were deployed. But the other major advantages are the mobility and longer range of your bows, which we would lose at night. Hah! my able commander, you are going to advance at night and rest in a tight defensive position by day. That way you gain ground, use less water and do not expose your tail."

"That sounds like a good plan for them. How do we combat it?"

"We don't. We wanted them to deploy further north so they miss the fort. They have played into our hands. Let them advance for a few nights. During the day you may run around their position and try to pick a few off here and there but it will be a ruse. I want them to gain in confidence. When they get to where the original line of OP used to be we will make them halt and set up for battle by deploying the mounted Infantry in their path on a front too wide to bypass. When they start their attack you will sweep their ranks from one edge with one troop while the other is picking up their Infantry Platoons. Then you will pick up the rest. The timing will have to be perfect or the enemy will not be committed. We don't want them to just call off the attack if we go too early and we don't want to be collecting our Infantry friends from under their arrows. I will join you before then. Perhaps as soon as tomorrow afternoon. If we two are able to pick off a few of their advance guard in the dark before they arrive at the OP line they will be spooked."

"Spooked, My Lord?"

"Sorry. Jumping at shadows."

"I missed you last night. My heart was racing with the excitement of the battle and my body was hot."

"So were you able to cool it?"

"Eloik assisted me as she did when we were girls."

"Good for you. Soon you will not need her."

"Nor you, Buyo."

"No. I look forward to that time. Though she pleases me greatly I do not feel the ébon for her as I do with you. Now tell your commanders of these developments. I will tell Izaki our plan is working."

"As you wish My Lord." At last he has told me of the ébon he feels. Soon we can stop all this fighting and planning and working and just settle down to a normal life. When that

happens I will allow his seed to germinate in my belly. For now, though, I will continue giving him the milkyweed tea. It is still too soon.

The watchers waited for the last rays of the sun to touch their position before they relaxed. Their day's work was done and they could unroll their blankets and sleep one at a time. Ch0n had given instructions that one of them had to be alert all day and all night. Every fourteen suns they would be relieved but during that time they were always working. He had also insisted that they put soot on their faces day and night. It was something they found strange, seeing as they never saw anybody close up but they knew the penalties for failure to obey orders and so they maintained the routine as though he were likely to walk around the nearest rock at any moment. Which he was.

"Did you hear that?"

"Yes. It came from the bottom of the slope. Quick. Wrap up your bedroll and follow me."

They sneaked silently along the narrow path they had created for just such a time. As they reached the lower slopes of the rise they saw the Matáng arcos climbing upwards close by, their pale faces shining bright in the wan moonlight. The watchers waited until the arcos had passed and then crept to their escape route. Moments later they were jogging as fast as the light would permit to their next OP. It took only a short time to reach it at a run and they were soon in place. The first thing they did was report in.

"Well done to you both. I watched the look on all your faces when I was laying down your rules of operation. Now you know why I was so strict with them. The alertness, the black faces, the escape routes. Had you not followed them all you would not be reporting this. You may well have been captured or

killed. Your helm would have been captured. The Lancers may
have ridden through the cutting and been slaughtered. Or you
may have escaped intact but the Lancers slaughtered in which
case you would have been tried and executed for failing to obey
your orders. Make no mistake, your diligence has been noted.
Set yourselves up there. I have a suspicion the Matáng will
move by night so you may be called upon sooner than you
think. Now. Another procedure to consider when you arrive at
a new site. As well as those we just mentioned, I want you to
prepare a place to hide the helm in case you get overrun."

*"Thank you, lord Ch0n. We are all here to serve the Arw'an and
Buq'ue in our own way. We are proud to have a small part to
play."*

Ch0n changed frequency.

"Karín. Are you there?"

"I am always here, My Lord."

"Yes you are. I have a change of orders for the Household
Cavalry. Tomorrow at first light I want you to split into two
troops. One of them I want you to take to the cutting where the
OP was stationed until just now. On the high side some thirty
or more Matáng archers have been deployed under cover of
darkness. I want you to take one troop of Lancers down the
approach to the cutting at a slow walk but do not enter the
cutting itself. Make sure you approach it so the archers can
watch you for as long as possible because I want their attention
focussed on you. The other troop will take their Infantry to the
base of the slopes behind the enemy and drop them off. They
will then provide archer support to the Infantry as they assault
the Matáng archers. I want none alive and I want their bows
and arrows."

"We would probably have ridden through that cutting tomorrow."

"I am sure your Lancers will find a way to thank the two observers who were so diligent with their work. Now I will leave you to plan your ambush of the ambushers."

The Matáng arcos watched their prey approaching in the distance. It was the first time they had had the chance to see the Lancers in relative calm. The lines were straight and the leader was making them manoeuvre on the plain as they advanced. Now they were in two files. Now they turned at right angles and walked in two long ranks with their lances vertical then horizontal. They put their beasts to a trot and then a gallop before slowing back to a walk and suddenly they all turned in their ranks and went about. What had been the rear rank was now the front and they repeated their walk, trot gallop back in the direction they had come. It was an impressive sight but in a short while their numbers would be decimated by repeated volleys of arrows. They were close to the entrance of the cutting now. The archers had orders not to fire until the leader was leaving the cutting so that all the riders would be in the killing zone. But they stopped short and performed more manoeuvres at the halt. Then they turned and walked back the way they had come and wheeled again as though to enter the cutting. It was then that the first volley of arrows from behind fell amongst them like rain. Fortunately they were well spread out and the terrain was rocky so they were able to take cover. Some of them were hit but the remainder repositioned themselves and tried to see what the situation was like below. Their commander was telling them to get to cover and return fire. Meanwhile, unseen and unheard, the Infantry started to swarm up the slopes. When they reached a point almost at the top of the rise they let out their battle cry and ran full tilt into the Matáng position. The archers were unable to fight back at close quarters. Their weapons were designed to be used at ideal ranges but in close they lacked swords or even daggers. They used their bows like staves but went down under the weight of the Arw'an assault. Below them, the Lancers shouted their encouragement. When it was over, the Infantry consolidated the position while their commander counted the dead and the cost. They had lost one man and the rest had nothing more than scratches and bruises. They counted thirty three dead Matáng and recovered all their weapons as instructed. Marik, the commander, famous for his run of sixteen hours to deliver the first of the oruk calves, went to the top of the rise and signalled to Karín with a mirror. She immediately gave Ch0n the news. He sat up in the bed and congratulated her and her troops.

"I will leave for your location after I breakfast," he told her. "This will set the Matáng back hard, losing so many specialist archers. We don't know how many he has but he has thirty three fewer this morning." He rubbed his hands together and laughed to himself.

"Are you feeling well pleased with yourself, My Lord?" Buyo stretched out her tiny nakedness like a cat in front of him.

"That I am, Buyo. Let me show you."

Ch0n rode out later in the morning leaving Izaki with detailed information about how he was going to wage the next few days of the war. Izaki was to prepare the fort for possible evacuation, although that now looked unlikely, and he was to send two companies of troops to the OP near the cave overlooking the lake. He told Alik to ride back to the castle with Buyo and prepare their quarters for the siege. He returned Buyo's smile and Alik's nod and turned the tlaque towards the battle front.

The Infantry clambered down the slope to the waiting Lancers and were greeted with laughter and general merriment. Eloik allowed a brief moment of celebration before calling for order and for the Infantry to mount. The Lancers lifted their feet from the stirrup cups so their passengers could mount and they were soon riding in column of twos to the rest of the Household Cavalry. The Infantry were holding on to their jockeys perhaps a little more intimately than they needed to but nobody wanted anybody to fall off so nobody complained.

Mastel was pleased with his night's march. They had managed a good ten miles in the moonlight and as the sun rose he halted the advance guard and the rest of the column closed up including the tail. It took a good time for them all to be securely established but as he did his rounds, Mastel could not help but think the position was far less vulnerable than yesterday's. He ordered breakfast and then fifty percent watches for the remainder of the day and he went to make his report to the king.

Karín examined the bow and compared it to one of their own. It was made of a different wood and was not dried into shape. When she released the string from the bow it straightened completely whereas theirs returned to a slight arc thanks to the type of wood and the time spent in the sun with the string attached. She called to her best two archers and asked them to do a comparison of capabilities with the Matáng arrows and then the Arw'an version. She picked five random Matáng bows and told them to report back when they had finished.

The Infantry soldiers who had been involved in the assault were teasing those who had had to remain behind. It was good natured at first but Karín had to step in and put it to a stop when it looked like getting too heated and swords were drawn.

"They need to come to grips with the enemy before their patience runs out," she thought to herself.

It was almost dark in the Matáng camp. Mastel was waiting for his archers to return. He had estimated that they would return long before sundown and now he was concerned they had either got lost or had been killed. He had no option but to wait and see. Sending a patrol to check was out of the question. In short order they would be marching again.

ChOn rode into Karín's position just on sundown. After a full day riding he was in no mood to go and join battle with the Matáng so he told Karín to move the position East after dark to their next pre-determined hide.

"If the Matáng are moving unhindered by night they will be making enough distance to get behind us if we don't move. Tomorrow we will take a good look at them while they rest and then we will make their night moves a little trickier. Another full night's march and they will be nearing the area where I want them to have to deploy for an attack. We have to get them back to moving during the day if that is to happen." He called the OP.

"Move back to your next position. When you are forced back to the original OP we will have a change of tactics. Meanwhile stay in front of them."

"They are just standing up My Lord. Shortly they will begin to shake out for their night move. We will leave here as soon as the light fades."

Both forces were on the move. The Household Cavalry moved quickly and efficiently led by ChOn and Karín to a pre-determined location. They arrived a few hours after leaving their old position. Behind them and to their left, the army of the Matáng king, Sith, shuffled forward in formation, led by Mastel who had no idea where he was going, what he would encounter *en route* or even how the terrain would be when he tried to establish his defensive position at daybreak. His men were wary of the riders and the rumour their arcos had not returned from a mission was sweeping like wildfire through the ranks. They all knew the fate of the battalion that had gone before them, massacred to a man and they all suspected deep down that Mastel and the other commanders were not as confident as they appeared.

When morning started to show its face they were in the middle of a flat plain with low hills to their front and no shade to speak of. Mastel was worried about the prospect of stopping in such open ground and declared the advance would continue after a short break. He sent scouts forward to the hills to survey the terrain on the other side and then they all sat down and waited.

It took the scouts more than an hour at the trot to reach the hills. They carried flags on staffs to signal their commander and when they saw the river snaking away to the south of their advance, they waved excitedly for the army to advance.

"They are ahead of schedule." ChOn commented to Karín. They were resting in the trees the Matáng scouts had seen. "Their commander is a good soldier and planner. The scouts have called them forward but that doesn't suit my plans. I want to delay them further in the sun. Quickly take the Household Cavalry and the mounted Infantry to the hills. Line them up on the crest where they are easily seen. Kill the scouts if they can be run down quickly. Go now. Wait until they are moving and then make them stop and plan their next move. The next phase of mobile defence has begun a day early." He called to the OP.

"Move back another line of hills to your original positions so you can relay to the Castle for us. Inform Sir Jez of our location and that of the Matáng. Tell him to prepare for an attack on the castle within the next seven days."

They rode to the hills and surveyed the situation to their west. The Matáng army was on its feet and moving towards them slowly. Karín looked at ChOn, who nodded. Karín had the Infantry march line abreast to the crest of the hill and then she walked the Lancers to form up in plain view behind them. They were more than two hundred strong. It was the biggest force they had deployed. Ever.

Mastel watched the Infantry appear over the hill and stand silently silhouetted against the early morning sun. The riders appeared behind them and stood waiting. The advance guard of the Matáng stopped. The vanguard stopped and the main body stopped.

"Mastel I believe we are getting close to somewhere important to the Buq'ue or they would not be willing to engage us. I will continue the advance to the hills. We can not split off a smaller force to clear the hills or it will be slaughtered. We have to just keep moving. Let the advance guard make contact and we will support them from behind with the arcos. The wind is more favourable to us this morning."

"I disagree, Sire. We need to separate the soldiers from the riders. If we can occupy the riders and attack the soldiers, we will prevent them from breaking contact. The riders will not be able to support them from under our spears. Give the Lancers a juicy bait. Press forward by all means but send another force at the double around the flank at the same time. They can not allow it to get behind them. They will have to assault it. Send the arcos with that force so they have the chance to fire at the riders at close range. I estimate there is less than a company of Infantry on the hill and the riders number the same."

"All right, Mastel. That sounds good. Call in the commanders and brief them. But do it quickly. I need to find some shade."

"Now we will see what their commander is made of. He has three options. He can do nothing and call our bluff, which would be a good option if he had some shade or could afford to leave his tail exposed. He could just continue the advance and push us off this hill with numbers or he could try something different like outflanking us at snail's pace to see what we will do. He has to cancel out our mobility or die by inches. I would try and pin the Infantry down by making the cavalry deploy and by attacking the Infantry while the cavalry is on their other task. For that to succeed, the timing would have to be perfect and we would have to allow our force to engage his. Learn from this, Karín and you others. We have stopped an army ten times our size. Every day in the field they eat and drink their way to defeat if they can not advance. Even this delay of a short time is costing them water and making them hungry. This is a mobile defence and can only be conducted if the defending force has better mobility or better static defences and a mobile logistic force. It causes attrition on the advancing force with few casualties on the other. He has made his plan now and will be calling in his junior commanders to allocate their roles. While we are waiting, make a show of drinking a lot of water. Splash some of it on the ground while you're at it. Every little bit counts in the war of nerves and morale. And tell me the results of your bow comparison. You were going to do it last night before we moved and after that I was too distracted to ask."

Karín smiled for it was she that had distracted him.

"Their bows are slightly longer than ours. I suspect it is because they need the extra length to flex. Their wood is not as flexible and if the bows were shorter they would break. Also they were not cut and shaped before drying so their natural shape is straight, not curved. The cords are of woven wool as are ours. We were able to draw some of the bows to breaking point, which means they are restricted with their range. They were unable to fire our arrows as far as we can fire them. We fired their arrows from our bows and they fly true but lack weight and do not penetrate at longer distances. In other words our bows are better and our arrows too. We could stand off and have a duel with them and they would fall short unless they had the wind at their backs."

"My trip to find the different wood was not wasted then. Nor the trip to the tar pit."

"According to Buyo they were not wasted My Lord."

"Hmm. Yes, well we will see what their commander chooses to do. Regardless, as soon as his plans are in action we will withdraw but not to the river. We will have to concede him the water in the river. But we will have cost him time and rations and Sir Jez is already preparing the castle. Now when we withdraw, take the Infantry over to that hill in the distance and drop them. It is an hour's ride and half a day's walk so they will be safe. Send half of the Lancers back to the tail of the Matáng advance while they are still moving. Do not engage their troops. Go back and join the rest and go to the next hide. AAh! Something is happening. They are advancing in force. Not very imaginative. No, there they go at a run. The bait. Karín. Walk the Lancers to the reverse slope so he thinks they are forming for an attack. But form up for the withdrawal instead and I will send the Infantry down soon."

"It is working, Sire. The riders have left and we will soon see them attacking the flanking force with the arcos. They are not so clever if something so simple can trick them. The lone rider must be their leader. He is dressed strangely and the sun shines off his face and that of one of the other riders. The timing is almost right. We should be able to take them now."

Ch0n was going through the same thought process. He could make out the king's entourage back in the column from the umbrellas but he was more concerned at the timing of the withdrawal. He waited and waited and then gave the order. His men ran back the fifty yards to where their girls were waiting, legs raised. In seconds they were moving and when the Matáng Infantry reached the spot where they had expected to do battle, all they saw was the Household Cavalry and their passengers trotting away well out of bow range. Mastel walked to the top of the crest and surveyed the terrain. In the distance the dust told him the Buq'ue force was well gone.

"Perhaps he is not so easily fooled, Mastel,"

"So it seems, Sire but at least they have conceded us the ground and the river. We will not want for water from now on. We will follow the river to where it takes us. He called to the commander of the advance guard.

"Change of axis. We will camp by the banks of the river. Move out!"

Almost two hours later, the first of the Matáng was arriving at the river bank. The commanders had to work overtime to get things set up before their men went swimming. At about the same time, One Troop of the Household Cavalry was sweeping through the rear elements of the camp followers slashing water bladders and porters and scattering bags of porridge. Twice the sixty riders swept through and then they were gone before the rear guard could even react to their presence. Many of the porters, slaves that they were, deserted at that point. Now they had a river to follow they knew they would find their way to their former Buq'ue families.

"They have hit the camp followers again, Mastel and most who were not killed have fled. The water containers and porridge have been strewn about. We will be marching on empty stomachs before long."

"We are close to their village, Sire. Their tactics have changed. Soon there will be food, women and treasure for everybody. We will follow the river until it takes us there. You will see that within one or two days they will try and move us from the river to the plains again. Their riders and arcos need space. In the trees along the river, Infantry is king. This is what we have been looking for and now we have it. Two or three

suns more and we will be in their village supping on their goats while their women serve us like princes. I am going to have the commander of the riders as a slave. I know her not but she must be formidable."

Gavan Connell

Chapter Twenty Nine: The Siege

Eight miles high, a computer clicked once and a vessel started to boot into life. A month before, it had detected an earth–like planet, had navigated towards it and finally moved into orbit. Now the long process of waking the crew would begin. The droids sprang into action. The fluids changed temperature very slightly to start bringing the almost-dead bodies to life. The on-board cameras started filming every square inch of the planet.

"I think we can let them come to us now. They will stay by the river for the water and soon they will find the fruit and the dáguia nests. In a week they will destroy every bit of natural beauty there is between here and the castle and then they will try to destroy that as well. Everything we have worked for comes to this. We will let them get to the outer walls and then we will give them everything we have. They can withdraw and try to starve us out but if we need to, I will send the Lancers out to attack their rear. The time of easy fighting is over, Karín. The Lancers and soldiers have learned well and trained well and won the skirmishes well but now they must also learn that casualties are part of war and their fellow Lancers and Infantry too will die or be wounded or captured and tortured. Talk to them about it. But the reality is that nothing can prepare them. Or me for that matter because this will be my first big battle as well. My dream tells me we will be together on the tower but it doesn't tell me if we will win or lose. That is up to them now and up to us as well. We will withdraw everything to the castle. The Lancers will operate from there, harassing their approach until we have to shut the main gates. The Infantry are no longer to be mounted. They performed their tasks well such as they were but now they will have to man their posts at the walls with the rest."

"We have done all we can. It is strange but had you never arrived, the Arw'an would be herders. The Buq'ue would be raiding the Arw'an and the Matáng would be raiding the Buq'ue. It was forever my dream to stop that cycle and to unite the Buq'ue and Arw'an against the Matáng but I thought it would involve strengthening the outposts so that the Matáng raiders would not think it worth their while. Now instead of a vicious circle of raids we have all-out war that will result in the Buq'ue and the Arw'an being enslaved by the Matáng king right here in Arw'an Castle or it will result in the three tribes being united under one king and ruled justly from this same castle. You have brought about this war and if we win, you will have brought about a lasting peace. If we lose you will have brought about a lasting life of slavery for us. There was never any middle ground. But we will win because we have you and we have what you have brought us and taught us. Now! Let's go home. In a few days we will beat the war drums and our future will be known."

"You go home. I have work to do here after dark and you can not help. Better you bed down the Lancers and in two days they can return to sweep the Matáng flanks and rear. I would like them to arrive at the castle with fewer men and less confident that they would be if they just walked there with no resistance. Tomorrow I will have communications with Jez. We will know the extent of the preparations but I have no doubt he will be ready.

The Matáng position was well established by the time Ch0n approached it in the early hours of the morning. He had left the tlaque tethered with the wolf and walked in. The mottled moonlight did nothing to illuminate his black-clad form under the trees with the gold visor raised and the clear, smoky, non-reflective one lowered. The thermal imaging and starlight scopes combination allowed him easy access. He didn't want to go into the depth positions of the camp but he wanted to create fear throughout the Matáng force. He unsheathed Shiew and ran his hand down the flat of the blade to still the humming. Treading lightly on the soft soil beside the river, he came to the first sentry who was half alert at his post. Had he been fully alert he may have had time to shout before his head was severed. Ch0n paused to see if the muffled sound of the body falling and twitching had roused anybody but he was able to continue towards the sleeping troops. Shiew sang her song a dozen or more times before Ch0n decided he should withdraw. He stole away into the mottled shadows where his animals were waiting and left for the castle without further incident.

Mastel heard the rumours before the company commander reached his tent. The news confirmed the rumour. Someone had walked into their position and removed the heads of fourteen soldiers from one platoon. That was bad enough but the rumour mill had it that the eyes of the victims were all open and nobody knew they were dead until they had been kicked by their cabot and the heads had rolled to one side.

"My Lord, Mastel, they are saying that whatever did this must have been able to see in the dark like an owl and could probably have moved from one side of the camp to the other and killed hundreds. They were already fearful of the riders but now they are talking of magic and beasts from the other side of death."

Mastel was a believer in magic and the thought of someone strolling through the camp randomly beheading his men turned his stomach but he was unable to show his superstitious fear in front of them.

"Tell them to stay awake on sentry duty tonight and they will be safe. I will personally do rounds tonight and if I find anybody asleep they will suffer the same fate as those from last night. Today we will march from here along this bank of the river. I do not want to separate the force by straddling it. The Buq'ue will

not join us in a set piece battle without their riders and these trees make it hard for the riders to operate. We are safe. We will up the pace of the advance today. It will be cooler where there are trees and we do not have to ration water. After the king has completed his morning routine I will give the word to move. Be ready. Runner! Tell the commanders to be ready to move when the king is disposed."

ChOn arrived at the castle after mid-day. He went straight to Jez and received a full briefing on the state of readiness of the defence. He was pleased with what he saw. Jez had also seen to the two oruk and he had fitted them both with breastplates made from the hide of the dragon they had killed some months before.

"My Lord, I have been riding them both and continued their training with the bamboo models. They now charge straight and true with no regard for what stands before them. They have learned that they can trample the bamboo soldiers. If we need them, they are ready to use in battle."

"They are still young, Jez but we may have no choice. If it appears the internal gates are threatened, we will lead the charge through them with the Infantry behind us. We will need armour for our arms and legs if we are to ride through the Matáng. And we need to make sure we get to the other side or it will be the end of us. It is a last resort. I do not believe things will get to that stage."

The herds had been dispersed to their far-away fields under the care of Doni and his herders. All the herders were now mounted and they were easily able to control the mixed herd of oruk, tlaque and goats. The villagers were still in their dwellings but their chattels had been stored in the castle's ground floor and they were living outside only to relieve the pressure on the water supply and the latrines. Mori and his birds were in the ramparts where they could be launched but they would not be able to retrieve messages from the Buq'ue fort. It was a failing that Ch0n had not foreseen, that the birds would home to their regular cage unless Mori could coax them down to the turret with food.

Ch0n went with Jez to the field works in front of the castle. They had constructed two earth bunds outside spear range. The archers would use them as cover while they unleashed their arrows on the advancing enemy force, which would have no option but to advance down the only strip of land that approached the castle. There was no question of their attacking across the river. When the enemy reached a certain point, the archers would run for the gates, supported by crossbows and longbows from the walls. It was assumed the enemy would gratefully use the bunds as cover and Ch0n would activate the buried explosives from the tower. The dead ground from where the Household Cavalry would operate was clear of obstacles and could not be seen from the attacking side but from the walls it could be observed and fired into.

"I think we are ready, Jez. You have done well. We have a few surprises in store for them yet"

"Thank you My Lord. I think we are and yes, we do."

"Alik. Ask Brigadier General Karín to come to me."

''Yes My Lord."

"Jez, after I speak to Karín, we will go to my stables and make the armour for our arms and legs."

Reny took the King's Troop across the river and trotted west towards the Matáng army. They came across them several hours later all on the other side of the river. The shouts from the other side told Reny they had been spotted but she was only worried that the Matáng had deployed a flank guard on her side and so proceeded in two files. The formation gave them the advantage of moving with a narrow front to any surprises on her side but it also gave her a broad flank to engage the force on the other side of the river. She gave the order and the Lancers started to loose their shafts among the Matáng. The trees offered some protection but they were still able to wreak havoc among the closest company. Meanwhile, Eloik had raced down the open ground and was now raining arrows on the left flank. She passed just once to share the confusion and panic and then wheeled back around and trotted slowly past in full view but well out of range. Mastel was growing more angry and frustrated every time his troops were engaged without the chance to make contact. The Matáng force had now lost more than a hundred and fifty troops and almost all their camp followers since they started the advance. As far as he knew, he had not inflicted a single casualty on the Buq'ue or Arw'an. The riders on his right flank continued to fire into his vanguard and there was nothing he could do about it. His arcos were returning fire but they didn't have the range of the Buq'ue weapons and were just wasting arrows. He called for the commanders to move away from the river another hundred paces. While the order was being relayed, Reny took her troop down the river engaging the entire line of advance. As they moved away, she turned and rode back down the line towards the castle. She forded the river and the two troops returned together through the main gate to cheers from the villagers.

Mastel decided to take the initiative and sent scouts out at the run. There were four to begin with but one dropped off the group every so often until only one remained. He kept running along the bank counting his paces and remembering everything of note. When he came around the bend through the bamboo forest and saw the castle on its peninsular, he stopped open mouthed. He tried to think of words to describe the scene. Finally he ran back to where he had left his comrade and told him to bring Mastel. There he waited. The scouts ran back in relays to where Mastel was waiting and planning. Five minutes after getting the message from the scout he was jogging out of the camp.

Mastel was no young man and he blew up badly on the run and had to walk and rest but he finally arrived at the bend in the river and for the first time, surveyed Arw'an Castle. It was late evening and what remained of the goats were being herded back through the gates. Smoke rose from within the walls and drifted upwards and upwards to the height of the tower and beyond. Mastel tried to come to grips with the enormity of conquering this layered position with the enormous stone structure in the middle on the remains of a rocky hill. The walled village had been sited and built in a tight bend of the river so it was almost surrounded by water. There was one land approach to the main gates across open grass with hardly anywhere to hide. The main gate was protected by a stone structure that could cause untold damage to a force trying to storm the gates. The actual wall around the village could be scaled quite easily in an unopposed attack but with soldiers defending it, it would be a daunting task and would cost hundreds of lives. Mastel decided that the best way to attack the site was in a solid phalanx concentrated on one small part of the wall so his men could get over it and spread out on the inside. From his position he could not see the second wall in front of the castle with its second set of gates. He knew his troops would be subject to a hail of arrows as soon as they came into range and that it would not let up until the two forces actually joined the fight at close quarters. And then there was the building itself. He had no idea how they would take it but take it they must because it dominated the site and no force could live beneath its walls for long. It simply had to be taken. Once again, it had to have a door and obviously that was the weak point, although it would be strongly defended from without and within. This battle was going to cost a lot of lives. He was looking at the approaches to the gates and asking himself just how many lives it was going to take to get through them when the thought occurred to him that he might not have to take the castle at all by force but that he could take the village and set up his force in such a way that they could not be shot with arrows but the people inside the stone shelter could be starved into submission. His own forces would loot the village of every item of food and the river would provide water. He would just sit and wait. He smiled at his own plan. Take the wall and starve the villagers in the shelter. He looked to the tower as three figures appeared atop it. One was the tall leader. He was talking and pointing at the approaches and waving his hands about. The second was a tall woman with her red hair blowing back in the wind. The third was a shorter man, perhaps the leader's army commander. He was nodding agreement and pointing along the approach and then all three looked directly at Mastel while the leader waved his hands some more. Mastel thought they had seen him but he was in the trees and the light was fading. He would have to make his way back in the dark. It would give him time to plan his attack.

"When they come, they will suffer their first big losses from the archers and then their morale will be tested by the explosives in the bunds. They will have to bring a second battalion up or a second company from the same battalion. Either way they will have a period of confusion when the two forces are mixed. That will be the time to ride through them from the flank. Do not go any further to the left than those trees short of the river." Ch0n was pointing directly at Mastel. "Turn there and ride back through and then cut for the gate. Jez, open the gate as the first ones come to it and keep it open as long as you can. Karín, your Lancers must hold their formations. If they break down you will suffer casualties and it will be hard for them to get through the gate. If we have to close the gate, you will give the order to ride for the open country to the west and wait for my instructions. They must not look back. They must NOT look back. Eloik and Reny or their cabots are just to ride at the head of their troops and lead them through the danger to the other side. They are NOT to stop for anything. Nothing is to slow their momentum. If they make it through, we will be able to use them to harass the rear and when the chance arises we will bring them back in. They will be safe outside the main battle. They must NEVER stop and fight. Their role is to fight on the move. Jez, any tlaque that loses its rider and looks like getting captured is to be shot by the archers."

He looked at them both and they nodded at him.

"My Lord, I have something to show you. I didn't show you yesterday because it was not trialled but now it has been. I have had Boro's men working on it for moons in secret, modifying and improving it. It is a large version of your crossbow. The mechanism was hard to duplicate with what we have but we are well pleased with it now."

Mastel backed away from his position and started to jog away. His mind was formulating his plan all the way back. It took him quite some time at his middle aged pace but when he arrived he was ready to give his orders.

Jez had the giant crossbow brought to Ch0n on the turret. The arc was seven feet long and made from a single sapling four inches in diameter and carved flat and smooth to two inches wide and an inch thick at the tip. It had been air dried on the stock with the bow slightly bent. The stock was six feet long and incorporated a winch mechanism at the back end to cock it. The hardwood bolts were more like four-foot long javelins almost an inch in diameter. They had been worked by hand to make them straight and their final test of straightness was to pass them through an aluminium tube from the landing craft. Each had a fire hardened tip. The fletches were made from tanned goat ears cut to shape and slid into slots in the back of the bolts.

"Today we test-fired this out to a range of a hundred paces. For the first thirty it flies flat. For the second thirty you have to raise this to adjust for the flight and for the last thirty you have to lift it again to sight it but it is used at that range against a group because the arrow loses its accuracy. We built two of these and we have made more than two hundred arrows. Would you like to fire it?"

"I would."

ChOn fired the crossbow at a spot on the ground in front of the area of the bunds and was surprised at its accuracy. Three arrows all struck within four feet of each other at about seventy paces.

"This is a good weapon. Well done." I want one here on the turret. Where were you thinking of putting them?"

"One here where you want it and the other is already in the gatehouse firing down the road. We might be able to get a commander or two."

"If the outer wall falls, cut the string of the one in the guard house and bring all the arrows here or they will be firing it back at us. And run a continuous line from the rail gun to the tower. If that tower looks like falling I want to be able to pull it and some or all of the ammunition up here and use it."

Mastel called his commanders in and gave them his plan. They would march on the morrow to the forming up place on the blind side of the rise in front of the fortress. There they would adopt the assault formations with shields to the front and march to the wall under a roof of shields. They would attack in a phalanx against a small area of the wall to the left of the main gate. The single aim of the first assault was to breach the wall with sheer weight of numbers. Once inside they would fan out and attack the gates from the rear while the second wave of troops similarly breached the wall to the right of the gate. They would consolidate on the inside and review their plan to breach the main fort or to just pull back and starve the occupants into submission.

Late the following day, the final OP reported the forward elements of the Matáng army had come into view. They withdrew to the castle and handed the helm to Jez, basking in the praise of the ChOn. Karín ordered the Household Cavalry outside the walls to their night hide in preparation for the next day's attack. Sentries were doubled and the special weapons checked and crewed.

ChOn and Karín were too excited to sleep. They lay together discussing the strategy for the Household Cavalry in the ensuing fight. ChOn kept emphasising that they had to stay mobile and never get bogged down in a fight or they would be slaughtered. He went through the sequence of assaults and the timing of their run for the gates. Unbidden, Buyo came into the room and lay down beside Karín and listened.

"I am sorry my lady, Karín but tonight is not the night for me to be alone," she said.

They rose before first light and dressed for the battle. Jez was already up and moving about his quarters. Alik was full of nervous energy. ChOn ordered him to dress in his full battle order and not his squire's tunic.

"Today you will find out your limits, boy. You are not yet a Knight but you will dress like one and do your best. Take this short sword. Stay by my side and do everything I say. There will be no time for me to look for you and no time for repeating orders. Are you ready?"

"I have been ready since the first day I donned this uniform of black in secret, My Lord. Fear not, I will be at your side until the end. To make it easy for you to see me, look for this." He took a silk cloth from his pocket. It had been dyed bright red. He

wrapped it around his head like a turban and tied off the knot. The loose ends hung past his shoulders and a sudden gust of wind lifted them. For the first time, ChOn saw he had a few wispy hairs on his chin and his top lip.

"Before the battle, report to Sonja. Give her my compliments and tell her to shave you. I will not have my men looking scruffy in the face of the enemy." The boy's face split in two and he raced below.

"Those are the things that make you a king, ChOn. Not the weapons and not your laws."

"Aah. The woman of my dreams. The time has come, Karín. By the end of this day we will know our fate. Come here. I wish to say something to you before we go to the roof." For a few precious seconds they stood together and then Jez's voice crackled in the helm on the bed.

ChOn mounted the tower with Karín and a freshly-shaved Alik. Karín's face was glowing and her heart was pounding but not only from the adrenalin rush. Below them in the faint dawn they could see things starting to take place. The archers marched through the open gates and out to the bunds. The walls were lined with soldiers and the reserve company was in place. The giant crossbow on its pivot mount was silhouetted against the lightening sky. Inside the keep, the villagers and all the domestic stock huddled together. ChOn checked communications with the two troop leaders, the guard commander, Jez and Karín. All were on line.

In the distance ChOn could just make out the Matáng army cresting the rise. He picked up a green flag and held it aloft. Below him a faint voice could be heard calling the archers to stand to. The ensuing silence was eerie. Karín moved to ChOn's side and slipped her arm though his. On his other side, Alik watched his master, the red turban fluttering occasionally.

The wolf sat quietly watching Ch0n with no less concentration than Alik. At the top of the stairs, Buyo stood alone watching them all.

Eight miles high, the commander of the space vessel was watching proceedings on his bridge. With him was his military commander, the senior cloned soldier. Scientists and others filled the space.

"This will be interesting. There must be two or three thousand dismounted Infantry against a force of perhaps three to four hundred in the castle. The leader of the defenders looks very much like a galactic soldier to me with his black uniform and helm. Perhaps he was marooned there with his team some time ago. Scan all frequencies and record anything you hear. Set the maxitron translator in motion. G2, watch this carefully. You will be landing there when the dust settles, no matter which side wins."

The clone nodded and set the scanner. In less than a second he was pegged to the same frequency Ch0n was using for the battle. The radio beeped twice to let him know that the frequency was fixed and registered. Eight miles below, Ch0n heard the sound and the clone saw him raise his head and look skywards as if he was expecting to see something there.

The clone G2 looked around him. He ordered them out of the space so he was there alone with just the commander. He pressed the talk button.

"Four o'clock."

Ch0n instinctively looked straight at the camera at his four o'clock high. He gave the field signal for 'silence' and returned his gaze to the approaching Matáng. Below him the commander of the archers was looking up at him. Ch0n waited until the front rank of the Matáng crossed the line in the dirt marking the range of the bows and he dropped the flag.

A good bowman could loose four arrows before the first one came to ground and most of ChOn's were able to loose three or four. The Matáng had their shields in place to guard their heads but the sheer volume of arrows ensured that many found spaces and took their targets to ground and opened up more spaces. The rain of arrows was constant and the toll terrible but the Matáng marched on, undaunted. A second wave of Matáng started jogging forward knowing the archers were concentrated on the first group. ChOn judged the distance between the forces and raised a red flag. The archers loosed their final volley and turned and ran for the gates. Behind them the archers on the wall covered their withdrawal. Of the original company of Matáng to cross the line of departure, barely twenty made it to the safety of the bund. The archers ran through the gates and Karín ordered the Household Cavalry to charge. They came from nowhere and hit the left flank of the second company at a run. The King's Troop charged them from the left rear and One Troop followed at their heels. One hundred and twenty mounted Lancers in four ranks against one hundred Infantry on foot produced a massacre. The lead ranks wheeled to the right and made for open ground well to the flanks of the Matáng and out of range of their arcos. The rest followed. In their wake, not a Matáng soldier remained alive.

"Eloik, Reny. Go to the rear of the Matáng and harass their caravan for one pass and return to your original hide," ordered Karín. She turned to ChOn.

"They are better served out there in the open. Once they come through the gates they are useless to us and occupy space we need to manoeuvre the reserve Infantry."

ChOn nodded and watched the third wave of Matáng jogging towards the gates; three platoons and a Company HQ. They were fired upon by the archers on the walls and sought the safety of the bunds. They crouched, tightly packed behind the earth shelters with their shields over their heads waiting for the next wave to reach them. Their commander had fixed a point on the wall where they would assault and he was pointing out the direction when ChOn detonated the explosives. The bunds moved skywards in a mass of dirt and body parts. The soldiers on the walls were shocked at the noise and instant violence the explosion produced. Even those on the ship were surprised at the sheer brutality of the tactic and G2 resisted the temptation to pass a comment to his brother below.

Mastel saw the bund blow before the sound reached him. The erupting earth and bits of flesh flying through the air almost weakened his resolve but he ordered the next wave forward. It consisted of three companies in block. Mastel had assumed that by now he would have a substantial force at the wall but all he had done was lose three hundred men on the approaches. The Battalion commander was running behind the first company with his standard bearer right beside him.

Jez was already directing the crossbow in the gatehouse. It was the first chance he had had to identify a target. He watched the smoke from the explosion and told his crew to aim one body width to the left. They loosed the shaft and the standard bearer was plucked aside. The commander looked around for him and saw his body about to be trampled by the next company. He shouted to the leading soldiers to save the standard. It was the commander's only means of signalling to his company commanders. While he was stationary and shouting, the second shaft, adjusted for flight took him through the side under the armpit and lifted him off the ground. Jez looked for and found the commander of the leading company and reloaded the bow. He directed the crew to the target and once he was sure they had identified him, he ordered the shot. The range was now considerably less and the crew had the wind and height adjustment. The shaft took him and the soldier behind him to ground. The attack continued but instead of concentrating on one part of the wall and lacking directions, the

Matáng troops continued on a wide front. The archers were cutting them down in their dozens and still they continued. When they were twenty yards from the wall, six pulse guns and six kinetic pistols opened up and the first company dissolved in a second. The second company faltered and the archers rained arrows down in their midst. The company commander was in the process of ordering them forward when an arrow from the crossbow caught him in the skull. The troops milled around as though lost and Karín put the Lancers through them. The result was the same as the previous occasion and Reny led them straight to the rear of the Matáng, passed again loosing arrows at the rear guard and returned to the hide.

Mastel was no fool. He sent a runner to the remnants of the leading companies and told them to withdraw. They limped back to the assembly area leaving five hundred dead on the plain with no known casualties to the Buq'ue. Sith was all for pushing on but Mastel would have none of it.

"Sire, they have weapons we have ever seen. They can kill a hundred at a time. We have to take away the advantage they have. I will put a blocking force of arcos on the right flank. If the riders sweep through again they will ride into the teeth of a storm of spears at close range. I will send scouts to the left flank to find where they are hiding. It has to be close. Once we know we can wait for them there as well. So they will be hit hard twice in succession. I will send the next wave just before dark when the riders are at the limit of their use and if they sweep we will have them in the half light on the right. By the time they recover and return to their hiding place we will hit them there as well. If they do not sweep we will be fighting at the walls. During the night we will send harassing parties to keep them awake while we rest. It is the only way I can see."

"Mastel. Send arcos behind and to the left of the next wave as well. If the riders come the arcos can prop and fire into them as they come and as they leave. That way we get them three

times in one pass. And cut long grass-tree trunks to make spear shafts. If they have their base on the ground and slope towards the riders, they will take the talaque through the chest as they run in. Each platoon should be able to manage several on their left flank. In addition, I want the front ranks to carry sections of bamboo bound together a man high and three men wide. They will protect against arrows and can be used at the wall as climbing frames."

"As you wish, Sire. Runner!"

"They have withdrawn to make another plan. Make sure all have rest, food and water. Get Kelda busy. Sentries only alert. Everybody else resting. They may come in the dark. Karín. Send the Lancers back out of harm's way. Tell them to stay out of the battle. They should return just before first light. Jez. Send sentries in pairs beyond the walls to the left and right flanks with flashlights. No more than one hundred paces. Tell them to make sure they can see the light on the tower at all times. I want them to flash to the tower every time I flash to them. I will flash one short flash. If all is well they are to flash twice but if they see any enemy they are to turn on the beam and leave it on until I flash to them. Then they will know I have seen their signal. Repeat the orders to me before you go."

Jez repeated the orders. Eight miles high, Clone G2 nodded to his commander.

"They are using a lot of English words in their transmissions. There is no doubt there is a marooned patrol or scout down there directing the battle. If that's the case we have to make sure he or they don't get their backsides kicked. There has been a lot of work put into that castle down there. He or they have been there a long time and will have all the information we need. If he gets killed we lose everything he has."

Gavan Connell

"We don't have any way to help. We are still three days away from being ready to land a party there."

"We can provide intel on the battle. We could send a capsule of rail guns right into the compound. One capsule, three rail guns and a huge quantity of ammunition."

"They belong to this mission. Not one already failed. He might be a rogue and they left him there on purpose."

"Not with all those explosives and the pistols. My guess he is the only survivor of a landing party and he is using all their equipment. The extra explosives and equipment were sent to him by the mother ship."

"Why didn't they send the second landing craft down to get them?"

"Out of service maybe like ours? They had to leave him or them so they sent all the capsules down with what they would hold. No point keeping anything on board the ship if you can't land anymore. They equipped him and went home. He made himself king of the sapients."

'We are not here to provide him with material assistance."

"We are here to gather intel on habitable planets, commander. If he has been gathering it for years and we lose it, we are failing in our mission."

"Don't forget who is in command here, Clone."

"How could I forget that, Commander?"

The radio came to life.

"Scan for new freq now."

Ch0n changed the frequency on his helm and started to count. He stopped at twenty.

"Have you come back for me?"

"Negative. We are a routine exploration vessel and your planet came up a possible. How come you're there?'

"Landing failure. All the other scouts died in the main cabin. I've been here about one earth year. Go away and forget about this place. We don't want you or anybody else coming to ruin what we have."

"You have war, soldier. And you have a tablet full of data. We will be landing in less a week right in front of the gate to your castle. Or his castle if he wins."

"He won't win. He hasn't got the heart for it any more or he'd have tried one more assault before he withdrew."

"I'll keep an eye on his movements and let you know if there's anything important. We want your tablet and you can come back with us. We lost a few this time so there are spare capsules."

"Tell me when you're ready but don't land in front of the castle. I'll tell you where to land. I don't want the locals to be scared. Stay off the air on my freq. If you need me, squelch twice and I'll come here."

"Roger that."

"Out."

Ch0n called Jez to the tower and they sat down with Karín.

"First the battle. What is he going to do? Karín?"

"He has to get to the wall and that means he has to take the Household Cavalry out of the battle. He has to destroy us as a viable force or assault where we lose the advantage. So he

either defends against our tactics using what we do against us or he attacks at night or along the river bank to the rear wall."

"Good. First point. You have assaulted twice from his left flank, consolidated on his right flank, rounded the rear of his army and returned to your hide. He may think that is your only option. So he might send archers to his right flank to ambush you or put archers on his left flank to fire as you approach. Either way we do not want to get caught out. I think it is time to leave the Lancers out of the battle until we see a need for them again. It will come but we are doing fine as it is and perhaps later when there is an area of the battlefield where they might be used we will call them in. Meanwhile, tell them to stay well away but within striking distance if we call them. If they come at night we have the helms and the crossbows."

"My Lord, to use the helms for the crossbow teams will rob us of communications. Perhaps one at the guardhouse and yourself here calling the general area we need to look into."

"Good point, Jez. Alik! Bring me Buyo please. Now Jez. What is he going to do?"

"He is going to somehow provide a way to get a large force through to the wall past our archers and your weapons. My guess is he will attack while it is still too dark for us to see out into the approaches. He doesn't know we have the helms but they don't help our archers anyway. They will be firing blind. My best guess is he will come during the night and follow up with numbers but the first wave in the dark will have to be a big force. Maybe another three companies in a block. If I were him I would sneak around the flanks as well and maybe try to get a small force over the wall by the baths where there is a bit of bank to walk on."

"I think you are right. If he comes at night we lose a lot of the advantage we have from the archers and also the Household

Cavalry. And we have to remember the night is long. We will use the thermal imaging to see if the attacks are probes or real attacks. They can't surprise us at all with a full on attack without us knowing a long time before it gets here. The pulses are area weapons at medium range, use no ammunition and are never going to run out of charge. They are our big advantage. And here comes another one. I want you to get the crew to show her how to sight and fire the crossbow. Let the crew do the cocking and loading and let her do the firing. You have a while in which to do it before dark. Don't ask why. Just do it. The back wall is a small problem but we have it manned to the level of risk. They may sneak a few soldiers around the side and maybe even a few will get over but they won't get far. If it looks like we are going to leak too many there we will look at the options. The Infantry company is standing by as a reserve if a small number get over the wall. I just thought of something. Alik. Bring me some cable ties, some frag grenades and a remote control. Jez, get your crew ready for Buyo in the guardhouse and go below and rest. It is going to be a long night. Buyo, tonight you will be posted temporarily to the guard house. You will be firing the crossbow after dark at whatever you think you can hit."

"You should rest Lord Ch0n. Let us do this thing until you are rested. You will not sleep tonight and we need you alert."

"I will try this thing I have for the crossbow and then I will rest, Karín. Not before."

When Alik returned, Ch0n was at the crossbow watching Buyo getting her training. She picked it up quickly and had her first shot at a target at thirty paces. It flew truly. Her second shot was a little off but she instinctively corrected and scored a hit. The target at one hundred or so paces was a group of corpses and she was able to put the shaft into their midst. Meanwhile Ch0n had studied the way the shaft sat in the stock and determined he had three inches of arrow sticking out when it was loaded and armed. He took a shaft, measured off the distance and attached a grenade to the tip.

"Alik. This will be your job if the first one works. You will fasten the grenades to the tips and then when the arrow lands you will detonate the grenade with the remote. Can you do that?"

Alik nodded once. Deep down he wanted to jump around with excitement but he was trying to be a man since his tryst with Marelik by the lake and his recent encounter with the razor.

"I can. My Lord. And I will."

With that ChOn went down to his quarters but instead of sleeping he went to the ground floor and walked among the villagers inside the keep. They were of good spirits and confident they would be back in their houses by the following night. ChOn said nothing but he was not of the same opinion. It was only after he had been seen, congratulated, slapped on the back and cheered on by everybody in the keep that he went to rest. He put the helm over his ear buds and let the minitron put him into a trance-like sleep.

Mastel had his troops assembled and resting. They had full bellies and he had managed to convince them that the cloak of darkness would help them conquer the wall. The arcos were waiting for night before they moved into their blocking position. The forward battalion was equipped with the new, long, anti-talaque lances, which were so light, a single man could carry one to battle and manoeuvre it into position to meet the charging Lancers.

When ChOn woke, Alik was shaking him.

'There is movement, My Lord. You should see it before we do anything."

He pulled on his armour and ran up the stairs to the tower. It was full night and there was almost no light at all on the tower because the moon had not yet risen. Jez was gone. Buyo too. Alik was standing by the crossbow with three shafts prepared, more standing nearby and a small box of grenades and cable ties at hand. Ch0n strode to the edge of the tower and looked where Karín was pointing. A group of perhaps thirty green blobs was moving in single file towards the left flank of the castle. Ch0n guessed they were probably archers moving into position to support the assault and that told him there would be no assault during the night but probably at dawn when the archers from both sides could see. He estimated they were some two hundred paces away and well out of direct fire range of the cross bows even though they could be adjusted on to a target at that range during the day. But not at night. The horse bows could make the distance firing at maximum range but the archers would have no idea of the fall of shot. Unless the group moved closer to the castle there was no point firing at them.

"Leave them," he told Karín. "If they come closer we will perhaps give them a loud welcome. Those over there, however we might try and hit if they come within seventy paces of the gates.

Buyo was standing behind the great bow above the main gates, watching twelve men walking cautiously down from the rise. They were on the main track and well-armed with six of them bearing swords, spears and shields and the remainder armed with bows. Obviously they were not going to storm the gates but they were going to try and take out some sentries or at least keep the guard awake. They apparently thought they could not be seen and soon veered off the track towards the left of the axis and halted. The archers took up positions at the front of the formation and a cabot stood behind them pointing towards the gate. The archers took arrows from their quivers and nocked them. The cabot leaned forward to give the command to fire and was at that exact moment knocked off his feet. Buyo watched the archers and soldiers turn in confusion. They could not really see the twitching body behind them. The crew finished loading and arming the weapon despite the total blackness inside the guardhouse and she took up her position behind the stock and reviewed the remaining Matáng. She decided to aim for the archer in the middle of the front line only because if she missed, she would hit one or the other next to him. She had aimed slightly left for the previous shot because there was a slight westerly breeze and she knew it would catch the arrow in flight and move it to the right. She aimed off a similar distance to the centre Matáng and let the shaft fly free. Even in the darkness she could watch it in flight. It wobbled just a little before levelling out and she grunted with delight as the shaft disappeared into the centre of the back of the one she had aimed at. This time the entire group turned to look at her. She knew they could not see her.

"Hurry!" she hissed at the crew. I want two more shots before they are out of range. The ten remaining were in a tight group looking to her and back towards their own lines when the shaft took two of them. Buyo jumped aside as the crew manned the winch and cocked the bow. The Matáng had started to jog back in single file when she looked down the stock and through the circle to the foresight. If she aimed at the front one, she should hit one of the others as they ran through where he had been when the arrow was released. Once again she watched it in flight and she saw the one fourth in the line go down but he had only been hit in the foot. He was screaming in agony and two of his comrades turned back to help him. Buyo let another shaft fly and it hit one of them squarely in the upper body. The wounded one was still screaming but now his comrade turned and ran for safety. The crew could not load fast enough to engage him as he ran. He was out of range in a few seconds. She turned to the guard commander.

"Ask the lord ChOn if I should finish him or let his cries fill the ears of his fellow Matáng for the rest of the night."

Karín was all for leaving him to scream but ChOn was more merciful. It took Buyo two more arrows before she hit him with a kill shot. She thanked the crew for their help and left the guardroom tripping over a stool and a soldier's foot as she left.

"Sorry, friend. Can't see a thing in this darkness." She could see the surprise register on his face but he could not see the smile that split her face. She ran up the stairs full of adrenalin, bounced to the tower roof and straight to ChOn.

"Did you see that? Well did you? Oh my, I was good! If we weren't in the middle of a battle I would....."

She looked at Karín.

"With your permission, my Lady of course."

"Take a look at what we have over there. There is a group of thirty or so archers but I think they are out of range of the crossbow. I would like to try and lob some grenades into the group. Can you see the arrows in flight?"

"I told you My Lord. Night to me is just like day. I can see everything by night that I can by day."

"Alik. Go down and find three stones the same weight as the grenades. Bring them back and attach them to three shafts. Thank you."

"This is almost as much fun as making íjon. Maybe better."

Alik returned breathless from the climb.

"Take a grenade arrow and put it inside your tunic for me. I want it warm when it leaves us." Buyo fired the first arrow with the rock attached, too long as ChOn had instructed. It went quite close to the spot he wanted it to land, having passed closely over the top of the Matáng arcos. ChOn marked the elevation on the stock. The second arrow fell short, which is also what ChOn wanted. ChOn marked the new elevation on the stock. Now they had the Matáng bracketed.

"Put this one into the group then. Elevate the bow to half way between the two marks and then make minor adjustments if you need to"

The shaft rose slightly and fell a long way before landing where the group was seated. It hit one of the Matáng in the top of the head and he went down mortally wounded.

"Alik. Warm grenade please..... OK, Buyo. Same shot exactly but this time we will detonate the grenade as it arrives." Alik took the grenade from under his tunic and the crew loaded the shaft. Through ChOn's thermal lens the grenade and the end of the shaft glowed green. ChOn took the remote from Alik and nodded to Buyo, who loosed the arrow. ChOn followed the long arc and pressed the remote as the green blob was about to land in amongst the green mass of Matáng archers. A loud explosion filled the night and ChOn's thermal imaging lens was filled with trails of green flying through the air. The sound of men screaming filled the night.

Mastel woke to the sound of the grenade. It was, he knew, something similar to what had happened with the bund and the loss of an entire company of Infantry. The breeze brought the sound of men screaming in pain and he knew the campaign was in serious trouble. He decided to make an all or nothing assault on the wall just before first light. He would commit the entire force in waves to the attack and trust the resolve of his men to keep attacking in the face of death all around them. Once they reached the wall it was only four men high and they would be able to scale it with their bamboo screens. He knew there was no point trying to sleep now. He was needed in and around his troops. He donned his battle dress and strode out of his tent towards the bamboo stand. On the way he called the commander of the front battalion and told him to send in another probe. He had not been made aware of the results of the first one. The information stopped him short.

"Single shot kills at seventy paces in the dark? This gets stranger as the night goes on. And what are they using that can loose a spear of that size that is accurate at seventy paces and more? We gain nothing if they can see us in the dark. What magic do they possess? Cancel the probes. The attack will go ahead before dawn as planned with the grass tree barriers. There is to be no turning back this time. We take the wall or we die."

Karín looked over the ground between the two forces with the thermal imager and saw nothing.

"My Lord, Chon. Go back to your bed. I will keep watch. If anything happens I will wake you again. Jez will take the watch when the tablet counts down the time you set and I will join you then until your turn."

Ch0n nodded at Karín and went below.

"Buyo. I know the burning feeling you have. I felt it out on the plains after our first big skirmish. I know it has to be satisfied. Go with him but let him rest afterwards."

Ch0n was back at the battlements when the helm showed the green mass topping the rise. He woke Alik and sent him to wake Karín and Jez.   He ordered the guard commander to call 'stand to'. Below him he watched the well-practised soldiers take their posts. He raised his gaze again to the rise and saw that there was no end yet to the troops crossing. The Matáng commander had at last showed his hand. This was it. The Arw'an had to hold the keep or perish. He waited for Karín to reach him. She was on full alert despite her broken sleep. She looked over the field.

"Well this is it. When the sun reaches us your dream will have become reality." He saw she had brought her precious crossbow and Alik was carrying what seemed like all the three hundred bolts. She noted his glance.

"If we win we may have no use for those that I do not shoot. If we lose it would be silly not to use them all."

The advancing Matáng drew closer and Ch0n was able to make out the bamboo barricades.

"Jez. Tell the archers to hold their fire until they can shoot into the depth companies. Same with the rail guns. We will have to let them get closer than before. The arrows and shot will not penetrate those shields they have made. The pulse guns should knock them down on full power but once again we need to pick the range. The crossbows may penetrate them. When they get to one hundred paces, fire some trial shafts from the guard house. Stand by the rail gun. Wait until they are almost at the wall and then sweep them from the flanks. Give them the kinetic pistols at the same time."

"It will be done, My Lord."

"Alik. Prepare grenade arrows. Lots of them. Karín. Get the Lancers to the rear of the Matáng. Be careful of archers. I want them to pick at the rear guard until they have to do something about it. Tell them not to attack unless they have split off a small group."

Eight miles high, the clone G2 listened intently. For two days he had had the maxitron translating what it could. He had slept with the buds in his ears along with the others in his team and they all had a vocab now of more than a hundred words. G2 was able to glean some of Ch0n's orders thanks to the maxitron and thanks to the liberal use of words, like 'arrows' and 'rail gun'. He was watching the Matáng army on the move. He could make out the bamboo shields. He could see the archers on the assault force left flank but they seemed in disarray for some reason. He scanned the log and found the entry from the night watch where Ch0n had fired the grenade. He spoke one word into the mike.

"Watching."

Ch0n looked straight at the camera eight miles away and nodded once.

The lead ranks were within crossbow range and the guard commander ordered a trial shaft. It left the crossbow and travelled the one hundred paces in a graceful shallow arc and struck the bamboo shield, ricocheting on impact. A roar went up from the lead company. It was the first small win they had had since killing a lancer weeks before.

"Too slow through the air at that range. Wait until they are at fifty paces and give them another!" ordered Jez before running to his position outside the door where the rail gun was stationed.

"Wait for my order to fire!" he shouted and then he repeated it through the mike to the guard commander.

At fifty paces the crossbow loosed another shaft. It penetrated the shield but stuck fast. Another roar went up from the leading companies but those at the rear suddenly saw a rain of arrows in the air above the walls and then another and then they were being hit and killed and wounded and the roar from the front was deafened by the cries from behind. The arrows continued in volleys and the dead mounted up. Ch0n nodded at Alik and the crossbow sent the first grenade on its way. Alik pressed the remote just as it crossed above the front ranks and it exploded in the faces of those behind. The crew armed the next grenade and on Alik's signal loosed it with a similar result. Alik told them to fire at the same spot so as to deplete an entire fighting unit and the effect was devastating. Holes appeared in the attackers with every blast and it was only pressure from behind that prevented the advance from faltering.

At thirty paces the crossbow went straight through the shield and so the crew pumped shaft after shaft into the front ranks, concentrating on just one section of the advancing bamboo wall.

Jez called the guard commander to open up with the six pulsers and they fired volleys at the front ranks which knocked them down but they were able to recover time and again thanks to the shields. He called for them to stop and so the assault finally reached the base of the wall. Mastel was watching from the rise and he smiled to himself. Now it was just a matter of when their numbers would prevail. His thoughts of victory were dampened when those on the walls opened up with the pulses again and then a faint rattling sound reached him above the din as the kinetic pistols opened up and then above that a deeper rattle and the front ranks went down as though the wind had flattened them. Jez had ordered the rail gun into action and the effect was devastating. As the gunners raised and lowered the barrel the Matáng were winnowed away. He signalled for them to fire into the next companies and they too fell before the withering bursts.

And then it stopped firing. The crew went through the fault finding but could not identify the problem.

"Send it up here," ordered Ch0n and Jez attached it to the line and winched it to the top of the tower.

The Matáng finally had the ladders against the wall and were swarming up only to be sent back by arrows or pellets. The pulses were taking a terrible toll and the Matáng company commanders were struggling to keep their men moving forward. They were climbing on the corpses of their fallen and the rear ranks were now half way down the slope with the Household Cavalry sniping at their heels.

Ch0n looked across the tower and saw Karín with the crossbow loosing bolts into the advancing Matáng. Her hair was flaming red in the breeze with the sun shining through it.

"Get the Lancers out of there and back behind the battle. They are in between the rise and the castle and there must be troops behind them. We can't afford them to get trapped in there."

Karín gave the order and Ch0n watched as they charged towards the west out of the melee. He screamed into the mike for them to go further north but by the time they wheeled they were in range of the blocking force and the Matáng arcos opened up with a volley at point blank range. Eloik went down in the first volley along with a dozen others but the rest had been well trained and they charged the arcos like demons. The second volley took another dozen or more and then the Lancers were among the arcos and the second troop followed through and the blocking force was no more.

"Reny! Get Eloik's helm. Lead the tlaque away with the wounded. We will recover the dead later but we have to get the helm and get away before they attack with Infantry," ordered Karín.

Reny raced to where she had seen Eloik go down. She dropped from her tlaque and striped the helm from her comrade. She took the reins of the tlaque and led it away calling for the others to do the same. They were milling around as the right flank of the assault changed direction and moved towards them.

"Get out! Get out!" Leave the tlaque and get out." Karín was screaming into the mike and waving the flag to the north. The

remaining Lancers followed Reny leaving twenty tlaque standing over their dead riders.

"Alik. Take down the tlaque. All of them."

Alik put the crossbow team to work and they systematically shot the tlaque as the Matáng were trying to capture them. Then they watched as the Matáng started to strip the women and hack the bodies to pieces. Karín was firing bolts into their midst and finally between her and Alik's crossbow they were able to get the Matáng to withdraw.

Down along the wall, the battle was being lost. The sheer weight of numbers was telling.

"Jez. Get the rail gun crew and all the ammunition up here. We will withdraw to the second wall when I give the order. Get the special weapons back now and leave the archers and Infantry till last. I want them to break at the same time the way we rehearsed it." ChOn went to work on the rail gun. He rebooted the computer and used his thumbprint to arm it. He had forgotten that the firer had to identify himself every five minutes if the gun was in constant use so as to prevent it being used by the enemy if captured. The crew arrived and ChOn reset the computer to the operator's thumbprint and they set it up to cover the keep.

"Karín. Get a report from Reny. Make sure she is OK. She has to take command of the entire Household Cavalry until this is over. We will have to repel the next attack and see if the Matáng have the heart to take a second wall or if they will set up a siege. Tell her we can do nothing to help her just yet. She is on her own for the time being. Jez. Tell the Infantry to move back now. The archers follow when the others are at the gate. Guard commander. Cut the string on the crossbow and have the crew bring all the arrows up to the tower. Do it now."

He watched the Infantry pull back from the wall and as they reached the second gates, the archers followed. For a short while there was no movement at all outside the keep and then the Matáng soldiers started to spill over the outer wall. The archers took up their positions and joined the battle again. The pulsers and the kinetic pistols were decimating the Matáng as they trickled over. Mastel watched and waited. He had ordered that the gate be opened after the wall was breached. He had no idea there was a second wall to be assaulted. The bodies continued to pile up outside the keep and within until either the word passed that there was another wall or one of the commanders realized something was amiss when the gates remained closed. The flow of Matáng stopped and the a few cautious heads appeared between the castellations and disappeared again. Karín used the lull to brief Ch0n on the condition of the Household Cavalry.

"My Lord. They lost twenty seven and recovered only six. We can assume any wounded are dead after what we saw. Reny says that of the six wounded, all were on their feet when they were recovered so she is hopeful they will mend. Some of them fell because their tlaque took the arrows and went down. Two have arrows in their arms still. One has a wound in the neck. Almost all the survivors had multiple arrows in their armour. They are running short of arrows. If they are to be of any use to us again we either have to get them some arrows or use them to sweep with lances. She says they are so angry they will happily die doing that."

"Tell her to take the arrows out and to wash the wounds with boiled water. Tell her to take the wounded away to a safe place, leave them there with the spare helm worn by someone at all times and then return with the remainder and sweep the rise behind the battle. There are a few trees there but I suspect there will be no troops. Maybe the commander or the king will be there and we can kill him or them. One pass only. Three ranks of twenty five. Then return to a safe distance along the river to the east. We will float arrows downstream to the second bend."

Karín started to talk immediately into the mike.

"Alik!" continued Ch0n, "you and Beny bundle up all the arrows you can carry. Tie them together and run to the baths. I want you both to climb down to the river with the arrows and swim them downstream to the second bend and wait for Reny. Do not come back. Your work here is done. Tell Reny to take you to the wounded Lancers. Go now. No. Wait."

He unclipped the pulse from his belt and handed it to the boy, quickly programming it to Alik's thumbprint.

"I want this back, son."

Alik nodded and turned to Karín.

"Before I go, could you please ask Reny if Marelik is among the dead?"

"I will signal to you when you reach the edge of the wall down there. Thumb up for good news. Thumb down for bad."

Some time later, the two squires rounded the bend at the baths and Alik looked up. Karín raised her thumb and they disappeared with the flash of a red turban.

The runner reached Mastel and the king.

"My Lord. There is a second wall inside the first. The Buq'ue dogs have withdrawn from the outer perimeter to the second. We can not scale the wall in numbers sufficient to open the gates. My commander says we should burn the gates and enter that way. He says if we do not act swiftly we risk the Buq'ue regaining the outer wall while we wait."

"Tell your commander to take the gatehouse and the tower on the right flank. They will give us a place to dominate the outer space and to fire arrows at the main tower. Go to the place where the riders were massacred and recover their arcos and spears. We will use them. By all means burn the gates. But get the tower and the gatehouse first so they can not reoccupy the outer wall. And tell him I want a casualty count as soon as possible."

Eight miles high, G2 watched and considered the situation. He was the senior soldier but he had no experience in a battle of this nature. He had programmed his minitron to the language translation provided by the maxitron but now he decided to look for battles involving castles. It led him to the sieges of the sixteenth and seventeenth centuries. He asked it for battle tactics of the iron-age and it took him to the Romans and Greeks and mentioned the Zulu wars and the use of iron weapons against guns. He knew Ch0n had viewed all this information and more. He looked at the way the battle was poised and thought Ch0n might still prevail. The rail gun was back in working order and the opposing force had lost momentum. Each day his charges were regaining strength from the long hibernation and he thought that they could land and intervene if necessary without using too much physical energy. He said nothing to his commander but warned his team they might be deployed sooner than usual and into a 'hot' zone.

Ch0n wanted to know where the Matáng commander was. His instinct told him that the rise was the likely spot where he could oversee the field but that would not be a sensible pace to be with the force all deployed forward and the headquarters vulnerable to attack by the Lancers. He would need a substantial force in place to protect himself.

"Karín! Tell Reny to call off the sweep of the rise. If the king is there he will have a big force to protect him. Hold them back until we can use them."

Reny told Karín they were still at the river with the squires and the arrows. Marelik and Alik it appeared had had a joyous reunion. The arrows were safely distributed and the boys would be taken back to the wounded by two Lancers and the rest would deploy to a safe site close to the battle.

The Matáng clambered up the walls to the gatehouse and the corner tower where the rail gun had been. From inside they would have an uninterrupted view of the inside of the village and the inner wall. They climbed around and entered the doors, somewhat surprised by the lack of resistance from the arcos inside the castle. The inside of the gatehouse was spacious. There was a hole in the floor to stab down on the heads of any enemy. The enormous crossbow stood facing the approaches in its own alcove, its string cut. The slit windows looked along the walls to the left and right and yet could not see towards the front.

"How stupid is this design. You can't shoot to the front," commented one.

"Nor can anyone from the front shoot you while you are shooting along the wall. It is a brilliant design and explains why our arcos had no effect."

"What is that thing up in the rafters?"

"What?"

"That thing hanging down."

"Don't know. I have never seen anything like it. Get it down."

"I can't reach it. You get it."

"Later. Tell the others to come in over the front window were the big arco is."

The rest of their section climbed up the ladders and into the gatehouse. Along the wall, a similar scene was being played out in the corner tower. Nobody could reach the mystery objects hanging from the roof.

Ch0n took the remote control from his belt and read some numbers on his tablet.

"1. Gatehouse. 2. Tower. 3. Gatehouse two. 4. Castle door."

He pressed the number 1 and there was a flash, smoke and a loud explosion from the gatehouse. He pressed the number 2 and the same thing happened in the tower. From the rise Mastel saw the two flashes and some time later heard the two explosions and he cursed himself for being so confident.

They have the magic to call on when we are gaining a foothold.

From the tower, Ch0n could not see what was happening at the base of the outer wall but he could see that the assault had lost its momentum. The rear ranks were pressing up against the milling mass to their front. Ch0n told the crossbow crew to fire a few more grenade arrows into the throng and the effect was instant. With each explosion, a hole appeared in the Matáng force and became bigger as those on the edges stampeded away from the blast.

"Karín I have to go down to Alik's quarters to recover some stores. I won't delay. Get the Cavalry here as fast as possible and put them in their hide on the east flank. Do it now." He ran down the stairs and looked in the stores he had recovered from his comrades. He had twelve WP white phosphorus smoke grenades and two remotes. Once declared illegal on earth, the WP had never been taken out of use because all sides had defied the ban. He also had twenty four conventional smoke grenades and two separate remotes. He took them all up to the battlements and started attaching them to the tips of the crossbow arrows. He decided to start firing them before he had attached them all. He looked for the breeze. It was drifting gently from the south east to north west. The smoke from a grenade fired near the wall to the left flank of the Matáng assault would drift back across their number. A WP grenade fired to their left flank into the grass would start a fire that would run down their left flank. He told the crossbow crew to fire the first, a WP into the throng closest to where they could be seen from the tower. He took a WP remote and nodded to the crossbow crew. They loosed the shaft and it passed over the outer wall and Ch0n detonated it above the heads of the Matáng. It exploded in a shower of white trails and the smoke started to drift across the Matáng troops. At the same time, those who were touched by the blobs of white phosphorus were burned. Their hair was burned. Their clothes were burned. Their skin was burned and their shields were burned. The screaming started a panic and soldiers started to run away from the smoke. The second grenade was placed a little further away but again on the left flank and the stampede started immediately.

"Karín. Get the Lancers to run through anybody that breaks off the main body."

He fired two normal grenades a little further out and started two more stampedes, even though nobody was burning. The left flank of the Matáng was a shambles with men getting trampled underfoot. When Karín nodded to him, he told the crew to put two WP grenades in succession a little closer to the centre of the force and the panic that followed caused many of the fleeing troops into the open. The smoke hid the Lancers from the main body of troops and they swept from the wall towards the rise unopposed along the entire left flank of the Matáng. They just rode and rode and knocked down running soldiers and lanced them and slashed at them until they reached the rear of the force. Marelik was wielding her short spear like a Zulu leaving dead and wounded in her wake. Two more grenades split the force again Reny turned the Lancers about in their tracks and they rode again down the flanks towards the castle wall. The thought of their fallen sisters was fresh in their minds and they showed no mercy as they went about their grisly work. The smoke drifted across the entire Matáng force and most had no idea what was happening to their comrades on the left. Mastel could see from his vantage point and it was then that he knew the battle was to be won or lost on his next move. He ran down from the rise and grabbed the first commander he came across.

"Storm the gate. It has long been burnt. Crash it and then take the main tower. If we lose the next skirmish we will be massacred to a man. We can not let them keep taking the initiative from us."

The company commander ran through his troops calling for them to follow him. They ran, gathering numbers all the way to the gate where the commander shouldered the remains of the burning gate aside and led his troops through. They poured in until they filled the outer section in front of the castle and they spilled through the remains of the village knocking down and smashing everything they could find. Ch0n let them come until he could see the main part of the force was inside the gates. He detonated the grenade above the front door of the castle and he let loose on the crowded space with the rail gun. He threw two WP grenades over the battlements towards the main gate and when the mass was packed tightly into the corner of the courtyard he detonated the explosive charge he had buried there. He looked towards the rise. There were bodies strewn all over the field but the main force of the Matáng had been decimated inside and outside the castle. He could now see Mastel and the king with their entourage on the rise.

"Jez! Prepare the oruk. We are going to hunt their commander. I have had enough of this. Karín. When Jez and I ride out I want the Lancers to fall in behind us in three ranks. We are going to charge through the Matáng remnants and into their security force on the rise. I am thinking their archers are or were all down here but there may be some on the rise. You take charge of the battle here. When I tell you, I want you to drop two grenades over the wall to clear a path to the main gate. After we pass, drop a WP into the space behind us. Have the Infantry standing by in case a few get through as we leave."

He touched her on the face and ran down the stairs. He met Jez in the oruk stables and they donned their extra armour. When they mounted the giant armoured beasts they looked a fearsome sight. Ch0n drew his pulser and unsheathed Shiew. He told Karín they were ready to leave and took his place behind Jez. They heard the two explosions and Ch0n nodded to the gatekeeper. The gates swung open and Jez charged for the main gate with Ch0n close behind. The Matáng soldiers in their way were just brushed aside or trampled and in a dozen strides they were clear and riding for the rise.

Mastel was telling the king it was time to withdraw before they lost every male Matáng in existence but the king was beyond reason. He was in the processing of replacing him as the commander when they heard a shout from the forward troops of their guard. They looked towards the castle and saw the two oruk burst through the outer gates and run towards them in a straight line trampling the massed soldiers in their path. Ch0n pulled alongside Jez and they fired the pulsers ahead of them wreaking havoc that the oruks compounded. The Matáng soldiers panicked and ran to the flanks, creating a path for the oruks. It was only half a mile from the castle to the rise and the force on the hill had nowhere to run. Mastel called the troops to stand to their posts and called for the few remaining archers to come forward. They watched the seventy-five Lancers form up at the canter behind the oruk and ride down the gap they had created. Mastel actually had the presence of mind to admire the poetry of what he had just seen before he drew his sword and told the king to take cover.

Eight miles high, G2 was shaking his head.

"It looks like our information on this planet is riding some sort of giant buffalo at the enemy command HQ. There must be a hundred cavalry on elk backing him up. I hope the video is rolling because they aren't going to believe it back on earth unless we send it with the report. He touched a button on the console.

"Go get 'em, soldier. I think you got 'em beat."

This time, Karín heard the transmission. It was not Ch0n's voice. She looked around her but saw nobody. She looked up into the sky without thinking or knowing why.

Ch0n and Jez charged two abreast into the outer circle of Matáng and didn't even slow down. The oruk was enjoying his first big run after being cooped up for days. Its giant horns and face were splattered with gore and the remnants of Matáng uniforms. Chon went straight through to the other side, shooting anything he could see on the way. Behind him, the Household Cavalry changed formation at the run and lanced and hacked at the Matáng and wheeled around for a second sweep. Ch0n had to call them off because the bloodlust was on them. He guided the heaving oruk back to the rise and called out.

"If any still live, stand up and know you will be spared for now!"

A few stood. They had been hiding under bushes and one was in a tree. There were six in all. Just six of many.

"Is one of you the commander of the Matáng Army?"

Gavan Connell

"I am Mastel, the commander."

"Where is your master?"

"I am Sith. King of the Matáng."

Ch0n slid down from the oruk and walked to the king.

"You are a cruel and unthinking king who would sacrifice his soldiers in the face of unthinkable suffering and death. As a soldier I could not forgive such a king." Without pausing he swung Shiew and severed Sith's head. He threw it up to Jez.

"Take the Cavalry to the gate and show this to the Matáng. Tell them their new king commands them to lay down their arms. Take these with you apart from this one."

"But My Lord! You will be alone here."

"I will not be alone. I will be with him. And he will not be alone. He will be with me."

Jez rode the oruk towards the gate and the Household Cavalry automatically fell in behind in column of threes.

"I hope your people lay down their arms, Mastel. If they do not we will just wait at the gate until they leave, fight or starve. We have food for a complete moon cycle inside the castle. The village has been stripped of every edible thing."

"Who are you?"

"I am Ch0n of the Arw'an, King of the Buq'ue and Matáng. I am pleased to meet you at last. I have been telling my commanders you are a formidable enemy. I found it hard to stay in front of you."

"So now you patronize me before you kill me?"

"There has been enough killing for one day. I would have you meet Izaki before I kill you. Izaki was the commander of the Buq'ue army, such as it was. A lot smaller than yours. He is currently a Knight in my army, Commander of the Buq'ue army and garrison commander of the Buq'ue fort, which lies four days walk along the river. He was my sworn enemy and now I trust him with one of the outposts of the nation. We have Matáng soldiers in our Army, by the way, survivors from an earlier skirmish."

"Palik?"

"No. He was a loyal servant of your good king Sith. He is no longer with us. Did you know Alengadale?"

"My brother's son."

"Oh how I wanted to save his life for never have I seen a man so brave. You may tell your brother his boy died with honour and is buried under a tree with the first of my Lancers to die in battle."

"You just took his head or you might have told him yourself."

"So what is it to be, Mastel? Do you wish to serve me as my Regent in the Matáng lands? If you do, we will have a united nation with access to trade and secrets of which you have no concept. If not, you will die here where you currently stand and I will appoint one of your other commanders. The one who led the troops through the gate might be a good choice. He is brave and the troops followed him into almost certain death.

"Yes. He will be a good choice. His name is Mastelik."

"Aaah. I see."

Ch0n unsheathed Shiew and Mastel heard the faint humming as Ch0n drew closer. He drew his own sword and faced up to the strange man now squatting side-on before him in his black uniform and fitted armour. The dull green blade pointed skyward behind his right shoulder. Mastel raised his own blade without ceremony and took one step forward into eternity.

So ends the first of the Arw'an Chronicles

"The Ever Queen"

The second book of the Arw'an Chronicles by the same author, follows.

"There shall be one of us who will return in the body of another but you will know her because she will be one of us. Look upon us now and know us. The red-fire hair and green eyes will be the sign and she will speak to the priests in the tongue we shared with them alone and no other. She will be in the company of others but you will know her and obey her as you have known us and obeyed us. To deny her will be to bring the wrath of all of us upon you, whom we have taught and with whom we have mixed our seed."

(from the ancient texts of the Eñame priests)

www.ingramcontent.com/pod-product-compliance
Lightning Source LLC
Chambersburg PA
CBHW052343020726
47503CB00001B/91